# THE SOLOMON KEY

## A NOVEL OF ANCIENT CONSPIRACY

SHAWN HOPKINS

This is a work of fiction. Names, characters, and incidents are either a work of the author's imagination or are used fictitiously.

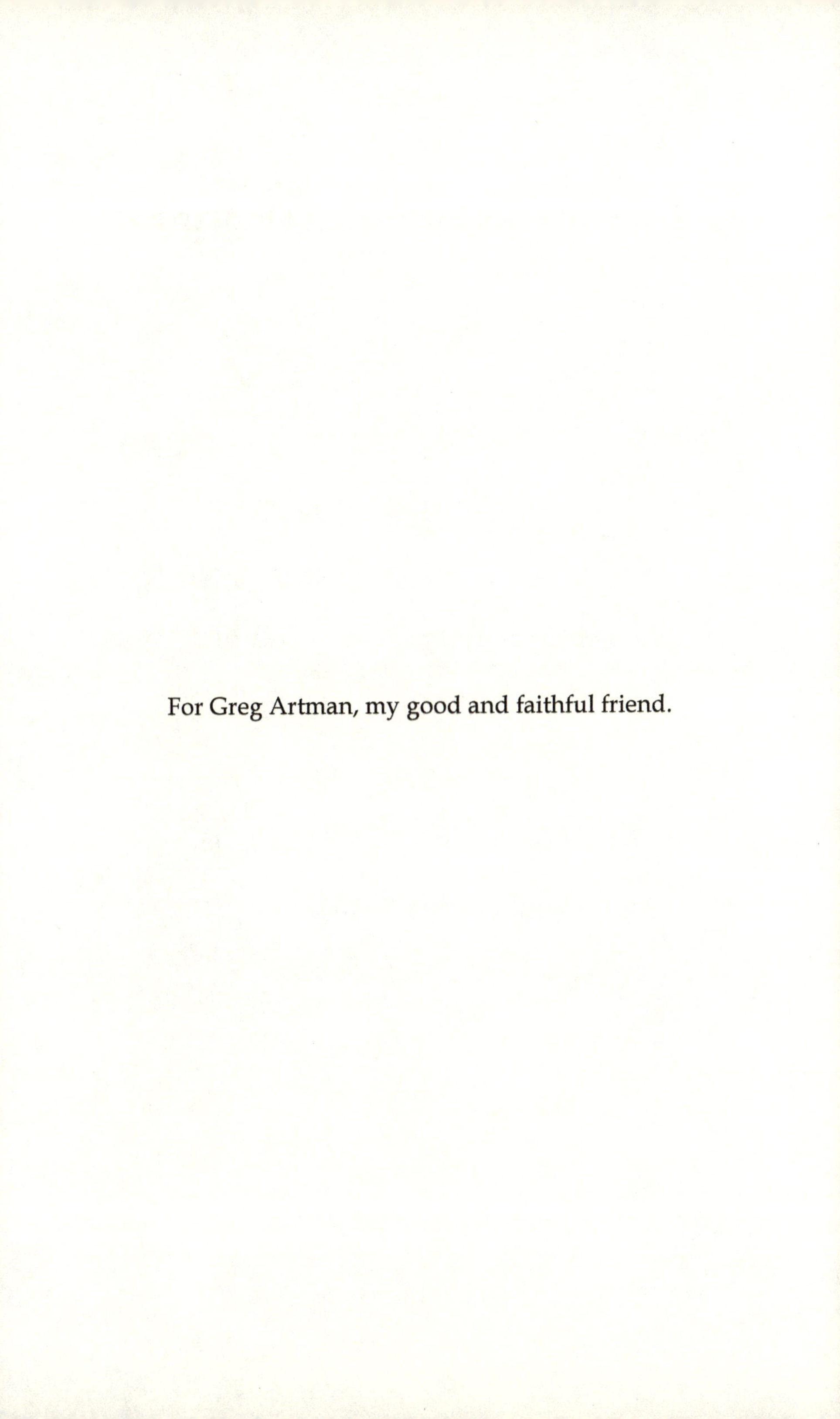

For Greg Artman, my good and faithful friend.

# Other Books by Shawn Hopkins

# Author's Note

This novel was formerly released by WestBow Press in January of 2011 under the title *Even the Elect*. It was then rewritten as *The Solomon Key* eight months later. During the rewrite, I snipped 60,000 words from the original story, deciding to leave the sociopolitical climate of the future setting as an insinuated backdrop rather than spelling it out in detail (I had also projected the story an additional ten years into the future). *Even The Elect* also had a bibliography of fourteen pages whereas *The Solomon Key* had only four. Ten years later, as I rewrite this second edition of *The Solomon Key*, I decided to go back to *Even The Elect* and resurrect some of what had been purged. The result was 2,000 fewer words in the *SK* rewrite, and then an additional 7,000 words added back from *ETE*. I hope that this will prove to be the definitive version.

Shawn Hopkins,
7/12/21

# I.

# HOLY SECRETS

*"For the mystery of iniquity doth already work: only he who now letteth will let, until he be taken out of the way. And then shall that Wicked one be revealed, whom the Lord shall consume with the spirit of His mouth, and shall destroy with the brightness of his coming: Even him, whose coming is after the working of Satan with all power and signs and lying wonders."*

—2 Thessalonians 2:7-12

Benaiah, the son of Jehoiada, concealed himself within the shadows of a large rock formation that sat reaching into the desert air like a man's disfigured arm breaking forth from the depths of Sheol and begging for water.

The sun had just finished its descent, and the Great Sea was ablaze across the horizon as she swallowed the ball of fire into her bowels.

And then darkness.

Even at such a great distance, Benaiah could feel the charging winds gliding over the sea's surface, freezing the desert air and pulling closed the curtains of night behind them. They circled around him, coming not only from the Great Sea to the west, but also from the Salt Sea to the east, and the sea

Moses split five hundred years ago from the south. Stars twinkled like ice in the sky, dancing before the moon. And though a deep chill was biting at his skin, his mind was too preoccupied with what had to be done for him to notice.

Below Benaiah was the camp, his army. He'd left its company to retreat up this jagged structure for some time to pray, to prepare. It was the son of Zadok who had suggested stopping here for the night, a spot just south of the Negev and enclosed by small mountains. Benaiah knew of its advantages—the blockage of wind and the concealment of torchlight and sound. But he also knew of its disadvantages. Attack. Being surrounded. Arrows storming down from the rocks above. Even if the king's army hadn't tracked them by now, there was a chance that the remaining Amalekite army had—the Negev desert south of Judah being their home. And though King David had struck them severely when recovering his wives and property from the raid on Ziklag, a small remnant had escaped on camelback. Had they since rekindled their old alliances with the Canaanites and Moabites? Benaiah didn't know. It was possible. He had indeed embarked on a dangerous journey, leading his handpicked army away from Jerusalem and into the wilderness of Paran.

Benaiah took his eyes off the camp and the scattered torchlight below and scanned the shadows dwelling among the rocks. They sat still and unmoving. Then the heavens drew his gaze, and the countless beaming stars seemed to sing with an intensity that would humble even the proudest of men. But instead of making him feel small and irrelevant in the face of its majesty, the sight only intensified the importance of his mission. The God who had created all those stars with a mere wave of His hand had dealt with Israel many times before, both with blessing and in judgment.

But it wasn't from coming blessings that Benaiah and his army were fleeing. No, King Solomon had broken the Lord's command and had disregarded the counsel of his father, David. Counsel that warned, *And thou, Solomon my son, know thou the God of thy father, and serve him with a perfect heart and with a willing mind: for the Lord searcheth all hearts, and understandeth all the imaginations of the thoughts: if thou seek him, he will be found of thee; but if thou forsake him, he will cast thee off forever.*

Solomon had indeed departed from the law of the Lord, offering sacrifices to the pagan gods of his countless pagan wives. So, surely, God would judge His chosen once again. Benaiah only prayed that God would bless this mission and deal with him mercifully as he attempted to execute it.

He set his gaze back down to the scattered camp. The stars seemed to spotlight the scene, drawing heaven's attention to their deeds and the vitality of their cause.

He was old now, and his service to King David seemed a lifetime ago. Someone else's even.

King David…

Benaiah had been one of David's mighty men, more honorable than the thirty, but not attaining to the first three. Adino the Eznite, who had killed eight hundred men with his spear during one battle, was the first. Eleazar the son of Dodo, and Shammah the Hararite were the second and third. He would have been the fourth.

Memories of those times projected against his mind's eye. The adventures. But they drew no smiles.

Joab…

Solomon had given the command to kill him, and even as Joab clung to the altar, Benaiah did slay him, cutting off his head and making himself captain of Solomon's army.

How things had changed.

A sudden noise came from behind, but he was not startled.

"What is it, Menelik?" he asked without turning.

Menelik, son of Solomon, came up and crouched beside him, ignoring the camp sprawled out below. "I know you have your doubts. I know your sense of loyalty must be confused. But you know that this is the right thing to do."

Benaiah looked at the young man through eyes weary with experiences Menelik would never come close to knowing. "I know." He paused, reconsidered. "I hope."

"You are unsure?" Menelik asked defensively. "It must have been done," he protested. "My father's idolatry will surely bring God's judgment to Jerusalem. It could not be left there under his care."

"And of the priests of Levi?"

"We have enough with us to reinstate the law when it is returned at a safer time." He paused. "Perhaps even the Temple itself will need to be rebuilt."

That thought was like a dagger into Benaiah's heart. Was it not so long ago that he'd watched with all of Judah as Solomon dedicated the finished Temple to the Lord and praised Him for His faithfulness? The memory brought a tear to his rugged and scarred face.

Menelik noticed the tear as it reflected the starlight. "What is it?"

"Better times, my friend."

"The Lord will not cast us off forever." He knew that from studying the books Moses had penned—the very knowledge that his once holy father, Solomon, had trained him in.

He nodded. "You should get some rest. The journey has just begun."

Menelik studied him for a second, lingering.

Benaiah knew what was going through his mind. It was the same thing that went through most minds that glimpsed his aged frame and tired eyes. The stories. His reputation as one of the thirty great warriors. Slaying the two lionlike men of Moab. The lion in the snowy pit. The great Egyptian who had been five cubits high and his spear like a weaver's beam. These were the things Menelik was thinking about, the things flashing through his mind.

"How long will you stay up here?" Menelik asked. There was a degree of care in his words.

"As long as it takes."

And it was then that Menelik finally noticed the swords leaning against the rock beside Benaiah. His eyes suddenly filled with panic. "You think they will come?"

Benaiah turned his whole body toward Menelik and looked straight at him, his gaze strong and unwavering. "Yes. Soon, I believe."

Menelik looked about frantically, across the way and to the other rock formations surrounding them. "But the scouts have not come back with any news of —"

"That is because they are already dead."

He shot to his feet, the finality of Benaiah's stoic words filling him with dread. "What should I do?"

Benaiah blinked. "Protect it at all costs. Get it to your mother's land and hide it until such a time as God makes clear. Then return it with all speed and diligence."

The implication was not lost on Menelik, and he frowned. His old friend's instruction suggested an absence during its performance. He swallowed the lump in his throat, reached out and grasped his shoulder with more emotion than he could contain. "God be with you, and may He bless you." He fought back tears. "Live." Then he turned and scurried down the craggy rocks and back toward the camp.

Benaiah watched the shrinking form of Menelik, son of King Solomon and the Queen of Sheba, finally disappear into a tent on the desert's sandy floor. Seconds later, he could be seen emerging with ten men, all with swords drawn and running toward the Levites.

Benaiah knew something that Menelik did not. Yes, his sense of loyalty *was* confused, which was why he had done what he had. He hoped Solomon would forgive him, that Menelik would forgive him. And that God would forgive him. He sighed. Stood. It was time. He prayed for strength even as he watched the skittering shadows stretch across the moonlit rocks and move toward him. He took one last look at the camp and the object he was most likely going to die protecting. It gleamed under the torchlight, another reminder of better days...of happier times.

"Oh, holy One of Israel, may your presence be soon restored..." Then he took hold of the ring that hung around his neck and dropped it beneath his cloak, where it rested against his skin. He picked up both of his swords. They were swords well acquainted with the shedding of blood.

The first attacker came from the shadows to his right and seemed to explode right out of the rock itself. Benaiah cut him in two. He then urged his aged legs to move, summoning strength he had not known for quite some time. As he began running back and forth, he was surprised by the degree of agility in his stride. He hoped it was a sign that the angels were with him, that they were the ones placing his steps along the edge of the jagged terrain. If they weren't, if he was alone in this, then there would be little chance of his tired frame stopping the marauders from killing them all.

An arrow flew by his head and bounced off the rock wall ahead of him. It fell harmlessly into the void that stretched beneath it. When he reached the gap, he threw both swords up into the air ahead of him and then jumped, sailing over the chasm and reaching out for the wall's serrated ledge. His hands found a small outcropping, and he pulled himself up, quickly rising to his feet between both his swords.

There was a man waiting for him.

Benaiah bent to grab one of the swords, but the man swiftly stepped onto its blade, pinning it to the ground. Benaiah pivoted, avoiding a swinging arc from the attacker's sword. He twisted, coming up with the other sword in his left hand and swinging it over his head, its blade flashing under starry light. With both hands, he brought the weapon down across the man's neck and sent his head bouncing down the steep slope behind him.

An arrow sank into Benaiah's back.

He grunted and turned to face three more men running to the ledge he had just leapt from. He stuck his foot under the dead soldier's sword and kicked it up into his free hand. He threw it at the lead attacker below, the sword flying end over end until burying itself into the man's chest. Benaiah bent over and picked up his other sword just as another of the men grabbed the outcropping at his feet. A cross-swing from both swords sent the man falling into the darkness, screaming until striking a rock, his hands still at Benaiah's feet.

The last of the three attackers turned and started running away, but Benaiah leapt back down, landing with perfect footing, and quickly caught up to him. He thrust his sword through the man's back, lifting him off his feet and propelling him forward and over the side of the cliff.

Blood dripping from his blade, Benaiah turned as someone jumped down from a hidden position above. But the soldier's landing had not been perfect, and the moment of unbalance cost him both of his feet. The next flash of Benaiah's sword severed his enemy's vocal cords and stopped another ungodly scream from echoing through the desert night.

Despite the cold air, sweat dripped from Benaiah's face, and his heart heaved violently in his chest. Standing over the dismembered soldier, he was once more aware of the arrow sticking out of his back. It annoyed him, but he did his best to ignore it. Instead, he looked down to the camp below. His people were moving, preparing to travel onward to a new location. There would be no rest for them tonight.

He looked up and down the mountains, but everything was still and quiet. Had he gotten them all? Could there only have been six? Not likely.

He ran across the rocky island, carefully descending its steep slope, and finally jumped back into the sand. But then another mountain began stretching up out of the wilderness floor, and he found himself standing in a gap…in a doorway leading out from the enclosed desert they had made their camp and into the open oceans of sand beyond. He stood motionless for a few seconds, watching his men in the distance. And then he looked back over his shoulder. The deep corridor that led to the vast deserts of Paran, formed by the two kissing mountains, was not empty.

Amalekites.

*Good*, Benaiah thought. These people had been a scourge in Israel's side ever since the Exodus, and he recalled God's words spoken to Moses and Balaam. That He would "completely blot out the memory of Amalek from under heaven" and that "they would perish forever." Benaiah could only hope that *he* would prove to be the instrument by which God finally fulfilled His word, finishing what King Saul had been commanded to do so long ago.

He raised both swords and, without another thought, charged through the gap and entered the corridor. He could hear the heathen army laughing at him, their amusement echoing off the rock walls around him. He didn't even feel the first two arrows that struck him.

Three horsemen charged away from the army, hooves kicking up sand in their wake. The torches the army held bounced light off the rock passageway, the horses and the charging Israelite lost in a confused spectacle of moving shadows.

Benaiah moved to the right, the sword in his left hand slicing through the muscled neck of a horse, his right hand swinging around and striking across the back of its rider. Both crashed into the sand.

The laughing stopped.

The two other horsemen had run past and were now coming about. They charged again, but before they even got near enough to use their weapons, they each had one of Benaiah's swords through the heart. Three dead Amalekites, one dead horse. Only about a hundred left. He smiled as he retrieved his swords and watched the whole Amalekite army rush toward him.

He had survived these odds before.

When the army met him, the sound of clashing metal boomed out of the passageway and drifted up into the watchful skies above.

He fought bravely for the secret sitting in the camp behind him. He fought for his God and for the glory of Israel. But it would be almost another two hundred years, under the kingship of Hezekiah, before the Amalekites would finally disappear from history. And, ironically, it would be a prince from the tribe of Simeon, also named Benaiah, who would be the one to finally bring God's promise to fruition.

And it would be thousands more years after that before his secret would be discovered. A secret that could prove to be the key capable of unlocking the end—the end the future prophets would describe as a time of great travail...

As the Time of Jacob's Trouble.

# 1.

*"The individual is handicapped by coming face to face with a conspiracy so monstrous he cannot believe it exists."*

—J. Edger Hoover

The senator punched the roof of the car with a meaty hand, swearing under his breath. Then he swore again, louder. Sweat formed on his brow and, in an attempt to ignore it, he turned his attention to his pockets, searching for his lighter and a pack of cigarettes.

He was angry. They got him. And this time they got him good. Those idiots had been there again despite the late hour and the scattered rain. Every weekend for the last month. It didn't matter how many of them were arrested or beaten, even tortured, they just kept coming. But this time it had been different. A major news channel had filmed it during a live broadcast. It was just bad luck. Had the news crew been there to cover something political, they wouldn't have been allowed to broadcast live. But they'd been there for something else—he didn't even know what—and he just happened to walk right through their shot. True, the presence of protestors should have made them cease broadcasting immediately, and he would find out who was responsible for that, sure enough, but still... He should've been more careful. And that was what they would tell him. What they expected of him.

He looked out the window and exhaled smoke into the bulletproof town car. He spread his legs, unbuttoned his suit jacket and slouched heavily into the back seat. The confrontation had ended badly.

He hated them. The "people." Hated that they were still able to agitate him. Hated that he couldn't just squash them all under his heel and finally be done with them. *Soon,* he told himself, and he tried to relax. But it wasn't working. He knew the media would spin the incident in his favor, but it was unnecessary work, and the people he answered to didn't like unnecessary work.

He lowered his hand to grip the edge of the seat beside him, the cigarette sticking up between his fingers and sending smoke throughout the yellowish lighting of the car's interior.

He began to panic.

Should he worry? But arrogance eventually chased the notion away. By his own esteem, he was much too important a figure to discard or demote. They needed him. And that fact made him valuable, untouchable. *Rest easy,* he told himself. *A subtle rebuke maybe, but nothing more.*

After the biological terrorist attack a few years ago, the country had practically begged for a police state, believing it a necessary evil that would ensure their safety against what most believed was just the beginning of an unending stream of brutal attacks. Attacks that had been escalating in magnitude and frequency for more than a decade. Eventually, this led to what had been called (and was still called) "the Transition." And the loss of liberty that had ensued had taken the "people" out of the equation altogether. Which was why the senator was sure there was nothing to fear from this last encounter. The power of the former Republic no longer threatened men like him. Or their agendas.

"Are you comfortable, sir?" the shadow from the driver's seat asked.

The senator blinked, tapped his cigarette with a free finger, and watched the ashes flutter to the carpeted floor at his feet. "Sure," he grumbled.

"We'll be there in about ten minutes."

He stared out the window, ignoring his own reflection, his mind dazed by the city lights blurred by the rain. He tried to get his mind back on the task at hand.

The driver pulled over on East 157th Street, where a man with an umbrella was waiting at the curb. He opened the rear door and ushered the senator out, escorting him under the umbrella and into the newly renovated Yankee Stadium. The game was just going into the seventh inning after two rain delays, but that was not why the senator was there.

They made their way through scores of local police and NAU soldiers before using an alternate entrance into the stadium.

Three police officers dressed in black uniforms scrutinized them as they approached, their fingers dancing on their triggers. The man with the umbrella flashed an ID, and the cops let them enter without a word. Once inside and on their way to the owner's box, a security guard ran up to the senator, ranting excitedly about the stadium being a smoke-free zone.

The senator stopped and turned, his overcoat swinging after him. "Excuse me?"

"It's an eco-crime, sir, and I'm going to have to ask that you get rid of it."

The senator smiled and blew smoke into the young guard's face. "I passed that law, son." Then he flicked the butt off his chest, turned, and continued on his way.

The security guard began to reach for his Taser, but the man with the umbrella stepped in front of him and waved a finger before he could draw it from its holster.

"Don't even think about it, young man." He folded the umbrella. "Or you'll be in a labor camp before the game is over." He turned and passed the senator in time to open the door to the owner's box for him. The senator stepped through, and the umbrella man followed, closing the door behind them and locking it.

"You look terrible."

The voice came from a shadow across the room.

The senator stepped forward, reached into the chest pocket of his jacket, and extracted an envelope. "I have the information."

A man emerged from behind the bar, carrying a bottle and two glasses. "Seriously, Bill, you look like hell," he said.

"Rough night."

The man was a good twenty years younger than the senator, dressed in slacks and a cotton shirt underneath a sweater vest. "A drink, then." He filled both glasses, handing one to the senator, who drained the whole thing in one gulp. The man raised an eyebrow, turned, and walked to an oversized chair, sitting to the sound of the crowd cheering a home run. "You hear that?" he asked, nodding toward the tinted glass that hid them from the fifty-three thousand fans on the other side. "The sound of ignorance." He took a sip and waved his hand at the air. "They care more about the pennant than anything they don't even realize we're taking from them."

It was an old tale, and the senator didn't need to be patronized with it, not by someone younger and from the same secret society as him. He tossed the envelope into the man's lap. "From DC."

The younger man sat up and immediately tore it open. "Is it what we thought?"

"It's all there," he said. "Can't imagine why it's so important."

The man pulled a coin-sized disc out of the envelope and smiled. "Have the loose ends been taken care of?" He placed the disc on the table next to him.

"As we speak."

The man nodded. "We can't be too careful these days. What's the narrative?"

"One of the scientists tried to steal it, to sell it on the black market. He murdered the others before being stopped by security."

He nodded his approval. "Will you stay and watch the remainder of the game?"

The senator swallowed the lump in his throat, beginning to feel the walls press in on him. "No. I have to get back. It's been an awful day." He made his way back to the door, where the gentleman with the umbrella opened it for him.

"Senator," the man called, standing.

He stopped and hesitated. Looked back over his shoulder.

"Did you happen to come from the Pratt House?"

He answered stoically, trying to sound as disinterested as possible. "No. I came from your wife's."

The man chuckled. "Senator—" He tossed the bottle of scotch to him.

He caught it. Looked it over.

"Relax," the man finished. "We're dealing with people"—he waved toward the windows—"who believe whatever we tell them to believe. They always have and they always will." He picked up the disc and walked back behind the bar.

The senator forced a smile. To which the man raised his glass and turned away. "See you later, Bill." He disappeared through another door.

The senator walked out of the owner's box.

"I'll escort you back to your car, sir," the umbrella man said as he closed the door behind him.

****

In the owner's box, the man turned the huge four-dimensional TV back on, its nanocrystals shining bright while the visible light technology stimulated his senses with high-frequency blinking—a pizza ad running behind the program. He knew it was a pizza ad because he could suddenly smell the pepperoni and melted cheese. He reminded himself again to get the feature removed. He hated being manipulated, especially by something he couldn't see. That was *his* role, to manipulate.

Trying to put aside the sudden urge for the particular brand of pizza, he focused on what was actually showing on the screen. The senator. Coming from the Pratt House, ambushed by protestors who seemed to come from nowhere. It was exactly at that moment the live feed should have been terminated. What a shame for the senator that it wasn't.

The sudden crowd was screaming and holding signs. And as the senator approached his car, one young man could be seen stepping out from the group with a small camera in hand. "America won't give in to your agendas! We know what you're doing, and we're not going to let it happen!" he yelled.

At that the senator turned, glared at the kid, and slapped the camera out of his hand. "There is no more America, you dumb piece of—" His voice trailed off as he punched the younger man in the face. "Better watch it! Someone could get hurt doing this sort of thing!"

The kid, blood running through his fingers as he held them to his nose, just kept yelling, "He hit me! The senator hit me!"

It was at that instant that the senator could be seen noticing a major news reporter standing nearby, face frozen in shock, his cameraman recording the whole thing. The look on the senator's face revealed guilt, realization in his eyes acknowledging that he'd been set up and caught in a trap of his own making. He quickly disappeared into the car as security guards and police began closing in on the crowd.

The tape ended, and the picture went back to the studio. The news anchor began talking about the protestors being a menace to society and how more laws needed to be passed against such treasonous rhetoric.

But the man had stopped listening. Instead, he drank the rest of his scotch and touched the earpiece in his ear, dictating a code word the phone used to connect with the desired recipient—the voice recognition software authenticating and securing the line simultaneously. "He just dropped it off. What do you want to do? Yeah, I'm watching it." He listened carefully to the answer. "Pity." Then he touched the earpiece again and spoke another name while he took the disc to the TV. He couldn't wait to see their conclusions.

He pushed it into the side of the television, activating its use as a four-dimensional computer.

****

The senator returned to the back seat of the car just in time to see the driver tap his earpiece.

"Home, sir?" the driver asked.

"Yes." He pulled the top off the bottle of scotch and started drinking. Then he hit a button on the door, and a TV swung down out of the ceiling in front of him.

There he was. On the news.

Punching a protestor in the face. *"Someone could get hurt doing this sort of thing..."* Had he been twenty years younger, he might have tried running. But not now. Now he knew it was useless. He drank some more. It wasn't as if the Council on Foreign Relations hadn't been suspected of conspiracy in the past, but it had always managed to come out unscathed.

And even now while the news was spinning the story in the CFR's favor, he knew that those he answered to would not be happy about the new enemies he'd just made for them. He'd just given the Resistance another recruiting tool and, at this stage of the game, that was not something the people over him typically tolerated.

He lit another cigarette, and it started to rain again. "Perfect," he muttered.

"What was that, sir?" the driver asked, looking into the rearview mirror.

"Nothing." He watched New York blur past the window. Like the rest of the country, the economic collapse that had accompanied the terror attacks had turned it into a trash heap. He glanced at the driver. "So what happens now?"

"Excuse me?"

"Don't play stupid with me, boy."

After a moment of silence, he answered, "You know how these things go, Senator."

His heart froze. "It'll look suspicious, me getting offed right after my statement. It'll lend credence to my words. To theirs."

The driver shook his head. "Your wife. She's twenty-three years younger than you."

The senator closed his eyes, tilted the bottle straight up, and drank as much as he could.

The driver continued. "You followed her to her lover's house. Shot them both; then turned the gun on yourself."

He stopped drinking, held the bottle away from him. "And I suppose I'm to be in a drunken rage?"

"Nothing personal, sir."

The senator's face flushed red, the alcohol emboldening him, but before he could utter another word, the driver turned around and shot him in the head.

# 2.



Melissa Strauss pressed her hand onto the shiny surface, and a red light turned green. The big steel door released its hold on the walls surrounding it, and it opened in a slow arc. Not for the first time, she found herself wondering at this special assignment. After all, it wasn't every day that her employers had her prancing through super-hi-tech facilities, touting around high-level security clearances, and keeping the company of armed guards. It was the desert that she was accustomed to, or maybe remote villages in South America if she was lucky, but a place like this? It had been years since she had the luxury of working in air-conditioning, let alone with all the hi-tech equipment that was everywhere in this place.

Just a few weeks ago she was in some disease-ridden part of Africa, overseeing the creation of a water reservoir, part of a two-year sanitary project to elevate Africa's state of living to meet UN law. But that came to an abrupt stop when an order from above suddenly changed her itinerary, sending her instead halfway across the continent and into the Middle East. Her new directive, which she understood to be top secret and a matter of national security, was to obtain an undisclosed object from another government employee and transport it back to

North America. To this place. Of course, there had been no turning it down. It had been an order. Though if it got her back to Vermont quicker, then she couldn't complain.

She walked through the door and down a corridor, her white lab coat floating on the cool, sanitized air. At the end of the corridor she came to another door, this one requiring her NAU Identification card, her voice, and a retinal scan.

*"Welcome, Dr. Strauss,"* said a synthetic voice.

She entered the lab. A loud click and a beep sounded as the door shut and locked behind her.

"Where'd all the security go?" Joe Theissen asked. He was hunched over a microscope and peeking over the top of his glasses. His fifty-six-year-old face was weather-beaten and serious, but his eyes glowed with a purpose that was known to be infectious—as they were now. Though relatively stern, his casual lopsided grin was continually blowing his cover and revealing to be true the rumored lightheartedness he enjoyed away from the work. Like Melissa, he was also employed by what was formerly known as the US Department of Agriculture, and the two of them had worked together on past projects.

Melissa looked around, suddenly aware of the military's bizarre absence. "I didn't see them on my way in. They just left?"

Joe shrugged and returned his attention back to whatever foreign artifact was under the lens. "You'd think they'd at least tell us they were leaving." He squinted, a free hand focusing the lens. "You see that guy Mark or Thomas?"

"No."

"Janice?"

Again she shook her head. "I'm sure they'll be back soon." She made her way to a closet.

"They should have been back ten minutes ago with my dinner." He stood and watched her as she hung up her coat. "Speaking of dinner..."

She walked over to him, ignoring his not so subtle suggestion, and placed a hand on his shoulder. She leaned over the microscope and peered through the lens. "We're supposed to be studying something else, you know."

"Blah, blah…" He waved his hand. "I don't care about that stupid thing. I was on the brink of a legendary discovery before they packed me up and sent me here to meet you."

She laughed. "Yeah, I bet."

"Besides," he continued, "I sent the diagnostics three hours ago. It's done."

A look of concern came over her. "Joe, what about the others?"

He gently nudged her away from his work. "Don't worry, I didn't cut any corners. I just didn't feel the need to sit around for another week trying to persuade those chimpanzees of its obvious spiritual implication."

"Chimpanzees?"

"With an emphasis on the last two syllables."

She left his side and walked over to a glass case, her mind grappling with what Joe had just told her. The other "chimpanzees" had actually been brought in from the recently internationalized NASA program. When they found out that Joe had cut all their individual research short by finalizing their findings and sending a report without their consent, there would be fireworks.

She looked through the glass case. At the object she had escorted halfway around the world. For some unknown reason, it seemed to be of major importance to the military. But she and Joe had learned rather quickly not to ask questions, and the amount of money they were promised for both their work and their discretion made the soldiers, the high-tech equipment, and this super-secret government lab beneath some building in Washington, DC, a little easier to cope with.

Joe looked up from his work again. "Oh, they said the power might go out tonight."

Melissa looked around the lab again, at the bright lights glowing from all the equipment. "What do you mean?" she asked, confused.

Joe stretched again, spoke his words through a yawn. "He just said they were doing some kind of drill or something. Said the power might go out for a little bit, no big deal. Light a candle or something." He winked at her.

She rolled her eyes. "It'd take more than a candle, Joe." But there was a subtle whisper in the back of her mind that told her something was off. From the time she had taken the object into her possession, she'd been escorted by a soldier. And from the time they'd arrived at this place, guards had covered their every move with automatic weapons. Complete and total secrecy was demanded of them, their communications to the outside world strictly monitored. Every day, NAU military personnel rotated in and out of the project, supposedly protecting them—though from what they were never told. And now, without any warning, they were just *gone?* With the power expected to go out? "I haven't been allowed near a phone since I've been back, haven't been allowed out of their sight. And now they just disappear, leaving us completely unguarded during a power outage?"

But his mind was elsewhere, and he just shrugged. "Maybe the thing isn't what they thought. Feels nice though, not having them breathing down our necks. Gives us some privacy." He winked at her again.

She smiled, but it wasn't genuine. "Don't forget the cameras," she said while waving at the small dark spheres dotting the ceiling. But despite the attempted humor, her heart rate was beginning to accelerate. Her eyes went to the object that lay suspended within the glass case. Whether she was turning to it as a means of escape, engaging her mind on a different matter, or whether she was subconsciously drawn to it as the suspected answer to her unvoiced concerns, she wasn't sure.

Then the power went out, and they were plunged into total darkness.

Joe swore. "No telling how long this *drill* is going to last. You want to get comfortable?"

"Joe." Her voice was shaky, worried. "I don't like this."

He had spent enough time with her in the past to know when she was scared, and the tone she had just used didn't attempt to hide her fear now. "We're fine, Melissa. No one even knows this place exists. And even if they did, they'd never be able to get down here." But he was trying to reassure himself with his own words, his subconscious whispering warnings of its own. "It'll probably just be a few minutes."

"All this high-tech equipment, all the blast doors, the cameras, the retinal scans… It doesn't make sense for them to just pick up and leave and then shut the power off on us, Joe. And no one else is back from dinner yet…"

"Maybe they were stopped topside, told not to come down because of the drill."

There was silence in the darkness as she thought about that. But before she could reject it, footsteps could be heard coming down the corridor.

Joe quickly shed his unconcerned act and ran through the darkness to a giant stainless steel counter that contained two large empty cabinets underneath. "Melissa, over here," he urged.

She followed his voice, and they climbed into the cabinet just as someone pushed open the heavy door and entered the room.

They held their breath, unable to see anything in the darkness.

And then a beam of light split the darkness in half.

"Joe? Melissa?"

It was Mark.

Melissa let out a sigh of relief and began to move, but Joe put a firm hand on her shoulder, keeping her still.

The beam of light swept across the room, bringing to sight whatever it fell on.

"Dr. Theissen? Are you here? Dr. Strauss?" The footsteps grew closer, the flashlight continuing to move back and forth through the room. Then the beam stopped moving and instead focused on just one thing. The classified object in the glass case.

They watched through the crack in the open cabinet door as the length of the beam shortened as Mark approached the case. Once he was standing over it, he raised the flashlight and swung it down. The glass case shattered. Alarms should have sounded, but with the power out…nothing.

"What's he doing?" Melissa whispered in Joe's ear.

Joe shook his head.

Mark picked up the object and held it under the flashlight. He stood there for a few seconds as if mesmerized by it, like he actually knew what it was. Then he pivoted, his shoe crunching broken glass, and headed back the way he'd come.

"What do you have there?" a new voice asked.

Neither Joe nor Melissa could see what was going on because Mark's flashlight was hanging uselessly at his side and pointing at an empty spot on the floor.

"What are you doing here? They sent you—"

"Where are they?" the new voice asked, cutting him off.

"They're not here."

"They have to be here. They weren't picked up leaving the lab."

"What difference does it make?" Mark asked. "I have it."

"They're here somewhere. Spread out and look for them." It was an order issued to more unseen figures, and the sound of moving feet suddenly filled the lab.

"Who sent you?" Mark demanded.

Melissa craned her neck to peer farther to the right, to try to see what was going on. When she saw Mark, he was raising the flashlight and pulling out what looked to be a gun. A shout came from one of the armed men when the beam from Mark's flashlight struck his night vision, and he jerked the headpiece off. Mark shot him in the chest.

The loud gunshot was followed by a barrage of others, and Melissa retreated against Joe, covering her ears.

"We can't stay here," Joe said into her ear.

Melissa threw the cabinet door open just as the beam from Mark's flashlight swept across the room and revealed two men in black shooting at him. He was hiding behind some metal crates, firing aimlessly over their tops while trying to focus the light on a glimmering object lying on the floor.

The artifact.

It was only feet away from her. She lunged for it, picked it up, and ran. She skirted the room's perimeter, going around the flashing gunfight, and went for the exit. She heard Mark scream and hoped Joe was right behind her.

But when the firing stopped, her movement could be heard echoing through the sudden silence. She was readying herself for the feel of bullets when she heard Joe call out, "Hey, you pieces of—"

His voice was cut short by more gunshots.

Melissa made it into the corridor with tears flowing from her eyes.

Another shot rang out, and sparks flew off the wall next to her, but she made it through the other door and to the elevator.

But the elevator wouldn't work without power, so she threw herself into the door next to it and entered the stairwell.

Her heart was racing out of control, her feet trying desperately to move her body up the stairs. The knowledge that guns could sound at any moment and end her life pushed her even faster. Before she knew it, she was leaning into the panic bar of a large steel door and throwing herself into a hallway within the main building.

She was topside.

She heard footsteps echoing through the stairwell even as the door closed behind her. She took off running again, looking for someone who could help. But she was on a restricted level, only personnel with top security clearance allowed on the floor, and there was no one around. She needed to go up one more floor in order to get to the main doors and out onto the steps that led to the street. Once outside, she could lose her pursuers in the crowd. But she was having a hard time figuring out which way to go even with the emergency lights shining above her. There were nothing but doors lining both sides of the hallway, the hallway itself dead-ending a hundred feet in front of her.

There was no time.

She picked a random door just as the stairwell door burst open behind her.

Hoping she'd closed the door fast enough, she made her way through the emergency-lit office and around a vintage oak desk. She crawled underneath it, pulled her knees to her chest, and tried to keep from convulsing. Her mind raced through a million incomplete thoughts, and she thought her heartbeat was so loud it might give away her location. She held her breath, praying the men would walk past the room.

They did.

She heard them open another door and walk up some other steps.

She fought the urge to go back to the secret laboratory and check on Joe. She wanted to know if he was still alive, but going back would only guarantee her death.

She opened her hand and looked at the relic resting on her palm. She didn't know what they wanted it for, but she would make it as hard as possible for them to get it. Her whole team had been set up from the beginning, she realized. And that infuriated her.

She crawled out from beneath the desk and quickly began looking for an envelope. It was a long shot, as no one used physical communication anymore, but then again, no one used big oak desks either. Had she picked the office of the only nostalgic person in Washington, DC, to hide in?

She found one in the second side drawer, and there was a pen already lying on the top of the desk. After scribbling a name and address onto the front of the envelope, she wrote a quick note on the underside of the flap by the crease in the paper. She took a tissue from the tissue box on the desk and wrapped the object in it before dropping it in the envelope. She sealed the flap.

Then she rummaged through the desk, looking for stamps. But that would've taken a miracle. People only used the postal service for packages.

She ran to the door and entered the hallway. The stairs were two doors down, and she made it to them without detection. She took them as silently as she could, at one point stepping over a black mask.

When she reached the main floor, she found that it was empty. The big glass doors that led to the street were within sight.

"Yes, sir, we're turning the power back on now."

The words were spoken by a man coming toward her, but they'd come from around a corner, and she couldn't see him. Knowing that the big doors would lock as soon as the power was back online, she moved as fast as she could, covering the empty floor with a speed she hadn't known since her high school track days. If the doors locked before she hit them, she'd break her shoulder or knock herself out. Maybe both. But they flew open, and she was out into the night and descending the steps.

Police cars. Roadblocks. Fire trucks.

An officer saw her come out of the building and came running over to her as she reached the street.

"Are you alright? You weren't supposed to be in there..."

She ignored him and continued running.

She rounded the block and ran into a small crowd that was being ushered away by police in battle gear.

She needed to get rid of the envelope.

She pulled whatever money she had from her pockets. Just a few ameros. She ran into the street, traffic screeching to a halt as the twilight faded behind her.

Running down the street, she turned her head just in time to see a black SUV bearing down on her. Another behind it.

A cramp gnawed at her side, but she couldn't slow down. If she did, she was dead. There were too many cameras and scanners on the street, so she couldn't get rid of the artifact here. If they found out about the envelope, they'd intercept it before it could reach its recipient—assuming she could even find someone to mail if for her. She had to get back indoors.

She turned down an alley, and one of the SUVs screeched to a halt. A man in a suit jumped out after her. The other SUV flew past and made a sharp turn around the block in an effort to cut her off.

Melissa turned. The man was too fast. She wasn't going to make it.

An open door ahead on the right. A restaurant.

She ran through just as the man came within arm's reach.

"Help me!" she screamed. "Help me! He's trying to kill me!"

The stunned cooks all turned to see the attacker behind her, and they stepped into his path.

Melissa ran out of the kitchen and into the restaurant. She excused herself to a couple who were sitting and eating, and quickly handed the man the envelope. "Will you do me the biggest favor in the world?" she asked, tears dripping down her cheeks.

"Uh…" The man looked around the room before stealing a nervous glance at his girlfriend. "Sure?" He took the envelope.

"Would you send that for me?" She looked back at the kitchen doors, knowing they would burst open at any moment. She threw all the money she had onto the table. "Please," she begged. "It's important." Then she turned and ran out the front door.

And straight into the arms of another man in a suit.

She started kicking and screaming, but he was strong and didn't loosen his grip. He carried her to the SUV like she was just an unruly child and threw her into the back seat just as the other guy climbed through the opposite door and slid in next to her.

"Come on, let's go," one of them said. The SUV took off, speeding down a road in what had formerly been the capital of the constitutional republic known as the United States of America.

Before Melissa knew what was happening, a plastic bag was pulled down over her head. When she inhaled, the plastic filled her mouth. One man held the bag while the other kept her from flailing.

A ring pierced the air.

The driver answered a phone. "Yes? Right." He turned and said, "Let her go."

They removed the bag without question.

She gasped, struggling to breathe.

"It's not there," the driver explained. "They think she took it."

As Melissa worked to catch her breath, her mind began connecting dots. Mark was supposed to kill her and Joe, and then the men in black would enter just in time to keep Mark from taking off with it.

"Ms. Strauss, you have something that we want." They stripped her but found nothing on her person. Then they searched in her person. Still nothing.

"See if she swallowed it," someone said.

Then there was plastic being spread and a searing pain across her abdomen. When she looked down, one of the men had her intestines in his hands.

She was unconscious when they threw her from the vehicle and off the bridge.

# 3.

*"If we understand the mechanism and motives of the group mind, it is now possible to control and regiment the masses according to our will without them knowing it."*
<br>—Edward Bernays

A lifetime of service to his country was etched into the fingers now sweeping over the ivory keys. His hands were large, masculine, but the piano had no quarrel with them. The melody was sad. The empty house in which it was being played could almost cry, its walls shrinking, the ceiling drooping. With eyes closed, the house and the world itself melted into a pool of sorrow. The sun outside pulled clouds over its face, dropping the world into shadow. Creation groaned, birds pouring out their broken hearts in seeming perfect harmony with the pitiful melody that resounded throughout the house before escaping out the open window and into the world beyond.

Edward Cairns sat at the grand piano, his bare feet pressing the pedals while his hands orchestrated a symphony of emotion. His soul was singing, though not with words. A heart like this couldn't be understood by words, couldn't be grasped with the same appreciation that such music allowed. And in that transition, where the brain comes so close yet fails to grasp the reality of another unseen world, there is understanding—though unexplainable. Tears dripped from the corners of his eyes and streaked down his old and hardened face, pooling under his square chin and falling onto the keys. Perhaps, in the end, it was his tears that were playing and not his hands at all.

In the other room, a recording was playing on the TV screen. A younger man, though with similar features, was standing behind a pulpit and pouring out his own heart. But unlike his father's heart, his was full of words that could express what he was feeling by using an inspired and emotional arrangement of the alphabet. The younger man, who appeared to be in his early forties, was found not only on the TV screen, but also within framed walls atop the piano.

Edward opened his eyes and set them on the picture before him. He stopped playing, the melody coming to a sudden, almost violent stop. The birds stopped singing, and it was quiet, though not completely. Now that the music had ended, the faint sound of the preacher's voice could be heard coming from the other room. Edward listened, just as he had a hundred times before.

Finally, he pushed his sixty-seven-year-old frame away from the piano and wiped the tears away with the back of his hand. He walked into the other room and sat down on the couch across from the TV. The German shepherd that was lying on the floor beside the TV looked up at him.

"Come here, Calvin." Edward slapped the empty cushion beside him, and the dog jumped to his feet and rested his head in Edward's lap. Edward petted the dog. "I know, boy. I miss him, too."

Calvin was Jack's dog. Named after the reformer, he supposed. Though some time after getting the shepherd, Jack had a sort of falling-out with Luther, Calvin, and some of the other reformers after discovering that they'd persecuted their own fair share of Christians who didn't agree with the state-sanctioned religion they were hoping to establish against Catholicism. But the dog had already learned his name, and it seemed a cruel thing to go and change it on him.

Now the poor thing was left trying to understand where his master had gone. Whenever hearing Jack's voice from the TV, Calvin would sprint into the room and look all over until finally surrendering and curling up in front of Jack's image, eyes filled with uncertainty.

Edward folded his arms and again turned his attention to the message that got his son killed.

> *"...We fell for every simple trick, evil men laughing at us as we marched to the beat of their drums, our faith so watered down that it became more than faith — it became idolatry! We put our faith in man and in so doing we turned the church of Christ into a political tool. For years we assumed the tool was being used by God, but now that we've seen the end game, we know that what has been guiding the political transformation of the church was certainly not the Holy Spirit. We joined a worldly agenda, forgetting about the Gospel of the Kingdom, and we turned against everything Christianity is supposed to be, using God's name in vain with every breath of political dialogue. Those of us on the Right and those of us on the Left..."*

Edward Cairns leaned back against the couch and stared up at the ceiling. He thought about his son. For a long time, the faith Jack had espoused had been a source of contention in their relationship, and even after Edward had finally succumbed and found God for himself, the particular loathing Jack had toward "patriotic Christianity" was something the two had never been able to resolve.

Edward had given his life to the country and considered himself a "great American" — a patriot. He believed in the Constitution and the Christian heritage of the nation. But Jack had insisted that there was no New Testament blueprint for building a Christian nation, that it was simply impossible. And after taking his father through many of the founders' own words and showing how much some of them actually *hated* Christianity and mocked it outright, he would simply ask, "Is this nation a Republic or a Christocracy?" To which, of course, Edward had no real answer. After all, even he knew that "turn the other cheek" had failed to make it into any of the land's sacred documents. First he had claimed a moral standing on his philosophy of Country and no God. Then on God and Country.

But Jack insisted that the two presented a conflict of interest. Which would start the arguments. Edward would accuse his son of letting Hitlers roam free on the earth, and Jack would say that his father was simply trying to justify the last sixty years of his life.

As Edward had watched the United States slowly dissolve into something else and the Transition finally birthed the North American Union, his frustration always found an explosive release against his son's seeming indifference to it all.

> *"The truth is not determined by what is popular and what isn't. It's determined by itself! It is absolute, unchanging, the knowledge of it available to all who are not too scared to seek it. To those who love God, for He is the truth! But for some reason, mostly due to that false reality we worship, Christians bought into the media doctrine and pledged their allegiance not to the truth, not to God, but to politicians. And too blind to see where this was all heading, we began voting against ourselves."*

With tired eyes, Edward watched his son for a few minutes longer before flicking off the screen. "Be seeing you soon, son." And then his voice drained into a whisper. "For whatever it's worth, I think you were right..."

A week after that sermon, Jack was assassinated. His head shot clean off his shoulders. The media had of course created an entire narrative that provoked sympathy for the shooter, who had just been fed up with Jack's "archaic" and "intolerable" Christian position on social issues. And rather than the shooter being judged as the intolerant one (murdering someone he didn't agree with), the event paved the way for the new thought-crime bill that had already been adopted by the EU. So while the media worked with certain elements of the government to falsify documents and even fabricate whole sermons meant to portray Jack's hatred of so-called progressive ideals, a war for those ideals had erupted across the nation. Soon thereafter, the NAU's ICSF (Inner Continental Security Force) began referring to the "fundamentalist" crowd as terrorists, and anyone caught teaching from an "unauthorized" version of the Bible got to spend a semester in a reeducation camp. Pastors were given the choice to either adopt new "enlightenment" doctrines or have their buildings seized, which led to almost half the churches in the country closing overnight. Not that Jack would've complained about that. He would have been all for the underground church. A church made of people rather than wood and glass and pulpits and offering plates. A church free of the rituals a pagan emperor had long ago shackled her with.

Edward got up off the couch, and Calvin ran to Washington and Jefferson, Edward's own two German shepherds. It was time to get the mail.

The sun broke through the clouds and warmed his tearstained face as he walked down the stone path to the mailbox. There was hardly any physical mail anymore, but he still went out to check every day. Holding on to the old ways, he supposed. He pulled the box open and stuck his hand inside and was surprised to find that there was indeed something there. Two envelopes. He looked up and down the empty street and then quickly took it back into the house.

He went to the kitchen table and sat, the dogs sensing his excitement and coming up beside him with tails wagging. The first envelope was nothing but junk, and his excitement took a nose dive. He wasn't sure what he was hoping for, but it certainly wasn't this garbage. As if all the subliminal advertisements on the TV weren't enough, the corporations still put some effort into targeting the elderly who might not have made the technological upgrades necessary to be victimized by their new marketing schemes.

He crumpled it up and tossed it into the trash can.

The second envelope seemed different. It was heavier and looked to have been addressed by an actual human hand. And it was addressed to Jack. No return address. Postmarked three days ago. He slid his forefinger into the envelope and dragged it from one end to the other. There was a lot of tissue paper inside, and when he turned the envelope upside down, something fell onto the table with a *clang*.

All three dogs looked up as his large hands moved fast to keep it from spinning off the table.

"What in the world?" he asked himself.

Washington barked.

He held the object up to what sunlight the clouds permitted through the kitchen window.

A ring.

He moved the ornament end over end, taking note of its design. He'd never seen anything like it before. Some kind of gem, large and shaped like a lens, sat fixed to the gold band. But it wasn't fixed in a setting because he could see directly through it. Instead, the band came around and fixed itself straight to the side of the gem. An artistic design engraved into the band expanded in the form of wings across the gem's two opposite corners, creating the illusion that the gem was in the care of an angel's wings.

His eyes were too old to make much sense of it, and his fingers were too big to wear the ring, but he was able to feel the underside of the gem with his pinky. It wasn't smooth and polished like the top and without an enclosed band would be pretty uncomfortable to wear.

A knock came at the front door, and the dogs barked, startling him. He set the ring on the table and went to the door.

"Who could this be?" he asked aloud. Speaking to himself and to the dogs helped to lessen the feelings of isolation and loneliness.

He looked out the peephole, his left hand reaching over and resting on the shotgun that he kept leaning in the corner next to the front door—something else that Jack had disapproved of. As did NAU gun laws.

He could make out a familiar face through the small hole and let go of the weapon. He opened the door.

"Hey, Ed," the man said.

It was Matthew Scott.

"Hello, Matthew," Edward answered. A friend's company was always welcome, and he smiled.

"You know they'll put you away for having that thing," Scott said as he pushed his way past him and entered his home.

"Yeah, well, they can—"

"Pry it from your cold dead hands, I know." He knelt to one knee and greeted the dogs.

Edward closed the door and locked it.

"When's Pop gonna get you guys girlfriends, huh?" Scott asked, trying to avoid tongues in his mouth.

"No way," Ed said. The number of pets, like everything else, was strictly regulated.

Scott looked up to his older friend. "Oh, come on. Don't be such a spoilsport." Calvin jumped up and put his two front paws on his shoulders while he walked his hind legs forward. Scott had to wrap his arm around the big shepherd and push back to keep from falling onto his back. "I know," he said to the dog, "I'm trying."

Edward walked into the kitchen.

Scott got back to his feet and joined him. Leaned against the island in the middle of the room. "How are you doing today, Ed?"

"Fine."

Matthew Scott was someone both Edward and Jack had met at the church just four months before Jack's death and, despite him being "unsure about the whole born again thing," the three of them had gotten along pretty good. And then Jack had been murdered. Since then, Ed and Matthew had spent a lot of time together, watching old movies, playing cards, and philosophizing about life—though Scott always seemed to let Edward do most of the talking. It was a friendship that was convenient for both of them, since they both valued the company and the suppressing of certain issues that company allowed.

"That's good. You got any food?" Scott went to the refrigerator.

"You didn't bring lunch with you?"

"Sorry, didn't have any cash on me."

Neither of them used the electronic means of payment, preferring to stay off the grid.

"There's some of that new genetically altered corn on the cob and some cloned chicken."

Scott chuckled as he pulled out a bowl of tomatoes. "These come from your backyard?" Anything unapproved by the FDA was illegal, including vegetable gardens.

Edward leaned against the stove. "You gonna report me?"

"Depends how good they are." And then the ring, still sitting there on the table, caught Scott's eye. "What's that?"

Edward pushed himself off the stove and walked over to it. "Beats me. Came in the mail today. It was addressed to Jack."

Scott raised his eyebrows. "Who's it from?"

"Didn't say."

"May I?" Scott asked, reaching for it.

"Sure."

He picked up the ring and examined it. "What the heck is it?"

"Your guess is as good as mine. Never seen anything like it."

"The band looks like solid gold. Are those supposed to be bird wings?"

"Angel wings, I think. What do you make of the stone?"

Scott peered closer. "Looks polished, almost transparent. It's not a diamond. Glass?"

Edward shrugged.

Scott flipped it over and caught a glimpse of its underside. "That's weird."

"I sure couldn't think of why anyone would wear something like that. It can't be comfortable."

"It looks like a lens, like you're supposed to look through it or something." He was growing more intrigued. "No return address. And it was sent to Jack?"

Edward nodded.

Edward had moved into Jack's house after he died, so he supposed it wasn't entirely strange that something would come bearing his son's name. However, it was the first piece of mail to do so since the federal database had updated his status to "deceased."

"Postmark?" Scott asked.

"Three days ago. Maryland."

"No letter, no nothing?"

Edward shook his head again.

The ring was indeed strange, but there was something else about it too...a kind of *feeling*. But it was a fleeting and elusive one they couldn't seem to grasp.

Scott tore his gaze away from it, the effort it took to do so somewhat surprising, and set it on the open envelope. "Who would send something like this to Jack"—he moved his eyes up to Edward's—"who wouldn't know how he died?"

Edward thought about it for a second. "There was this one girl that he was corresponding with for a while. She was an archeologist or something. They met in Jerusalem, I believe. About three years ago, right after that thing with Syria. I always thought he liked her, thought he would finally settle down."

"What happened?"

"Nothing. She went off to Africa before anything could really develop. As far as I know, that was the last Jack heard from her."

"And if she was gone for a few years, she may not know Jack was killed."

"Yeah, but then why send it with no note or return address or anything?"

"Maybe it's something between them, something that didn't need a note. Something that she didn't want to bring attention to in the event it was intercepted."

Edward scratched his face. "Maybe a hint? Like 'hey, mister, when am I gonna get one of these?'"

Scott shrugged. "How the heck would I know?" He picked up the envelope and noticed something he'd missed. "Did you see this?"

"What?" he asked, the inflection in Scott's voice moving his feet closer to the table.

"There's something written here on the inside of the envelope." He held it up, trying to make out the scribbled letters.

"What are you talking about?"

"Look."

Edward squinted, but it didn't help. "My eyes. Just tell me."

"It looks like 'HELP—MS.'"

"MS…" He sat back into the chair that he'd left pulled out from under the table as his mind searched. "It's got to be her."

Scott dropped the envelope back onto the table. "Her who?"

"The girl he liked." His eyes couldn't hide the sense of mystery that was at work behind them. "Melissa Strauss."

"You think she's in trouble?"

Edward moved a hand over his scalp again. "Well, I'm not sure," he answered sarcastically, "why don't you keep reading."

"You know," Scott replied, "you're pretty crabby today."

Four hours later, the afternoon having been spent pondering the mysterious ring over a game of chess, Scott finally made his way to the front door. He passed a small table and brushed a hand over the book that was resting on it. It was one of the books Jack had written. The front cover was illustrated with a cemetery, the stone in the forefront inscribed "America." And while one might assume the headstone would be in the form of a Christian cross, it was instead an obelisk. He opened the door and turned back to Edward. "Thanks for lunch. Maybe I'll see you tomorrow."

Edward watched out the window as Matthew Scott drove away in his old 4Runner. "He won again, boys… Every stinkin' time." He was speaking to the dogs and referring to the chess match. But that wasn't what was really on his mind. After the three years of keeping his company, there was still something about Matthew Scott that Edward just couldn't put his finger on, something that often had him wondering just who this friend of his really was.

# 4.

*"We shall have world government, whether we like it or not. The only question is whether world government will be achieved by conquest or consent."*
　　　　　　　　　—James Paul Warburg to the US Senate, 1950

Matthew Scott leaned back and crossed his feet on the coffee table in front of him. The house was dark except for the light projecting from the TV. He was surfing through pages of thumbnail previews, the constant flicker mirroring the frantic nature of his own restless world. It was just after midnight, and like most nights, he couldn't sleep. He yawned, and his eyes watered.

He was just over forty, but the shape that he was in was almost uncanny. In the rare instances he had to go into town, people stared. And not just women. It was inconsequential to him, the vanity of it. In fact, he despised the attention. Which was why when he did have to go out, he wore loose-fitting clothes to help hide his muscular frame. There was, of course, a reason for his size, and a reason he didn't strut around showing it off. A reason no one could ever know. It was rare in these times for one to focus so much on his or her physical appearance, which was why most people stared. Sights like him were so rare that most probably assumed he was some noteworthy celebrity or perhaps a porn star. Someone who had the luxury to spend hours in a gym, who *needed* to spend hours in a gym.

*But if only they knew.*

Knew what he knew. And how he knew it. Though that was knowledge he would be taking to the grave with him, the how. And while the grave was inevitable, the longer he could hide his past, the longer he could prolong the appointment. Staying alive was all he cared about right now (and even that was open for debate). He tried not to think of the things that would someday surely condemn him. The things that had been asked of him. *Ordered* of him. He tried to forget what he'd done. But to forget completely was impossible. All he had to do was select the news.

Which he did.

CNN. The wars in Russia, Turkey, and Iran. More terrorist cells found in Canada. Different religious groups denouncing each other, the World Atheist Association once more condemning both.

His bright blue eyes took in the sights and sounds as he brought every current news program up in thumbnails all at once. Waving his finger at the screen, he made the cursor appear and directed it over one of the preview windows with the thimble-like remote, selecting it with an imaginary click of his finger. The station was announcing a developing story, the news anchor referring to an incident in Washington a few days ago.

*"...and as if you couldn't forget just how close the threat of terrorism actually is to us here in North America, we have a breaking story coming out of Washington, DC, just blocks from the White House."* A picture of a woman appeared behind the news anchor's head, up in the right-hand corner of the screen. Her NAU ID photo. *"A woman, who the ICSF says has ties to terrorist organizations around the world, is in a coma today after attempting to evade capture by police."*

The scene switched to the White House press secretary, the date on the screen revealing it to be a recording from yesterday. She was speaking in response to a question one of the reporters had asked.

*"No, sir. The woman blew up her lab and her co-workers."*

The reporter asked why.

*"We're not sure yet, but there is evidence enough to suspect that this is yet another attack on our way of life."*

Another reporter inquired about that evidence. *"That is classified at this time, but we will have more for you as our investigation into this terrible act unfolds."* The woman cleared her throat. *"This woman seemed just like a normal woman. She was born and raised in the United States, she was employed by the NAU, and she seemed very patriotic. So, I think this attack means that, even with the security that has been granted via the North American Union, we still have to be vigilant."* And then, right at the end, she added, *"But we can't let them change how we live."*

Scott frowned, but before he could flick the channel away, the news anchor came back on the screen and mentioned her name.

Melissa Strauss.

Scott sat up straight, his heart pumping fast. He was out the door and in his car before the next story.

****

Scott ran a hand through his short dark hair as he tried desperately to keep the 4Runner from going above the posted speed limit. Though he had removed the microchip from his license plate, created his own registration tag, and his car was too old to have one in the serial plate, it was even more of a reason to be cautious. If one of the scanners tried processing his plate number to send a fine and update his license by adding the necessary points, the computer wouldn't be able to read the chip—which was required by law—and the picture it took of his car would be sent to the authorities with a raised flag. That would bring scrutiny, and the path to a shovel and six feet of dirt would suddenly be a lot shorter. If anyone even bothered digging him a hole.

He didn't want to use his phone. If they had any indication that the letter might have gone to Ed's, they would most certainly be listening in. Even if not, just uttering the word "ring" would be picked up by their word-recognition software, and his records would automatically be pulled. Though everything he owned was registered under false identities, he didn't need any of his records being looked at. So it was worth the slow and torturous drive over to his friend's house. He hoped. He was also concerned about driving past curfew, but he had little choice in that matter. The curfew was only a few days old, so he thought it unlikely the tools would already be updated to transmit immediate coordinates to the local authorities. He could be wrong, of course. Either way, he figured he'd finally worn out his welcome in this town anyway.

Scott turned the lights off as a precaution and rolled the truck to a stop a few houses down from Edward's. Sitting silently in the dark, he picked up the old night-vision monocular from the seat next to him and pulled on the head mount. Designed for the Special Forces ages ago, the monocular went over just one eye in order to maintain the adaptation to the darkness in the other. The world was green and white, but visible. Too visible. He looked to the streetlights. They were out, their solar cells having been taken offline. While opening the door, he looked over Ed's house for signs of other guests.

He saw one.

A figure walking in front of a second-story window. Scott knew it wasn't Edward. He took a quick look around the house to make sure there were no guards, and then he was out of the truck, leaving the door open a crack to avoid the sound of it closing. He ran quietly across the street and into a neighbor's backyard. The grass was wet with dew, and he had to be careful with his footing. He used the bushes and trees for cover. Moving quickly and fluidly, his mind worked through all the possible scenarios that he might find himself in once inside the house.

He ducked behind a bush that stood up against the last fence before Ed's yard and checked his surroundings. He noticed that the lights mounted to the side of Ed's house were dark. He was only ten feet away and knew they were supposed to become active within fifty feet of either heat or movement.

He sprang forward, grabbed the fence, and hopped it in one single motion, landing on the other side without a sound. He ran to the side of the house, the world blurring past him in a sea sickening wash of green light. He put his back against the house and peered through a window beside him. There was someone in there, walking to the back door. He had a rifle in his hand, night-vision goggles strapped to his head.

Scott ducked below the window and moved to the back of the house, toward the back door. Sweat began to bead on his forehead. He spun to the side of the door just as it pushed outward and arched past him.

A man in black fatigues stepped outside.

Scott grabbed him from behind and broke his neck. The person was dead before he'd even realized there was a threat. The vertebrae had snapped much easier than he'd expected.

Scott lowered the intruder to the concrete patio and quickly searched his pockets. No ID, of course. But he took the knife, pistol, and semiautomatic rifle that had been slung over his back. It had a silencer fitted to the end of the barrel. When he pulled the night-vision goggles from his face, he saw that it wasn't a "him" at all. It was a woman.

His stomach clenched, and bile rose in his throat. He hated killing women. Not because he saw them as weak or vulnerable, but because it just made him sick to do it. He knew that most of the women who had fought so hard to win equal standing with men did not foresee their victory as being a direct ticket into an NAU draft. But women being killed in war was a solution to one of the world's many overpopulation problems. Some even believed they were being overdrafted, which, ironically, resulted in more women deciding to identify as men. Was this one of the women who had been tricked by the World Population Project (the global organization that had supported the women's movement the most and the first to point out the threat males transitioning to females presented to all the progress the movement had made over the last century)? He didn't have time to think about it. Ed was still inside somewhere. He swallowed the emotion and guilt (guilt upon guilt upon guilt) and went through the door.

Immediately he saw what she'd been doing.

Three German shepherds were lying dead in the hallway, streaks of blood across the floor from being dragged. Calvin, Jefferson, and Washington—three of his only four friends. All dead. He took a deep breath and cleared his mind. Then he raised the rifle tight against his shoulder and began moving through the house, room to room.

The ground floor was clear. Which meant they had to be upstairs.

Scott walked through the living room and past the grand piano, suddenly catching a glimpse of another intruder across from him. He swung the rifle toward them before realizing it was actually a reflection in a mirror hanging at the bottom of the stairs. In reality, the person was standing at the top of the stairs above him. Scott quickly stepped out of line with the mirror, hoping he hadn't been spotted.

A scream came from above.

There was no more time. He stepped back into the living room and swung the rifle up, pulling the trigger one time. The barrel coughed, and the person above him was flung backward and onto the hallway floor, out of sight. Scott ran up the stairs and saw a door ajar at the end of the hall. He moved toward it, stepping over the crumpled body and squeezing off another silenced round into the masked head as he passed. The casing landed on the carpet at his feet.

He heard a voice. Crept down the hall, following along the banister that guarded the second floor from the first.

"Where is it?" the voice asked. It was the voice of a professional, of someone in control.

But the question got no response.

Scott imagined Ed bound to a chair, face bloody.

"We know it's here. There's no use in hiding it from us."

"Why are you doing this?" Edward's weak voice finally responded.

"It's a matter of security, Mr. Cairns. You of all people should understand."

A weak laugh transitioned into coughing.

"Don't make this more than it needs to be."

Scott was right at the edge of the door, trying to learn who was in the room and where they were positioned. When he entered, he'd need to take them down before they could react.

"Mr. Cairns, where is the ring?" It was another voice, this one even colder than the first.

"I don't have it on me."

Ed screamed in pain.

Scott was out of time and could only hope that the three of them were alone. He was square with the door and knew the two voices were coming from in front of Ed. There was a three-inch gap between the door and its frame. It opened inward. If it didn't squeak when it opened, the two intruders should be dead before they even looked up. But if the hinges were to make a noise…

Scott crouched low, the rifle tight against his left shoulder and already level with where he imagined the combatants to be standing. His right hand pushed gently against the door, and he moved forward, following its arc.

The hinges squeaked.

There was a light source somewhere in the room that created indiscernible bright spots in the night vision, and he could barely make out the greenish figures hiding within its glow. One of the forms turned to face him, thinking it was one of their own people. A soft cough from the end of the sound suppressor proved that assumption to be fatal. But the second person was more cautious and had already begun bringing their weapon around. A shot flew through the space Scott would have been occupying had he not gone in low. The bullet whizzed over his head, and Scott shot the intruder in the face.

Scott stood and quickly swept the smoking barrel back and forth throughout the room. Only Edward was left, and he was indeed tied to a chair. Scott moved fast to untie him, wondering if maybe all the people he'd just killed were women. Best not to know, he thought.

"It's me. Matthew," he whispered to Edward.

"Matthew?" he asked, confused. "How'd you…"

"We'll talk on the way. Let's go." He helped him to his feet and pushed into his hands the night-vision goggles he'd taken off the woman. "Put this on."

Edward began stumbling forward and groaned in pain. "My leg," he muttered. "They stuck a knife in it."

Scott helped Edward back into the chair and quickly examined his bloody leg in the green glow of his monocular. "They missed the artery. Can you walk?"

"I'll try." He reached up and wrapped his arms around Scott's neck. Then, through gritted teeth, he asked, "Did you get them all?"

"Four."

Edward stopped abruptly, halting Scott's progress toward the door. "No, Matthew," he said. "There were five."

"Okay." Scott quickly moved Edward over to the wall, where he could lean against it for support. "Stay here." He handed him the pistol he'd also taken from the woman and then crept out of the room.

Scott saw the fifth intruder just in time and dove to the floor just as bullets flew over his head, tearing apart the railing and punching into the wall surrounding the doorway behind him. The gunman was below him in the living room and firing up through the floor. Pieces of sheetrock, wooden studs, plywood, and carpet exploded all around him, and he threw himself through another door, escaping the overhanging hallway.

He got to his feet. The shooting stopped. All he could hear was the sound of his own breathing.

Then the door he'd just come through shattered to pieces, and wood splinters flew at his face, cutting his forehead. He spun away from the opening and put his back against the wall next to it, sliding down into a squat as chunks of drywall exploded into clouds around his head. He stuck the rifle out the doorway and fired blindly toward the stairs, where he knew the person had to be in order to shoot at the door.

The fifth intruder went seeking cover, and Scott used the opportunity to run back into the hallway. He leapt over the chewed-up section of floor and threw himself back into the room Edward was in, coming up in a tuck and roll.

"It's me, Ed," he shouted in a whisper before his friend could shoot him. He ran past Edward, who was still leaning against the wall with the pistol ready, and went to the window. He used the butt of the rifle to break the pane. "Now get in the closet and don't move."

"What are you gonna do?" Edward asked as he struggled to get to the closet on the other side of the room.

"I'm not sure." Scott lifted one of the dead bodies up onto his shoulder, confident that it weighed over two hundred pounds and sure it was a male. He went to the window and threw the body through the broken glass and onto the roof.

A noise came from the hallway.

Scott dove out the window, using the dead body to stop him from going over the edge of the roof. He regained his footing and walked back to the window, positioning himself off to its side. Then he reached for the corpse and began pulling it by an ankle, dragging the man across the tiled roof until he could grab an arm. He lifted the lifeless body up and held it in front of the window.

Just as soon as he had the man standing, his corpse started to dance, and blood sprayed all over the place. The bullets ripped the body from Scott's hands and sent it tumbling backward and off the roof.

As Scott gripped the rifle, waiting for the person to come to the window, a loud gunshot sounded from inside the room. The unsuppressed shot seemed to echo throughout the silent neighborhood. Somewhere a dog barked.

Scott jumped through the window and back into the room, ready to fire. But the intruder was already sprawled on the floor, blood beginning to pool from a head wound.

"Sorry, I had the shot," Edward said from inside the open closet.

"Your idea was better than mine," he mumbled, though he was afraid the loud shot might end up costing them valuable time. "Come on, we gotta go before the police get here. The neighbors will definitely report the discharge."

Edward worked his way down the hall and into his bedroom, where he grabbed a pair of pants hanging over the back of a chair. He pulled the ring out of its pocket. "Okay," he said, and hobbled toward the stairs.

Scott followed him to the back door and watched as his friend paused before the dead dogs.

"Why don't we take my car?" Edward asked. His voice was somewhat detached, his feet frozen.

Scott knew it would be a struggle getting Edward across the street to where he'd parked the 4Runner, but he shook his head. "I can't leave my car. They'll find us if I do. You can make it." He put a hand against the small of his back and urged him forward. "C'mon, we have to go. Now."

They crossed the dark street and got into the 4Runner. As Scott pulled away and steered the car back toward his house, he looked in the rearview and saw the streetlights flickering back to life behind them.

"Where are we going?" Ed asked.

"There's a few things we're gonna need," Scott said.

# 5.

*"All of us will ultimately be judged on the effort we have contributed to building a New World Order."*
— Robert Kennedy, 1967

Matthew Scott dressed and cleaned Edward's wound. He worked fast, knowing there was a lot to do and very little time to do it in. The TV was on, and more 3D terror alerts were scrolling through the air in front of the screen. The terror alert had been red for a week now, indicating to both Scott and Edward that something was about to take place.

Just as Scott finished with Edward's leg, they saw headlights out the window.

"Shhh." Scott shut off the TV. "Get on the couch and lie down. Stay there."

Edward eased himself out of the chair and over to the couch. "Police?"

"Yeah." And he ran upstairs and slid into bed.

The armored vehicle drove slowly down the street, its headlights grabbing the street in front of it while a searchlight swiveled on its roof. The bright light flashed through the windows and for a moment turned night to day. Scott knew the vehicle was also equipped with thermal technology and laser microphones that enabled the operators to see and hear beyond walls. Scott had tossed the confiscated weapons into a creek on the way back, so he wasn't worried about the RFID tags in the triggers showing up in the police scans.

The vehicle passed by.

Scott waited another few minutes before getting out of bed and rejoining Edward in the living room. "I'm going to pack. You should get some rest. Tomorrow's gonna be..." But he couldn't bring himself to finish the sentence.

Edward nodded, knowing exactly what Scott didn't want to say. But without his dogs, he didn't really care. He was suddenly having trouble coming up with a reason to stay in this world. As he looked into Scott's eyes, he read his concern. "I'll be fine, Matthew." Then he rolled onto his side and closed his eyes.

"I'll wake you when it's time," Scott said. He went to the window and split the blinds with his fingers. No sign of the police. He looked at his watch. It was a little after one. Curfew didn't end until five. They'd leave at 5:30. But where they would go was still uncertain. He left the living room and moved down the hallway.

He was ready for this day, always knew it would come, though he had imagined different circumstances creating the need for it. He also hadn't counted on anyone being with him, especially not an old man with an injured leg. He'd have to make some alterations to his plan. Though, he had to admit, he never thought he'd be able to hold out this long. He reached for a backpack that he kept on the top shelf of the hallway closet and wondered if he was grateful for the extra time, for what it had allowed. It hadn't restored his marriage or brought back the friends he'd once had. Hadn't taken away all the shame, hadn't restored peace or mended the nation...

Whatever.

With the pack at his feet, he began lifting the floating shelves and leaning them against the hallway wall. Then, once the shelves were out of the way, he stepped into the closet and removed a three-foot-by-three-foot section of sheetrock. Behind the hole was another wall, this one holding a compact M4 rifle. He lifted it off the hook and stole a peek around the corner, back to Edward sleeping on the couch. His friend was going to want to know about all of this. Who he really was. He wondered how much he should reveal and how much would be better left unsaid. He let his brain work on that problem as his body went about the preparation, pulling the ammunition and other equipment out of the compartment and setting it alongside the assault rifle.

He was packed and had a story ready for Edward within an hour. He set his watch, crossed the living room, and went up to his bed.

But he couldn't sleep. Too much going through his head. He thought of Edward, how he'd managed to outlive everything in life he'd held dear. His wife, his son, his dogs, and even the country he'd served. And, in an indirect way, Scott had something to do with the latter, didn't he? He would omit that little fact when giving Ed his story.

From there his thoughts traveled randomly and without direction, just one leading to the next. The ring, Jack, this archeologist girl, Indiana Jones, the old movie theatre by his house, his first date… And by the time he arrived at what always proved to be the ultimate destination, he wouldn't be able to decipher the labyrinth of ideas that led him here. To *these* thoughts. Thoughts of his wife.

The last time he'd seen her was just a few months after the "terrorist" attack in Los Angeles. A long time ago. He could still feel that last kiss they shared before he crossed the tarmac and boarded the plane. The plane to hell. He turned onto his side and, as with every night, tried chasing that image of her from his head—the short strawberry hair that blew down across her green eyes as she waved goodbye…the tears that passed over her quivering lips.

He pulled a pillow over his head as if that might help vanquish the picture that was so engrained into his mind's eye. It was like an ever-present picture hanging on the underside of his eyelids, always there whenever he closed them. He wished he could take it down, to erase her memory and forget she ever existed—that *they* ever existed. He didn't know where she was, how she was, or even *if* she was. All he knew was that it was all his fault. Everything.

It was times like these that he wished he were back in that dark room and all he could hear was his own screaming and all he could see was his own blood. It was a better reality than the one that paraded the only thing he ever loved so mercilessly through his thoughts. To have his head sawn off with that rusty blade would have been a wonderful thing compared to living with the guilt of leaving her. If only he'd been killed, then he'd have an excuse for why he didn't return to her. But death wouldn't justify what he'd done *prior* to that, the very reason he was unable to come home. It was the largest and most damning of all his sins, the watershed to all that tormented him.

He had been strong enough to escape the physical danger and to stay alive all these years, but every new day that passed chipped away at the resolve it took to withstand the emotional anguish that came with the surviving. The thought of ending it all was a nightly one, usually tempting him the most after all efforts to take down the picture failed, and all he wanted to do was to fall asleep. It would only take one single moment, less than half a second to put himself into the deepest of sleeps. One trigger pull, that was it. And if he never woke up from that sleep, even better.

But he deserved to wake up. Over and over again for all of time. Life was his punishment, and he would continue to use it as self-flagellation.

Then, suddenly, it wasn't just his fault anymore, and a crowd of faceless men came front and center before his mind's eye, blocking the picture of his wife from view. But they weren't men, just shadows of men. His muscles tensed beneath the sheets, and a tremor ripped through his body. He thought of what he would do to those men if ever he was before them.

# 6.



A faint red glow broke the horizon, the line it struck across the distance a fire signaling the end of the world. Or maybe just the beginning of another day. Either was a possibility.

Mathew Scott stood next to the coffee table, his eyes fixated on the ring resting on its surface. He'd been intending to walk past the table and into the kitchen when he caught a glimpse of the thing, and it had stopped him in his tracks. He was still staring at it when Edward came into the room, and it wasn't until Ed's hand was on his shoulder that he blinked and was able to look away from it.

"You okay?" Edward asked.

"Tired." He turned away from the table and changed his mind on the kitchen, going for the packed bag instead.

"How did you know I was in trouble?" Ed asked.

Scott answered around the corner. "News report came on saying Melissa Strauss blew up a building in DC."

Silence from the living room.

"Said she's in a coma now."

"She must've known she was in trouble and thought Jack could help her somehow," Ed said.

"That's what I figured. Knew they'd be looking for the ring." He walked the bag and the rifle back into the room and saw that Ed was staring at his bulging forearms.

"She was trying to keep it out of their hands…"

"Whose hands?" Scott asked.

Ed looked up, but his face was blank.

"How's your leg?" Scott asked instead.

"We need to talk."

Scott set the bag down. "I know you have questions, but we gotta get moving. I don't know if they can trace you back here, but we're not sticking around to find out."

"I'm not going with you."

Scott blinked. "What do you mean?"

"I'll only slow you down."

Scott didn't have time for this, and he said so.

"Matthew, I can't do this. Look at me. I've become an old man. I just don't have—"

"Am I gonna have to throw you over my shoulder like a child, then?" Scott interrupted.

Edward could tell from the look in Scott's eye that he was prepared to do just that. And he knew he could. He sighed. "I guess there are better ways to go than being tortured to death."

Scott could certainly think of one.

Ed grimaced as a jolt of pain raced down his leg. "Where are we going?"

"North."

"What's north?"

Scott shrugged. "If we go far enough, nothing."

Edward turned his head, motioning back at the ring. "What about that?"

"Toss it in a lake. Story over."

Edward answered quickly, already having considered such a solution himself. "I'm not sure. Why would she send it to Jack instead of getting rid of it herself? I think she wanted him to have it, to figure out what it means."

"We could speculate all day, Ed. But soon we're gonna hear choppers, and then we'll never find out what it is because we'll be dead."

They both looked at the gold ring with angel wings, intending just a casual glance at what they were referring to, but again it seemed to hold their eyes, whispering of mysteries they could sense but not explain.

"I would like to find out what it is," Edward said under his breath, more to himself than to Scott.

"We need to go. Now," Scott said.

# 7.



Scott backed the 4Runner out of the driveway just as a shadow flew over them. He craned his neck to look up through the windshield and just saw the black tail of a helicopter disappear over the tree line.

"Didn't even hear it," he mumbled. It had been traveling low and fast, nearly invisible against the dark rainclouds already gathering in the north.

"Hear what?" Edward asked, looking up at the sky.

"Nothing." He put the vehicle in drive and began heading south.

They drove in silence as if simply breathing too hard might give them away. The sound of the engine thrummed in their ears, and they kept glancing at the sideview mirrors, expecting to see flashing lights racing up behind them.

No one else was on the road this early in the day, and that was a problem. Not that they had much choice. Leaving before curfew expired would have been way too risky, and waiting until later would have subjected them to roadblocks. Hopefully, their exodus was in the small window between the two.

They would find out in a second.

Rounding a bend, Scott made a turn away from Jamaica, Vermont, his home for the last decade.

They could see the highway up ahead. It was their only real option of getting out of town before everything was locked down and they found themselves trapped. But a few army trucks and some police cars were already there, blocking its entrance.

They were too late.

Scott turned the headlights off and brought the 4Runner to a slow stop. The 4Runner was matt black, and there was a chance they hadn't been seen. But before Edward could even say something, Scott had the car in reverse and was backing down the road and around the bend. Then, once the checkpoint was out of view, he hit the brakes while jerking the wheel hard right. The 4Runner spun 180 degrees, and Edward's head cracked against the window. Scott threw the vehicle into drive while in mid-turn and slammed on the gas as soon as they were facing north.

"Sorry," Scott said.

Ed rubbed his head as he leaned back into the passenger seat, his left hand going forward and gripping the dashboard. "If we can't get to the highway—"

"Just hang on."

But Edward knew that there was only one other road out of here and that it too would be blocked off. Jamaica State Park was their only option now. "Drop me off at your place," he said.

"What?"

"The park is your only way out, and I'll just slow you down."

Both things were true. In fact, the park had been Scott's original plan. The very reason he'd settled in Jamaica. He'd always intended on ditching his vehicle in the park and disappearing into the wilderness on foot. There would be plenty of options for him at that point. But Edward's wound had changed all that. Traveling slowly through the park would only ensure detection by the NAU troops that patrolled it.

"No," Scott stated.

"I'm serious, Matthew. Leave me." Edward's voice was stern, like he was giving an order to a subordinate.

But Scott would have none of it. "I'm not leaving you behind. And if you say another word about it, I'll break your jaw."

Edward blinked, taken aback by Scott's tone and seeming sincerity. He'd never seen this side of him before, and again he wondered just who this man really was.

Flashing lights appeared behind them.

"Company," Edward stated. The black police car just happened to be turning off a side street when they passed it at sixty-five miles per hour.

Scott took the old Toyota up to eighty as an awful siren obliterated the early morning calm. Scott's own street flew by in a blur as he sped past it and continued toward the only other street that could get them out of here.

Until a few armored security vehicles broke the horizon ahead, coming straight toward them.

"You should go back to Worden Street," said Edward, leaning into the back seat for the M4.

"Yeah, I think you're right."

The ASVs' DARPA-designed 90mm electromagnetic rail guns would more than complicate their odds of escaping in that direction. Scott pulled a pistol from his pants and put both windows down. The morning air came rushing into their faces, and again Scott slammed on the brakes, this time turning the wheel hard left. The world beyond the windshield blurred dizzily into a half-spin, ending with them rocking side to side on the 4Runner's wheels and facing the oncoming police car, the ASVs now behind them.

Edward leaned out the window and fired the M4. The car and its flashing red lights were only seventy-five yards away and closing fast. The 5.56x45mm NATO rounds splashed against the car's hood and pierced both front tires, sending it off the road.

"Well, you're committed now," Scott said, referencing the severity of Ed's actions — of which summary execution was the state's required punishment. He pressed the gas pedal to the floorboard, and smoke erupted from the spinning tires. They shot forward just as machine-gun fire erupted from behind, exploding the back window. "Get down!" Scott yelled. They flew past the broken police car and back toward his own street. The military would squeeze them from both directions now.

The park was indeed their only option.

Scott turned hard, and the 4Runner screeched as it skidded back onto his street. A wave of 5,400 mph conductive projectiles screamed from the rail guns and pierced the passenger side of the Toyota with a rapid series of *thunks*.

"You okay?" asked Scott once they were heading straight down the street and out of range. He glanced over at Edward. "You hit?"

"No, I'm fine." Ed turned to look behind them. He started counting and got to six before the three ASVs turn the corner behind them. "Here they come," he said.

Scott looked into the rearview and saw the metal beasts for himself. He knew the military vehicles were equipped with wheel independent suspension that gave them superior mobility, but his main concern was the rail gun. If they got within range, they'd reduce his car to scrap metal in mere seconds—even with the reinforcements he'd made to it over the years.

"Hurry," Edward muttered.

The park offered nearly eight hundred acres of cover and was only half a mile away. But they needed to put enough distance between them and the ASVs if they stood any chance of exiting the Toyota alive.

Ninety-seven miles per hour. They passed his house. "How much time will we have?" Scott asked.

"Ten seconds if we're lucky."

Three paved roads wound through the park, everything else walking paths. And though his vehicle could handle the bumpy terrain, the ASVs could handle it far better. Their only hope was to ditch the truck and force the soldiers to come after them on foot.

They sped through the park's entrance, leaving the town behind.

Helicopters approached from the north.

They got beneath the forest canopy just in time. The leaves had already begun to turn their reds and oranges, but hadn't really begun to fall yet, so Scott didn't think they'd have a problem with the choppers. "How close?" he asked.

Edward looked back over his shoulder again. "Don't see them yet."

"Hold on." And without further warning, he suddenly veered off the asphalt road. Foliage flew up into the windshield as the 4Runner went off-road, underbrush striking the headlights and scraping against the doors. Scott and Edward bounced in their seats as they navigated the uneven terrain.

Scott hoped that the damage to the plant life wouldn't be noticeable to the soldiers operating the ASVs, and that they'd pass right on by them.

He drove a little farther into the shadowed forest and then brought the 4Runner to a stop, killing the engine. He knew that the better trained soldiers would be stationed in the big cities and other areas of conflict, and that the ones assigned to their little Vermont town were most likely far less experienced. If so, there was a good chance that they wouldn't notice the bent foliage.

"They're going too fast," Edward whispered.

They watched the ASVs' headlights race toward them through the thicket. And then pass them by.

"Let's hope they take the road to its end," Scott said. He started the 4Runner back up. "That should give us enough time." He turned on the headlights. The canopy was shielding the rising sun, and it was too dark to try navigating the forest without at least a little light. He didn't think the helicopter pilots would be able to see the two beams through the treetops. "I have a spot where we can spend the day," he said.

Edward stared at him. Watched him drive. Watched his eyes. The look on his friend's face, that set determination in the midst of everything falling apart around them, was not a new sight to Edward. He'd seen it before. In other men. Men who'd experienced combat. Men who *excelled* at combat. Special Forces types. The elite. Until now, Matthew Scott had shown no indication that he was one of those men. "You plotted this path a long time ago."

It wasn't a question.

Scott offered a slight nod, keeping his eyes locked on the near-invisible ground ahead. "I made it," he clarified.

"You *made* it?" Edward asked. "Made what?" And then he noticed how the ground in front of them seemed less dense, more forgiving. "You cleared a path?"

"Every summer I'd take just a little off the top so that I could see the path without attracting any soldiers."

"You knew this day would come."

Scott's eyes darted over to him. "You didn't?"

Edward didn't answer, just stared up at the colorful leaves that were the park's sky. "So where does it lead, this path of yours?"

"A cave."

"They'll send dogs."

"I know."

"You picked this place out." He waved his hand. "Not the park, your house, I mean. This area. You wanted a getaway route. Access north. Why? Why would you need that?"

"Why *wouldn't* I need it?" he deflected.

"You know what I mean."

But he didn't answer. Instead, he brought the Toyota to a stop. "Get out. I'm gonna ditch this thing, and then I'll come back to get you."

Edward nodded without argument and pushed the door open. He climbed down into a bed of wet ferns, then softly closed the door. He hugged the rifle's stock against his shoulder.

"I'll be back," Scott said.

And the vehicle began moving away, disappearing into the darkness. Edward hobbled over to a large tree and sat. The sound of Scott's car began to fade, and the living forest filled its void. He looked at his watch. It was 6:34. He rested the weapon on his lap and pulled at his jacket, fighting against the cold October morning. As his breath materialized in front of him, he listened to the sound of a nearby stream. The wind was blowing through the trees, rustling the leaves. A few fluttered to the ground around him, and he remembered when he used to take Jack to places like this when he was a boy. It had always seemed to help gain some kind of perspective in a world that seemed to have none. It had been their little retreat center, their refuge from the harsher realities of the world.

Edward leaned his head back against the tree and closed his eyes, feeling the cold breeze move over his face. He thought about Jack and his late wife, Naomi, who had died of cancer a number of years ago. He thought about their reunion one day—a day that would certainly be sooner rather than later. But for now, when he opened his eyes, there was only the multicolored forest there facing him. No loved ones welcoming him into Paradise. Just Vermont.

And then a noise.

He sat up straight, his eyes darting back and forth through the underbrush.

A doe.

He relaxed and leaned back against the tree. He watched the animal, thinking about the danger she faced and the fact that she didn't even know it. Had no idea there was even a threat. The world beyond the forest didn't exist to her, yet that ignorance would not protect her. A missile could destroy her entire world at any moment, the fingers of a global evil no longer limited by boundaries of distance.

She looked up, and even from thirty yards away and with his bad eyes, Edward could see those big black eyes, the twitching ears. *That's right, my friend. Not all is as it seems.* But then she dipped her head back to the ground and resumed eating.

Edward moved his eyes off the deer and took in the trees. They didn't know either. Didn't know that a third of them would be destroyed according to the book of Revelation. Or maybe they knew a lot more than anyone gave them credit for, the book of Romans saying that all of creation was groaning for the day all will be restored.

"Soon, I think," he whispered. And he closed his eyes again.

****

Edward nearly had a heart attack when a voice sounded behind him and startled him from sleep. Turning with the M4, he saw Scott standing just a few yards away.

"Come on," Scott repeated.

"Must've dozed off…"

Scott helped him to his feet. "Can you walk?"

"Are you offering to carry me?"

"No."

"Then I guess I don't have much of a choice." Clenching the muscles in his jaw, he stretched out his stiff leg. "Hurts."

Then a sudden blast of wind roared through the treetops, pulling leaves away from their branches and moving them like giant clouds around them.

"It's gonna rain," Edward said.

Scott nodded.

They reached the cave in twenty minutes, and just in time. Somewhere out there in the woods, they could hear the faint barking of dogs while more helicopters beat the air above them.

# 8.


*"To achieve world government, it is necessary to remove from the minds of men, their individualism, loyalty to family traditions, national patriotism and religious dogmas."*

—Brock Chisolm,
former director of the World Health Organization

Edward brushed dirt from the shoulder of his jacket and raised his eyes to the ceiling again. It was hanging just two feet from his head, and he couldn't help feeling a little claustrophobic within the cramped confines of Scott's hideout. He kept glancing upward, expecting the tree that sat above them to come crashing through.

Scott noticed and said, "That tree is nearly a hundred years old. It's not going anywhere today."

Ed nodded, but his eyes continued searching for cracks in the cave's structural soundness.

The entrance to the cave had been an opening so small that they needed to crawl on their stomachs to get through it. It was really nothing more than a den inside a one-tree hill.

Ed shifted his weight on the homemade chair. His leg was killing him, and it felt good to get off his feet for a little bit. He moved his gaze off the ceiling and throughout the candlelit space. There was a small table and a shelf that held some bowls, pots, and other utensils. Beyond all that, he could just make out Scott's silhouette about ten yards deeper into the cave. He was kneeling beside a pile of dirt and digging with his bare hands.

"What are you doing?" Ed asked. He wiped sweat from his brow.

Scott threw another handful of dirt onto the pile. "Getting my supplies."

"How long did this take?"

"The cave? A few years. Once I found it, I just had to dig it out and reinforce it."

Ed nodded, though Scott wasn't facing him to see it. "You're six hundred and eighty-eight feet above sea level, with the park at the end of the street, Ball Mountain a little northwest, access to West River, and all in a county with a population of only five hundred people."

"Like I said," he grunted, "it was a good location to settle down in."

"Who have you been hiding from?"

Scott stopped digging and wiped his brow with the back of his hand. Then he looked up through the shifting candlelight and the myriad of shadows it was creating. But he said nothing. Instead he turned back and pulled a large army bag out of the darkness. He swung it around and plopped it on the ground between them, the work it took to do so indicating how heavy it was. He turned and pulled out another one, dropping it beside the first.

Edward watched as Scott took a breather, his chest heaving, hands on hips. "Weren't you afraid they'd find this place?"

"The UN troops?" Scott shook his head. "You saw how the tree roots come over the entrance. Something would have to lead them here, and I switched up my route every time to avoid making a path. But even if someone did spot the hole, no UN or NAU soldier is gonna crawl through it without being ordered to."

"I'm surprised. It was before your time, but the 1972 World Heritage Treaty and the Man and Biosphere Program saw to buffers around state parks that were operated by UNESCO."

Scott nodded. "In the name of protecting ecosystems, they were able to get UN troops on American soil, I know. But like I said, the few who patrolled this area were bored and lazy and just looking to put in their time so they could get back to whatever country they came from."

"So were you actually planning on living here?"

"Figured I could if that's what it came down to. I'd take it one day at a time though."

"You'd go insane living underground like some hermit."

"Maybe. But if I wanted to go out fighting, I got New York to the west, Massachusetts to the south, and Quebec to the north."

"You really did think this through."

Scott turned away from him again, reaching for something else. This time it was a large metal box that he pulled out of the dark womb. But unlike the two duffel bags, he set the box down with an awkward sort of reverence. He flipped open the two latches on its side and swung the lid open.

Edward leaned forward for a better look. "Are those—"

"Yup."

Edward stared at the grenades and claymore mines that were stacked within the box. "Who are you?"

Again, Scott didn't answer. He unzipped the army bag and pulled out a huge M107—the army's first semiautomatic .50-cal. sniper weapon system. He leaned it against the wall. "An oldie but a goodie," he said. "Effective on multiple targets up to two thousand meters. But too loud for this."

"*This*? What is *this*?"

He went back into the bag and this time extracted a fully assembled AS50 semiautomatic sniper rifle. "Designed for special ops. Twenty-seven pounds dry weight. Fifty-three point nine inches long."

"I know what it is, Matthew," Edward said. "My question is just what you're planning on doing with it."

Next came an HK 417 assault rifle, an M249 Squad Automatic Weapon (or SAW), a few pistols, another M4, and a whole lot of ammo.

Edward got back onto the chair and sighed. "I'd really like to know what you're planning, Matthew."

Next, he laid camo for each season out across the floor. He took off his jacket and picked the digital bushland pattern with a four-color autumn palette.

"How are you holding up?" Scott asked, deflecting the last question.

"Fine. A little sore and out of breath and a little upset about my dogs—"

"I meant about killing that guy last night."

He shrugged. "Self-defense." He watched the flame flicker on the wick. "Not the first person I've killed."

"Oh yeah? Back in your military days?"

"Yeah. Right about when everything started hitting the fan." He paused. "I hated it. Killing men who were ordered to do the same things I was." He rubbed his bald head. "Making widows and orphans out of people I'd never met just because someone said I had to."

"That's war. Old men playing chess with the lives of the young."

"Yeah. But last night they came into my house."

"What if they were ordered to?"

"Then they had a moral obligation to reject those orders."

"What if they were told you were planning on blowing up a school the next day?"

Edward fell silent. He knew what kind of stories got invented in order to make following orders more appetizing.

"My point is," Scott said, "I don't ask the questions you ask. I just do what I was trained to do."

"So you suppress it?"

"Of course I suppress it. The things that I've done would make any normal person stick a gun in their mouth."

Edward stared at his feet. "It will come. Someday you won't be able to outrun it anymore, and it'll jump on your back so hard..." He looked up. "Unless you start to like it. In which case maybe you should put the gun in your mouth."

Scott smiled as he got undressed. "Good people depend on bad people to do the dirty work for them. To win their so-called just wars. To keep them safe."

"Is that what you were doing? Keeping people safe?"

*On the contrary*, Scott thought. "Is this the thanks I get for saving your life?"

"I'm sorry. I just don't want to see you put a gun in your mouth is all."

"This is the part where you tell me about forgiveness and redemption and all that stuff Jack preached, right?" He shook his head. "Not interested."

Edward sighed. "Will you at least tell me who you are?"

Scott pulled on the pants. "Who I *was*."

"Okay, who you were."

"CIA."

"Data entry, right?" Edward quipped.

"Black ops."

"And the story?"

"Sold my soul to a flag. Then found out it didn't mean anything anymore." He reached over and grabbed a water bottle out of his backpack. After taking a sip, he offered it to Edward.

Edward took it and drank. "Go on," he said, wiping his mouth.

"Got captured in Iran." He put the jacket on. "Just about had my head sawn off. Wasn't one of my favorite days. Anyway, the Agency offered to bring me home for a while, but I didn't really trust them, so I decided to stay put." His eyes were focusing on his fingers as they worked the buttons. "Then I heard that some of the guys I'd gotten involved with in the past were starting to turn up dead. Heart attacks, hit and runs, airplane crashes. There was no doubt that someone was tying off loose ends."

"Loose ends?"

"Something we were involved in before Iran. Anyway, the Agency suddenly wanted to fly me home for 'debriefing,' but people like me aren't allowed to retire, and I wasn't looking to disappear on their terms. The base I was staying at was attacked by rockets and machine-gun fire, and I managed to slip out during the chaos."

"How'd you get back into the States?"

"I knew plenty of people who'd take money without asking questions. Got a new identity and laid low. Avoided places overly friendly with surveillance and police."

Edward tried recalibrating what he thought he knew about his friend, but it was going to take some time. He asked a more personal question. "You have any family?"

"Had." And he quickly deflected that line of questioning too. "What about Jack?"

"What about him?"

"It's gotta kill you what they did to him."

"Of course it does. The way the church denounced his works while at the same time endorsing any sleazeball politician who called themselves a Christian..." Again, he bowed his head. "My son was right about everything. Even I couldn't see it at the time. How we separated faith from politics while trusting political princes who were said to have faith. We were a walking contradiction."

"Hypocrites."

Edward accepted the accusation with a solemn nod.

But before either of them could say more, a noise louder than thunder echoed off the cave walls and spilled dirt from the ceiling.

"That's my signal," Scott said, and he tucked a 9mm Beretta into the back of his pants. He knelt over the open backpack and quickly began transferring the ammo, claymores, and grenades into it. "Stay here. I'll come back for you when it's safe." He put the sniper rifle and the M4 over his back so that the straps crisscrossed his chest. Then he pulled the backpack on over top of them. "I'm leaving the SAW and the other M4 with you. You shouldn't need them, but..."

"What do you think you're gonna do?" Edward asked, shocked. "There could be a hundred troops searching the woods by now."

He grabbed the HK 417. "Don't worry."

"Don't worry?"

"Be happy." He flashed a smile. "Just stay here."

Edward didn't find it funny. "And what about the ring?"

"What about it?"

"If anything happens to me —"

Scott moved past Edward and toward the exit. "Nothing's gonna happen to you as long as you stay put."

And then he was gone, leaving Edward alone with the flickering flames and moving shadows. He took another sip of water and thought of the biggest part of the story that Scott had left out. What he'd been involved with prior to ending up in Iran. And why he had to come to Vermont to hide from it.

Reaching into his pocket, Edward delicately removed the ring Melissa Strauss had sent to his son. He stared at it and prayed for Matthew's safety. For his own clarity within the vast ocean of insanity that seemed to be rising all around him.

# 9.



*"The drive of the Rockefellers and their allies is to create a one-world government combining supercapitalism and Communism under the same tent, all under their control... Do I mean conspiracy? Yes, I do. I am convinced there is such a plot, international in scope, generations old in planning, and incredibly evil in intent."*
—Larry P. McDonald, Congressman, 1976

Scott slid out of the cave, wiggling his way through the roots that covered the entranceway. Once free of them, he got to his feet and walked to a nearby stream. It was raining now, and thunder rumbled in the distance. He looked up to the sky and gladly welcomed the huge drops that pelted his face. Rain was a good thing. It would help conceal his presence, turning dry and brittle ground into soft, pillow-like silence.

Squatting beside the stream, he thrust both hands into the cold mud along its bank and smeared it over his face. He kept doing it until his whole face was covered. How long it would last before the rain washed it all off, he didn't know. But he didn't think this would take long.

He stood and searched for a state of mind that he hadn't been in touch with for a long time. Where was that old audacity that had rendered him invincible? Lethal? He needed to remember...

The explosion had come as a result of someone trying to open the door to the 4Runner, so he knew exactly where they were.

He began walking in that direction.

Fifty yards later, he was sprinting through the freezing rain, ice once more filling his veins.

He remembered.

He jumped off a small ridge and landed on his feet, using the momentum to propel himself forward onto his stomach. He scurried to his right, seeking the cover of a tree and the dense undergrowth that had been growing in its shadow. The remains of the Toyota were about two hundred yards ahead of him. He could just make out its charred and smoldering frame.

Scott maneuvered the AS50 semiautomatic sniper rifle from off his back and opened its bipod. After setting the rifle up in front of him, he peered through the high-powered scope, and the distance between him and the 4Runner nearly vanished. There were a few badly burnt and dismembered bodies strewn around the Toyota's remains. A little to the right of that was a circle of troops and loitering police. They were gesturing into the woods, angry and confused.

Scott knew they couldn't see him through the thick undergrowth. Not with the naked eye and from two football fields away in the rain. And there was no sign of the dogs he'd heard earlier. Still, he tried not to move any more than he had to.

He continued to scan the woods through the scope but didn't see any more soldiers in the area. Seven from the circle by the 4Runner began to fan out, moving away from him.

Scott had left the 4Runner at the center of a depression in a spot where the trees were spread out and thin, ensuring that he would have a clear line of sight while his targets wouldn't be able to pick him out against the dense forest behind him.

The crosshairs fell over a soldier holding a satphone to his ear, and the four data lines split his head into four quadrants. Sever communication to the outside first…

He lay still, allowing his heart rate to slow.

Two hundred yards wasn't a distance great enough to have to worry about the geophysics of the shot. Just needed to be still and calm down after the long sprint. He looked back through the scope. He had pre-adjusted the sights for this distance and now only needed to make a minor alteration. He accounted for the wind and held his breath.

*One. Two. Three. Four* —

He pulled the trigger.

The shot rang out all the way to Ball Mountain before echoing back. It could have been mistaken for thunder if it weren't for the exploding head that came as a result.

The group of soldiers stood there, blood splatter covering their faces, in their eyes. They stared in shock at their fellow soldier suddenly dead at their feet.

Scott moved the crosshairs slightly to the right, splitting another magnified head into fourths.

He fired, a red mist left hovering in the rain where the next target's head had been. Picked up another confused NAU trooper and shot him too.

That was when the remaining men finally took off running for cover, stumbling over rocks and slipping on wet leaves. They didn't know where to go, which direction to flee from.

Scott had the face of a frightened trooper in his sights next, but just as he went to squeeze the trigger, the rifle dipped, and he shot him in the leg instead. The soldier fell to the ground, clutching what was left of his calf and screaming.

There was one round left in the magazine, yet Scott found himself hesitating. Which allowed the soldiers fanning out more time to home in on his position. It was strange — the delay. He couldn't get his mind around it, to forget about it and move on. The fact of it just stood there blocking his ability to calculate, to act. Why had he chosen to let the man live? It was a decision that could come back to haunt him and a decision that went against everything he was trained for. It raised questions from the dead, stalling his mechanical precision. Yet, somewhere far off in his innermost being, there was relief. He blinked, trying to get his finger to operate the trigger. Something was different. Maybe Edward's warning of his past sins finally catching up to him was already starting to come true. Or maybe it was the woman he'd killed last night that was giving him pause. He didn't know. But what he was sure of was that his little mental breakdown had given them too much time to react.

The crackle of machine-gun fire burst out against a background of thunder, and a nearby tree began spraying splinters of wood at him. He resisted the instinct to move, to seek cover as bullets flew past him. To move a muscle would be suicide. The soldiers were shooting blind, firing in the general direction of the attack. They didn't know where he was, and it was best not to tell them. He lay still, unmoving, holding his breath.

When no immediate return fire answered back, the soldiers stopped shooting. They were spreading out now, using the trees for cover as they walked toward his position.

Scott cursed himself for his hesitation. He should've fired his last shot and reloaded before the rest of the soldiers could fan out. Now that they were getting closer, the SA50 would be useless. He'd have to reload at least three times to finish them off, and he'd be dead after the first. He rejected the thought of using claymores or grenades—the thick forest would protect most of the soldiers from the blast, and he'd have to get up to throw it anyway.

Setting his sights on the closest soldier, he could see his face clearly—even the water drops running off his smooth skin. Brown eyes, high cheekbones, thinly pressed lips. Maybe twenty years old. He was dipping below the intersecting data lines and then coming back up between them as he moved across the uneven ground. Scott's last round went through his neck.

Scott jumped to his feet and spun toward the tree, leaning his back against it. He threw the AS50 over his shoulder and replaced it with the M4. He could hear the soldiers' voices and the confusion in them as they shouted to one another. They weren't well trained, just warm bodies with guns. Expendable. Scott moved away from the tree and began running away from the dozen or so NAU troopers now quickly closing in on him. He would circle around and come up behind them.

Once he was sure he'd gotten behind them, he crouched down and tried to catch his breath. A helicopter passed by overhead. He sprang back to his feet and began charging their flank.

****

He was looking at their backs. They were fanned out in a crescent formation, their eyes and weapons focused on the ground ahead of them. The sniper rifle was out of the question. The first shot would throw the target forward onto their face, and then all the soldiers would know he was behind them. Only this time they would be the ones with the dense forest as their cover, and he wouldn't be able to get them all before they got him.

Scott could make out the seal on the armbands of the soldiers to his right. The North American continent inside a circle. They were NAU troops just like he'd thought. But the soldiers to his left had a different seal, comprised of just two black letters. UN. And between them was one lonely police officer. They were stretched out, left to right, over fifty yards. He watched them walk, allowing them to get deeper into the forest. He'd need to have the cover of the woods himself when he started his attack.

A deep breath. Another.

He ran.

With the rain concealing his movements, he came up on the NAU soldier positioned at the line's end. He fired the M4 at his back, sending him to the ground.

Scott spun and disappeared behind a tree, waiting for the response the loud report would invoke. Once the shouting began, he quickly darted from his cover and moved to a tree closer to the next trooper.

Another breath.

He leaned away from the tree and fired, striking the disoriented soldier in the arm and stomach.

But this time some of the others spotted him, and a moment later they were all shooting in his direction.

Scott ignored the tree being shredded behind him and removed the HK 417, SA50, and the backpack from around his shoulders, dropping them at his feet. Then he fired some more shots around the tree and managed to send the converging troops looking for cover.

He opened the backpack. Removed two grenades and stuck one in his pocket. Then he stepped out from behind the tree, firing the M4 from his hip. When the soldiers ducked for cover, Scott used his teeth to pull the pin from the grenade and then tossed it as high and as far as he could.

Even over the rain, the soldiers could hear the metal bomb falling through the trees above them, bouncing off branches, knocking leaves loose.

While the troops' attention was focused above, Scott switched to the 417 and ran to a fallen tree. He dove behind it as the explosion rocked the park.

When all he could hear were screams, he got back to his feet and gathered the stuff he'd left at the tree. Then he approached the dead and dying, shooting them one by one.

It was over.

Standing in the pouring rain, his muddy mask nearly gone, Scott swept his eyes over the casualties. One of them must've been closer to the blast than the others, their clothes burned off, the shrapnel nearly severing them in half. But there was still enough anatomy left intact for Scott to recognize its female characteristics. He closed his eyes.

And this time he did vomit.

Whether it was the adrenaline crash, the smell and gore, or the fact that he'd killed his second woman in two days, he wasn't sure. He only knew that something within him had changed over the years. Nothing like this would have bothered him so deeply before. But whatever it was, he wiped his mouth and ignored it. Reinforcements would be here soon.

He started jogging back to the cave. Back to Edward.

****

The rain was coming down harder, and now lightning was flashing through the sky. That was good. No more helicopters.

As Scott ran along the stream's bank and approached the cave, he moved his eyes back and forth, looking for signs of anything out of place.

Nothing. Just sheets of freezing rain obscuring the fiery red and orange hues of fall. He continued to wade through knee-deep ferns. But then he got a glimpse of the cave's entrance and stopped.

Running in front of it was a set of tire tracks.

He brought the M4 to his shoulder and stepped closer, now noticing footprints in the mud too.

Scott shed his equipment and ducked into the hole, crawling on his chest through the darkness. "Ed!" he called.

Quiet.

"Ed, it's Matthew. I'm coming in." There was no light to greet him, just a black void. All the candles were out. He knew the tracks had been made by an ATV, and he wondered if its driver was down here waiting for him. Would he finally get that bullet out of this world? He moved about his hideout, finding the table with his outstretched hands. The pots and pans, the empty army bags, the chair Ed had been sitting in. "Ed!"

No answer.

He continued searching the room, not sure whether he wanted to find a body or not.

But there was nothing there.

# 10.



He crawled toward the waterfall that covered the exit as fast as he could. When he reached it, he grabbed the roots hanging over the opening and thrust himself through the wall of water and back into the day.

He jumped to his feet, pausing only long enough to grab the M4. There was no time to worry about the backpack or the sniper rifles. If he could, he'd come back for them. There was another magazine duct-taped to the side of the one already loaded, so at least he had that.

He chased the tread marks east, guessing that whoever had been driving the ATV wouldn't have been heading for the mountains west. He slipped in the mud and nearly went down.

Eventually, the tracks led him out of the dense woods and onto a trail. Scott knew it was a tactical blunder to keep on the path, out in the open, wooded hills on either side of him, but his only concern was catching up to Edward, and he took the risk.

Thunder and lightning continued to converse above him as he tried coming up with a theory as to why there was only one set of tracks. If the military or police had somehow found Edward, they would have been traveling in a group. At least two or three. And why would Edward have left the cave? Was it possible that someone else could have known about it? Was this the work of the same shadow force that had tried acquiring the ring from Ed last night?

*No way*, he thought.

The topography ahead of him began to change, the sides of the small valley evolving into a steeper and denser ridge on his left while evening out on the right.

But that wasn't what he was looking at.

Peering through the sheets of rain, he saw the tire tracks begin to swerve, driving in and out as if the driver had been struggling to keep the vehicle on the path. And then the tracks went straight off the trail and into the woods to his right. Had Edward put up a fight, sending them off the path?

He felt something graze his forehead, and when he touched it, there was blood on his fingertips. He took off, sprinting through the slippery muck, speed his only chance at survival. He could hear the bullets smacking into the trees twenty yards to his right, proving the sniper was up on the ridge to his left. He blindly fired the M4 in that direction and could only hope the rain would provide him with enough cover.

He broke right, running toward the trees in a zigzag pattern, not wanting to give the shooter a steady shot at his back.

He made it through the tree line, shielding his face with his arms as splinters rocketed past him. He continued following the tracks down a slight decline. Saw that they disappeared into a sea of ferns.

He jumped into the feathered undergrowth and started calling out for Ed, not sure if he was still being fired at or not.

And then he saw it. Turned on its side, three bodies still straddling it. "Edward!" he yelled, raising the rifle and covering the other two men on the quad as he approached. But they were both dead. One shot through the heart, the other missing half his skull. "Ed," Scott whispered. He kneeled beside him and tried pulling his body out from under the vehicle. He stole a glance back through the trees and to the ridge beyond, but the sniper (or snipers) was no longer shooting. Scott knew that was because they were already on their way down the hill and closing in on his position.

"Edward, it's Matthew," he said. He noticed blood dripping off his friend's hand, running down out of his sleeve. Scott stole another glance back toward the ridge and spotted movement through the trees. He counted at least three bodies making their way toward the trail. He ran through the ferns and took a kneeling stance, firing the rifle from his shoulder and forcing them to go for cover.

He saw three more.

Six of them.

But why weren't they firing back?

He didn't know, didn't care. He went back to Ed and dragged him behind the quad. He quickly opened his jacket and discovered the source of the blood. A bullet had pierced his chest.

Scott leaned over him, placing his ear over his mouth. He was still breathing. Barely. Though there was nothing Scott could do to delay the inevitable. A flood of emotion surged through him as he ejected the taped magazines, flipped them over, and rammed the full one into place.

The six people were crossing the trail, just a hundred and thirty feet away. Scott leaned over the quad and shot at them. Struck one, the others parting for cover again, still not shooting back. And then Scott spotted at least ten more of them still up on the ridge. He looked back down to Edward, but his friend's eyes were still closed. He looked back to the trail.

They were gone.

He swung the weapon to the left, then to the right, his finger already starting to pull the trigger. He peered through the pouring rain, but there was no sign of the remaining soldiers anywhere.

A hand grabbed his ankle.

Startled, Scott looked down and saw that Ed's eyes were half open.

"Matthew," he whispered.

Scott turned away from the ridge and the trail and slid into a sitting position against the ATV. He cradled Edward's head in his lap, ignoring the bullets that were finally beginning to ricochet off the quad. "Shhh..." It was the only thing he could say. *Just a moment longer and it will all be over. For both of us.*

Then a strange smile curled Edward's lips. "Jack..." And his eyes grew wide and he reached up, grabbing Scott's hand. *"Israelis..."*

His hand opened, and Scott felt something drop into his palm. He looked down and saw the ring sitting there. When he looked back up, Edward's eyes were closed.

He was gone.

Scott closed his eyes, the fight out of him. But he wasn't so sure he was about to be welcomed through celestial gates. Not by a long shot, and no smile crossed his lips as he prayed to the Great Nothingness to take him away. It seemed the better of the two remaining options he'd heard about.

He stared at the picture of his wife, thinking of the last time he'd seen her. Kissed her. And then the picture fell off the wall, the event and the hell that followed it shaking the room.

Judgment was coming.

*No! I'm not ready!*

He opened his eyes and saw that they'd surrounded him. His fate was out of his hands. He started to reach for the grenade still in his pocket when a huge explosion came from behind, engulfing him in its heat.

With ringing ears, he twisted to get a look behind, and saw that the ridge was in flames. He didn't understand.

And then he felt something sting his neck, and his vision began to fade. He shook his head, and the park rolled like an ocean out before him. He thought he saw a figure approach him, and he wondered if it was Lucifer coming to claim his own. With one last faltering remnant of consciousness, he managed to drop the ring into his pocket.

Strangely enough, Ed's last word was also Scott's last thought.

*Israelis...*

# 11.



Sounds came from another room, a whisper gliding through the crack beneath the door.

Talking.

It was his mother, but he could only make out bits and pieces of what she was saying through a dense fog of obscurity. Still, he perceived enough of it to understand that it was intelligent.

*"People are trained from birth to think within a small designated space..."*

But it was strange, as if her voice was stolen and being used by someone else. Someone in the future who would understand the importance of what it was she was saying. He shifted, straining to hear more of the once familiar voice. *The voice...* No, his mother had died when he was thirteen. So it couldn't possibly be her voice that he was hearing.

And it wasn't. In fact, it never had been, the voice instead masculine. His father's voice.

*"The Orwellian creed — 'ignorance is strength' — put forth in 1949, is the perfect example of man's inability to think."*

He was familiar with that creed. But no, this wasn't right either. His father had killed himself after his mother died.

*"The extent of the hypnosis is almost unthinkable. People still waving flags of countries that no longer exist."*

His teacher at the Farm, giving a lecture to all the young recruits! He remembered that day well, what he was feeling, what he was thinking, wondering if he'd get operations or intelligence. He'd been assigned by the Directorate of Operations and sent to Tehran. No, Baalbeck. Or was it Salah Al-Din? Whatever, he knew he was in Islamabad. Or at least Iraq. But then he was pretty sure he'd been in all of them. As a matter of fact, he was there right now, in all of them. Every single one. New Delhi, Kabul, Medina, Jerusalem, even London. What he was doing there, he couldn't tell. Something important. Something dangerous.

He tried to focus on his teacher's voice…

*"The real war that is waged is a war for the mind, but the people won't fight it. Why? Because it doesn't exist? No, because those waging war on them tell them it doesn't exist. And so it doesn't. The pairing of ignorance with the death of history has become the ultimate form of patriotism."*

He was confused, disturbed. Nothing he'd ever heard from his teacher at the Farm had sounded like this.

No, he couldn't be at the Farm, could he? Not in the Middle East or Europe either.

Slowly, he regained consciousness, and a growing semblance of cognitive awareness began to enlighten the words he thought had been spoken by people once familiar to him. In fact, there were no voices. Just products of his own thoughts mixing with past faces.

When he finally opened his eyes, his pupils retreated in the face of a blinding light. He blinked, allowing his eyes to adjust, and noticed the bare bulb hanging over him. Instantly, he was back in Iran, back in that room he'd spent years trying to forget.

He shut his eyes. Concentrated.

The disorientation faded, and he began to get a sense of his surroundings. There was the light above him. He was lying on his back, restrained. A cold stale smell was in the air. He had a headache and could hear faint voices coming from somewhere distant.

He checked his motor skills and was happy to learn that he could wiggle his toes, clench his fists, and turn his head. But he couldn't sit up. He could tell he was under a blanket, and though he couldn't see them, he could feel the restraints securing him to the table.

"What do we do with him?"

It was one of the voices coming from…where? He looked to his right and saw a doorway concealed in shadow.

"We find out who he is," came the response.

It took Scott a few seconds to realize that the people talking were not speaking English but Hebrew — a language he knew well enough from the crash course he'd gotten from the Agency as well as his time spent in Jerusalem (his ability to pick up on languages was one of the things that had made him an attractive recruit). Though he was suspicious as to why the sacred tongue was the language of choice here. Wherever *here* was.

He ran through the last series of events, allowing his mind to catch up with the here and now. The NAU and UN troops, the ATV, Edward…

The people on the ridge.

His head was pounding, and he tried to think through the pain. He didn't think they were UN, NAU, or local law enforcement. But whoever they were, they'd been positioned to either take out the ATV or to cover its getaway. And the explosion — where had that come from?

He pushed the loss of Edward and everything else that didn't make sense into the background of his mind, and instead focused on getting out of there.

Whoever secured him to the table had done a good job keeping him from rolling off it, but that was about it. So the person responsible was either polite or incompetent. Scott wasn't going to assume the prior and wouldn't count on the latter. With enough slack in the restraints to allow some wiggle room, he began inching his way toward the end of the table.

"Why did you bring him back here?" The discussion was still going on behind the door.

"Don't you think it would be wise to find out what he knows?"

In Scott's experience, things usually took an interesting turn once talk like that started. A pair of pliers came to mind.

With his head positioned as an anchor, he used the muscles in his neck to pull his body along the table while helping himself along with his fingers. Soon his head was hanging over the side of the table, and he was able to sit up. He squirmed out of the bonds, leaving the blanket behind, and hopped off the table. It was only then that he realized he was naked. He swore under his breath and looked around the small room, but he found no trace of his wet fatigues. Having no other choice, he snatched the blanket from the table and flung it around his waist.

His bare feet pitter-pattered across the cold floor as he frantically searched the four walls, looking for another exit. But other than the table and the light bulb, the room was empty. There was no other exit.

Scott approached the door and put an ear against it, trying to better hear the language of the Chosen.

"I will not let you do that!" They were still arguing. But it didn't seem to be about him anymore. That was good.

"He is the only one who knows where it is," another voice interjected.

"Yes, if you believe the stories."

Another voice spoke, this person's Hebrew tainted with a European accent. "Friends, we do not have time for this. Any second now the camp may be stormed, and our mission will end in failure."

Scott didn't think it possible to be any more confused, and part of him wondered if this could still be part of his dream. He tried to control his breathing, sweat beading on his forehead despite the cool air. He wiped it away and saw a line of blood on his hand. Whether from the splinters of wood or the sniper's bullet that had grazed him, he wasn't sure.

"Wake him up," someone commanded.

Footsteps approached the door.

Scott jumped back, quickly studying the door hinges. They were on his side, so the door would swing toward him. He flattened himself against the cold wall, chills running up his bare flesh.

The door swung open right at his face, hiding him between it and the wall.

The person entered the room, passing him, and then stopped when he saw the empty table, the straps loose on top of it.

Scott leaned his shoulder into the door and rammed it shut, knocking backward a few men who were just about to enter.

The man who was left in the room with him drew a pistol, but he'd been late getting it out, and Scott snatched it from his hand before he could even raise it. He grabbed the guy from behind and had the pistol pressed into the soft tissue behind his ear before the guy even knew what was happening. It took all of Scott's self-control not to pull the trigger. It was too much like last time, like Iran, and he felt himself beginning to lose it.

When the door opened again, four men with semiautomatic pistols were standing before him.

"Drop them," Scott ordered, jamming the point of the gun further into the back of the man's ear.

The four men hesitated.

"Now!"

One of them, a bearded man, spoke in English. "And what will you do if we do not? Shoot him?" He stepped closer. "I do not think so."

"Stay back."

"How about you put down the gun, and we will forget this ever happened," the bearded man said.

Scott quickly swept his gaze over the other three. As fast as he was, he knew nothing about these men. If they were Jewish, then it was quite possible they were Mossad, and if that was the case, then he'd stand little chance against four of them. Though what reason the Mossad would have for being here was far beyond anything he could imagine. "Forget that you killed my friend?"

At that point, the man lowered his own pistol, and a twinge of sympathy flashed in his eyes. "We did not kill your friend."

In that split second, Scott swung the pistol up and fired, dropping to a knee while pulling the man down on top of him, using him as a shield, and shooting the other three.

Or at least that was what he saw himself doing in about two seconds. He blinked, looked around the room. "Where am I?"

"Please, I can see that you are upset and understandably so. Why don't you lower the gun, and we will have a civilized conversation."

"We do not have time for that," one of the others interjected.

But the bearded man ignored him. "Perhaps you would like some pants?"

Scott could feel the knot in the blanket begin to loosen. "Pants would be nice," he said.

"Then please put down the gun."

The man Scott was holding at gunpoint finally spoke up. "It is okay. We are men of our word."

With his world spinning upside down, the effect of the drug they had used still prominent in his system, he realized that he had little choice.

The bearded man sighed. "Please, I am begging you. We are pressed for time here, and we will shoot you if you force us to. There are more pressing matters that require our immediate attention."

Scott figured he'd be dead already if they'd wanted to kill him. Heck, they'd had him unconscious and strapped to a table. They could've done anything they wanted to him. He stepped away from the man, though he kept the gun trained on him. And then, with a deep breath, he lowered the pistol. He could feel himself shaking.

Turning to face him, the one he had held hostage said, "Thank you. It was a wise decision."

Scott shot him a look that said it better have been.

One of them walked back out the door, hopefully to get a pair of pants, while the others came closer. "Can we have the pistol back, please?"

"I don't think so."

He nodded, acknowledging the unspoken terms, and everyone else lowered their guns. "So, who are you?"

"Who are *you*?" Scott retaliated.

After a second, the man answered, "You can call me David."

"Okay, David." He leaned against the table, fatigue almost causing him to collapse. "You can call me Matt."

"Are you a soldier?"

"No." His head was getting heavier.

"You handle yourself like one. You have obviously been trained."

No response.

David tilted his head to the side as one of his men whispered into his ear. He didn't look all that happy with what was said. He nodded, however, agreeing to whatever it had been.

"Matt, it is essential that we understand who you are *not*."

The puzzle wasn't coming together by any means, Scott still feeling as if he were on some kind of hallucinogenic, but he was starting to sense that these men simply wanted to know whether or not he posed a threat to them. "I'm nobody. Just someone trying to survive."

"And your relationship to Edward Cairns?"

"A friend."

"I see." David brought his hand to his mouth and stared at the floor, thinking. "I do not have time to keep asking questions, Matt. So I am going to risk exposing myself in the hopes that you...cooperate with us."

Just then, the man who had left returned with a pair of pants. "They should fit." He threw them at Scott.

"Thanks." He kept the gun ready while struggling to pull them on.

David continued. "We are Israeli Mossad."

Scott's eyes narrowed, and a dark chuckle escaped his lips. "What are you doing here, in *North America*?" And he couldn't keep from his tone a sarcastic undertone that accused the man's home country of having something to do with the former Republic's current world status.

Detecting this, David answered, "We are operating outside of national scrutiny. You could say that we are 'off the grid.'"

"Rogue agents."

David flinched. "That is a bit harsh. Let us just say we owe our primary allegiance to the Promised Land and to our faith."

"So then you're *not* part of the global cabal running things back in the Holy Land…or you are?"

David shook his head. "No. On the contrary."

And all of a sudden, through fatigue and all, Scott realized in part what had happened out in the woods. "You took out the people on the hill."

"Yes."

"So then who took Ed from the cave?" Even as he asked, Edward's last words floated through his mind.

*Israelis…*

"That was us."

But before Scott could work out the arithmetic in his head, David added, "You took the ring from him."

And the world seemed to drop out from under Scott's feet. "You were after the *ring*?"

"Why else would Edward be of interest to us?"

Scott forced himself to stand tall. "And the little visit he got last night?"

"That was NAU Intelligence." He looked to one of the men next to him and signaled for him to leave. Then he walked closer to Scott. "Look, you cannot understand what is taking place, what is on the verge of happening. Not now. And we simply do not have the time to explain it to you. I do not know who you are, but for some reason I believe that you are on our side, or at least not opposed to it. You were Edward Cairn's friend, so I assume you share a common belief about what is happening in the world now. That it is the end of days."

Scott frowned. "I neither espoused nor rejected his prophetic views. I didn't share his faith."

"That is unfortunate. I am sure he would be sorry to hear you say that. Nevertheless, your attempted escape and your fight with the soldiers suggests that you have no love for them."

Scott raised his heavy eyes. "*Them?* I don't know what you're talking about." He brought his hand up to his head as a sudden sense of vertigo swept over him.

"I am sorry that we had to drug you, but under the circumstances, you would have been confused as to who we were and would have mistaken us for the enemy." He smiled sheepishly. "In a way, we saved your life."

"Why wouldn't you just shoot me?"

"We are not like that. Not when we do not need to be," said a new voice behind David. And the person who'd spoken walked into the room. He was a tall man with silver hair and eyes that beamed with purpose. He was also wearing the white collar of a Catholic priest. Without any introduction, he held up the ring and asked, "Do you know what this is?" His tone was forceful, not one to play games and against the clock.

"No." Scott eyed him suspiciously. This was the guy he'd heard speaking with a European accent. "You guys all friends?" he asked. History didn't necessarily paint the two groups as the best of friends.

The priest ignored him. "They say rings were introduced as a symbol of power. Probably in Egypt. Evolved from the signet or seal in about the sixteenth century BC." He smiled, his eyes locked on the clear lens. "You have felt its power, haven't you?"

He didn't answer.

"You know there are many legends and myths surrounding rings." He seemed to be entranced by it. They all did. "In medieval times, rings made from certain materials were thought to have occult powers. They were made to protect a person or to influence another. Inscribed cabalistic words and astrological signs were believed to hold mysterious powers." Then he let his eyes slide upward to meet Scott's. "Some wonder whether or not those myths and legends were born of a truth."

Though Scott could not deny the strange way the ring made him feel, he surely wasn't going to admit it. Not to this clown.

The room started spinning, and he was growing too weary to keep up with the unfolding present. He just wanted to sleep.

That was when the priest looked him straight in the eye and asked, "What does the year 1947 mean to you?"

"1947?" repeated Scott. "Is this a game?" He was so tired.

"First week in July."

David looked uncomfortable. It was obvious that he either disagreed with what the priest was about to say, or that he didn't trust Scott to hear it.

Scott smiled sarcastically. He knew the reference. "Martians invaded Earth?" He leaned back against the table.

"Whether or not they were Martians is a subject of debate. What is *not* is that something significant happened and that the government covered it up."

"Roswell? What does —" He grabbed his head and closed his eyes. So tired. So confused. He began to sway from side to side.

Just then, another Israeli burst through the door. "They're here!"

David took one long look at Scott before turning and fleeing through the door along with the rest of the Mossad agents.

"Who's here?" Scott asked, managing to lift his heavy eyes to the priest.

"The enemy."

Gunfire began erupting somewhere far away.

"What's going on?" Scott stumbled away from the table. He needed some kind of foothold on reality, but he was afraid he would be too tired to hold onto it once it was offered.

"I am sorry, but there is no time to explain now. We are under attack."

"By who?"

The priest shook his head as if he almost didn't know how to answer. "I guess it depends."

"Depends?" *Why is everything a riddle?*

Ignoring him, the priest turned and exited the room, leaving Scott in just a pair of pants and trying to maintain his balance. "Wait!"

Somewhere above him an explosion rocked the earth, and clouds of dust fell from the ceiling.

He stumbled forward and chased after the priest.

# 12.

*"There is a chance for the President of the United States to use this disaster to carry out what his father...a phrase his father used, I think only once and hasn't been used since, and that is a New World Order."*

—Gary Hart, September 12, 2001

Explosions rocked the ground and rattled the walls, and he had to reach out to steady himself as he ran up the stairs. All hell seemed to be breaking loose, and all he had was a pair of pants and a pistol.

He came to the top of the stairs, his feet freezing on the cold concrete floor, but didn't see any sign of the priest. It looked like he was in a cafeteria, tables lining both sides of the room. He noticed bars over the windows.

After quickly checking the 9mm he'd taken from the Israeli agent, he began moving across the room.

And then there was a blinding flash of white, and the room was gone.

His ears were ringing. He tried to open his eyes, but all he could see was smoke. He was lying on the ground, the pistol gone from his hand. Everything was moving in slow motion. His brain pounded in his skull.

He rolled onto his side. Saw the gun lying in some burning debris nearby. He tried to get up, but it took a few moments to regain control of his limbs and to hear beyond the alarm bells still sounding in his head. The smoke started to part, moved along by the sudden presence of wind blowing through the room.

He started crawling, trying to get a sense of what had happened. Something had exploded, but he didn't know what. He became aware of a fierce burning in his back, but he ignored it and kept moving through the dizzying chaos, things on fire all around.

Then he saw the far wall. It seemed to be missing, reduced to rubble and scattered throughout the room. He could make out the dark shapes of people running by outside.

Suddenly, what was left of the hovering smoke shot away in big curling wisps as a loud thumping noise began hammering his swollen brain. And then the head of a monster appeared, descending from the floor above and staring at him through the hole in the wall. It just sat there, watching, its scorpion-like tail extending away from its body and ready to strike.

Scott forced his body to move, getting up off his hands and knees and back onto his feet. He ran, veering off balance to his left and right, stumbling over debris, trying to stay upright. To get away from the hovering locust that was watching him.

He dove for the gun just as the black AH-64 Apache helicopter tilted to its side and moved laterally away from the opening while simultaneously releasing a burst of fire from its automatic cannons. The deafening rounds struck the floor, tables, and the back wall, filling the room with more concrete shrapnel. Scott covered his head with his hands.

And then it was gone.

Whatever lingering effect the drug had on him, the explosion and the helicopter attack seemed to have taken care of it. His head still pounded, and he still felt a little dazed, but he no longer felt the need to curl up and go to sleep. He got back to his feet and went to the crumpled wall, unaware of just how cold he was. That he couldn't feel his feet.

He climbed over the broken wall and stepped out onto the wet grass. And entered a war zone.

Three Apaches circled the facility, strafing it with rockets and missiles. They were farther away though, their flight pattern taking them away from him. But he knew they would be circling back around soon. He had to get to the woods.

Without a second thought, he began sprinting toward a barbed-wire fence that was lying across the ground, twisted, its posts bent downward at sharp angles. Like it had been run over by a tank.

As he sprinted across the fifty yards of open grass, he turned to see where the Apaches were and saw that one was already beginning to swing back toward him. He wasn't going to make it.

Ahead of him, a figure suddenly emerged from the tree line. There was something on its shoulder. Scott tensed, expecting to be ripped in half by a grenade. Instead, a surface-to-air missile went screaming from the person's shoulder and over his head. Scott turned and watched it climb into the sky, heading straight for the Apache.

The missile struck the helicopter's tail and exploded. The chopper started to spin in circles, a trail of smoke spiraling from its broken tail. Then it crashed into the building and burst into flames, its rotors snapping off on impact and flying through the air like a huge lawnmower blade. It flew right past Scott, chewing up the grass and sending clumps of dirt spiraling into the air as it passed.

The person who had fired the missile began jerking involuntarily and then collapsed beneath an umbrella of blood.

Scott's eyes darted back and forth, searching for who had shot him. But it was ultimately the two remaining Apaches swinging toward his position that captured his attention. They rose above the building, elevating together like uncoiling twin serpents about to bite. But they were still on the other side of the—

For the first time, Scott was able to get a good look at the complex. At the guard towers. The razor-wire fences.

It was a gulag.

Explosions continued to blow the deserted prison camp to pieces, but even through the blasts, Scott was able to pick out the sound of machine-gun fire coming from his right. He swung in that direction and saw two men running toward him.

They were fifty yards away and shooting weapons from their shoulders. But Scott didn't feel anything, which, considering their rate of fire, he thought was odd. He should be dead by now. Then one of the men stopped shooting and began yelling something in Hebrew while pointing. Scott turned to see what it was they were shooting at, if not him, and saw four men in black ski masks moving back and forth between scattered debris. Whether they were shooting at him or the two Israeli agents didn't matter. Either way, he was in their line of sight.

The Apaches opened fire.

The two agents who had been covering him were instantly shredded to pieces by the Apache's large rounds. Then the four masked men began concentrating their aim solely on him. Geysers of mud peppered the ground around him, their bullets homing in on his route to the woods.

But then there was another explosion, and when he looked back, he saw only a crater where they'd been, body parts strewn all over the ground around it.

He made it through the tree line and sought cover behind a large rock. Peering over its top and back to the camp, he watched as the Apaches began taking fire from somewhere within the demolished building. The two helicopters pulled back, intent on coming around for a better angle of attack. More masked men were engaged in a firefight with what Scott assumed to be more Israelis, but he wasn't interested in sticking around to find out. The sun was dropping, and colder temperatures were coming.

He turned his back to the fighting and pressed on into the trees.

****

Darkness had spread itself over the woods, bringing with it frigid air.

Matthew Scott was rolled up into a fetal position beside a small fire, too cold to fall asleep. It was maybe a degree or two above freezing. Too cold to spend the night in the elements with no shirt or shoes. How he'd even managed to start the small fire was a miracle in and of itself.

He thought about trying to make his way back down to the gulag. To scavenge clothes and materials from the dead, but the thought of walking in his bare feet all the way back there... He'd rather stay here and die.

*Snap.*

Scott heard something over his chattering teeth. Something in the woods, making its way toward him. But he was so cold that he couldn't bring himself to care. If only he could get more wood into the fire. But he couldn't move. Couldn't think.

He tried raising the pistol at the emerging form, but the gun just shook all over the place. It was no use. The pistol fell to the dirt as his will dripped away, and he closed his eyes.

# 13.

*"The real rulers in Washington are invisible and exercise power from behind the scenes."*
—Felix Frankfurter (1882–1965),
US Supreme Court Justice.

He wasn't sure what to expect when he next opened his eyes—whether he'd be an ice sculpture, or standing within the innermost circle of hell. So when he looked up through tired eyes and saw the sun breaching the jagged horizon on its way up through a cloudless sky, he was confused.

He turned his head and saw trees in every direction. Colorful deciduous and evergreen pines, their tips glowing orange beneath the morning's early gaze.

But that wasn't right. There's no way he should be—

He looked down and discovered that he was wearing an army jacket. And wool socks on his feet.

*What the—*

Then he noticed the charred earth where the fire had been. A few charred remains burned red in the morning breeze, but the scorch radius was far too big to have been from the same fire he'd made.

He got himself onto his hands and knees, feeling the stiffness in his joints. Then he got to one knee and stood. Pain shot through his feet and blew away the remaining cobwebs of fatigue. He adjusted the jacket and began taking a more careful look around.

Footprints that weren't his around the blackened earth.

Scott checked the pistol to make sure it hadn't been tampered with. It looked fine.

Strange.

He continued searching for clues and found one in a broken branch. Delicately making his way over to it, he bent to one knee and peered into the thick undergrowth beyond, looking for more signs. And there were plenty.

Had they been made intentionally? Were they left behind for him to follow?

What else was he going to do?

He started walking after the trail of broken sticks and crushed foliage, leaving all the confused and agonizing events of the prior day free to continue their stories around the scattered remnants of the mysterious fire. But not with him. Not now.

An hour or so passed, and his feet were about ready to quit on him. The socks were beginning to come apart over the hard terrain, and as he climbed up a slight rise, he —

A house.

At the top of a hill about a hundred yards away. Not a bunker or another prison camp, but an actual house. With siding. A deck. A shed.

Scott gripped the pistol with both hands while searching every inch of the house for signs of activity. It didn't appear to be occupied, but he knew better. Whoever had given him the jacket had wanted him to follow them here.

He navigated the surrounding woods and approached the steps leading up to the deck, careful to stay beneath the windows. He crept to the back door and reached for the handle.

It was unlocked.

Would opening it set off alarms or trigger an explosion? Only one way to find out. He took a deep breath and pushed it open.

Silence.

He raised the pistol and aimed it into the kitchen. It was a pretty nice kitchen, too. State-of-the-art appliances, lots of cabinets, an island.

But no sounds of rushing feet to greet him.

He left the door ajar behind him and continued making his way through the kitchen and into the den, his socks not making a sound across the wooden floor.

Coughing. From the second floor.

The den led to a hallway that ended at a staircase. He climbed the stairs one cautious step at a time, following the noise. When he reached the top, he was faced with another hallway, doors lining both sides of it. He tiptoed to the one the coughing was coming from and stood before it. Should he knock? Kick it down?

He decided to knock.

*Click.*

He could feel the cold steel press against the nape of his neck.

"Drop the gun, please," demanded a soft and unfamiliar voice.

Scott set the safety lever and did as he was told. And before he could determine whether or not the person with the gun was a threat that required neutralizing, the door in front of him swung open.

And there stood David.

Scott wasn't sure if he was surprised to see the Israeli agent or not, though now he knew where the jacket had come from.

David was holding an automatic rifle, the shoulder strap of which was looped down toward the floor. "Hello," he said.

"Hey," Scott replied.

"This the guy?" the voice behind him asked.

"Yes," David responded.

The cold pressure against Scott's neck vanished.

David spread his arms. "Welcome," he said.

"Well, you look considerably worse than the last time I saw you," Scott said. David looked as if he hadn't slept in ten years and had cuts and bruises all over his face. His hair was disheveled, and a portion of it even looked like it had been scorched.

David nodded. "It has been a long night."

Scott turned to get a glimpse of the man behind him and came face-to-face with a six-foot-tall, blue-eyed, medium-built character dressed in light jeans, combat boots, and a long-sleeve shirt under a sleeveless jacket. His face was made up of sharp angles that were mostly hidden beneath a few days of stubble, the color of which matched his medium-length black hair. He was holding a modified AK-47.

"You're pretty quiet," Scott said.

"Name's Mayhew. Titus Mayhew."

"Matthew Scott."

"Pleasure."

David stepped beside them and grabbed the jacket Scott was wearing. "How did it do?"

"Kept me alive. Thanks." He looked down and wiggled his toes. Then he glanced at David's boots. "No more boots?"

"I fed your fire and gave you my jacket and socks. It was all I could do at the time."

"Were you gonna come back for me? You know, invite me to breakfast or something?"

"I figured the trail we left would suffice as an invitation to join us." He turned and walked back into the room. "Do you remember the priest?"

Scott followed after him. "How could I forget."

"He is badly wounded, and I do not think he will survive."

"Sorry to hear that." Actually, he didn't really care.

"We went back to the facility after dark to try to find something that might help him. We came across you on the way back."

There was a bed in the room, and Scott recognized the face of the priest protruding from beneath a blanket, his head propped up on a pillow.

"Here," Mayhew said, handing him the pistol back.

"Actually, I think it's his," he said, motioning toward David.

David waved him off, and Scott took the gun from Mayhew and stuck it into his waistband.

"Any chance of getting a change of clothes around here?" Scott asked.

"There is a closet in the other room," David said.

Scott nodded and turned his back to David and the dying priest. Walked past Mayhew, who was not an Israeli, and made his way down the hall and to the door David had pointed to. He went in and found two couches positioned around an old seventy-inch 8K television. There was a bookshelf full of old novels and movies.

Walking past all that, he went to the window and pulled the curtains aside so that he could survey the area around the house. There was an ATV parked by the front door and a path that led into the woods. Other than that, he saw nothing.

He left the window and went to the walk-in closet. There were plenty of clothes to choose from, and he grabbed some dry socks, a pair of running sneakers that were only half a size different from his own, a pair of jeans that might just fit him better than the ones the Israelis had given him, and an old red Nike T-shirt with a big white Swoosh across the chest.

There was another door in the room, and when he opened it, it was like he was opening the gates to paradise.

A bathroom with a shower.

"David," he called out into the hallway, "we safe here?"

David appeared in the other doorway and shrugged as he pulled something out of his pocket. "We will never be safe so long as we have this." He held it up so that Scott could see.

It was the ring.

"But we do have some time," David added.

"Does the hot water work?" It was all he wanted to know right now.

David nodded. "This house belonged to the man who oversaw the prison camp. He—"

Scott didn't wait for the rest of the story. He pulled his head back into the room and went for the shower.

He turned the knobs, and water fell from the showerhead. In a matter of moments, steam was clouding the room. He pulled off his socks and jeans and stepped into the stand-up shower. Water splashed against his back where the fiery debris had burnt him, and he quickly turned away from it, instead leaning his back against the shower wall. He closed his eyes and let the hot water melt his frozen joints and relax his stiff muscles.

The ring. Israeli agents. A Catholic priest. Roswell. Edward. His three canine friends. The two women he'd killed…

He opened his eyes.

So much for relaxing. But he stayed in the water until his body felt somewhat restored, and then he got out.

It was time to find out what was going on.

# II.

# UNHOLY SECRETS



Gondamer stepped out of the Al Aqsa Mosque and onto the Temple Mount itself. He paused, resting a hand on his hip while running the other through his long and disheveled black locks. A cool evening breeze traveled over the one-hundred-forty-four-acre expanse and pulled at his white habit. He watched as the sun disappeared below the Holy Land, taking the relentless heat with it. He sighed and moved his gaze away from the sight and set it instead on *Templum Domini*, the converted Dome of the Rock, which sat adjacent to him now.

His soul was troubled this night, and as he gazed at the cross transfixed atop the church, he found that the symbol actually stirred *more* conflict within him rather than quenching it.

Torches began lighting up around him, and he heard footsteps.

A shadow stopped beside him, staring off toward the Kidron Valley. He knew it was Rossal.

"What is it that troubles you?" Rossal asked, his own white habit whisking around his ankles.

Gondamer didn't bother looking over at the figure beside him. He didn't have to. They were all family, the original nine, and the familiarity between them was so great that he need not see Rossal's face to pick from his voice more than mere concern but intention as well. "You know what I struggle with, Rossal. The conflict that I feel."

Rossal crossed his arms and looked down at his feet. He waited a good while before speaking, the faint sounds of Jerusalem echoing in the distance. "The Holy Father wills it, Gondamer. *God* wills it."

"Yet, still we have found nothing."

"Patience is often the sacrifice required in order for God's will to be realized."

Gondamer finally set his eyes on him. "Or made known."

"He does that through the mouth of the Pope. We must continue with our part, trusting."

"We have been here for nearly three years," Gondamer quietly objected. "And what have we to show for it? Empty caverns, stale cisterns?"

Surrendering any thought of debate, Rossal simply put a hand on Gondamer's shoulder. "Come, let us observe the ruins before the others leave their work for the night. Perhaps, with prayer, God will provide a nugget of hope for your weary soul."

And with a gentle nudge, he allowed Rossal to lead him to the ruins below the Temple Mount, to reunite with the rest of the new Order and its mission to find what Pope Urban II insisted had to be there. But if it *is* here, Gondamer thought to himself once again, why then had the Babylonians, the Romans, and the Muslims failed to find it? To him, it seemed like a mystery somewhat easy to solve. But to question such things was to doubt the infallibility of the Holy Father.

As if reading his mind, Rossal said, "God's power has kept it hidden from His enemies. That is why it has yet to be found."

"Then why have we yet to find any trace of it? If God's power keeps it hidden from His enemies, then certainly His power can reveal it to His children."

"And that is precisely why we dig."

Gondamer sighed with frustration as they descended into torchlight and a myriad of tunnels. The sounds of digging came echoing about them, and just as Rossal was about to continue on, Gondamer grabbed his arm, stopping him. In a whispered hush, he asked, "How much longer can we pretend to escort pilgrims from Jaffa's coast?"

"We are not pretending, Gondamer."

It was both true and not true at the same time.

After the Crusaders drove the Muslims from Jerusalem in 1118, they had considered their vow fulfilled and thus returned to Europe, eager to spend their spoils of war. In their absence, pilgrims journeying from the coast to the Holy Land were often harassed and killed by bitter Muslims still living in the Islamic territories that surrounded Jerusalem. So it served as a good excuse for nine pious knights to appear humbly before Baldwin II, King of Jerusalem, and to offer him their services. Impressed with their dedication, the king was delighted to have them as protectors of those traveling to Jerusalem. But that was only for appearances' sake. The reason the Pope sent them to Jerusalem was much more important than that. And it was no coincidence that the king made their dwelling place the mosque that now rested over the very ruins of Solomon's Temple—an arrangement encouraged by the Pope, to be sure. The whole thing was his idea, the Order of the Poor Knights of Christ and the Temple of Solomon.

So while it was true that they protected those traveling from the coast, such a mission was only to mask the real reason they were stationed in the Kingdom. But before Gondamer could speak according to these things, a loud cry arose from somewhere in the darkness.

"Did you hear that?" asked Rossal, concern in his voice now.

"Of course I heard it. Where did it come from?"

Then they heard it again. But this time it lasted longer and seemed to be growing louder. Suddenly, from a tunnel adjacent to them, Andre de Montbard emerged, laughing and hollering with excitement. He was covered in dirt and sweat. And he was holding something in his hand.

"What is it? What did you find?" asked Rossal.

"I found a golden scroll!" He was dancing in circles, hopping up and down like a child.

With great doubt, Gondamer grabbed hold of him and forced him to settle down. "Let me see it!"

It *was* a scroll.

"Be careful with it!" Rossal warned. "It must be brittle with decay."

But Andre de Montbard disagreed. "No! It is in perfect condition!"

So Gondamer took it from him and examined it. Some kind of metal for sure, though not gold. Copper perhaps? He wasn't sure. Very carefully, he started to unroll it, curiosity and anticipation making his hands tremble as he did so.

De Montbard was right. It was as if the scroll had been hidden just yesterday. It unrolled with ease, no threat whatsoever of corrosion. That, in and of itself, was strange.

Hebrew inscriptions. Greek letters.

"Where did you find it?" he asked.

"In the cavern, under the floor." He was pointing back into the darkness.

"What is happening?" It was Hugues de Payens. He emerged from the tunnel they were standing in front of— Godfrey de Saint-Omer, Geoffrey Bison, and Payen de Montdidier with him.

"I found a scroll!" Andre exclaimed.

Gondamer handed it over to the co-founder of the group, also his relative. "It does appear to be something of significance."

Hugues de Payens looked at it, his eyes intensely searching it over, marveling at the bizarre discovery. "It seems impossible that it should be this well preserved." Then he looked up to Andre. "Show me where you found it."

They all went into the tunnel.

The torches hanging along the walls on either side gave off enough light to see what had happened. Up ahead, the tunnel widened and disappeared into a huge room. They could see, before even entering the room, that Andre de Montbard had been working at one of its walls, crumbled rocks lying in a pile by some tools.

"I was just striking the wall, trying to knock out that adjoining piece, when I noticed that the ground beneath my feet seemed to move. I brushed the dirt away and found that stone slab." He pointed toward a large flat stone now resting beside a dark spot in the ground—a hole, indiscernible beneath the shifting light. "The stone had a word carved into its face, so I worked it free and flipped it over." He was still excited, talking fast. "I could not see into the hole, so I just reached down into it. It was deep, deeper than the depth of that stone. I was just able to get my fingertip on it."

Hugues de Payens approached the hole and kneeled beside it himself. Then he looked up to the ceiling far above, wondering out loud if it could be right where the Holy Father said it would be. And then he bent over and stuck his hand into the blackness. Immediately, he retracted his hand, shaking it. "It is cold." The statement was full of bewilderment and shock.

Andre agreed. "I thought my fingers would fall off before I could retract it."

He tried again, this time his arm disappearing up to his shoulder.

The Knights all stepped closer, anxious to see if there was anything else to be found.

Slowly, and in almost melodramatic fashion, de Payens pulled his hand out of the darkness.

Wanting a better look, and feeling impatience overtake him, Gondamer grabbed the torch out of Geoffrey Bison's hand and held it over the hole, hoping to see if there was anything in de Payens's hand. But the torchlight didn't help at all.

Hugues de Payens lifted his hand to examine what was in it. "Light," he commanded.

Tearing his attention away from the hole, Gondamer moved the flame over to illuminate de Payens and whatever he was holding.

A ring.

Hurrying to his feet, de Payens scrambled out of the room and into the tunnel, calling back over his shoulder, "Bring the scroll! Bring the scroll!"

Everyone followed after him, eager and excited to see more closely what it was they had discovered.

Except Gondamer. He stood unmoving by the hole, the torch still in his hand. His eyes narrowed as he tried to look into its depths. The hairs on his neck stood tall. Bending to one knee, he brought the torch closer. But the flickering flame wouldn't shed any light into the darkness. In fact, when he stuck the tip of the torch into the hole itself, the fire failed to even illuminate its sides. It was as if the hole itself swallowed the light.

He stood straight and looked around, suddenly not enjoying the solitude. Before he left though, he dropped the torch into the hole.

He watched it fall.

And fall.

Until it was just a little speck of light. Until it disappeared.

He grabbed the nearest torch off the wall and ran.

By the time he reached his relatives and fellow Temple Knights, they had split into two groups, one examining the scroll and the other the ring. As he walked past those bent over the scroll, Rossal looked up from it with a big grin and called out to him, "How is this for a sign? I told you it is His will!"

Gondamer continued walking straight into the mosque, where Hugues de Payens was holding the ring up to the light. He was mumbling something. Gondamer couldn't make out what it was though. He walked quickly, calling out to him as he approached, his voice full of warning.

Hugues de Payens, the French Knight and veteran of the Crusade and the Grand Master of the Order, turned and looked at him with a strange gleam in his eye.

"Wait, I must tell you—" But Gondamer's warning was ignored.

Hugues de Payens smiled and slid the ring onto his finger.
And then everything changed.

# 14.

*"The World is governed by very different personages from*
*what is imagined by those who are not behind the scenes."*
— Benjamin Disraeli, Prime Minister of England, 1844

The man thrust his hands into his pockets. The cold bitter air bit at his face, and the wind disheveled his graying hair while whipping his tie back over his shoulder. He squinted down at his watch and then resumed scanning the landscape.

Loitering anywhere near the White House was prohibited. The days of sightseeing and educational tours had become a thing of the past, and even the government employees themselves were too intimidated by the troops in black battle gear to linger any longer than necessary. It was for this reason that the man's contact should have been easy to spot.

He began walking, staring at the ground until he reached the foot of the reflecting pool. The obelisk's capstone stretched across the water's smooth surface, pointing at him like a spear. He raised his eyes, taking in the resurrected 555-foot Washington Monument. Rebuilt after the earthquake a few years ago, its esoteric significance was now close to being fulfilled. *Close.* That was why he still had to exercise such caution, why the senator in New York had to be "quarantined" the other day. Now was no time to get sloppy, not with the finish line in sight.

He wondered how many presidents prior to this one even knew of the obelisk's true meaning. Maybe James K. Pulk. He'd laid its cornerstone on the fourth of July, 1848. And he was a Mason. That was what was so nice about the current Commander In Chief. He didn't need to be manipulated or babysat. In fact, perhaps his greatest weakness was wanting to advance things too fast. Most, like Wilson or Carter, had just been puppets on strings, though a few had openly called for the New World Order. But then you had your JFKs—people who actually stood opposed to the Great Plan. People who didn't think they had to play by the rules. People who got themselves shot.

Another glance at his watch. Only fifteen minutes until the "glitch" was corrected and the facial-recognition cameras would be able to identify him.

He swore under his breath and shot a quick sideways glance at some people walking along the pool toward him. They had coffees in their hands and were quickly making their way back to whatever building they worked in.

His eyes drifted back to the obelisk, and his mind began reciting its history. How it was originally supposed to align with the White House, but the ground was too unstable there, so it had to be moved. How, in contrast to a normal obelisk being cut out of a single block of stone, the Washington Monument was made up of many stones in order to convey the idea of *e pluribus unum*—out of many, one. How the top of the Monument was made up of thirteen levels, just like on the seal of the now obsolete dollar bill. How its aluminum capstone was set on December 6, 1884. How it wasn't aligned with the White House, but would be aligned with the Masonic House of the Temple built in 1915.

His gaze settled over a bare piece of land just a few hundred feet away from the towering phallic symbol where he knew there was a twelve-foot replica of the Monument resting beneath a manhole. It was missing its capstone—just like the pyramid that had been on the Federal Reserve Note.

He pondered the connection between America's symbols and the ancient mystery religions that birthed them. That the

Great Pyramid, said to have been missing its capstone for most of history, had been showcased for so long on the now obsolete federal reserve note with the all-seeing eye of Horus illuminated by the light of Sirius behind it. He thought about the esoteric traditions claiming that the return of the capstone to the Great Pyramid would signal the return of the Great Initiate, which would finally bring to reality the Latin words on the nation's Great Seal, *ANNUIT COEPTIS NOVUS ORDO SECLORUM*. And of course he recalled the date at the base of the pyramid. 1776. The year the Illuminati had been formed.

He spotted a figure leaning against a nearby tree, and his heart started beating faster. Half a dozen more men suddenly appeared, stepping from behind other trees, all of them in black suits and sunglasses. But they were not part of the Secret Service entrusted with protecting the man across the street.

A black car with tinted windows rolled to a stop along the curb.

"About bloody time," the man whispered.

The door opened, and a large man struggled out of the car as three more security guards exited around him, their eyes searching the grounds, the nearest windows, the streets, everything.

The fat man walked toward him, and they met with a cold handshake.

"You're late, Marcus."

"You are very fortunate that I am here at all," replied the shorter, older man. His accent was thick, his hair white, his face pudgy. His real name wasn't Marcus.

Looking at his watch again, the man who had been waiting said, "We only have thirteen minutes left, so make it quick."

Marcus smiled, pulled the hood from off his head and pointed at his face, at some kind of barcoded stickers he had over his chin and cheeks. "Keeps me safe from the facial-recognition scans."

The man didn't like Marcus, and he didn't care to hide it. "With a nose like yours, putting stickers on your face is a wasted effort." He looked away and sighed. "And you're fat."

A flash of fire erupted in Marcus's eyes.

The guy held up his hands in defense. "I'm just saying you don't want to get fined is all. Obesity laws won't be kind to you over here."

Marcus grumbled under his breath. "I hate this godforsaken country."

"And I, yours. Now can we please get on with it?" The only downside to this game of global conspiracy was whom he was forced to be friendly with—the whole "enemy of my enemy" thing.

"I need to see him," Marcus said.

His eyes widened. "The President?"

Marcus moved closer. "There are things we need to discuss before the next phase."

"So call him."

"Things that cannot be uttered over a phone."

The man looked around as if he were contemplating the possibility of such a request, but ultimately shook his head. "No. You can't. It's just not possible."

"Maybe you are not understanding me." A sharp tone came with his accented words. "So let me make myself clear. If you do not get me an hour with the President, immediately, I am going to leave this whole situation unresolved, and it will be up to you to clean up."

He swore. "You know there's a million people just waiting to catch you with the President. And if they do, we'll have to postpone again. The public will crucify us. And then there'll be war."

"I understand the risk involved," Marcus answered, clearly not going to take no for an answer.

"Fine, I'll see what I can do. It can't be today though. He's got a joint meeting with the Canadian and Mexican presidents. If we change something last minute, it'll draw way too much attention."

A simple nod.

The thin man glanced at his watch. "About that situation you spoke of…"

"It is *our* problem. Get me an hour with the President, and my people will deal with it. You can call your troops off."

"Personally, I don't understand why it's so important," he grumbled.

"And nor could you."

"Whatever. Is that what you need to speak to the President about?"

"All I will tell you is that I would like to have the ring in my possession and my people off the continent before the next phase goes into effect."

He stared at Marcus. "He's not going to call off the next phase, whether you have your stupid ring or not. I guarantee you that."

Marcus just nodded. "Do you have the identity of this mystery man, this *Rambo*, who took out your intelligence team and slaughtered your NAU troops?"

He clenched his teeth and mumbled, "We're still trying to get a lead from his vehicle. The license plate was a dead end. He knows what he's doing. Until we have a name or a face, there's nothing we can do."

"And Cairns?"

"Dead. Your people, I believe."

"What about the girl?" Now Marcus was looking at his own watch.

"She just came out of the coma. She'll be sedated so she can't talk to anyone, and in a day or two she'll be taken to an old FEMA camp to satisfy many a lonely guard. Until of course she hangs herself in order to escape her grief."

Marcus nodded as if he was okay with that. "I lost some of my best men up in Vermont to this man."

"How do you know it was him?"

"Who else could it be?" Marcus responded, trying not to sound uncomfortable. But his eyes said that there was a lot he was withholding. "Get me that meeting," he said. And without another word, he flipped his hood back up, turned, and began walking back to the car, his security guards quickly taking up their positions around him.

"Enjoy your stay!" the thin man called out as he stole another glance at the time. Five minutes before his window closed and the cameras recorded his presence. Something that was completely out of the question. There would be hell to pay if someone found out about his meeting with the Prime Minister of Israel.

He pivoted on his heel and began walking back along the reflecting pool.

He had told the Prime Minister that he didn't know what the fuss over the ring was about. That was true. What wasn't true was that they were going to sit back and let Israel tidy up the mess alone. Because there were more people who wanted this ring than just the Prime Minister. And though he didn't know why, the Secretary of State did know that his friend, the President of New America, was one of them.

# 15.

*"It is therefore our duty to surround them with its [the Illuminati's] members, so that the profane may have no access to them. Thus we are able most powerfully to promote its interests. If any person is more disposed to listen to Princes than to the Order, he is not fit for it, and must rise no higher. We must do our utmost to procure the advancement of Illuminati into all important civil offices. By this plan we shall direct all mankind. In this manner, and by the simplest means, we shall set all in motion and in flames. The occupations must be so allotted and contrived, that we may, in secret, influence all political transactions."*
— Adam Weishaupt, founder of the Illuminati

Scott tucked the pistol into the back of his pants as he came down the stairs. He found David and Mayhew making breakfast in the kitchen. Bacon was frying on the stove, and the smell of it sparked a memory, a happy one — one of her working over the stove in that white lingerie the first morning of their married life.

But that wasn't what was in this kitchen. Not even close. That life was gone forever.

"Thought you were Jewish," Scott said as he entered the room.

David looked at him, confused.

He pointed to the stove.

"Oh, the bacon." He nodded. "It is for you two Gentiles."

Scott leaned over the stove, the smoke filling his nostrils as Mayhew referenced Peter's vision in the book of Acts. "Rise, kill and eat."

"Amen," Scott mumbled.

"Are you hungry?" David asked.

Scott's rumbling stomach answered for him.

David slid two fried eggs off a frying pan and onto a plate before handing the pan over to Scott. "Eggs are in the refrigerator."

Scott set the pan back onto the burner and opened the fridge. He grabbed two eggs, though he really wanted to grab six, and took them over to the stove, where he cracked them on the pan's edge and jettisoned their innards onto its sizzling surface.

Mayhew was standing over the bacon at the next burner over. "Feel any better?" he asked.

Scott nodded. "Much." He wondered where the eggs had come from. Figured there must be a chicken coop somewhere close by. It wasn't like there were supermarkets around the corner. "Who are you?" he asked Mayhew.

Mayhew smiled. "You mean, what am I doing hanging out with the Mossad and a Catholic priest?" He looked up from the bacon. "Joined the Marines after Los Angeles, went to Iran and Syria. Got out, went to school, became a teacher, got married."

Scott flipped the eggs. "Still married?"

"No. I became a Christian, and she started hanging out with cooler guys. By that time the Constitution was being replaced by the NAU Charter, so I went underground and joined the Resistance."

"The Resistance, huh?" He looked out the window. "And where are we now?"

Without looking up, and through a mouthful of egg, David answered for Mayhew. "New York."

"Adirondack Park?"

Mayhew nodded. "Just west of I-87."

"That's a hundred and forty miles away from Jamaica. How'd we get here?"

"Helicopter," said Mayhew.

"Helicopter," Scott repeated. "I see. You just fly around in restricted airspace at will, then?"

"Not exactly."

Scott waved a fork around the kitchen. "And this house. You said it belonged to the warden or something?" He dumped his eggs onto a plate and sat down across from David.

"Yes," David answered. "We killed him. Took his house, took his prison. Made it ours."

Scott leaned back in the chair and looked up at Mayhew as he came over to push some bacon onto his plate. "Doesn't seem like a very Christian thing to do."

Mayhew didn't respond.

David explained, "The attack on the camp yesterday was most likely a response to what happened in the park and did not have anything to do with our capture of the camp or the ring. The military simply tracked us and sent a strike force to eliminate us."

"But even if they hadn't tracked you, they would have eventually come to retake their camp. You wouldn't have stood a chance against them."

"We would not have been there when they arrived. *If* they ever arrived."

Mayhew sat down beside them.

"So you weren't trying to establish a base of operations, then." He put eggs into his mouth.

Mayhew shook his head. "We move around a lot, guerrilla warfare. Makes it hard for them to concentrate a large force against us."

"Why this particular camp?" Scott asked.

David fixed him with a serious stare. "There were reports that they had started to use the incinerators."

Scott held his gaze for a moment and then shifted his eyes to Mayhew. He'd heard rumors but had dismissed them as exaggerations. "It's gotten to that point, then."

"I am afraid so," David said. "And it will only get worse. By the time the public finds out, it will have already been common practice. And even then, most will refuse to believe it. Just as before. People cannot grasp the wickedness of man, and denying that something like this could happen is the very thing that allows it to go on."

"Okay." Scott held up his hands and closed his eyes. He was going to have to try to process that later. "Let's reel this back in. Melissa Strauss—"

"Was caught on surveillance cameras inside a restaurant in Washington, DC," David said, cutting him off.

"You have access to the security feed throughout Washington?"

"We have insiders everywhere, Matthew," he answered. "We knew the ring was being kept in an underground NASA lab in DC, so we knew what was really happening when it broke on the news." A slight pause. "We were hoping to intercept Melissa Strauss before they did, but unfortunately that did not happen."

"Yeah, about that. Why didn't they seize the envelope before it even got to Ed? All they had to do was stop the mail and go get it."

"Because, by the grace of God, the video did not reveal whom she had given the envelope to, or that she even still had it on her person at that time. They had to consider the possibility that she had gotten rid of it prior to entering the restaurant, so they spent hours going through footage from the streets. By the time they found out whom she had given it to and were able to analyze her file and piece it all together, the ring had already arrived in Vermont."

"And you knew she'd sent it to Ed because they knew."

A nod. "We knew about Edward because they knew about Edward. About his son. His whole profile. And we knew you were in the park because they knew that too, though they do not seem to know who you are. We were monitoring your escape and knew you ditched the vehicle in the woods. A drone pinpointed your general position, but you neutralized the troops before they could use the information, which allowed us to. We found Edward sitting nearby, presumably waiting for you to get back."

The knowledge that Edward hadn't stayed in the cave made Scott frown. "So you just happened to be the nearest Mossad agent on call?"

Again he nodded. "If not me, then it would have been someone else."

"So then who killed Edward?"

"An Israeli death squad."

He blinked. "Why would an Israeli death squad want to kill Edward?" And then he realized. "They were waiting for *you*. They were positioned to cut off your escape, and you rode right into them."

"They didn't know whom they were shooting at. Only that Edward was with them and that he had the ring. They killed our agents, but you showed up in time to hold them off until we could get there."

"And get the ring."

"And get the ring."

"Is that all you care about?"

"It is."

"Why?"

"Because if the secular arm of my country acquires it, it may be buried for the rest of time."

Scott finished his eggs and pushed the plate away. "So what?" Then he looked over at Mayhew. "So let me guess, David and his band of merry Mossad agents ask if they can come alongside your local chapter of Resistance fighters. You don't ask too many questions, because you need all the help you can get. Meanwhile" — he looked back to David — "you're just biding your time, hoping that the ring pops up on your radar."

"We came into the country as soon as we discovered that the ring was discovered and had been taken to Washington," David explained. "In the meantime, yes, we lent our hand in the war against the World Order."

Scott turned back to Mayhew. "And you're okay with the Mossad using you like that?"

But David answered for him. "He is okay with that because I have explained to him what is at stake. And he has been persuaded by those facts."

"Is that true, Titus Mayhew?" Scott asked.

Mayhew sighed. "Yeah. If what he says is true, then keeping that ring out of their hands is the greatest priority."

"Because they'll make it disappear?"

David smiled. "It is more complicated than that."

"Of course it is."

David dropped his gaze. "I apologize for having to include you in all of this. But I did not see another way in which your life could be spared." Then he met Scott's eyes with his own. "Seems that God has bigger plans for you than you might have imagined."

"Like dying tomorrow instead of yesterday?"

"At least your life would have been worth living, if you were to die well."

The comment hit him in a place he hadn't thought to guard. He needed no reminder that his life had done little good for anyone.

David stood up. "It is time to do a perimeter check. I trust the two of you can manage to clean up?"

"David," Scott said, "what about the others who were at the camp with you?"

David walked to the door. "They are all dead," he said. He went outside, closing the door behind him.

Before Scott could finish his last piece of bacon, Mayhew stood, leaned forward, and whispered into his ear, "Talk to the priest."

But before he could respond, Mayhew was out of the room too. Scott turned and looked after him. Watched Mayhew walk to the door David had exited. The look on his face as he peered through the screen and off in the direction David had gone, however, was not one of ease but one of suspicion. Or maybe even malice. Scott couldn't tell which, but he found himself thinking that he was the only one not holding a secret deck of cards.

Then Mayhew left the door and continued on to wherever it was he was heading.

Scott walked out of the kitchen and climbed the stairs to the room the priest was dying in. Mayhew had said to talk to him. And for some reason he had whispered it. *What else am I going to do?* he thought.

He eased the door open, not sure what to expect or what to say. Death made him uncomfortable. Not necessarily the quick death that had been his profession, but the drawn-out process of dying. He found it revolting. Edward dying in his arms was enough to occupy his mind for a long time. He didn't need to look into the eyes of a dying priest on top of it. Whether he liked the guy or not. But David had managed to avoid answering any of his questions about the ring, so maybe the priest would have some answers for him.

The priest was sitting up. "Where is the ring?" he asked in such a strong voice that it startled Scott.

"David has it." He closed the door.

"Where is he?"

"He went outside to secure the perimeter."

"You need to get it back."

Scott shook his head. "The only thing I need to do is get the hell out of here."

"Then why did you come up here?" But he didn't wait for Scott to answer. "I'll tell you why you came up here. Because it intrigues you. Because God is calling you to it."

"Sure he is." And he turned to leave.

"We're all going to die, Matthew," the priest called out to him. "Every single one of us. The only question is, what awaits us when that happens? What awaits *you*."

Scott turned and faced him once more. "I know exactly what awaits me," he seethed, "and there isn't a thing you can do about it, *priest*."

"Stop."

He had no idea why his feet obeyed the priest's voice, but they did. With a resentment that didn't even make sense to him, he glared at the man from the corner of his eye.

"Over there. Under the table," the priest said, pointing to a table across the room.

Without protest, but with enough body language to demonstrate his pride, Scott walked over to the table.

"Go ahead. It's underneath," the priest urged.

Scott bent over, slid his hand beneath a small space, and pulled out a worn messenger bag. "What is this?"

A twitch of pain swept over his face. "A piece of the puzzle." He nodded toward the door. "They're just hired guns with half the story. They don't know anything."

"So why are you telling me this?"

"Because you don't have *any* part of the story. And that makes you the only person I trust."

He looked down into the bag, noticing two leather-bound books tied together with twine. "This is about the ring?"

"It's all about the ring. Everything. That is why you have to protect it."

"From who?"

The priest closed his eyes, exhaustion sweeping over him. "Everyone. You can't trust anybody."

Scott took a step forward. "Why is the Vatican interested in it?"

With eyes still closed, he answered, "The Holy See is very much involved with what is going on in the world." He sighed heavily. "I can only pray that I have exposed that in time." He opened his eyes. "Get the ring back."

"But, David—"

"Don't let him have it!" The sudden outburst made him wince again.

Scott took another step closer and looked back at the closed door that led to the steps. He lowered his voice. "What *is* it?"

The priest took a deep breath. "It is the key to—"

But the door burst open behind him, and Mayhew was suddenly in the room.

"We need to go! Now!" he yelled, grabbing Scott's shoulder and pulling him away from the priest.

Scott tried resisting, but Mayhew was using all of his strength to drag him out of the room. "What the—"

"They're coming! It's gonna blow!"

Scott looked back to the priest. "What about him?"

"There's no time!"

The priest looked at Scott, and the expression on his face was one of acceptance. This was his fate, and he would not fight it. Still, there was that fire in his eyes that told Scott just how severe the situation was and that somehow it was up to him to reconcile it. He opened his mouth and said, "Rose—"

But Scott was already out of the room and didn't hear the rest.

# 16.



*"The government, which was designed for the people, has gotten into the hands of the bosses and their employers, the special interests. An invisible empire has been set up above the forms of democracy."*

—Woodrow Wilson

Scott followed Mayhew out the front door. "What's happening?" he yelled.

Without slowing down, Mayhew threw a hand up over his shoulder and pointed into the sky behind them. "Look!"

Scott turned and saw the unmistakable form of an unmanned combat air vehicle. A strike drone. And now he was running forward of his own volition, sprinting to get as far away from the house as possible. He didn't even bother looking for the tiny tubes he knew had already started falling from the sky.

The house erupted with a deafening roar, and the explosion turned their world into a dizzying blast of blinding heat as flaming debris rocketed deep into the woods. The shock wave picked Scott and Mayhew up off the ground, tossing them like rag dolls through the air.

****

When Scott opened his eyes, he found himself staring up into a smoke-filled sky, pieces of fire streaking through it like meteors falling to earth. It looked like the end of the world. Like the apocalypse. And then a piece of flaming debris landed on him and burnt through his soot-stained shirt, searing his flesh. He sat up and brushed the ember away as a high-pitched whine screamed in his ears. Like the old emergency broadcast system was running a test in his head.

The house was gone. Just a section of its burning frame left standing. Pieces of it strewn all over the place. Ash falling like snow.

He struggled to his feet and found that the 9mm was still tucked into the back of his pants. He stumbled down the scorched path, looking for Mayhew. He'd only gotten ten feet when a micro air vehicle suddenly emerged, gliding laterally from the burning woods to his right and hovering five feet off the ground in front of him.

MAVs were an older technology first used to detect IEDs, and Scott had seen them evolve over the years. But this model was new to him. There was a big UHD optical lens focused right on his face, no doubt scanning it against countless others within the Central Database. When no results came back, his facial print would be immediately uploaded into the NAU's intelligence data bank with a red flag tagging him as an unknown. Or rather "a suspected enemy of the state." What the MAV would then do once targeting him as a suspect, Scott had no idea. But he didn't intend to find out.

Before he could even reach for the pistol, however, a shot rang out, and the vehicle fell to the ground in a shower of sparks.

Mayhew jogged over to him, slinging the AK-47 over his shoulder. "David took off on a quad," he said, out of breath.

Scott looked around for any sign of the Mossad agent but couldn't find one.

Mayhew continued, "I saw him talking on a satphone. I asked him who he was talking to, and he pointed up to the sky. That's when I saw the drone. Before I knew it, he was mounting a quad and heading off into the woods. I came back in to get you."

Scott didn't have the necessary background information to properly process the news, what it could mean. All he knew was that these guys had been playing cloak-and-dagger with each other long before he showed up.

"That path hits a road three miles northeast of here," Mayhew said, talking fast and pointing. "But it's only half a mile if we go straight east. If he's headed north, then he's long gone. But if he's going south, we can cut him off."

"Where's the ring?" Scott asked.

"David had it."

The priest's lasts words swarmed in his head, and as much as he wanted nothing to do with it, to just turn and run in the opposite direction, he found himself running alongside Mayhew through the woods.

****

After running hard for five minutes, they reached an old highway barrier. It stood ten feet high and stretched northeast to southwest. Scott could tell that the overgrown area around it was once an on/off-ramp that connected whatever town this used to be to its major highway. He figured its abandonment was probably the work of the UN's revamped Rewilding Project—isolating small rural towns as a way to force their populations into the cities, where they could properly regulated.

Scott moved to a tree that was leaning against the wall and began climbing it. Once he was high enough, he could see over the concrete barrier and down the southbound lanes. They eventually disappeared into the horizon. But there was a median between the southbound and northbound lanes that was now thickly lined with evergreens, so he couldn't see the other lanes. He turned his head north and saw that the southbound lanes went on for about three hundred yards before bending out of sight. "Is this 87?" Scott asked.

Mayhew climbed up beside him and straddled the wall. He handed Scott the AK-47. "Yeah," he answered. Then he hopped down, nailing the proper landing form. He motioned for Scott to toss him the assault rifle, but Scott wasn't looking at him. He was staring off to the left, north up 87.

And then Mayhew heard it too.

It was a vehicle, the sound of its engine ricocheting off the barrier walls lining the highway.

"Come on!" Mayhew yelled, urging Scott down off the wall.

Scott tossed the rifle down and jumped, landing on the ground with less perfect form and needing to go into a tuck and roll. By the time he was back to his feet, Mayhew was already stepping out onto the asphalt with the assault rifle raised and pointing at an approaching white van.

Scott started toward Mayhew, not fully understanding what the Resistance member intended to do. Did he think David had hitched a ride with whoever was driving the van, or did he intend to hijack the vehicle himself?

The van was a hundred yards away and going about 70 mph when Mayhew squeezed off two rounds, blowing apart the front right tire. The van slowed as its driver struggled to keep control. Mayhew fired again, this time taking out the front left tire. And as the van got closer, still slowing, he put a few rounds into the engine block.

The van rolled to a stop fifteen yards in front of them.

Mayhew signaled for Scott to check the van as he crossed in front of him, moving to cover the driver's door. Scott complied and circled around to the left, covering the side door with the 9mm in case anyone came out shooting. As Scott passed the front passenger-side door, he noticed that the windows were tinted, the large pines behind him reflected in the glass.

"Get out of the van!" Mayhew yelled.

No response.

"What've you got over there?" Mayhew yelled over to Scott.

"Nothing!" Then he kicked the side door. "Anyone in there?"

When nothing happened, Mayhew smashed the butt of the rifle through the driver-side window. He quickly stepped back, flipping the AK-47 back around and aiming it into the van.

There was no one in the front seats.

Scott ran around to the back of the van, anticipating the driver's only remaining option of escape. But when he got there, he found that the back doors were already open. Turning to look back up the road, he spotted two people running for the row of trees separating the north- and southbound lanes.

"Stop!" Mayhew yelled, coming up beside Scott. He raised his rifle into the air and was about to squeeze off a few shots to get their attention when another noise suddenly erupted all around them.

Machine-gun fire.

Blasting down I-87 and rebounding off the barrier behind them and through the woods in front of them.

Scott and Mayhew hit the ground, covering their heads.

When Scott looked up through his arms, he saw that the two people were now lying sprawled at the road's edge.

Then the shooting stopped, and the rumble of engines took its place.

Scott turned toward the bend in the road. "Sounds like a convoy," he said. He jumped to his feet.

"The ring..." Mayhew got up and started moving toward the bodies.

"What?" Scott yelled. He looked back down the road just as the huge muzzle of a sophisticated rail gun cannon came into sight, rounding the turn. "We gotta go, now!" He started moving back toward the van.

But Mayhew ignored him, instead breaking into a sprint and running full tilt toward the median. He was almost there when the sound of a machine gun once again blasted down the highway. Chunks of asphalt jumped up around him, pelting him, but he just covered his face and kept going.

Scott reached the van, not understanding what in the world Mayhew was thinking. He had no cover and nowhere to go with an entire line of NAU military vehicles heading straight toward him. Scott could already make out three APC Strykers and two MGS Strykers, followed by a line of Humvees that was still wrapped around the bend. The High-Mobility Multipurpose Wheeled Vehicles alone were equipped with .50 cal. machine guns and automatic grenade launchers. The Armored Personnel Carriers were fitted with an upgraded PROTECTOR Remote Weapons System that housed an M151 with an MK-19 automatic grenade launcher, while the two Mobile Gun Supports needed only their heavy rail guns to strike fear into anyone looking at them from the wrong end. Which in this case was Mayhew.

With only a hint of remorse, Scott turned away from Mayhew's pointless endeavor and instead began concentrating on his own escape. But before an option could present itself, a new sound came, transcending even the M151 that was still firing at Mayhew.

Shouting. Screaming. Explosions. Small-arms fire.

It careened down the wooded slopes west of I-87 and echoed onto the northbound lanes before crossing the wooded median and ultimately sounding off against the concrete walls behind him.

Scott was shocked to see men and women spilling out of the median and attacking the convoy with guns, grenades, and even shoulder-mounted rocket launchers. At least a hundred of them came storming onto the road, screaming like warrior barbarians from some distant century.

The assault was just the miracle Mayhew needed, as the vehicles turned their attention away from him and focused instead on the attacking guerrillas.

Scott sprinted across the lanes, coming up on Mayhew as he reached the two fallen figures and turned one of them over. Even though he was still a good twenty yards away, there was no mistaking the man's face. It was David.

As he got closer, he could see that the Mossad agent who had saved his life was lying in a lake of blood. Mayhew searched through his pockets, looking for the ring. Scott stood behind him and saw David open his eyes.

"Did you think you'd get away?" Scott heard Mayhew say.

David coughed and spit up some blood. "The ring belongs to Israel, and so does all that it unlocks…" His voice was weak, defeat heavy in his eyes. "I failed. The future is lost."

"You shouldn't have lied to me about the ring," Mayhew growled. He found the ring in David's front pocket.

That was when Scott grabbed him and lifted him to his feet. "Come on!"

Mayhew nodded, and they both began moving toward the cover of the trees.

David lifted his head out of the sticky puddle and yelled after them, "It belongs to Israel! It belongs to the Jews! To Jerusalem!"

A line of machine-gun fire peppered the ground in front of them, cutting them off from the trees. They turned away from it and ran for the van as blasts of heat swept over them from nearby explosions.

They needed cover, and the van was their nearest option.

Scott saw a Humvee break out of the chaos and head toward them. They were ten yards from the van.

Five yards.

Five feet.

The .50 cal. erupted, bullets flying past them and sinking into the van as they dove through the open rear doors. They frantically made their way over the bench seat as bullets ricocheted through the van after them. The Humvee roared past, the gunner pivoting and lining the side of the van with holes, a hundred rays of light now beaming through the torn metal. The seat they were hiding behind was almost down to its frame, its insulation scattered all over the place. Scott couldn't believe they were still alive.

Looking out the front window, Scott could see that the Humvee was coming back. He threw the side door open on its track and hopped out, Mayhew right behind him. But another burst of fire from the Humvee chased them around to the rear corner of the van. As the Humvee drove past, Mayhew fired off two short bursts from the AK-47, the second of which struck the gunner in the face.

The driver of the Humvee slammed on the brakes and brought the vehicle to a grinding halt as the gunner's lifeless body was pushed up and out of the vehicle. Another soldier climbed up behind the machine gun, but the driver hadn't gotten out of Mayhew's range before stopping, and Mayhew shot the new soldier out of the turret too.

Scott started for the Humvee. "Cover me!" he yelled.

Mayhew stepped away from the van, trying to get the attention of anyone who might be left in the Humvee while firing a couple of harmless shots at its frame, careful not to strike the tires.

Beyond them, the Strykers' rail guns were firing into the woods on the other side of the median, splintering huge evergreens and sending earth spraying like geysers high into the air. But the guerillas were escaping their fire with relative ease by swarming around them at close range. They had already taken out most of the Humvees' gunners, and the Strykers were now hitting each other more than them. A few of the Resistance fighters even managed to toss grenades into some of the vehicles, and flames were slithering out of broken windows. A rocket screamed from somewhere beyond the tree line and slammed into one of the MGS Strykers.

To combat the elusive band of rebels, the NAU vehicles began unloading their troops, and immediately combatants from both sides began falling amidst the sudden roar of small-arms fire.

But Scott didn't see any of that. He was too focused on the Humvee in front of him. He watched another soldier try to squirm up behind the .50 cal. And prayed it wasn't another woman. The soldier was too distracted by Mayhew shooting the AK-47 to notice him, and Scott shot them in the back of the head as he climbed up the back of the Humvee. The dead soldier dropped back down into the vehicle, and Scott climbed into the turret and dropped down after them. He fired the 9mm as he landed on top of the two corpses, taking out the driver. Then he opened the side door and pushed the bodies out onto the highway. He climbed out and ran around to the driver's side. Pulled the driver out from behind the wheel. He stopped only long enough to commandeer the NAU jacket from him and then slid behind the wheel himself. With adrenaline pounding through his veins, he slammed on the gas and sent the Humvee shooting forward. He skidded to a stop beside Mayhew. "Get in!"

Mayhew hopped into the empty passenger seat and turned to look out the back window. Scott floored the gas, and the Humvee shot south down I-87, the battle quickly fading into the distance behind them.

"Who were those guys?" Scott asked as he tried pulling the army jacket on while still controlling the wheel.

"Local militia. Guess they knew the convoy was coming."

"It's a good thing they did, or you'd be dead." He looked over at Mayhew. "What were you thinking?" He didn't respond, and Scott didn't press the issue. "How did you know that was David?"

"I told you. I saw him talking on a satphone right before he took off. I knew he was making a break for it, and it didn't seem likely that he was planning to four-wheel it all the way down the interstate."

"Did David call in the drone?"

Mayhew shrugged. Stared out the window. "I don't know."

Scott didn't know either. Didn't know how long they had before the army hit the kill switch on their stolen Humvee. Didn't know where they were going. Didn't know who this Titus Mayhew really was. Didn't know what had really been going on between him and David. Didn't know what the stupid ring was or how a piece of jewelry could be so significant that people were willing to kill and die to get it. Didn't know what the priest had tried to tell him about a rose...

All he knew was that the gas pedal would stay against the floorboard until they ran out of gas.

# 17.

*"I am concerned for the security of our great nation; not so much because of any threat from without, but because of the insidious forces working from within."*

—Douglas MacArthur

North would have taken them into Canada, which was exactly where Scott wanted to go. Where he had planned to go. But Mayhew wanted to regroup with his Resistance people in Pennsylvania, and for some odd reason, Scott felt like he should help get him there. After all, a lot of what the Resistance was doing was trying to clean up his mess. Maybe helping them do it would ease his conscious a little. To make up for what he'd done. Of course, it wouldn't be enough. Nothing would ever be enough.

He looked into the rearview mirror as he sped south down I-87 and said farewell to the Canadian wilderness. It would have to wait. "Does your resistance group have a name?" he asked Mayhew.

"Not in the way you mean. It's too easy to discredit a name."

Scott squinted ahead. "How do you differentiate between all the different groups in the country, then?"

"We're fine simply being referred to as the Resistance, but I guess to others within the Revolution, we're characterized by the name of our leader. But it's not an official designation. We don't have a flag or anything."

Scott didn't really care if they had a name or not. Wouldn't mean anything to him one way or another. Besides, he knew what they were called; he'd heard it every time he turned on the news — terrorists, right-wing extremists, Nazis…

But Mayhew kept talking. "As with most of the Constitutional Resistance groups, our creed or ideology would probably parallel that of Orwell's 'Brotherhood.' Though fighting to uphold the Constitution should be considered the true mark of American patriotism. We're just following the founding fathers' instructions."

That might be all well and good, Scott thought, but he knew the difference between being a terrorist or a patriot would be decided, as always, by whichever side won this war. Mayhew and his Resistance would either go down in history as heroes of the Republic or hanged as villains. And he was pretty sure which side was going to be writing the history books. Despite his conversations with Edward, he knew that the people had given up too much for too long. There wasn't anything anyone could do about it now. Just ask Jack. Or Melissa Strauss. Or all the dead Mossad agents back at the camp. Or the priest. Or the Resistance members sprawled out over the highway. Or countless others who had thrown themselves into the churning teeth of the reigning technocracy. "There is no Constitution anymore."

"The Constitution will always be alive, living in the hearts and minds of men…"

Scott smiled. "Like the word of God." It was a jab at Mayhew's self-expressed faith, at his conflicting philosophies. But Mayhew didn't take the bait, just looked out the window.

"Why'd you want me to talk to the priest?" Scott asked next.

Mayhew looked over at him and thought for a moment. "Never really trusted David. Couldn't get a feel for what side of things he was on. I sensed a tension between him and the priest, like they were working toward two opposite ends. I saw that David had a satphone, and when I asked him about it, he lied, said he didn't have one. I thought that maybe the priest might confirm some of my suspicion to you. He obviously wouldn't trust me, since he thought I was in league with David."

"So you never talked to the priest yourself?"

"No."

"How'd the priest even get in the picture?"

"They showed up at the same time, which is why I assumed they came together. They both wanted to help the Resistance."

"The Mossad told you about the ring right away?"

Mayhew shook his head. "No, not right away. And then they only confided in a few of us, asked us not to spread it around. We didn't even know they were Mossad at first. Not that we really cared who they were as long as they were willing to fight alongside us."

Scott drove in silence for a little while, none of this helping him to make sense of what was happening. "The priest told me that David only knew half the story." He wasn't going to tell him what else he'd said.

"Probably."

They drove another quiet mile before Scott said, "So David made off with the ring just as the MAV and drone show up..."

"I know what you're thinking, but I don't think so. Whoever bombed the house wasn't interested in recovering the ring. The MAVs were probably sent out from the prison camp. I think the van had already been waiting for him, that it was prepared to wait all day for him. But then he spotted the MAV and knew we'd been made. He came in and shouted a warning to me before taking off on the quad. When I went out to see what he was doing, I noticed the drone."

"Thank God for clear skies. Okay, so David didn't call in a strike. What did he want with the ring?"

Mayhew leaned back in the passenger seat and closed his eyes. "We found out David was Mossad when he came to some of us and told us about this ring, how important they thought it was. They told us it was actually nearby and that they needed to retrieve it while they could. We didn't argue. They could leave if they wanted to. Besides, David and the priest were staying back. But that's when I heard the two of them arguing."

"About what?"

"I don't know. It was in Hebrew. But the rest of the Mossad agents took a helicopter — don't ask me how they got one — over to your neck of the woods. When they came back, they had you and the ring with them. Naturally, I had some questions for David, but before I could confront him, we were being attacked. Myself, David, and the priest were the only ones left standing when the fighting stopped."

Scott thought back to the conversation he'd had with David and the priest right before the prison was attacked. About Roswell. He reexamined David's response to the priest's mention of it and wondered if he'd misinterpreted what David's uneasy look had meant.

Mayhew was still talking. "So all that talk back at the house was just me going along with his act. To let him think he was in charge and that I had joined his cause. And I didn't know who you were either. Still don't, actually."

Scott thought about it. He couldn't find a glaring hole in Mayhew's story, yet something still wasn't sitting right. He glanced at the fuel gauge. Half a tank left. He hoped they'd be able to get through it all before the kill switch was activated or they ran into more trouble. If they could just get to a small town and lie low for a little while, they might just have a chance. Though the money he'd left back in the cave would have been nice to have. People tended to look the other way when handed three months' worth of state support. He wasn't counting on them being able to secure more fuel. The little oil that was left in the world was being stretched out with various methods of dilution and becoming harder and harder to find.

"What did David say the ring was?" Scott asked. He was starting to feel like he was never going to get the answer to that question, and he still for the life of him couldn't understand how it could be so important. This wasn't Middle Earth, after all.

Mayhew shook his head, his eyes still closed. "Just said it has some kind of power the globalists want to use against the world."

"And you believed that?"

"No, but for the Mossad to show up here with a Catholic priest in tow, the thing had to be important."

"So if you didn't believe David's story, then what do you think it is?"

Mayhew opened his eyes, pulled the ring out of his pocket and stared at it. "I don't know what it is."

"But you risked your life to get it."

He nodded. "Stupid thing to do, I guess." He put it back into his pocket.

If the ring was important enough to be stored in a secret underground NASA facility in Washington, DC, with both the Mossad and NAU Intelligence going after it, then Scott wondered if Mayhew should be the one entrusted with it. Or, if he didn't know what it was, why he'd even want it himself. He figured he was planning on giving it to the Resistance leaders, to let them decide what should be done with it. Yet, it hadn't been given to Mayhew or the Resistance to make that decision. It had been sent to Edward's son. To Jack.

Scott tried to convince himself that he didn't really care. That it wasn't any of his concern. Tried to forget how the ring had made him feel. Back when Edward was still alive.

He stole a glance at Mayhew, but his eyes were closed again, and he seemed to be asleep. *No,* Scott thought. *It doesn't make sense.* If Mayhew didn't have any clue what the ring was, then he wouldn't have risked his life for it.

Scott shifted uncomfortably in the Humvee. Taking another look at Mayhew to make sure he was still asleep, he reached beneath the army jacket and adjusted the priest's canvas bag.

Maybe there were answers in there.

# 18.



Matthew Scott pulled the Humvee over onto the side of the road.

"Out of gas?" Mayhew asked, sitting up and looking around.

Scott pushed the door open and slid out. "No." Then he shut the door and stretched on the shoulder of I-87. He heard Mayhew get out of the vehicle behind him. "I think there's a town ahead." He could make out two twin bridges farther down the road.

Mayhew followed his gaze and nodded. "Probably."

"We're not gonna want to leave the Humvee near where we're staying."

Mayhew looked behind them and spotted the moving water through some trees. "In the river?"

"Yeah."

If there were people in the town ahead, then certainly the lane whispered down would be a short one that would end at the police station. No way could they drive a stolen NAU

Humvee through the heart of town if they were hoping to hole up there without any problems.

Scott looked up the road again, half expecting to see a line of flashing lights. "Think they'll notice their missing vehicle is transmitting from the bottom of a river?"

"It's been over an hour. I'm sure they know exactly where we are."

"Maybe. Maybe not," he said as he opened the door and got the vehicle running again.

Mayhew stood to the side and kept watch for anyone coming down the road as Scott drove onto the grass and between two trees.

Scott jumped back out, the front wheels just a foot from the moving water. "It's in neutral," he said.

Both of them went to the back of the Humvee and pushed it into the river. The current caught it, and it floated toward the middle, drifting to the left and toward the bridges in the distance. Until it got stuck on something along the riverbed and stopped moving. The water just covered the hood.

Scott looked up at the fall trees. "Maybe it's concealed enough," he mumbled.

"Yeah, sure it is."

Scott nodded at the AK-47 Mayhew was still holding. "You planning on walking through town with that sticking down your pants?"

Mayhew heaved it into the water after the Humvee. "You still have your pistol?"

Scott nodded and began heading toward the bridges, trees to the right, the northbound lanes across the median to their left.

"You have some kind of idea where we're going?" Mayhew asked, thrusting his empty hands deep into his pockets.

"Not really. But that's Albany ahead, across the bridges." Scott looked up to the sun and figured it was about one o'clock. His watch was back with the priest in a billion pieces.

A gust of cold air came down the road, and they folded their arms across their chests.

"Do you have any money?" Mayhew asked.

"No."

A car passed by them but didn't stop. It crossed the bridge and drove out of sight.

"I do."

Scott looked over at him, his stride slowing. "How much?"

"Three thousand."

"Ameros?"

"Yeah."

"That should cover a motel for the night."

"It'd better cover a lot more than that," Mayhew stated.

"We'll see."

After a few more minutes of walking, Mayhew asked the question Scott had been waiting for. "What else did the priest say to you?"

He began the response he'd prepared. "To protect the ring."

"From who?"

"He said everyone."

"What does that mean?"

"No idea. He started to say it was a key, but that's when you came running in."

"Anything else?"

Scott stared ahead. "Just something about a rose."

They continued to the bridges in silence.

They were an architectural beauty, the bridges. A scene one would expect to see hanging framed on office walls. It was named the Thaddeus Kosciusko Bridge after Thaddeus Kosciusko, a Polish man who served as a colonel for the Continental Army during the Revolutionary War. The Continental Congress honored him by making him brigadier general, and in 1794, he went on to lead the Kosciuszko uprising against Imperial Russia. At least that was what the plaque hanging on the bridge said. Scott thought it strange that the sign was even still there, all references to the Revolutionary War having been scrubbed from most public places years ago. Maybe it was a good sign, that the town they were entering wasn't all that fond of their new NAU overlords.

The bridges were actually a pair of identical arch bridges made of steel, cables connecting the deck to the arch. There were three northbound lanes on the east bridge and three southbound lanes on the one they were crossing now. The Mohawk River flowed beneath them.

Scott looked over the side and watched multicolored leaves float past. "Mohawk River..."

"What about it?"

"Some kind of importance during the French and Indian War and the Revolutionary War. Can't remember what."

"Was that on the plaque?" Mayhew asked.

"Mohawk River was, yeah. We just walked out of Halfmoon."

"Halfmoon?"

"The name of Henry Hudson's ship."

Mayhew nodded ahead of them. "And this is Colonie?"

"That's what the sign said."

The view from the steel bridge was even more beautiful than the twin bridges themselves. The water reflected the colorful trees along the riverbank, their leaves turning and fluttering away with the coming winter. For the next few days, the sight would be a remarkable one. And then for the next few months, there would be no colors at all.

They walked off the bridge and went another half mile down 87 before crossing over the northbound lanes and stepping into a grass clearing. They could see the town from there.

Ten minutes later, they were walking down a street lined with houses on both sides.

Scott scanned the homes, hoping no one inside felt the need to report the two out-of-towners like the law said they should.

They were almost to the last house when a man working on an old car looked up and took notice of them. Then he was crossing the front lawn. "Excuse me!" he called out, stepping onto the street behind them.

They stopped and turned to face him.

"Yeah?" Scott's heart was thumping in his chest.

The guy looked him up and down before shifting his gaze over to Mayhew. Their condition—soot-covered clothes, cuts and bruises marking their faces—was not lost on him. "Where you guys headed?"

"We were on our way to Manhattan, but our car broke down a few miles back. Now we're just hoping to find an auto shop or a motel we can spend the night in." Scott looked past the man and quickly appraised his living conditions. The guy was barely getting by, most of his house in disrepair. Scott knew what he wanted.

"Well, you're a long ways off from Manhattan. If you're lookin' to spend the night though, there's a motel off Loudon Road 'bout two and a half miles from here." The man was wiping grease off his hands with a dirty rag.

"Loudon Road?" Mayhew asked.

The guy smiled again, about to play his hand. "Yeah. You want, I'll give you a lift."

Scott nodded, deciding it was better to play the game than to go against it. Besides, times *were* tough, and he couldn't just kill him because of that. "That would be very nice of you, sir. I think we'd appreciate it."

"No problem at all, it's just a few minutes down the road." He turned and walked back up the lawn, pulling his keys out of his pocket. "Hop right in." He went to the front of the car and slammed the hood shut.

"You sure about this?" Mayhew whispered to Scott as he opened the front passenger door.

"Just have your money ready."

They got into the stranger's car.

It was only a two-minute drive, and the motel was right off the road like the guy had said. "Thank you very much," Mayhew said as he climbed out.

The man turned away from the steering wheel and looked back at Scott. "If by chance anyone were to come around looking for you, what is it I should tell them?"

"We only have two hundred ameros," Scott lied, cutting to the chase.

The guy frowned. He'd been hoping for more. But then he managed a smile. It was still more than he'd get for reporting them. "If that's all you got."

Scott waved at Mayhew, and Mayhew handed him a hundred and twenty ameros. Scott then slapped it down into the man's open palm.

A huge smile beamed from his face. "Your secret's safe with me, boys. But I wouldn't be here come sunup. Not unless you can scrounge up another hundred." He winked at them.

Scott leaned forward, his eyes suddenly ice cold, and said evenly, "I don't mind giving you the money. I know you need it. And I appreciate you not alerting the authorities. But if we get visitors tonight, I know where you live."

The look of fear that passed through the man's eyes let Scott know that his point had been received. He stepped out of the car and stood beside Mayhew. Watched the guy turn around and drive back to his house.

"Think he'll talk?" Mayhew asked.

Scott turned away from the road and began walking to the motel. "I don't think so."

When they reached the counter, they were confronted only by a sign that read *NO PAPER ACCEPTED—PLASTIC ONLY.* Scott hit the bell and, while they waited for service, swept his gaze through the room. There was a camera aimed right at them up in the corner behind the counter.

"I doubt it's linked to anything but an old recorder in the back room. This place looks like we could buy it with the money I have in my pocket," Mayhew said.

A minute later, an old man wearing big glasses and a flannel shirt hobbled through the door behind them. "Oh, didn't see you come in. Sorry. Was out raking the yard."

As he rounded the counter and approached the computer, Scott asked, "You take ameros, right?" He pointed to the sign.

The man stopped and squinted up at him through his thick lenses. "Why? You don't got no card?"

"Stolen," he lied.

The old guy hung his head, wagging it back and forth. "The NAU is all about electronic transfers. They want everything on record, and they give me a tax break on plastic sales."

Scott smiled as he nodded. "I understand. Do you have any rooms open?"

"Yeah, pretty much all of them."

"Well, how about you skip the whole computer part of the process, and we'll throw in a few extra ameros to make up for your loss?"

The old man's eyes looked magnified behind his thick lenses, and he looked like a cartoon when he blinked. "How long?"

"Just the night."

He flashed a gapped smile. "You were never here." He reached for a key.

"Thanks," Mayhew said, handing over more of his stash.

The old guy squinted through his glasses, noticing the cut on Mayhew's head. "Nice little gash you got there. Guess you fell, right?"

"Right."

Then the guy smiled again and shoved the Union notes into his pocket. He walked out from behind the counter. "Follow me."

# 19.

*"The New World Order cannot happen without US participation, as we are the most significant single component. Yes, there will be a New World Order, and it will force the United States to change its perceptions."*
—Henry Kissinger

It was five o'clock, and all that remained of the sun was an orange glow over the horizon. Scott was sitting on an old chair and leaning back with his arms folded. Mayhew was asleep on the queen bed that occupied most of the small motel room. There was a television hanging on the wall. It was showing an old black-and-white Jimmy Stewart movie, and the alien portrayal of what life had once been like in the Old Country was tormenting Scott's sense of reality. He knew that the program had been an illusion masking the troubles of its own day, but it was accurate in at least showing how truly blissful the ignorance of a generation could be—as long as it wasn't that generation that paid the price for it.

The last bits of sunlight were coming through a pair of red curtains and setting the room on fire with dark oranges and reds.

Scott looked at Mayhew and wished he could fall asleep the same way. But there were too many nightmares awaiting him in dreamland. Most of which involved innocent people jumping out of buildings. And now another dead friend, lost pets, and the lifeless gaze of two women dressed in tactical gear were all new characters waiting to be cast in horrifying new episodes.

So instead of sleeping, he was thinking.

Until he began to feel the room creeping in on him, the walls getting closer. Familiar feelings of claustrophobia—a product of his time spent in that Iranian interrogation room—trying to convince him that he was trapped. That there was no way out. And of course they were right. He *was* trapped. Trapped by his circumstances, trapped by his memory, trapped by his conscience, and trapped by his future.

He studied the beam of light sneaking through the edge of the curtain. It was striking a laser line up the wall beside him. He wasn't sure why Mayhew hadn't asked about the messenger bag yet. He'd obviously seen him wearing it while they were running from the house and fighting on the interstate. Had he assumed it was his bag and didn't know it had been the priest's? He wasn't sure, but if he wanted to find out why the priest wanted him to have it without Mayhew looking over his shoulder, now was the perfect time to do so.

He reached down and grabbed the bag. *A piece of the puzzle,* the priest had said. Hopefully it would be a corner piece, something to anchor the rest of the nonsense to.

Scott stood, ignoring the pins and needles in his legs, and walked over to the nightstand. He placed the 9mm on it. It was the least he could do. Then he walked out of the room, shutting the door behind him without a sound.

****

The road was quiet. There were no houses around that he could see, and only an occasional car passed by. He didn't know where he was walking to, but walking itself was the end, so he didn't really care.

Eventually he came to a flickering neon sign that peered down at him, shouting, *Danielle's.* He followed the sign and found himself standing in the parking lot of a diner. He adjusted the bag hanging from his shoulder and walked to the door, realizing he was about to put his assumption of this town to the test.

Stepping inside, it took just three seconds for him to process the layout of the diner and everyone in it. The space was small, the seating area shaped like an L with bar stools wrapping around the front counter, the kitchen through the doors behind the register. There were three people in the diner. One guy sitting alone in a booth next to the window at the bottom of the L, and a man and a woman facing each other at the top. The guy sitting by himself had his back to the door. Balding, broad shouldered, slightly slouched posture. He looked like he was around two hundred pounds. Out of shape, older. He was staring at a digital device and sipping a coffee. Hadn't touched his half-eaten burger in a while. He was holding the coffee mug in his right hand, and the empty sugar wrappers and creamers on the table were also positioned to his right. So he was right-handed. And since he was sitting with his right side against the wall and facing away from the entrance, Scott quickly concluded that he wasn't carrying a gun. Anyone carrying a gun these days would be aware of their surroundings and ready to draw if need be. They would sit facing the entrance, gun hand ready to draw in an open aisle rather than find himself hindered by having to clear the table. This guy was no threat and definitely not interested in Scott's presence.

The other guy was too busy trying to sneak a peek down his date's shirt to even notice him, both his hands holding hers on top of the table while they waited for their food.

Scott made his way to the counter, where he waited to be seated. There was no one there managing the register, and he was about to seat himself when a guy wearing a dirty apron opened one of the kitchen doors and peeked out.

"Take a seat. She'll be with you in a second." And then he disappeared again.

But not before Scott was able to get a glimpse past the cook and into the kitchen. There were no NAU troops lying in wait for him. Turning away from the counter, he went for the last booth in the room, where the young girl would be the only person able to see him. He pulled the bag off his shoulder and dropped it onto the table as he sat down. He was facing the door, and the window beside him gave him a panorama of the parking lot and a good portion of road leading to it. He eavesdropped on the conversation ahead of him as he leaned back against the bench seat and scanned the ceiling. He couldn't find any cameras but knew they were there. Had to be for the state to approve their business.

The waitress came out through the kitchen doors. She didn't have a notepad in her hand or in her apron, so either she'd been working here for a while, or the menu was pretty simple. He didn't care. He wasn't buying anything.

"Good evening." Her voice matched her face. Friendly and soft. She was an attractive woman, tall in heels, brown hair, great eyes. About thirty-three, give or take a couple of years. No wedding band.

Scott smiled politely. "Hi."

"What can I get for you?"

He was instantly attracted to her. "If it's all the same to you, miss, I'd just like to sit here." He wasn't sure how she'd take being referred to as "miss." He thought it had been considered polite once but then vaguely recalled being slapped by a woman a few years ago for it. He'd slapped her back, but lesson learned. Or not, apparently.

But the waitress didn't seem offended. Rather she gave him a curious smile. "No money?" Her eyes couldn't hide their teasing.

Scott figured that in a small town like this, any guy who was even remotely attractive would probably earn such attention. He shrugged. "Lost my wallet."

"Well, since we're so busy and all..." She looked around and laughed.

He smiled. "Thank you. I appreciate it."

She smiled back and turned away in a manner that was obviously meant to tempt him into following. He sighed and hoped Edward couldn't read minds from his heavenly abode.

Reaching into the bag, he pulled out the two books and set them on the table in front of him. Their covers, brown calfskin leather—the smell of which had faded long ago—were beaten from constant attention, and the pages they contained were yellow with age. There was a long piece of twine in the bag, indicating the books had once been tied together. Whatever was written on these pages were things the priest hadn't trusted David or Mayhew with.

He noticed the waitress watching him from behind the counter, and smiled again. She smiled back. Then he turned one of the covers back and brought the diner's lighting across a loose piece of paper. It was folded and resting against the first page. He removed it, gently unfolding it to discover a drawing of North America with what appeared to be the spirit of a man whimsically emerging from out of its center like some floating genie or ghost. He was holding scrolls in his hands, and over his head was an eye enclosed within a triangle. And then Scott noticed a rose and a cross on his cloak. *A rose.* Scott stared at it for a moment, but there were no other markings that could explain its meaning. He folded it back up and replaced it, instead turning to page one of the mysterious book.

The page had no lines, and the priest (presumably) had filled the blank page with another sketch—Christ on the cross, a double-headed phoenix behind Him, a Bible passage in Latin encircling the symbol. He wasn't sure what that meant either and turned the page.

## THE TESTAMENT OF SOLOMON

Scott had never heard of it and wondered if it was the title of the priest's own work, or if it was an actual piece of history. Notes scribbled beneath the title seemed to answer his question.

> Old Testament pseudepigraphical work. Considered a haggadic-type folktale and commonly dated between the first and third century AD. Standard Greek text contains comments on fourteen Greek manuscripts written in Koine Greek and generally not believed to be a translation document—though believed by some in 1896 to have been translated from the Hebrew. Other scholars think it a Christian revision of a Jewish document, the original being the very collection of incantations which, according to Josephus, was composed by Solomon

himself. Still others believe that if it was written by a Greek-speaking Jew, it was later edited by a Greek-speaking Christian. Most, however, attribute it to a Greek-speaking Christian. Origin is unknown, but common candidates include Galilee, Egypt, Asia Minor, and Palestine. In 1945, Coptic translations of fifty-one tractates were discovered in Egypt. One of them—"On the Origin of the World"—mentions "the book of Solomon" and seems to refer to the eighth chapter of the Testament's demonology. Though it is also possible that it refers instead to the first-century BC "Hygromancy of Solomon." If, however, it is referring to the Testament, then it would provide further proof of it originating from third-century Alexandria…

He looked up from the page, turning his attention out the window and into the parking lot. *Demonology?* He felt like he was trapped inside a joke. Roswell and now demons? He turned the page.

Chapter 1:5–7.

He moved his eyes over the penned words and found that a strange feeling accompanied them.

> When I, Solomon, heard these things, I went into the Temple of God and, praising him day and night, begged with all my soul that the demon might be delivered into my hands and that I might gain authority over him. And it came about through prayer that grace was given to me from the Lord of Sabaoth* through Michael his archangel. He brought me a ring, having a seal consisting of an engraved stone. He said to me, "Take, O Solomon, king, son of David, the gift which the Lord God, the highest Sabaoth, has sent you. With it you shall imprison all the demons, male and female, and with their help you shall build Jerusalem. But thou must wear this seal of God. And this engraving of the seal of the ring sent thee is a Pentalpha.**
> *transliteration of Heb. *Sabah* (army): the Lord of (heavenly) armies.
> **"some manuscripts include this. Pentalpha being a 31-letter word written in the 2nd and 3rd of a series of concentric circles, an engraving with 'O Lord our God' plus a group of Semitic-sounding names." —DC Duling

Scott turned the page to find verses from the next chapter, this time with more drawings in the margins. Among the doodles was a cross wrapped with a single rose. He flipped through the rest of the book, and it was all more of the same—selected verses from *Testament of Solomon.*

He leaned back against the seat and stared up at the ceiling, wondering if what he just read could possibly be speaking of the same ring Mayhew now had in his pocket.

The waitress came back out and checked on the couple. Then she walked back to him.

"Everything okay?" she asked.

Scott shrugged, and she squinted playfully. He was about to say something that would ensure him spending the night with her, when a sudden twinge of guilt erupted from his conscience. Though his wife was probably remarried or maybe even dead, he had still left her, and this feeling something for a stranger only fanned those flames of shame. "Are you Danielle?" he asked instead.

She leaned against the booth and placed a hand on her hip. "Nope. I'm Cindy."

"Would you care to join me, Cindy?" He didn't know what he was doing anymore, his morality on and off the merry-go-round faster than he could keep up with it.

She laughed, flashed him another killer smile, and turned away from him, confident as to how this game would end.

He forced his attention back to the book, though with a bit less interest than he'd had just a moment ago. Images of what could be with Cindy were flashing through his mind while his wife came riding around the carousel, condemning them. But before he could purge it all from his head and settle back into the strange book, something in the parking lot caught his eye.

A police cruiser.

He swore under his breath, all thoughts of the girl and the books in front of him gone. The cop was getting out of the car and making his way across the parking lot. Scott looked at the waitress. She was looking at the cop, and then she was looking at him. She wasn't stupid. Bored perhaps, but not stupid. She disappeared into the kitchen.

Scott picked up the menu and pretended to read it as the cop entered the diner. Scott could feel the cold gaze of authority sweeping over him, processing him. He forced himself to focus on the menu, the prices.

A shadow fell across the table, and he looked up to see Cindy smiling down at him. She poured him a cup of coffee.

"On the house," she whispered. She winked at him. And then she began talking loud enough so that the cop could hear her. "Indecisive tonight, huh? Well, I think I'd personally recommend the club sandwich with a side of French onion soup."

"Sounds great, Cindy." And he mouthed a silent "Thank you."

She bent over, the smell of her perfume seductive, and her lips touched his ear. "There's an exit in the back." Then she quickly kissed his ear before retreating back into the kitchen. "It'll be right up, Frank."

Scott lowered the menu, and saw that the cop was now on a bar stool at the counter. He didn't seem too interested in anything but the menu. Scott sipped the coffee and watched Cindy come back out through the kitchen doors and lean on the counter in front of the officer. She talked to him like she knew him.

Best way to avoid attention was to not act like you deserved any. So he played the part of a hungry local who was just ordering a late dinner while huddling over a book. Blending in is what had kept him alive over all the years spent operating in enemy territory. Only now, everywhere in the world was enemy territory.

Setting the menu aside, he willed his eyes back to the priest's book.

> "At the moment the demon appears to you, fling this ring into his chest, and say to him: 'In the name of God, King Solomon summons you,' and come running back to me as fast as you can without having any misgivings or fear in respect of what you may hear on the part of the demon."

That was enough of that.

He closed the book and reached for the other one, curious to see if it held anything more useful. But as he stretched out his arm, his elbow knocked over the coffee. He was fast as lightning in that he was able to catch the mug and prevent it from smashing onto the floor. Had even managed to preserve half of its contents. But the other half had splashed across the table, wetting the *Testament of Solomon*. He cursed his clumsiness, picked the book up and started shaking it off. Then he grabbed a handful of napkins and threw them on the puddle before it could stretch to the other book. He could feel the cop's eyes on him again. In all his years of clandestine behavior, this was by far the stupidest mistake he'd ever made. How could he have been so careless? Was he getting old? He heard the cop ask Cindy about him, who he was. He said that he didn't recognize him, and she told him that it didn't surprise her, that he wasn't the sharpest cop on the block.

Scott looked up, trying to feign innocent embarrassment, and the cop locked eyes with him. Scott gave his best attempt at a disarming smile, but the cop didn't return it. Instead, he turned to look into the parking lot.

*Uh-oh.*

The cop got off the stool and came walking over, one hand hooked into his belt beside the butt of his service pistol. He sat down in the booth across from him.

"Hi there," the officer said through a classic patronizing smile.

Scott looked up from the wet napkins. Now he was annoyed. "Can I help you, Officer?" There was an edge to his voice that he hadn't meant to let slip through.

"Never seen you before," he said.

Scott shrugged. "Name's Frank."

"How'd you get here, Frank?"

"Is there a problem?"

The cop laughed. "No, I don't think so. But I was just curious because there's only four cars in the parking lot. None of which belong to you. Hitchin' is illegal, so you must've walked from somewhere."

"Got dropped off. Not 'hitchin'.'" He saw the cop look at his ringless finger.

"Girlfriend?" he asked.

"Boyfriend." He stared at him. "Is that what this is about?" He let the question hang there between them for a second, allowing the cop to interpret the question in all its various ways. Was he interested if he was? Or was he homophobic? In which case NAU laws would prosecute him, cop or no cop.

"My mistake. I thought I saw you were flirting with Cindy."

"Nope, just being polite." He thought the cop was about to get up, but he didn't. Instead, he asked another question. The wrong question.

"Can I see your identification card?"

"I left it at home."

The corner of the cop's mouth pulled into a grin. "And where might that be?"

He gave him the name of the road he and Mayhew had walked down after crossing the bridge.

The cop nodded and then got up. "Well, now that I know where you live, Frank, I'm sure I'll be running into you again soon."

"Look forward to it." But Scott knew it was an act, and he watched the cop walk straight out of the diner, waving to Cindy as he went. Then he climbed into the patrol car and got onto the computer.

It was time to leave.

Cindy came over. "Everything okay?"

"Not exactly." He put the books back in the bag and looked out the window. The cop was already on his way back in.

With a shotgun.

Scott wondered if the MAV back at the warden's house had transmitted his image before Mayhew shot it. Or maybe the Humvee had been found. He jumped to his feet, put the bag over his shoulder, and told Cindy to get him a steak knife. Then he looked at the young couple, who had suddenly become aware of what was going on around them. "Get out."

They didn't even hesitate.

The cook came out. "What's going on here?"

"Just get back in the kitchen and shut up!" Scott yelled.

Cindy ran back to him just as the cop came in through the doors, shotgun held tight against his shoulder. The couple ran past him, fleeing the diner.

"Freeze!" the cop yelled.

In one smooth movement, Scott had the knife out of Cindy's hand and pressed against her throat. "Put the gun down." His voice was cold and flat.

But the cop just stood there aiming the shotgun, not seeming to mind that he wouldn't be able to use it without killing Cindy.

Scott could feel Cindy's fear running through her body, making her tense in his grip. He leaned his head forward and whispered, "I'm not going to hurt you."

The cop took a step closer.

"Take one more step, and I'll cut her head off."

The cop almost smiled. Like he'd enjoy seeing that. Images of the urban training exercises that had been taking place in the country over the last fifty years flashed through Scott's mind, and he suddenly realized that the cop wasn't just hoping to stall him until backup arrived.

Scott let Cindy go and slowly raised his hands. The cop responded by using the shotgun to motion him away from Cindy and over toward an imaginary spot nearby. So that he could blow him in half unhindered. Scott nodded and lowered his arms. He took as much time as he dared, forcing the cop's patience. He was hoping the cop would repeat the gesture with the gun.

"Come on! Step away from her!"

And the barrel moved away, back to that imaginary location.

Scott didn't know if the cop was using slugs or not, but at only ten feet, any pellets would be relatively concentrated anyway. He bent his right knee forward, dropping it hard into the back of Cindy's and sending her down to the floor. Scott went down with her, mimicking her movement and using her as a shield. He was hoping the suddenness of the move would confuse the cop.

And it did.

As the cop brought the barrel back around, he hesitated, trying to figure out what had happened, why they were suddenly falling clumsily to the floor. The hesitation only amounted to half a second, but that was all it took for Scott to let loose the knife. He threw it as he went down. He'd aimed for the chest but let go too early, and the trajectory was too high.

The cop pulled the trigger just as the steak knife sank into his neck, and a deafening boom rocketed throughout the diner, shattering the glass window in the back.

Cindy lifted her head and moved the hair out of her eyes, watching in horror as the cop collapsed to the floor, slipping in his own blood while trying frantically to pull the knife from his throat.

Scrambling to his feet, Scott grabbed Cindy underneath the arms and lifted her up, pushing her forward. "Go!"

She jumped over the flailing cop and went to the door while Scott paused to grab the shotgun and take the pistol from the officer's holster.

Cindy ran straight to her car and fumbled with a set of keys, dropped them, picked them back up, and finally got the door open. She slid behind the wheel. Scott got into the passenger seat beside her.

"Go," he said.

She started the car and peeled out of the parking lot. As they drove north, two police cars flew past them on their way to the diner.

Scott looked over at Cindy. Her face was pale, her knuckles white on the steering wheel. "Thanks," he said.

She swallowed. "This is bad, isn't it?"

He knew that once the cops saw the video feed, his face would be everywhere. Cindy's too. There wouldn't be a camera out there that wouldn't be trying to match every face it saw with his and hers. And once that guy in the diner told the cops that he went with Cindy, they would simply hit the kill switch on her car and come get them. Yeah, it was bad.

And now he had even more decisions to make.

# 20.



indy pulled the car up alongside the motel just as Scott instructed.

"Stay here. I'll be right back," he said. Then he jumped out of the car and left her trembling at the wheel.

Scott flung the motel door open so hard that it slammed off the adjacent wall. Mayhew was sitting on the edge of the bed and staring at the television. He didn't even turn his head, his attention wholly captivated by the images flashing across the screen.

"Let's go," Scott said.

But still Mayhew didn't respond.

"Mayhew! Let's go! Now!"

"Look at this," he whispered.

Scott grabbed him and yanked him to his feet. "We don't have time for this!"

Snapping out of his stupor, Mayhew quickly began looking for his gun and jacket. "What's going on?"

"Come on," Scott said, pushing him out the door and into the parking lot. Before closing the door, however, he glanced at the television himself. The images being broadcasted were indiscernible, the camera jerking all over the place. He could tell there was fire and that people were running. And then he caught the words across the bottom of the screen.

*NEWS ALERT: TERROR STRIKES NORTH AMERICA.*

He closed the door and ran to Cindy's car. "Come on, over here," he said to Mayhew, pointing.

Mayhew looked confused. "What—"

"Do you have the ring?" Scott cut him off.

Mayhew blinked, staring at the car. "How did—"

"Do you have the ring?"

"Yeah."

"Just get in the back!"

As Scott climbed into the passenger seat, as calmly as he could manage, he told Cindy to go.

"Where?" she asked. She wiped her eyes with the back of her hand.

"Who is *she*?" Mayhew asked, leaning forward from the back seat.

They both ignored him.

"Just drive," Scott answered. "Anywhere. Go the speed limit. We'll see how far we can get before they hit the kill switch."

"Kill switch?" Cindy asked.

Scott didn't answer her.

She pulled back onto the road.

"What happened?" Mayhew asked again.

"Killed a cop." Then he thought of something else and turned to Cindy. "Do you have a phone on you?"

"Yeah."

"Give it to me."

She dug it out of her pants, hesitated, then handed it over.

Without a word, he tossed it out the window.

"What are you doing?" Cindy screamed. "That was my phone!"

"They're tracking it."

"It was off!"

"It's always generating a signal."

Another tear slipped out from the corner of her eye. "That was my life…" she whispered.

Scott wasn't sure if she meant the phone or her job or what they were fleeing from in general. But she was right. He had walked into her life, and now the life she had was ruined. *Join the club*, he thought. It was getting to be a big one.

As confused as Mayhew was, he could interpret the situation well enough to know there was one question more important than all others. "How long?" he asked.

Scott looked out the window. "I don't know. The police are on the scene now, two possible eyewitnesses, the surveillance feed…"

"So any minute, then."

Scott didn't answer, but Cindy did. "The cameras weren't on," she said.

"What do you mean?" Scott asked.

"They weren't on," she repeated.

"Why not?"

She seemed to blush and turned her eyes away from the road for a second. "Because we turned them off."

*We?* He didn't care. "When?"

"Last night."

"And no one else turned them back on?"

She shook her head. "We closed, forgot to put them back online before we left. When I came in today, I saw that they were still off. I wasn't going to point it out."

It didn't take any great amount of imagination to figure out why she'd shut the cameras off, but Scott was relieved nonetheless. It meant that the security feed couldn't have been tied into the central surveillance system. They wouldn't have gotten away with shutting it off if it had been. It was just a simple security feed copied to discs for insurance purposes. Maybe the town wasn't so bad after all. Still, the two guys in the diner had seen them leave in Cindy's car. It would take them a little longer to find them, but they would. If their AI computers could determine where Melissa Strauss was most likely to send an envelope, then they could certainly find Cindy's car. "Is this car registered in your name?" he asked Cindy.

"It's not mine."

That was why she'd fumbled about with keys instead of just using her thumbprint. "Who's is it?"

"A friend's."

At the moment, he didn't care if she had a hundred "friends". Maybe they might just make it out of the state after all.

Mayhew was watching the road ahead. "We need to stay on the smaller roads," he said. "If we get on the interstate, they'll just set a trap for us."

He was right. If whatever agencies were looking for them found them on a major road, they'd have enough time to set up a blockade. They'd hit the kill switch on the car just as they approached it, leaving them trapped in front of a line of tanks. Better to keep them guessing on the back roads. They couldn't block every one of them, and any extra hoops they could throw at them would just amount to more minutes of freedom.

Cindy looked over to Scott, then up into the rearview mirror at Mayhew. "You're not terrorists, are you?"

"Depends who you ask," Mayhew sneered.

"No, we're not terrorists," Scott added before she could fall apart.

"Then why didn't you show him your ID card?"

"Because I don't have one."

"But only terrorists don't have identification cards."

Scott watched the light from the streetlamps pass over her face. Her eyes were fixed ahead, and like cracks in a dam, the wideness of them signaled the pressure that was building in her brain. He could tell that she no longer wanted to be in the car with them.

"We're not gonna hurt you, Cindy. You don't have to be afraid of us."

"Afraid of you? What about all of *them*?" She ran a hand through her hair and fidgeted in her seat. "You're like some secret spy guy from the movies, right? So you know how to do all this run and hide stuff. I mean, how do you not have an ID card? How do you live?" And she started to cry. "I don't know how to do any of this…"

"Can you take us to the state line?" Mayhew asked.

Scott stared at her, the feelings of guilt and ownership and responsibility building to a crescendo within. Again she was right. She didn't know how to survive off the grid, probably had never even thought of terms like "the grid" before. She was dependent on the technocracy for her very breath and would have no clue how to operate apart from it. Which meant she would make a mistake mere minutes after being left on her own. And then they'd have her, and she'd be right next to Melissa in whatever black site they had in mind. Unless they claimed she was an accomplice in killing the cop. In that case, they would just execute her on the spot. He couldn't just leave her. Yet he couldn't take her with him either.

She shrugged. "Do I have a choice?"

"Just stay off the major roads, okay?" Scott said, speaking in as soft and reassuring tone as he could manage. Then he turned around and looked at Mayhew. "What was on the news?"

"Turn the radio on."

Cindy flicked a switch on the steering wheel that activated the HUD on the windshield in front of her. She hit another button, and the heads-up display slid across the glass before stopping in front of the passenger seat.

Scott reached up and tapped the glass, selecting the local news station. Though if he was right about what he thought he saw on the TV, and why Mayhew had been so entranced by it, then it wouldn't matter which news outlet he selected. They'd all be under the control of the North American Emergency Management Agency and playing the same state-issued report.

And there it was.

Unconfirmed reports of terrorism all across the Union. Dallas. Manhattan. Seattle. Phoenix. Boston. Miami. Mexico City. Tijuana. Cozumel. Toronto. Montreal. Vancouver. Ottawa.

The voice coming through the speakers reported an estimated half million people dead, major infrastructure collapse, power outages all across the continent, possible biochemical agents in the air… It said, as synthetically sweet as can be, to locate your emergency kits and to stay in your homes until further instructions were received.

All three of them sat in silence as the two beams of light continued to stretch over the empty road ahead of them.

Dallas, Toronto, Tijuana… It might as well have been the moon. Other people, other places. But Scott knew that was all about to change, that the ramifications of what happened in those places would spread like a dark, suffocating cloud over every inch of the country.

As if reading his mind, Mayhew said, "This could be the crisis they use to bring in the New World Order."

"The what?" Cindy asked.

# 21.

*"Out of these troubled times, our fifth objective — a New World Order — can emerge. A new era, freer from the threat of terror, stronger in the pursuit of justice and more secure in the quest for peace. An era in which the nations of the world, east and west, north and south, can prosper and live in harmony."*

—George H. W. Bush, September 11, 1990

Scott was at the wheel, Mayhew asleep beside him, Cindy stretched across the back seat behind. Scott had let Cindy drive for a while, hoping that operating the vehicle would give her more to do than just sit there mourning the loss of everything she knew. He'd also wanted to be free to aim the cop's pistol and shotgun out the window if needed. But he could tell that she'd started to get tired. The adrenaline had begun to wear off, and she'd declined quickly. So he'd taken over, and she got into the back while Mayhew climbed into the passenger seat.

Scott lifted his own tired eyes up to the rearview mirror and studied what he could see of Cindy's body, trying not to think about how this was all going to turn out for her. He wondered what her story was. Why she was helping them. Did she really feel threatened by them, or did she want to be with them? With him? Could this be an opportunity to escape something back in her hometown? He blinked. What did it matter? She had no future now. Though he wouldn't mind a few hours—

When he could no longer take the shame of his dueling thoughts—some more selfish than others—he returned his eyes to the road ahead and instead thought about the priest's books.

"Mayhew," he whispered. He reached over and shook him.

"Yeah?"

"Here." He handed the messenger bag to him.

Mayhew sat up in the seat and took it. Pulled out the two books. "This is what you've been carrying around?" He held them up to the moonlight shining through the window. "What are they?"

"The priest gave them to me."

"What?" he asked, surprised.

"I didn't tell you earlier because I wasn't sure I could trust you."

Mayhew didn't comment, just reached up and hit the interior light.

"Spilled some coffee on one of them."

"That's what the smell is…"

"Any idea what they are? What it means?"

He flipped through the pages. "Did you read them?"

"Only a paragraph or two."

"What did the priest say about them?"

"That they were pieces of the puzzle or something." He looked down at the fuel gauge. Quarter of a tank. "Why don't you read it." It wasn't a question. "And then paraphrase for me."

"Okay." He flipped to the first page in the first book. "Says it's the *Testament of Solomon*."

"You've heard of it?"

"No." He started reading.

As Mayhew read in silence, Scott retreated into his own thoughts and wondered what nationwide martial law would look like. He was sure that most of the units were already in place, conveniently running drills or handing out food or administering vaccines in exactly the right locations. He, more than anyone else, knew how it went. And now everyone would finally get to witness the secret things added to continuity of government legislation that even Congress hadn't been allowed to see. Things like incinerators, apparently. He wondered how long he had until everything was locked down and his getting to Canada would be just as likely as getting to the moon.

Fifteen minutes later, Mayhew closed the book and stared out the window.

"What?" Scott asked impatiently.

"Some pretty weird stuff is what."

"Does it say what the ring is?"

"It talks about *a* ring. But if it's the same one..." His voice trailed off.

"Tell me what it says."

"It starts off with this boy who's working on the Temple. His soul is being sucked out of him by a demon."

Scott looked at him.

"Yeah. But Solomon really likes the kid, so he decides to do something about it."

"*King* Solomon? From the Bible?"

"Yeah, as in the son of King David. You remember David, right? Goliath, Bathsheba..."

"Yeah, yeah, whatever."

"So First and Second Samuel records that David wanted to build a temple for the Lord, but the Lord wouldn't let him. Said his hands were too bloody. But He told him he could gather all the material for the Temple so that his son could build it. So that's what Solomon did, built the Temple. *Solomon's* Temple."

"Yeah, I got it."

"So anyway, Solomon prays for help, and the archangel Michael shows up and gives him a magic ring that can control demons."

"Demons..."

"Yeah. Michael tells Solomon that he can use the ring to force demons to help build the Temple. So the next day Solomon calls the boy over and gives him the ring along with instructions on what to do with it." He opened the book back up again. "This demon Ornias comes to him, and the boy throws the ring at his chest, capturing him. Ornias then pleads with the boy, promising him great wealth if he'll let him go. But the boy takes him to Solomon instead."

"Sounds like a bunch of horse crap," Scott said.

Mayhew ignored him, continuing on. "Solomon then starts interrogating all these demons." He waved his hand in the air. "There's all this astrology stuff that's mentioned…" He flipped through more pages before coming to a stop and reading aloud, "'And I Solomon having heard this, and having glorified the Lord, ordered her hair to be bound, and that she should be hung up in front of the Temple of God; that all the children of Israel, as they passed, might see it, and glorify the Lord God of Israel, who had given me this authority, with wisdom and power from God, by means of this signet.'" He closed the book. "The signet. The ring."

"*The* ring? As in the one in your pocket?"

Mayhew shrugged.

"So what's it supposed to be the key to?" Part of him just wanted to grab the book and throw it out the window after Cindy's phone.

"I don't know, but I'm not done yet. Solomon uses all these demons to build the Temple, and then people from all over come bearing gifts to see the Temple of God and to witness the wisdom of Solomon. One of those people was the Queen of the South. She's described as being a witch. But she hears his wisdom and glorifies the God of Israel… But then Solomon falls into idolatry, turns his back on God and begins sacrificing to pagan gods." Opening to the back of the book, he read, "'And when I answered that I would on no account worship strange gods, they told the maiden not to sleep with me until I complied and sacrificed to the gods. I then was moved, but crafty Eros brought and laid by her for me five grasshoppers, saying: Take these grasshoppers and crush them together in the name of the god Moloch; and then will I sleep with you. And this I actually did. And at once the Spirit of God departed from me, and I was obliged by her to build a temple of idols to Baal, and to Rapha, and to Moloch, and to the other idols. I then, wretch that I am, followed her advice, and the glory of God quite departed from me; and my spirit was darkened, and I became the sport of idols and demons. Wherefore I wrote out this Testament, that you who get possession of it may pity and attend to the last things, and not to the first. So that you may find grace forever and ever. Amen.' There are all kinds of footnotes here about various other translations and stuff."

"It all makes sense now," Scott grumbled.

Mayhew opened the other book. "This one looks pretty similar to the *Testament*. Same handwriting, I think. It's got a title, but it doesn't look like a translation, just simple notes on the book of Tobit."

"Tobit?"

"I think it's a book in the apocrypha."

There was some movement in the back seat and then a tired feminine voice. "That was a strange story," Cindy remarked.

Mayhew slipped the books back into the bag.

"Tell me about it," Scott said.

"How long have I been asleep?" she asked.

"For a while."

"Where are we?"

But before Scott could answer, the lights flickered off, the engine died, and the car rolled to a stop.

# 22.



Headlights appeared from all directions as vehicles surrounded them. Scott went to push the door open, but a sudden blinding light filled the car, and he brought his hands away from the handle and instead slowly lifted them into the air. There was no point in resisting now. There were probably ten guns trained on him, the men holding them hoping more than anything that he would try making a move. He squinted into the white glow and tried to think of something to say to Cindy. Something that would assure her everything would be alright. But he couldn't get his lips to form the lie.

The sound of feet came stampeding toward them, and then hands were grabbing him and ripping him out of the car. He still couldn't see anything in the shining light, only silhouettes whenever a figure passed in front of the beams. His world was a symphony of ambient noise. The mass of boots stepping and sliding over asphalt, breaths of exertion against the back of his neck, the fabric of clothes being pulled…

And then he was being slammed against the car, hands moving up and down his body, his arms twisted violently behind his back. A *zziiiiiipp* noise sounding out as plastic ties dug into his wrists. Duct tape slapped across his mouth and a hood pulled down over his head. The light vanished, replaced by outer darkness as another *zziiiiippp* came with a tightness just above his Adam's apple. He tried to swallow, but the zip tie wouldn't let him. He tried to breathe through his nose, nice and steady breaths to regulate his heart rate.

He could hear Cindy resisting and could see her squirming body in his mind's eye as she fought uselessly against the men restraining her. No voices answered her screaming questions, and he could only hope that she'd be spared from discovering just how depraved man could be.

They zip-tied his ankles together and then pushed him over. Without his hands to break his fall, he crashed into the street head first. He felt blood ooze above his right eye. Then strong hands grabbed him under his armpits and thighs, and he was being carried facedown to one of the vehicles. He was sat upright in the back seat and could feel two men slide in on either side of him, neither one of them making a sound. The doors shut, and he knew Mayhew and Cindy must have been taken to other vehicles. Or maybe executed on the side of the road. Though why they'd want to keep him alive if not the others, he had no idea.

The vehicle (which Scott figured was an SUV) started to move, and he imagined the others falling in behind it as they sped off into the night.

With the hood on, all concept of time evaporated, and flashbacks of Iran—blindfolded with the feel of rusted teeth against his flesh—came filling the void left in his senses. He was going to snap if he couldn't bring his mind into submission. *Think,* he told himself. Something mathematical, objective. He tried counting the seconds, listening to the sound of the car, feel the way it moved over the road. Tried to hear the men breathing around him, the way their equipment jostled on their persons when the car hit a bump. But it wasn't working.

The saw was beginning to glide, teeth tearing skin.

*The puzzle! Solve the puzzle!*
What puzzle?
*The Testament of Solomon.*
He rehearsed what Mayhew had told him. About an angel who gave Solomon a ring that controlled demons. A ring that had something to do with the one Mayhew had. But even if it was the same ring, why would the priest relate it to what was taking place in the world today? Why did different governments want it? To control demons themselves? It didn't seem remotely plausible that, outside of Hitler's supposed obsession with occult artifacts, any government would even believe in magic rings let alone fund black operations in order to attain them. He was obviously missing something that two factions of Jews, the Holy See, NAU Intelligence, and the CIA (who he was sure was the present company) were not. And whatever it was they knew, or thought they knew, had to be of monumental importance on the current world stage. Was it something about Roswell? Was the ring brought to Earth by aliens? Maybe it was the Green Lantern's ring. With all the terrorism that supposedly just went down, why the CIA would still be coming after them made zero sense.

A bump in the road dispelled the absurd thoughts, and he started to wonder if his captors might know who he was. If this could be something entirely unrelated to the ring.

He tried to talk, but the tape over his mouth just turned his words into muffled grunts.

But it did finally earn him a response, a voice icily whispering into his ear, "Extraordinary rendition."

The extrajudicial transfer of a suspected terrorist from one state to another, usually to places known for their practice of torture. Scott knew all about it. Had practiced it himself for years. It had started way back in 1995 when President Clinton gave the CIA permission to use rendition. But during the War on Terror that had spanned beyond the first decade of the new millennium, its use exploded. No judge, no jury, no evidence, no phone call. Just disappeared. He supposed it was poetic justice. Karma. Reaping what he'd sown. Whatever.

The SUV swerved suddenly and began bouncing over uneven ground. They were driving off-road.

Then the vehicle came to a stop, and doors began opening.

*Is this it?* Scott wondered. Was this the end of the line? A muzzle pressed against the back of his head at the edge of a shallow grave? And suddenly everything seemed so pointless. Surviving Iran, hiding out all the years since…for what?

He was shoved from behind, and he fell to his knees. He struggled to swallow the saliva trapped in his mouth by the tape. He was no longer controlling his breathing, and his heart was beating fast.

He heard the other SUVs pull up behind him and their doors open too. He envisioned the ditch before him, the one that he would share with Cindy and Mayhew for the rest of time. He pulled against the plastic ties around his wrists, feeling his muscles bulge beneath the jacket. Blood dripped into his palms.

Then, seemingly from out of nowhere, the sound of a huge engine began filling the empty expanse around them. It whined loudly, and there was no mistaking what it was. And he knew, even as they carried him toward the noise, that they were in a field.

And about to board a jet.

He almost sighed with relief. It meant that the story wasn't over yet, that there was at least one more chapter to his pathetic life. And he found it strange that he suddenly cared so much about living when so many of his nights had been spent contemplating suicide, chasing the footsteps of his grief-stricken dear old dad. If there was a later, then he'd ponder that inconsistency then. Right now he was concentrating on listening to Mayhew and Cindy being carried up the steps behind him.

Once inside, he was pushed down into a seat, his hands still bound behind his back. He could sense someone standing over him, and he anticipated either the removal of the hood or a sound-suppressed shot that would render the darkness permanent. Though the latter would have made more sense while still in the field.

There was a *snap* and then a pinch on his neck as someone used a knife to cut the plastic tie off his neck.

Then the hood came off.

Scott blinked in the light of the plane and looked past the shape standing before him. He saw men in black jumpsuits and ski masks strapping Cindy and Mayhew down five rows ahead of him. When they were done, they turned and exited the plane.

Scott finally moved his gaze and let his eyes adjust to the close proximity of the person standing over him. This guy was wearing a suit and tie, and there was a strange smirk stitched across his face. He was holding a syringe.

Scott thought about head-butting him, leaning forward and swinging his head down like a wrecking ball right into the guy's nose. It was a move he'd perfected over the years, the proper technique able to cave a man's face in. Then he could whip his hands up under his feet and take his gun —

But the syringe…

Its plunger had already been engaged.

*Wait.*

This was all wrong. Why was this suit standing over him? Mayhew was the one with the ring.

The man's face seemed to come apart as his mouth opened and he said, "Have a good flight, Mr. Cavanaugh."

Scott's heart froze in his chest, and the rusted saw went back to work with a vengeance.

As darkness swallowed him, he thought that maybe his head was somewhere else.

# 23.



*"Behind the ostensible government sits enthroned an invisible government owing no allegiance and acknowledging no responsibility to the people."*
— Theodore Roosevelt

It was Operation Midnight Climax, and he could already feel the effect of the drugs running through his system. He was in San Francisco, in a hotel room with Cindy. Though he was more interested in the two-way mirror across from them than he was in what Cindy was doing to him. The CIA agent who was watching them and taking notes was too distracting.

No. This wasn't Cindy. Wasn't anyone he knew. Just a prostitute on the CIA's payroll who had taken him to the safe house after lacing his drink with LSD.

Or no... *He* was the CIA operative taking the notes from the other side of the mirror.

And the ring the hooker was wearing... It was glowing.

Demons started to crawl out of the walls, out of the ceiling — sick scorpion-like creatures. They were salivating over the man and the woman, and their saliva was setting the room on fire.

Bombs were exploding.

And then he was suddenly across the street, watching the safe house collapse.

The demons circled like vultures over its ruins, and now he could see their faces. He recognized them. They were world leaders. They held a flag in their clawed grasp, the image on it ten stars arching over a pyramid. They tore it to pieces. Became one single entity, a third eye opening on its forehead, the face no longer one he recognized.

He looked around and noticed that he wasn't in San Francisco anymore, but Africa. Piles of dead bodies stretched in all directions as far as he could see. Syringes were sticking out of them, and men in white suits were walking around and spraying them with something. They had swastikas on their arms but UN written on their backs.

Without warning, the ground swallowed everything whole, and stillness settled over the empty plains. Until the earth belched a volcano of sand up into the sky. It twisted into a tower that disappeared into the clouds.

Light caught his eye. He looked down and saw that *he* was wearing the ring.

****

Scott opened his eyes. Or at least he thought he did. Flames were licking the air around him, and he could hear gunshots echoing back and forth somewhere close by. Thinking he must still be dreaming, he closed his eyes again.

But then he felt the heat, and his eyes snapped wide. It was no dream.

He tried to move, but his hands and feet were still bound. What was going on? Had the plane crashed? He looked up and found that he was actually looking down. Vertigo swept him away and pounded his aching head.

But still the fire was getting hotter, closer.

He could feel a body leaning against him, and he tried to push it away with his shoulder. It rolled away from him and floated up into the air, landing on the ceiling. He looked to his right, out a window, and could make out a road, rays of light, and feet running back and forth. But it was all inverted.

He understood.

*Oh no.*

He was upside down, strapped to a seat not inside a plane, but in an overturned SUV. He tried to wiggle his body free, knowing there wasn't much time before the flames reached the fuel tank. He twisted at his waist, trying to reach the seatbelt with his bound hands. It was no use.

He looked around and noticed that the driver was still sitting behind the wheel, covered in blood and staring hypnotically through holes sprinkled across the windshield. A moan escaped his lips. The guy was still alive.

And then the fire reached him, and he erupted into flames, his moaning turning to screams.

The sight pushed Scott's mind to the brink of hysteria, and he yelled, shaking his body like a lunatic trying to get out of a straightjacket. The fire was coming for him.

The dead guy lying on the roof below him caught fire next, and the flames licked Scott's hair as the driver still screamed, the flesh melting off his body.

Then Scott's jacket caught, and he added his own screams to the driver's chorus. He looked around for any signs of salvation but saw only smoke. The fire spread up his arms. He stomped his feet against the floor, his ankles no longer tied. He could smell flesh dripping like wax, but didn't know if it was his or the driver's.

*Welcome to eternity*, he told himself.

Then the door beside him swung open, and someone was leaning across him. The seatbelt came undone, and he was suddenly flying through the air, out of the smoke and flames. He landed in the street, was turned over, and his hands came free. He jumped to his feet and ripped the jacket off, beating it against the ground until the flames were gone. Then he pulled the tape from his mouth and took in the night air, his chest heaving, tears streaming down his face.

He saw Mayhew and Cindy through the shimmering heat. They were waving for him to get away from the SUV.

The gas tank.

Scott forced his legs to move, and he ran after them, away from the burning fire. As he got off the road, he stole a glance back at the overturned vehicle and understood what must've happened. Two men in suits were lying next to it, their blood pooling onto the street and reflecting the blaze, while another SUV was lying on its side. There were four men sprawled around that one, spent casings scattered everywhere. A third SUV had gone off the road and slammed into a tree. More suits lay scattered around that one as well. Scott realized that their little convoy must've been hit by rockets.

A gunshot sounded out, and Scott saw that there was still an agent alive and peering out around the back of the SUV that had rammed into the tree. He was shooting into the darkness. A wave of bullets answered, engulfing the SUV, the tree, the road, and the last agent standing.

Then the SUV exploded and plunged Scott's world into heated oblivion.

****

Once again, Scott found himself lying on his back and staring up at the sky. Only this time he was in a field of grass and looking into a cold starlit night. He figured he'd only been unconscious for a few seconds, but he wasn't sure. He turned his head and saw Cindy lying beside him. Her eyes were closed, and she wasn't moving. He moved toward her. "Hey," he said, nudging her.

No response.

"Cindy."

Still nothing.

He looked over her body and saw that there was a piece of metal sticking out of her back by her left shoulder blade.

"Is she okay?" came a voice from behind him. It was Mayhew.

"I don't think so." It was too dark to see the full extent of her injuries. "She needs help."

People appeared moving in the grass around them, their shadows stretching across the ground in the flickering light cast by flaming debris. Mayhew ducked down, but all Scott could do was hold his breath.

"Stand up," a voice commanded.

Scott could barely see Mayhew, so there was no use in trying to communicate with him.

"Stand up, please," the voice insisted.

Please? Not that they had a choice, but in Scott's experience, the bad guys were rarely polite. He got to his feet and stood into a blinding light.

"Don't move," the voice said.

Someone was patting them down. He spoke into a radio when he was done. Said something in Hebrew.

The light fell away from their faces, aimed instead at the grass by their feet. Scott realized the flashlights were fastened to the underside of assault rifles.

Before Scott or Mayhew could say anything, two beams came slicing through the darkness, a black van driving behind them. It came to a stop a few feet away, and another voice urged them toward it.

Scott caught a glimpse of the guy when one of the other flashlights passed over him. He was in all black, flight gloves, body armor, the whole deal. "It's okay," he told Scott and gently nudged him toward the van.

Scott looked back over his shoulder. "What about her?"

"She is coming too."

More men materialized out of the blank night and carefully picked Cindy up off the ground. They carried her to the van, and Scott and Mayhew followed.

While Scott waited for the men to secure Cindy's broken body into the back of the van, he looked over at the burning SUVs. He had been mere moments from that being his fate.

Four of the Hebrew-speaking men ran back to the van that had struck the tree and began going through it. Scott knew what they were looking for. If only he knew why. Why he'd been marked out as a pawn in some game being played out amongst the elite. These people had known ahead of time the exact route the CIA would be traveling, where they were heading, and what their cargo was.

He climbed into the panel van, and the door slid shut and locked into place.

"You okay?" Mayhew asked him.

"Never better."

And the two of them laughed at the absurdity of it all, laughed until tears rolled down their cheeks. Laughed until it wasn't funny anymore and the hysterical relief they felt at still being alive faded into anger and frustration.

The two front doors swung open, and the driver and another person climbed in.

"Are either of you injured?" the driver asked through his mask.

They shook their heads. Nothing that required any attention, anyway.

The driver put the van in drive and left behind half a dozen of his fellow agents to find the ring and then cover their tracks.

Scott appreciated that these people hadn't killed them and that they were helping them escape. But the fact that they could've been killed by the rockets that took out the SUVs told him that whatever mission they were on was more important to them than his well-being, and that he would become expendable the moment they believed he complicated that mission. So he remained silent, fine with the fact that he was in this car with them rather than on that plane with his former employer.

As the van drove through the night, the demons Scott had dreamt about seemed to have come back with reinforcements. Only now they were the familiar demons of his past rather than those from the future. And as Cindy struggled to cling to life in the back, those winged creatures continued marching at him from out of an ocean made up of past sins. Sins that could never be forgiven. Sins that had always brought thoughts of suicide. But again he knew that suicide was only a cop-out, that he deserved to feel this way, to fight with these demons. And so he *wanted* to feel it, *needed* to feel it. It was his punishment. Yet there was a voice within that rebuked such thoughts, scolding the logic behind them as utterly foolish and circular. Feeling guilty can't possibly be any sort of payment for sin, just the evidence of its presence, the voice said. That feeling itself was no retribution, the guilt of having sinned not cancelling out the sin. But then, he argued back, he never wanted to cancel it out, just wanted to pay for it. And going through life with this burden felt like he was serving his time. To which the voice responded by stating that there was no redemptive quality to his suffering, that it isn't a satisfactory punishment. The guilt wasn't payment for his sins but merely the natural consequence of having committed them.

It was his cycle of insanity, and he wanted to stop thinking about it. There were more important things at hand. Like why the guy on the jet had called him Mr. Cavanaugh.

His real name.

He wasn't sure how they knew, but what he *was* sure of was that he was now back on the grid and in their crosshairs whether he had the ring in his possession or not.

He turned and looked back at Cindy. "How is she?" he finally asked the man who was working on her.

He looked up from her wound and answered softly, "Not good. This is all that I can do for her here." His two brown eyes peered out from behind the mask. "I am sorry. We did not mean for this to happen."

"Me neither," Scott mumbled. He closed his eyes and brought the framed picture of his wife into full view. Cindy was standing there beside it, smiling at him from the diner.

# 24.

*"The people never give up their liberties but under some delusion."*
—Edmund Burke, British Statesman, 1784

They switched vehicles twice in the hopes of throwing off anyone who might be trying to track them, but so far there were only empty roads and clear skies. Now they were in a minivan and driving into the dawn.

Scott woke up when the sun rose over the skyscrapers ahead of them and shone in his eyes. He rubbed his neck, his bruised and cut wrists, and gently touched the cut by his eye and the small channel the sniper's bullet had carved out of his forehead. Then he turned to look in the back seat of the minivan. Cindy was there, but the person who had been watching over her had driven the cargo van away after their first vehicle swap. Since then, Cindy had woken up only once and hadn't spoken. Not that she needed to. Her eyes said it all.

"What do you think?" Mayhew whispered while nodding toward Cindy.

Scott just shook his head.

The man in the front passenger seat turned and looked back at them. Neither Mossad agent was wearing their mask now, and Scott could see sympathy in his eyes.

"Well, I'm going to pray for her," Mayhew said.

"Go for it," Scott muttered, and he watched the driver run his hands through his curly black hair.

"You understand that we could not take her to a hospital," he said.

"I know." He leaned back into the seat. "So you're Mossad?"

They locked eyes in the rearview.

"We are almost there, and then you can ask your questions."

"Almost where?" he said to himself, looking back out the window. They were driving into a city that obviously hadn't been mentioned on the news report last night. Though there didn't seem to be anyone around. No police or military, no traffic, no one walking the streets. It was like a ghost town. The clock on the dashboard read 7:14. So where were the demonstrations, prayer vigils, protests, riots, commuters, shoppers, or morning joggers?

They turned into a parking garage, and the driver took a ramp up to the next level. Construction equipment was everywhere, cones, caution signs, and arrows all warning that the level was restricted to construction personal only. But the driver drove right up to it.

Suddenly, four men in hard hats and orange vests appeared, clearing the equipment away so that the minivan could pass through. Once they were past, the workers put everything back behind them.

The driver parked the van beside the elevator. "You can get out," he said to Scott and Mayhew.

Scott opened the side door and stepped out onto the concrete floor just as a man and a woman came running out of the elevator doors, pushing a gurney. They went straight to the back of the van and carefully transitioned Cindy onto the gurney. Then they wheeled her back into the elevator.

The doors closed, and Cindy was gone.

Scott stared after her. Blinked.

"I think she'll be okay," Mayhew said, coming up beside him.

Scott looked at him and realized that this was only the third day of them knowing each other. He'd known Cindy for only hours. But apparently that was all it took for him to destroy someone's life.

The elevator doors opened again.

"Come," the driver said, and he ushered them toward the elevator, where men with guns stood waiting for them.

Scott took a deep breath and stepped inside.

It came to a stop on the fortieth floor and opened to a common office setting. They passed through a sea of cubicles, computers, phones, and piles of paper. A shell company for sure.

They came to a door that had a security pad above its handle, and one of the armed men from the elevator stepped forward and swiped a key card through it. Then he punched in a sequence of numbers, and a beep sounded. The door opened, and they went in.

The new room was full of file cabinets with a large wall safe along the back wall. Its steel door stood six feet high.

"Is that a vault?" Mayhew asked.

The big door swung toward them, away from the wall.

As Scott stepped closer, he could see that there was no money in it. No stacks of paper currency, no bars of gold, no piles of diamonds, and no columns of drawers with keyholes. Just a hallway that led into darkness.

"You first," said one of the armed men to Scott.

Figuring he didn't really have a choice, Scott stepped in. And then the door swung shut behind him.

"Hey!" He turned back and banged his fists on the cold steel, but of course that did nothing. He peered back into the darkness and saw a light come on at the end of the corridor. The silhouette of a man stood in the rectangular glow.

"Please, come," the silhouette said.

Scott walked down the dark hallway and found himself standing before a man who was holding out his hand. He had dark hair and brown eyes, and Scott guessed that he was in his late fifties. His black slacks and white shirt were accented by a bright blue tie. Scott shook his hand while surveying the new surroundings. Two black touchtables, a coffee table, some radios, and a map. There were a few books piled up on the coffee table, and a few chairs facing the desk. There was another, smaller safe in the wall behind the desk. There were no windows.

The man spoke as he waved Scott to a chair, shutting another steel door behind him. "I imagine you must have some questions."

Scott thought he sounded a little too cheery considering all that was happening in the world. "A couple."

"You probably want to know who I am."

Scott just stared at him.

The man sat on the edge of one of the touchtables and folded his arms. "Ask away, then."

"Where am I?"

"Columbus, Ohio."

"Where is everyone?"

"They were told to stay indoors until further notice."

"How bad is it?"

The man shrugged. "It is still too early to be sure, but I imagine a few million people when all the smoke clears."

Scott almost fell out of the chair. "A few *million*?"

"Easy. The nuke itself—"

"A nuke?"

"I am afraid so. In Texas."

*Nuke.* Scott sat frozen, the magnitude of the word not fully registering. Like it was too big to fit through the space of comprehension. He lifted his eyes. "Who?"

"You mean who are they blaming?"

"Yeah."

"No official word yet, but no doubt they will say Russia or Syria."

"What about all the other places?"

"You are referring to the reports on the news. Thankfully, they seem to have been exaggerated. Our intelligence indicates a couple of nuclear power plants, some explosions in Canada, but the nuke was the central act." He sighed. "But like I said, it is still too early to tell."

As hard as it was to do, Scott set the world events of last night aside and instead inquired about his own predicament. "Who captured us?"

"The CIA."

"How'd you find them?"

"We knew exactly where they were taking you, so we set up an ambush."

Not exactly the answer to his question, but he went with it. "And where were they taking us?"

"A DARPA science and engineering laboratory in West Virginia."

Scott was glad he'd missed that trip. "What's your name?"

"You can call me Mr. Smith." And then he laughed. "Or anything you want." He unfolded his arms. "And what about you? Do you prefer Matthew Scott or...Joshua Cavanaugh?"

He leaned forward. "How do you know who I am?"

"I am an agent for the Israeli Mossad, Matthew. I know pretty much everything they have in their computers." He waved behind him toward the glass touchtables. They were displaying some sort of technical readouts.

Whether the "they" he was referring to was his own government, the NAU, or the UN, he wasn't sure. "Am I in the global database?"

"Oh, you could say that." He got up and began pacing, his hands in his pockets. "I am not sure how you managed to stay hidden for all these years, but they are coming for you now."

Scott's heart was beginning to race. "Do you know what I did?"

A softness settled in Mr. Smith's eyes. "I do. But then many of us were ordered to do things that we did not quite understand, and questioning orders was not an option."

Scott looked away, clenching his jaw.

A door that he hadn't noticed before, one that blended perfectly into the white walls around him, suddenly clicked open. A woman wearing black fatigues walked into the room. She was a glaring contrast to their bright surroundings.

Mr. Smith turned away from Scott and focused his attention on the visitor. "Do you have it?" he asked. There was an urgency in his voice.

"Yes." And then she reached forward and handed him a ring.

*The* ring.

Mr. Smith studied the object in awe, mesmerized. "Thank you," he said to her.

She nodded and exited the room, the door shutting behind her.

Mr. Smith set the ring down on the touchtable he'd been sitting on and then went to the door. He put his ear against it and seemed to be listening for sounds on the other side, making sure the woman had really left. Then he returned to the table and pulled a radio out from a drawer beneath it. He brought the radio to his lips and pressed the transmit button. "Okay."

Scott narrowed his gaze, trying to detect the game being played here. But before he could say anything, the door opened again. But this time it was a man who entered, and he went straight to the ring. He picked it up and looked straight into Mr. Smith's eyes. "Are you sure about this?" he asked him. He had still yet to acknowledge Scott's presence.

Mr. Smith nodded. "Yes." And then added, "My prayers are with you."

Without another word, the man turned and left with the ring.

"What was that about?" Scott asked.

Mr. Smith sat behind the desk and folded his hands on its surface. "As I said, I work for Mossad."

Scott noticed he only had a slight accent, like he'd spent most of his life in North America. "So?"

"So I'm also an Orthodox Jew."

"Congratulations."

"Are you familiar with the various Jewish beliefs—Orthodox, ultra-orthodox, conservative, progressive?"

"I'm familiar with Zionism." He let a hint of hostility flavor the statement.

Mr. Scott sighed, understanding from Scott's tone that he was holding the movement somewhat responsible for the deteriorating condition of his own country. He held out his hands. "Political Zionism? Christian Zionism? Religious Zionism? There are several forms, Mr. Scott."

"Which is the one that conspired with the Devil to set the stage for this hell? Which is the one responsible for the USS *Liberty* and the Mossad agents who danced with joy after taping the collapse of the Twin Towers in New York? Which form of Zionism is that?"

Mr. Smith paused and then nodded solemnly. "The historical events you speak of..." He sighed. "In both instances, though I do not believe Israel was responsible for both, we were hoping for an American war with our enemies."

Scott looked at him blankly. "Thanks."

"You are thanking the wrong person. That was a very long time ago. Different generations. But I am not a Zionist, Mr. Scott. I am from the traditional Orthodox position that actually condemns Zionism. So I can understand your feelings toward my Land, and I can only apologize on her behalf."

Scott turned his head and took in the room. "What about David and the other Mossad agents?"

"I assume you are referring to the man who acquired the ring from Edward Cairns?"

He nodded.

"He was a Zionist with interests opposite of mine." He nodded toward the door behind him, the one the ring had come in and gone out through. "As is theirs."

Scott frowned. "You're a double agent?"

He laughed. "I am simply trying to prevent a great catastrophe from occurring, Mr. Scott."

"A bigger catastrophe than a nuke going off in Texas?"

"Much bigger than that, I am afraid. Do you know of the Six-Day War?"

"The war you started against your Arab neighbors? The reason for the attack on the *Liberty*?"

He shook his head. "The NSA's USS *Liberty* was not attacked because she had evidence of Israel starting the war, or because she was within earshot of the El Arish massacre. The most decorated ship in American naval history was attacked by unmarked Israeli planes and Israeli patrol boats because that was the plan that had been drawn up between Israel and the United States. After sinking the *Liberty*, the attack was to be blamed on Egypt, and then America would enter the war and help take over the entire Middle East. Fortunately for those on board the *Liberty* who had managed to stay alive during the three-hour attack, a Russian spy ship entered the area, and the Israeli forces were forced to flee the crime scene."

Scott nodded. It was something he'd suspected back when he first learned of the event. Why else would then-President Johnson park the ship in the Mediterranean, call off the 6th Fleet's attempt to help, and then threaten the survivors with death or life imprisonment if they ever spoke of what really happened that day? Why would Commander McGonagle be given the Medal of Honor in secret and then told not to tell anyone he'd earned it? Given the history of the Joint Chiefs of Staff, of America's war appetite, it was more than feasible, it was likely. It had been the same with Cuba, Vietnam, Iraq, Iran, and Syria. And now it was looking like it was Russia's turn.

"You do not seem shocked," Mr. Smith said.

"I'm not. The staged Gulf of Tonkin incident that led to the Vietnam War. Operation NORTHWOODS that the Joint Chiefs presented to Kennedy, wanting to commit acts of terror in the US and then blame them on Cuba. Operation AJAX. PNAC. It's a long list." He felt his guts clench, knowing he'd signed his own name to the list. "I've seen firsthand what we're capable of when we want to go to war." He leaned forward. "But you were talking about the Six-Day War..."

Mr. Smith waved a hand over the touchtable and sent the scrolling readouts into some kind of hibernation mode that rendered the desk blank. "The evil forces that operate behind the scenes are responsible for the creation of both Zionism and radical Islam. It is their plan to have both religions exterminate each other."

"Okay."

"Do you hate us for what we have done?"

Scott knew that many believed political Zionism to be the peak of the invisible world government. Right above the Bilderbergers, Business Advisory Committee, Council on Foreign Relations, and so forth. While there was no doubt in his mind that Israel's government was just as guilty as any other in scheming to align things for the so-called "New Order of the Ages," he doubted the operation was unfolding at their sole discretion. Besides, how could he be angry at any other country after what his own had done? "I have nothing against your people. They should be entitled to what is theirs."

"Ah! And what *is* ours if God has chosen to take it away? Of course I believe in the ancient prophecies, of Messiah reigning from the Temple in Jerusalem, but I do not believe, as do my Jewish brothers, that we, by our own strength, can hasten that day through political and secular conniving. Like Abraham trying to bring about God's promise by taking Sarah's handmaiden, or like Moses slaying the Egyptian, we are only complicating the situation by our human intervention. So while they try to coerce His coming, they are only heaping up more judgment upon us. And the Messianic Kingdom will not come until we are purified from our sins."

Scott wasn't sure how this was at all relevant to why he was here right now. What it had to do with the ring. "I've spent time in your country. I know the different viewpoints concerning how your 'Day of Restoration' will come. But what does that have to do with any of this?"

"It has everything to do with all of it." He stood up from the chair and began pacing again. "Do you know what the ring is?"

"No."

He stopped in his tracks, baffled by the answer.

"I have no idea," Scott promised.

"The priest must have told you."

"He was blown up before he got the chance." Scott saw the man flinch at that. It was subtle, as if he'd tried to hide any reaction, but the news had obviously affected him. Though Scott had no idea why.

"If you didn't know what the ring was, then why keep it? Why risk your life, your cover?"

He waved a finger. "That's a misunderstanding. I don't care what that thing is. When they came after it, they came after a friend of mine."

Mr. Smith looked at him with new understanding, realizing he was a player in a game of which he didn't even know the object. "Do you *want* to know?" he asked.

"I'd like to know why everyone's willing to kill for it. Why Ed died."

"Did you read the priest's books?"

"Only one of them."

"Then you only have part of the story."

"I've had it with all the riddles. Are you going to tell me or not?"

He nodded. "But first let me tell you what it is that I am trying to prevent."

"The Six-Day War thing?"

"My Zionist brothers are planning on taking back by force what God has taken from us in judgment."

"You said it yourself, nothing new there."

"I'm talking about the annihilation of the Muslim presence in Israel. I'm talking about plans to destroy the Dome of the Rock. An operation to wipe Mecca off the map."

That was new.

Scott leaned back. "And by pulling it off, they'll just be playing into the hands of the New World Order."

"The elite have no love for my Land. Never have. They wish to destroy us along with the Muslims. The nations will see it as a necessary act to bring peace to a world that has never known it. The dawn of the New Age."

"What if you're wrong and their plan works?"

"My religion forbids us to take anything by force. As I said, the Messiah will come and sort all of this out Himself."

Scott sighed and began wondering how Cindy was doing. "So again, what does the ring have to do with it?"

Mr. Smith looked at his watch.

# III.

# UNTOLD SECRETS

*"Let no man deceive you by any means: for that day shall not come, except there come a falling away first, and that man of sin be revealed, the son of perdition; who opposeth and exalteth himself above all that is called God, or that is worshipped; so that he as God sitteth in the temple of God, shewing himself that he is God."*

–2 Thessalonians 2:3-4

Their hooves sounded like thunder, beating the ground in a frantic stampede toward the coast. Yet the lead rider swore he could hear his own heart pounding above the shaking earth below him. Pivoting in his saddle, he stole a nervous glance behind him. It was hard to see through the darkness, but he could tell that all four of his brethren were still behind him.

He turned around just in time to duck beneath a low-hanging branch that he barely saw. What they were doing was suicidal, the moon the only light keeping the forest from disappearing altogether. They had little choice, however. They were being followed.

Hunted.

At midnight, eighteen ships would set sail from the port of La Rochelle for Scotland, and they needed to be on one of them.

But even with the articles the fleeing knights had in their possession, the ships could not risk waiting for them. And finding another means out of the country would be impossible with the King's men closing in on them.

The five knights pushed their beasts harder, yelling, kicking, and urging them to run faster through the invisible forest. And as they approached the countryside, they wondered about the fate of the Order, for it rested heavily upon their weary shoulders this night. The contents of their cargo had come directly from the hands of Grand Master Jacques de Molay — sacred objects that only a handful of men within the Order's inner circle even knew about.

The lead rider turned his head to look behind him again, and this time what he saw made his eyes bulge in their sockets.

Torchlight. In the distance, through the trees.

The King's men were gaining on them.

Without thinking, he sat up straight in the saddle and began gesturing to his brothers, attempting to warn them of the approaching danger.

He never saw the branches that cracked his ribs and threw him from his horse. The only thing he did see, as he painfully rolled onto his back, was the hoof coming down on his head.

The rest of them continued on without even looking back, for their fallen brother had not been the one charged with the articles' safekeeping.

They burst out of the forest and into the open country, streaking through moonlit fields of grass. The noises from the magnificent beasts — the air exploding from their nostrils and the loud rhythmic pattern of their feet charging over the soft ground — were the only sounds accompanying them in their race for the port.

Everything they had achieved over the last hundred and eighty-nine years, all the wealth and power, was on the verge of extinction, for King Philip IV was no longer going to tolerate being in their debt. The charges of blasphemy had provided a convenient excuse to outlaw the Order and thus free himself from its control. That the charges were true was inconsequential. The Pope would have seen that such confessions were tortured out of them regardless. The Pope and the King would learn, however, that Gnostic teachings, coupled with Arabic influence, had corrupted the Order, bringing it into contact with something sinister. Or perhaps they would find it to be the other way around, that something sinister had brought them under the corrupting influence of their Arab neighbors. Did it matter to them what history would say? No, only that they were around to hear it.

They could see the water ahead, the moon reflecting off its surface. But the King's men were too close. They would never make it without giving away the escaping ships. Someone had to make a sacrifice if the Order was to survive. If the Grand Master's will was to be fulfilled.

Slowing to a trot, the knights began circling around each other, their watchful eyes waiting for the sight of torchlight.

"I will stay and fight them off," one of them said through a thick beard.

Another knight nodded and pulled his sword out of its sheath. "As will I."

The one with the red beard addressed the other two. "When you get to the ships, tell them immediately that Philip's plans for Friday the thirteenth have been confirmed. Tell them the Grand Master himself promised protection under Bishop Lamberton, and that the Order ought to find favor in the eyes of Robert the Bruce."

The two other knights, one of which had the objects on his person, didn't respond. Instead, they pulled on the reins, turning away from their brothers without a word, and took off toward the coast, kicking their horses with their heels.

Red Beard and his sole companion watched them gallop to the seacoast and disappear into the night.

"Do you think they will make it?" the other knight asked.

"If I can help it."

There was silence for a second, the sudden realization that death was just a few moments away clashing against their recent hopes of living out long lives in Scotland…or perhaps somewhere even more distant.

"The ring de Molay gave him… Do you think it was the same one worn by de Payens?"

Red Beard looked at him impatiently. "Of course it is."

"And the scroll?"

He didn't answer, just turned his horse away from the seacoast and back into the field. Toward the torchlight that had just broken the horizon.

The two Templar Knights stood little chance against the vast number of French soldiers, but the little resistance they offered did allow for the escape of the eighteen ships and their cargo—the secret treasures from beneath the Temple Mount in Jerusalem found by the Poor Fellow-Soldiers of Christ and of the Temple of Solomon almost two hundred years ago.

# 25.



*"Since I entered politics, I have chiefly had men's views confided to me privately. Some of the biggest men in the U.S., in the field of commerce and manufacture, are afraid of something. They know that there is a power so organized, so subtle, so watchful, so interlocked, so complete, so pervasive, that they better not speak above their breath when they speak in condemnation of it."*

—Woodrow Wilson

He was thinking about November 1910. Jekyll Island and J. P. Morgan. The goal to establish a private bank that would control the nation's currency. The Aldrich Bill, later reformed into the Federal Reserve Act. President Taft vowing to veto any such bill. The bankers first supporting Teddy Roosevelt in the Republican primaries and then, when he didn't get the nomination, Woodrow Wilson, who promised to sign the bill in exchange for their support. The Bull Moose party created to take enough Republican votes away from Taft to ensure a Wilson victory (thank you, Teddy). December 23, the senators and congressman on their payroll signed the legislation while the rest of the government was already on holiday. Enter the Federal Reserve Bank, which was not federal and a breach of Section 8 Article 5 of the then United States Constitution. An engine responsible for the creation of incredible private wealth that allowed an imperial elite the ability to manipulate the economy for its own purpose, using the government itself as its enforcer. Private banks creating money out of thin air and lending it to the government and charging interest on it forever. *The few who understand the system....will either be so interested in its profits or so dependent on its favors that there will be no opposition from that class, while on the other hand, the great body of people, mentally incapable of comprehending...will bear its burden without complaint,* stated an old Rothschild communiqué. And now here he was, sitting at the end of the line of what they'd started in 1913. Only he wouldn't be repentant of it like Wilson had been. No, he would embrace it. Already had, in fact. This was his time. The Dawn of the New Age rising over and crowning *his* head. Sure, he could admire Kennedy for having the guts to print four billion dollars' worth of "United States Notes" to replace the Federal Reserve Notes, but look where it ultimately got him. His head all over Dealey Plaza.

The President of New America sat in the Oval Office, waiting for the call. For instructions. The Prime Minister of Israel needed to speak with him in person, and though he wished more than anything to avoid such a meeting, the powers that be were insisting upon it. Unfortunately, as much as he hated the man (and his country), Israel was in fact the centerpiece to their entire scheme. They needed them. Yet, some of the very men the President answered to were Jews— political Zionists.

Spinning in his chair, he stared at the phone as another flash of dread swept over him. He had woken up with a bad feeling about this day, and the sensation hadn't yet subsided. He just wanted to get this over with. There was no doubt the fat man would be angry. He had wanted the ring and his men out of the country before the next phase went into effect. That hadn't happened, and now it would be harder for his death squads to pursue the ring without detection.

But that was the whole point. The Masters didn't want Israel to have the ring. And thus the President's confusion. Was it possible that the Prime Minister didn't know about the NASA hoax? Had he been kept in the dark about their plans for the

Middle East? Because if the Prime Minister was hoping that some Israeli national interest was going to be realized at the end of all this, he was being gravely misled. And though the President enjoyed this hypothesis—the old goat left out of the loop and headed for destruction—it would only make his conversation with him more awkward. Especially if he'd discovered the CIA's recent attempts at securing the ring. Which was another mystery that haunted the President, for it wasn't every day that both NAU Intelligence and the CIA (which were still in the process of being brought under the same roof) were so easily embarrassed. At first he thought it must have been the PM and his Mossad who had foiled their attempts in Vermont. But that didn't add up. Instead, he thought it more likely that there was another sect of Jews working to get the ring. But could they really be that good? And this Jack Cavanaugh character who had just popped back onto the grid—one of the operatives who had been instrumental in pulling off the Los Angeles incident... What was his involvement in all this?

The President sighed. It didn't matter. They had plans for him.

He turned his thoughts away from all that and set them on the more pressing issues at hand—like last night and what it meant for the future. He rehearsed to himself all the executive orders he would be putting into effect on national television later on in the evening. Even the older executive orders like the 10990s and 11921 that had been left in place during the Transition would be put to use. The state of emergency would allow for the NAU takeover of everything, and all of the stubborn remains of the former Republic would be purged once and for all.

The New Age was here indeed, illuminating his horizon.

A noise sounded from the desk's speaker.

Startled, the President reached for the flashing light on the touchtable. It was the call he had been waiting for, the one signaling the beginning of a dreadful confrontation with the Prime Minister. The image of a man abruptly appeared atop the desk before him, and he listened to what it had to say.

When the report ended, the President stood and left the Oval Office, Secret Service agents trailing him down the hall.

He stepped out of the White House and into the sunlight, surrounded by agents touching their ears and talking into electronic instruments too small to be seen. He straightened his tie as a convoy of black cars pulled up to the curb. The Prime Minister was in one of them, waiting for him. He swore under his breath and tried faking a smile as an agent walked to one of the cars and opened the back door for him. This was not going to be the most pleasant moment of his day. He slid into the car, and the agent shut the door.

They were alone in the back seat of the limo, facing each other. The barrier between them and the driver was soundproof. No one outside the need-to-know was even aware that the Prime Minister was in the car, the President just making his scheduled trip to a nearby site that had been affected by the previous night's acts of terrorism. Once they arrived and the President exited the limo, it would immediately take the Prime Minister to a jet waiting at a secured location.

"Hello," said the Prime Minister.

"Hi."

"Thank you for speaking with me." He was well aware of the President's hatred for both him and his people. Though there was no love lost for the US or the newly formed NAU on his end either, in this case their interests were the same. He just hoped he could get the racist egomaniac to realize it.

"What do you want?" the President asked.

"I want the head of your Secretary of State." He took a sip of something in a martini glass. "I told him that I would take care of the ring. I assume you got the message. Why then did you not tell me this was happening last night?"

The President stared at him. "I guess you're on a need-to-know basis."

The PM's face flushed red with anger, and he took another sip. "I want that ring, and I do not care what they say about it."

That earned a raised eyebrow. "Are you going rogue on the Group, Prime Minister?"

Another sip.

The car started to move.

"Besides," continued the President, "what good would it possibly do you without the other pieces?"

The Prime Minister waved a hand in dismissal. "That does not concern you, but I am here to tell you of something that does."

"And what is that?" *You fat piece of trash.* He leaned back into the seat.

"We have been betrayed."

The President nearly laughed. Seeing himself as the blessed child of the New World Order, he couldn't fathom that anyone from the Group would betray him. He was the face of their future. Had been recruited and put in power for just that purpose. *"We?"* he asked.

The Prime Minister shook his head. "You cocky bastard. What I would not give to see you—"

"Yet you are here to *warn* me?" He laughed.

"Only because it is in my own best interest that you survive."

The President stopped laughing as that unsettled feeling began creeping back up his spine. "What are you talking about?"

"Do you think they would hesitate to kill you if it served their purpose, if it molded public opinion in their favor?"

The President leaned forward. "You are the one who had better watch his back."

But there was no response from the Prime Minister. Instead, an explosion engulfed the entire limousine—reducing it to pieces of metal, glass, and flesh that fell like rain all over the street.

# 26.


*"The governments of the present day have to deal not merely with other governments, with emperors, kings and ministers, but also with the secret societies which have everywhere their unscrupulous agents, and can at the last moment upset all the governments' plans."*
— Benjamin Disraeli, Prime Minister of England, 1876

Mr. Smith looked up from his watch. "Did you read the *Testament of Solomon?*"

Scott nodded. "More or less."

"And according to that work, what was Solomon's ring used for?"

"To control demons."

"Control them to do what?"

Scott tried to remember. *Oh yeah…* "To build the Temple."

Mr. Smith laughed, amused by the facial expression that had accompanied Scott's answer. "You are very warm, Mr. Scott." He chuckled some more. "I will tell you a secret though. Demons did not build the Temple. However"—he held up a finger—"that does not mean that there is not a truth hidden somewhere beneath the fable."

"So the ring does have something to do with the Temple, then?"

"What is it that you know of the Jewish Temple?" he asked as he sat down behind the desk again.

Scott was tired of his questions being answered with more questions. "It was built by King Solomon."

"And then destroyed by the Babylonians. Built again by Zerubbabel, embellished by Herod, and then Titus destroyed it again in AD 70. Do you know what the Temple means to the Jewish people?"

Scott shrugged. He didn't really care.

Reading his mind, Smith said, "You should care. It is why they want it."

"Who?"

"Everyone."

"I don't understand," he answered, frustrated.

"We believe that the Temple Mount is the physical locus of God's manifestation on this planet, what we call 'the camp of the *shekinah*.' It was once the site of the Temple, of the Holy of Holies, and the very center of creation." He folded his hands and leaned forward. "For more than one thousand years, the Jewish sanctuary occupied this specific spot. Until, as I said, it was destroyed by Titus on the ninth of Av, AD 70. But ever since, the hope of rebuilding the Temple has remained at the very center of our religious consciousness. That is because, in the Jewish tradition, the Temple represents the heart of God, of Israel, and the heart in each one of us. So, with this heart lying desecrated and desolate, the Land itself and all her people are also broken along with it. The Jerusalem Talmud states that for each generation in which the *Beit HaMikdash* is not rebuilt, it is as if that very generation is responsible for its destruction. And since one of the greatest sins is to destroy the Temple, my Orthodox brothers believe that atonement can only come from fulfilling the divine commandment to rebuild, triggering a process of national and universal redemption. They see God's instruction through Haggai, encouraging the Jews back from Babylon to rebuild the Temple, as the living standard."

"But you don't agree?"

"Many Orthodox see the building of the Temple as a prerequisite to the Messiah's coming. That is why they recite three times a day, 'May it be Thy will that the Temple be speedily rebuilt in our time.' Personally, I do not think it wise to say 'May it be Thy will' about anything. It is only more of the same, trying to manipulate His will to meet *our* timetable through our own selfish means of fulfillment."

"Some might argue that it's God's will for things to come about this way, *through* human means."

A patient smile crossed Mr. Smith's lips. "Ultimately, we all know that the Temple must be restored to fulfill the prophecies. But any temple constructed that is less than what is prophesied is not what we religious Jews are waiting and hoping for. The Second Temple was inferior to the First because it lacked the very things that made the first glorious. Among them the *shekinah* itself, according to the sages. It is for this reason that some Jewish sects, like the Dead Sea sect, separated themselves from the Second Temple and establishment Judaism in Jerusalem. They did not believe that the Second Temple met the prophetic requirements necessary to be considered the prophesied Day of Restoration's Temple. Therefore, they believed that its priesthood and the sacrifices being offered were ritually defiled. Because the First Temple was destroyed due to defilement, they believed the second was likewise doomed from the start. They considered themselves a continuation of the purer Jews of the First Temple, or First Temple Judaism."

"And this is your view?"

Mr. Smith leaned back and seemed to contemplate his answer, his brown eyes going up to the ceiling as if it were an open window into history. "When Herod built his Temple, he tried to prove his loyalty to both the Jews and the Romans. He put a Roman eagle above the doorway to the Temple, corrupting the character of the Temple as a place of peace. This was certainly not the Temple promised to us in the Time of Restoration, built by the permission of Gentiles...by our enemies. God's glory was not in it." He returned his gaze to Scott's. "History has seen other efforts at erecting a temple, ones the people hoped would be responsible for ushering in the King. One such time was under Shimon ben Kosiba. He led the second Jewish revolt against the Romans in AD 132, probably because Emperor Hadrian had not kept his promise to rebuild the Temple.

"After liberating Jerusalem, the leading sage of the time, Rabbi Akiva, proclaimed Shimon as the Messiah and changed his name to Bar Kokhba—Son of the Star. Jewish reckoning accepted this claim because they saw him kicking out the Romans and establishing an independent Jerusalem as evidence of such. Akiva himself believed the sage's claim and went so far as to declare his conquest of Jerusalem the start of the Messianic era. He started a new calendar system based on the delusion. And even though most of history seems to have forgotten it, he also built a third Temple."

"I never heard of that."

"Most have not. But what do you suppose happened to his Temple? Was it the beginning of the Messianic era as he declared? No, of course it was not. Instead, Hadrian recaptured Jerusalem and, according to the Midrash, dashed the temple stones. In its place he put up a temple to Juno, Jupiter, and Minerva. A statue of himself erected on top of the Mount also went a long way in making clear to the Jewish people that the Messianic era was still far off." He looked down and smoothed his tie. "And then there was Julian, the ruler of the Roman Empire after Constantine. A hater of Christian exclusivity, and himself a pagan, he favored the sacrificial system within Judaism because it seemed to him more pluralistic. He promised the Jews that he would not only build them their Temple, but that he would even worship with them in it. The Jewish people were ecstatic as he began gathering the materials for the new Temple. But again, Mr. Scott, what do you suppose happened?"

Scott didn't answer, just waited for him to continue.

"An earthquake destroyed all the site materials the day before building was to begin. May 19, AD 363. Julian died the next month." He stared into Scott's eyes. "Do you understand what I am telling you?"

*Not exactly*, he thought.

"Through many annual events that occurred on one very specific day of the year, the ninth of Av, God confirmed something to His people. On that one day, the Jewish people were sentenced not to enter Eretz-Yisrael, the First Temple was destroyed, the Second Temple was destroyed, the city of Bethar—where Bar Kokhba made his final stand against the Romans—was taken, and the Temple Mount was plowed over by the Romans. All on the same day in different years. Coincidence? I do not think so. I believe it means that God is in control. It means we ought to *let* Him be in control."

Scott leaned forward. "So you're saying that your brand of Orthodoxy condemns trying to bring about this Messianic era through human efforts, that it's prophesied Messiah will come and build the final Temple Himself in the Day of Restoration?"

He nodded. "Correct. Zionism wishes to take something that can only be given. All of the holy writings point to a future Temple that will be the center of the world. The Messiah will reign from this Temple, the *shekinah* will fill it, and both Jew and Gentile will be welcome there. *This* is the day that Israel will be restored and not a second sooner. If we take it upon ourselves to fulfill the prophecy by going to war with the Muslims, it will just be more of history repeating itself."

Trying to get all this straight in his head, Scott attempted to offer a summarization of all Mr. Smith had said. "So secular Israel doesn't want anything to do with a Temple, with Judaism at all. But the religious sects are divided, some thinking it's their responsibility to build the Temple whenever possible through whatever means necessary, that doing so might even bring about the Messiah's coming. But others, like yourself, believe any human effort to bring about the prophesy is a sin."

Mr. Smith smiled a smile that seemed to say, *Good try but not quite so simple*. "My brothers want to rebuild the Temple, and in so trying they will bring more suffering to our Land...to the whole *world*. They will indeed go to war with the Muslims just as the demons of this world want. They need only a spark to set everything in motion."

"The ring."

"Yes, the ring. If they get it, they will find all the justification they need to go to war, to usher in another false Messiah like

Bar Kokhba. To push the nation further from God's good graces."

"And why does the CIA want the ring?"

"Because the elite need the Middle East. It is the centerpiece of the puzzle. The edges are constructed, and everything else is in place. The Middle East is their last hurdle. They want to be in control of everything that happens there. That means they have to introduce the ring on their own terms and in their own time. If the Temple Movement or the religious Zionists get their hands on the ring, they may try to take matters into their own hands. The globalists cannot afford that spot of the world to spiral out of their control."

And for what seemed to him like the hundredth time he'd asked this question, Scott said, "What is it?"

"Part of a formula, and whoever gets their hands on it will be able to figure out the equation. Or keep anyone else from solving it."

Realization flashed through Scott's mind. "You want to hide it in order to take the whole situation out of human hands."

Smith nodded. "I cannot let my people make another disastrous error by further defiling the Holy Land by getting into a religious war. I love it too much. And allowing the globalists to attain it for whatever deception they have planned is equally out of the question."

"But if the ring justifies taking the Temple Mount by force, why wouldn't they just give the ring to your people?"

"As I said, they want to control and monitor everything that happens. Zionism is working for them at the moment simply because they have the reins. But if Jews were to get their hands on what this ring unlocks, they will not only go to war with the Muslims, but with anyone who stands in their way. Including the New World Order. They will try to force the Messianic era into existence, while the elite only want to give them the *illusion* of the Messianic era. An era *they* will control."

Scott ran a hand through his hair.

Mr. Smith stood. "It is very complicated. The inner circle where Lucifer resides may be the only place on earth where there hangs a picture of the completed puzzle. Even the outer rings of the conspiracy know little or even nothing about what role they play in the whole thing." He shrugged. "The conspiracy is as old as the fall of Lucifer from heaven. For thousands of years it has been expressed through humanistic philosophies hiding behind veils of democracy, freedom, and human progress. Volumes could be written on just one chapter of its existence, and there are thousands of chapters. You could spend your entire life researching the occult, following it through the centuries and into the ancient mystery religions, the secret societies, the political and religious systems of our world. Hundreds of years of political planning." He took a breath. "How could one know all that the Devil has been up to for the last six thousand years, and that within every society of which he has been working to prepare the way?"

He waved his hand over the surface of the desk, bringing the touchpad to view. "Here, and I have hundreds of quotes like these." His fingers danced on the projected keys, and a block of text suddenly appeared, staring up at him from beneath the glass surface. Leaning forward, he spread his fingers out over the quote and grabbed it. Then he flicked his wrist, spinning the words around so that they were facing the other side of the table. He pushed the words away from him, and they slid across the desk toward Scott.

Scott stood and stepped closer.

"We shall unleash the nihilists and the atheists and we shall provoke a great social cataclysm which, in all its horror, will show clearly to all nations the effect of absolute atheism, the origin of savagery and of most bloody turmoil. Then, everywhere, the people, forced to defend themselves against the world minority of revolutionaries, will exterminate those destroyers of civilization; and the multitudes, disillusioned with Christianity whose deistic spirits will be from that moment on without direction and leadership, anxious for an ideal but without knowledge where to send its adoration, will receive the true light through the universal manifestation of the pure doctrine of Lucifer, brought finally out into public view; a manifestation which will result from a general reactionary movement which will follow the destruction of

Christianity and atheism, both conquered and exterminated at the same time."

—Albert Pike

After a moment of quiet thought, Scott said, "You still haven't told me what the ring is."

But just then there came a knock on the invisible door—the one Smith's Mossad comrades were behind, some of them like David. Zionists.

"Come in," called Mr. Smith.

The big door swung open, and a short man wearing a suit walked in. His face was full of bottled-up information, his breath short.

"What is it?" asked Smith.

"There was an explosion in Washington. The President is dead."

Scott whipped his head around, unsure if he'd heard that right.

Mr. Smith went and stood in front of the messenger, ignoring Scott. "The Prime Minister?"

"We think he was in the car, too."

After a second to get his thoughts in order, he nodded to the Mossad agent and said, "You know what to do."

The man hurried out of the room.

Scott swiped the words of Albert Pike from the air and leaned onto the desk. "The President of New America and the Prime Minster of…"

"Israel."

Scott swore. "What's the Prime Minister doing here meeting with the President?"

"It was a secret meeting. My sources tell me that the Prime Minister had something to tell the President, something that could only be told in person. Israel has no idea that he even left the country. He will be declared missing. They are orchestrating their war. They are molding the public's opinion. Now everyone in the world will be crying for the Arab states to pay." He paused. "This is how they are finally going to get the Middle East. To destroy religion."

Bringing his hand to the raw spot above his eye, Scott felt a wave of dizziness come over him, and he stepped back toward the chair.

Mr. Smith walked over to the door. "There is much more that I should explain to you about my people. About the Temple Mount, what we believe lies beneath it. The battle between secular Israel and religious Israel. What the ring of Solomon unlocks. But, unfortunately, I cannot continue conversing at this time." He opened the blank door. "My people will help you disappear again if that is what you want. But I have a feeling that God has a specific role for you in all of this." Then his eyes grew soft, sympathetic. "And I doubt that you have finished exorcizing your demons anyway."

Scott fell into the chair, his world spinning. It was not lost on him that Mr. Smith had decided to have this conversation with him instead of Mayhew. Though he had no idea why.

Mr. Smith smiled politely and then left, closing the door behind him.

Scott needed air, needed to get out before the walls moved in and crushed him to death. Everything that once offered stability to his uncertain life had just been erased with one conversation.

The huge steel door he had entered through opened behind him.

# 27.

*"...It would have been impossible for us to develop our plan for the world if we had been subjected to the light of publicity during those years. But, the world is now more sophisticated and prepared to march towards a world government. The supranational sovereignty of an intellectual elite and world bankers is surely preferable to the national auto-determination practiced in past centuries."*

—David Rockefeller

The man had a medium build and was a full three inches shorter than Scott. He was dressed in gray slacks and a black silk shirt. A leather belt circled his hips and supported a holstered pistol. His eyes were vivid and intense, his lips pressed tight. "You have two choices," the man said without wasting time on an introduction. "You can try to get to Canada and disappear just as you had planned, or you can help stop what is happening here."

But that wasn't what Scott heard. What he heard was "...or you can help stop what *you* started." He blinked. "Are you offering me a job?"

"No. Just direction."

"You don't think I know where I'm going?"

The man answered straight-faced. "That depends on the choice you make."

Scott thought about it for a second (finding it strange that he was even doing that), and he saw Canada fade a little further away. But why? He didn't owe these people anything. Or did he? Mr. Smith's words, *And I doubt that you have finished exorcizing your demons anyway,* flew in circles about his head. But that wasn't fair, was it? It was the people who had engineered the sociopolitical climate of the day and all those who had let themselves be brainwashed by it. Yet he knew that didn't excuse him. He had been ignorant too.

His mind blanked. *Why do I even care?*

Why?

It was a question aimed at an endless parade of events, of their consequences. A word that went all the way back to the beginning of time. It could be addressed to anything and everything. But what was the point when it could only be answered by an eternal omniscience? And again he found himself, as he often did, hoping there was no Great Answerer who could address the question. Because if there was no reason behind the why, then there could only be pointlessness, and pointlessness was something that he would actually prefer. Because if he was *pointless,* inconsequential and trivial, then nothing he did could possibly be significant. And, of course, a pointless existence would be better than a guilty one—no supernatural court upholding the virtue of what didn't matter. But of course he knew he was only trying to fool himself. That what he wished he could believe only testified to what he did believe. Whether he wanted to admit it or not.

"Alright. You win," he finally said.

"It is not a game that anyone can win, Mr. Scott. It is only an opportunity to be used as an instrument of good. There are but three categories in life. Those doing evil, those doing good, and those doing nothing. Nothing, as I suspect you have finally figured out, does not aid the forces of good as much as it does the forces of evil. Therefore, there are really only two categories." He shook his head. "It is not a game. It is life and death. It is light and darkness."

He knew he was being manipulated, but what other choice did he have? They were coming for him whether he had the ring or not. If he turned the Israelis down, the facial-recognition cameras would identify him before he even got to the curb. If he was ever going to make it to Canada, he'd now need help to get there. And if he helped them, maybe they would help him. Besides, he had something to say to these monsters who were running the world, something on behalf of Edward. Of Jack. Melissa Strauss. Cindy. His wife. The three German shepherds. Of the countless millions who had suffered through all their wars. "Whatever you say."

The agent looked into his eyes and nodded as if he could see what was going on behind them. "There is someone Mr. Smith wants you to meet. Someone who can answer your questions. Once you speak with him, then you will know what it is that you should do."

If playing along would get him out of here, then Scott was fine with whatever they said, though he had no intention of doing so any longer than was necessary. "Okay."

The man reached behind his back and pulled the priest's books out of his waistband. "Mr. Smith recommends that you read these on the way."

He took the books from him. The book of Tobit and the *Testament of Solomon*. "Can't wait," he muttered.

Then the agent turned and walked back into the corridor, signaling for Scott to follow. And so he did, his conscience a raging sea, and every one of his thoughts contradicting the next. The priest and Mr. Smith, a Catholic and a Jew, had both said God had plans for him in all this. But maybe they were wrong. Maybe he had his own plans. He certainly didn't care about Jerusalem or a ring that could allegedly rebuild its temples.

Titus Mayhew was sitting at a desk, waiting for him. The clock above his head indicated that half an hour had passed. He looked distressed, and Scott could guess why.

"Cindy?" he asked as the Mossad agent closed the big vault door behind them.

Mayhew shook his head. "She didn't make it."

A sorrow-laced spike plunged into Scott's heart. She was dead because she'd helped him. He killed her.

"We leave in ten minutes," the agent said as he walked past them.

Mayhew stood up and placed a hand on Scott's shoulder. "She was conscious right at the end. I got to pray with her."

"Good," he mumbled. He couldn't swallow the lump in his throat. He stepped out from under Mayhew's hand and walked after the agent.

"Wait," Mayhew called.

Scott turned. "What?"

"What are you going to do?"

"They want me to talk to someone."

"You're getting involved?"

He shrugged. "Got nothing better to do, I guess."

"Can I go with you?"

"Sure." He didn't think it was his decision anyway. For the time being, he was following someone else's set of rules.

They walked out of the office together and entered another hallway. The elevator was to their left, and three men were standing by it.

"We going with you?" Scott asked them.

"Yes, but we have to move fast," one of them said. "The military is about to descend on Columbus."

The elevator doors opened, and they all stepped in. Hit the button for the parking garage.

Mayhew watched the floors light up on the control board as they descended. He seemed to be concentrating on something, and Scott wondered if they were wondering the same thing. Like why Mossad would use precious fuel and risk the lives of their people just so he could have a talk with someone?

When the doors opened, Scott stepped out into the same garage they'd arrived in less than an hour ago. Back when Cindy was still alive.

"Hurry," said one of the agents. He walked toward a black SUV with tinted windows and government plates. "We do not have much time."

The five of them loaded into the vehicle and took off for whoever this person was who could explain everything.

Because it was the least the Mossad could do for the people who brought them the ring.

Scott didn't buy it. Not for one second.

# 28.



*"None are more hopelessly enslaved than those who falsely believe they are free."*

—Van Goethe

The Mossad agent's foot pressed the accelerator against the floorboard, propelling them down Columbus's vacant streets and through the standing red lights that stood hovering over empty intersections. They needed to be out of the city before the military began setting up checkpoints, banging on doors, and rounding people up. Scott wanted no part in the loudspeakers, barbed wire, and detention centers, so he didn't say anything about the ridiculous speed they were traveling, though he was a little nervous that the slightest bump in the road might send them spiraling out of control.

He was getting out of Columbus, which was what Scott wanted. But he wasn't exactly sure which set of convictions the Israelis around him were allegiant to. Were they Mr. Smith's orthodox friends, or were they secular or even religious Zionists? Were they the ones who had brought the ring to Mr. Smith or the ones who had taken it from him? There were two of them in the front seats, and the third was in the back behind him and Mayhew.

Mayhew turned in his seat to ask the agent behind them a question when he caught a reflection off the back window and paused.

Scott noticed and sensed Mayhew tense up beside him.

Something was wrong.

The SUV flew down a one-way street and passed straight through another red light. A bread truck, apparently still making its morning deliveries, slammed on its brakes as it entered the intersection. The agent behind the wheel managed to avoid being broadsided by the truck but never saw the vehicle coming the other way.

Scott noticed it in the corner of his eye and barely had time to brace himself.

The collision was enormous. Metal crunched. Glass exploded. Tires screeched. And everything went spinning.

Not wearing seatbelts, they were all whipped around like rag dolls. Until another huge collision brought everything to an instant stop, and the SUV rebounded up and backward a few feet, everyone inside it flying forward.

Scott tried to move, and glass spilled off him. He was on the floor with a pounding headache, but he managed to pull himself up onto the seat and look around. Everything was still out of focus, and he had to blink a few times before he noticed that the front of the SUV was gone. It had been pushed inward and shoved up through the dashboard. Now there was a brick wall where the driver had been, the driver himself smeared across it like an insect. The agent in the passenger seat was still alive, but he was spraying blood everywhere and wouldn't be for much longer. Mayhew was bent over the end of the bench seat, his head on the floor by the door.

"Mayhew," he whispered, reaching for him. But before he could get a response, another black SUV came screeching up alongside them, its front end smashed, its doors swinging open.

Men in black suits stepped out of the vehicle. They held automatic rifles tight against their shoulders, and the sound of their footsteps tapping across the street grew louder as they approached the wreck.

Then they opened fire.

The blasts echoed off nearby buildings and charged down the vacant streets as empty casings tinkled off the asphalt.

Scott was afraid to breathe much less move. The first shot had exploded the head of the agent in the front passenger seat, but so far they didn't seem to be shooting at him or Mayhew. Not wanting to give them a reason to, he slowly raised his hands into the air, fingers spread apart.

The side doors opened, and glass emptied into the street. One of the men from the other SUV stepped close, checked Mayhew's vitals, and then pulled him out of the wreckage.

Scott stared ahead as a guy in a black silk shirt, gray slacks, and an automatic rifle slung over his shoulder asked him if he was okay. It was the same guy from Mr. Smith's office.

Scott nodded and lowered his hands. He could taste blood in his mouth.

"Come on then," the guy said.

Scott struggled toward him, feeling pain in every step. "What's going on?" he asked. Then, "You could've killed us."

The man helped him out onto the street and walked him around to the back of the SUV as two more men in suits pulled open the rear doors. There, lying in the back with a bullet hole in his head, was Mr. Smith, his eyes frozen open and staring into nothingness.

Scott swore under his breath and realized that was what Mayhew must've seen in the reflection just before they were rammed into. He put his hand out against the vehicle to steady himself. He needed to sit.

Another suit came walking back around from the front of the vehicle. "Got it," he said.

"Is it damaged?" asked the guy from Mr. Smith's office.

"No."

"Okay. Let's go."

They bent over to help Mayhew, who was just starting to regain consciousness, up into their SUV.

"What's your name?" Scott asked as he climbed in beside Mayhew.

As the sound of rotors suddenly materialized over Columbus, he said, "Call me Malachi." Then he said something in Hebrew to the driver and shut the door. Ran around to the front passenger side and jumped in. "Go," he said.

The driver slammed on the gas and swung them away from the twisted heap of metal protruding from the building's side. When they were twenty yards away, one of the two suits sitting in the back pulled out a device and pushed a red button.

The mangled wreck disappeared in a massive fireball that brought half the building down on top of it. Black smoke billowed upward into the morning sky, signaling the helicopters.

"What's happening?" asked Scott.

"We were betrayed," Malachi answered. "There was a mole. They were just waiting for us to get the ring. Using us." He held the ring up between two fingers. It gleamed in the morning sunlight.

"What did they want with us?"

"I cannot be certain, but I would assume they just wanted you out of their way. You interrupted their escape, so instead of allowing you to delay it, they just invited you along."

It dawned on Scott that the three men had been waiting for the elevator and not for them. "But how did they get Smith down into the truck?"

Malachi shook his head. "It was another man who murdered him and transported him to the vehicle. He used the gurney we brought your woman friend in on. We caught him coming back up in the service elevator. He was not planning on leaving with the other three."

Mayhew blinked and looked around. "Where are we?" he muttered.

But just then three black helicopters swooped down on them, and soldiers in black uniforms began firing at them, their feet perched against the landing skids.

The driver swerved and punched the gas as Malachi leaned out the window and fired his assault rifle. He struck two of the shooters, and they dropped to the street, one of them landing on a parked car and exploding the windows, the other just striking the blacktop. The helicopters were attempting to drop down and cut them off.

"Turn right!" yelled Malachi.

The agent pulled the wheel hard to the right, and they shot down an alley just as the hovering helicopters opened fire with their six-barrel rotary machine guns. Sparks flew past the windows from prolonged brushes against the alley's sides.

The black helicopters climbed back into the sky for a better position, and the Mossad driver kept the SUV in alleyways and small side streets, trying to hide between the larger buildings that would obstruct the helicopters' view.

"An underground parking garage," Malachi instructed. Immediately, the driver shot out of their current alley and turned left onto a two-way street. They could see the helicopters circling in the air a few blocks to their right.

"Were they Mossad?" Scott asked, referring to his previous captors.

He nodded. "Zionists who will stop at nothing to have the ring."

"Even if it means killing their own?" Though he realized as the words came out of his mouth that the same could be said of Malachi.

"We Jews have been fighting amongst ourselves since before the northern and southern kingdoms."

Mayhew coughed.

Scott leaned forward. "And the helicopters?"

"NAU military. Though I doubt they know anything about the ring."

"But this vehicle has government plates."

"They are fake. Only meant to deter the curious."

*Great.* "Where are we going?"

"I told you, to meet someone who will help you."

"Where?"

"Here. In Ohio."

He touched his aching head. "What are you going to do with the ring?"

Malachi looked back out the window just as the helicopters appeared to spot them. They began coming around in an attack pattern. "I am going to take it to my boss."

They shot into a parking garage and followed the ramp down into its sublevels, passing parked cars on both sides.

Then the driver slammed on the brakes and brought them to a stop in an empty parking slot. The question now was whether or not the men in the choppers would be coming in after them.

The four Mossad agents jumped out of the SUV and ran to where the ramp circled back up to the street. And sure enough, ropes began dropping down in front of the entrance, and soldiers were fast-roping down onto the street. But standing out under the rising sun, they couldn't see into the darkness of the garage and the Mossad agents who were waiting for them.

Scott watched from within the SUV as the Jewish agents operated from a silent count and opened fire simultaneously, the two on the ends working from the outside in and the two in the middle from the inside out. The sound of the automatic fire rebounded throughout the concrete tomb and set off scores of car alarms. The NAU soldiers were dead before they could even hear it.

Malachi then led the men back to the SUV before wiser soldiers could begin rolling grenades down the ramp at them. "Come on, Scott," he called into the vehicle. "We need a new ride."

Three minutes later, tires screeched as two newly acquired cars flew up and out the other side of the garage, leaving behind another group of soldiers creeping toward the abandoned SUV.

Scott and Mayhew were in a black Mustang with Malachi behind the wheel, while the other three agents were ahead of them in a red BMW. And though there were no black helicopters waiting for them on this side of the building, it was only a matter of time before the microchips in the cars' E-plates showed up on some agency's radar.

"Do you have the books I gave you?" Malachi asked Scott.

"Yeah."

"Perhaps you should look through them. It will be about a two-hour ride."

Scott didn't feel like reading because his head felt like it was still being jackhammered, but he knew he wasn't going to be sleeping anytime soon either. He took *Tobit* out of his pocket, opened to page one, and tried to ignore the blood that was dripping down his head and onto his shirt.

# 29.


*"They who can give up essential liberty to obtain a little temporary safety deserve neither liberty nor safety."*
　　　　　　　　　　　　　　　—Benjamin Franklin

Malachi drove the stolen Mustang down East Broad Street and then made a right onto South Grant Avenue. Three-quarters of a mile later, the city was behind them.

"Are you okay?" Scott asked, turning in the front seat to see Mayhew sitting in the back.

"I'm fine. Just a headache." He met Scott's eyes. "The guy in the back of the SUV… What happened? What's going on?"

Scott realized that Mayhew hadn't been in the room with Mr. Smith and thus couldn't know about Texas or the President. Not any of it. So for the next twenty minutes, he brought Mayhew up to speed with what was going on in the world. After which Malachi ran through the conflicting agendas existing within the Mossad and the differing perspectives pertaining to the Holy Land—not that the Mossad itself was divided, but that some of its agents had higher allegiances to other religious dogmas than did the secular state.

Mayhew just sat there massaging his temples. He looked like he was trying to digest a brick.

"So where exactly are we going?" Scott asked Malachi. And though Malachi had pretty much repeated to Mayhew the same summarization Mr. Smith had given him, there was a fatal flaw in Malachi's rendition of it. A certain hypocrisy that undermined its said conviction—namely the refusal to use force in order to accomplish anything. Something that Malachi and his three friends had just blatantly disregarded when executing the other agents. But Scott didn't say anything about it, just tucked it away for now.

"Athens County. It is about ninety miles southeast of here, near West Virginia."

West Virginia. Wasn't that where they said the CIA wanted to take him? To that DARPA facility?

The red BMW continued ahead of them, its brake lights yet to shine through the morning sunlight, and by the time Scott set one of the old books on his lap, the landscape outside the window had already gone from city to suburb and was now making the transition to rare farmland.

Book of Tobit, chapter 3.

There was a summarization of the text before a verse-by-verse translation spilled over onto the next two pages. Scott skipped through it, paying attention only to words that were either underlined or circled, presumably by the priest. He found a few references made to the *Testament of Solomon* scribbled beside the body of the text and then an excerpt from Milton's *Paradise Lost:*

> Better pleased
> Than Asmodeus with the fishy fume
> That drove him, though enamoured, from the spouse
> Of Tobit's son, and with a vengeance sent
> From Media post to Egypt, there fast bound.
> - Paradise Lost , iv. 167–71.

Scott ran his finger down a list of names that followed Milton's excerpt. In the margin near the top of the list was written its explanation.

References to the Catholic authenticity of Tobias.

The list started with St. Polycarp and a date. AD 117. Next to it read,

Cites Tobit 4:10 and 12:9 (Ad Philippenses).

That was how the whole page was laid out. A name, a date, and the references used.

Deutero-Clement, St. Clement of Alexandria, Origen, St. Athanasius, St. Cyprian, St. Ambrose…

Tobias was present in Old Latin Version from AD 150 until replaced by Jerome's Vulgate. Earliest canonical lists contain Tobias (Council of Hippo, Councils of Carthage, St. Innocent I, St Augustine). Fourth- and fifth-century Septuagint manuscripts contain Tobias. Council of Trent confirmed canonicity of Tobias (April 8, 1546) as well as Vatican (April 24, 1870).

Scott looked up from the pages and stole a glance back at Mayhew. He appeared to be sleeping.

"You read this thing?" Scott asked, turning his attention to Malachi.

Malachi looked over. "I am familiar with *Tobit*."

"So why do you think Smith wanted me to read it?"

But Malachi only shrugged. "His name was Benjamin, by the way."

"Did he know the priest?"

Malachi nodded. "Very well."

Scott was confused. "Did they share the same—"

"The priest was Catholic. Obviously there existed differences of opinion. But as far as the ring was concerned, they wanted the same thing."

"For it to disappear."

"To keep it from the wrong hands."

"And whose hands are those?" Scott asked.

"Everyone else's."

He thought about it, and some dots began to connect. "The priest was working with Benjamin."

"Yes."

"Against David."

He nodded. "David was a Zionist. He wanted to use the ring as a means to reestablish Israel, to bring the Messiah."

"And you think the idea is blasphemous?"

"Like Benjamin told you, some of us Jews are still hoping in a future fulfillment, and we see all these human efforts as simply delaying it."

Scott was about to bring up the seeming contradiction that was bothering him when Mayhew's voice entered the discussion from the back seat.

"I don't understand. The Zionist movement seems to *be* the process of prophetic fulfillment."

Malachi's eyes rose to the rearview mirror. "We do not believe in any process. We believe that Messiah will return and do all things at once. Our Zionist brothers, both secular and religious, are planning on destroying the Dome of the Rock and building another Temple there. But the Temple they build will have to be destroyed in order for Messiah to build *His* Temple when He comes. The Temples that have already stood in Jerusalem have fallen victim to God's judgment, and if another Temple is to be built, it too will face the same end. And perhaps our conquest to gain back what God has taken from us will be the very grounds for such punishment."

Mayhew leaned back again. "So David was working for Benjamin, and the priest was working for Benjamin, but David and the priest were working against each other?"

"Benjamin was a top-ranking Mossad agent whose orders came from the secular state of Israel. All Mossad agents work for the secular state. But there have developed religious cliques within the agency, cliques not in agreement with the direction the secularists wish to take us. But the religious factions are in disagreement with each other too. David reported to Benjamin but was acting according to his own interests, not aware that Benjamin had his own agenda. That was the priest's role, to keep an eye on David and his findings."

The car was silent for two miles.

Finally, Mayhew asked, "Who are we going to see?"

"His name is Isaiah. He knew Benjamin."

"Jewish?"

"Messianic Jew."

Mayhew squinted. "I thought the Orthodox considered Messianic Jews to be heretics and apostates."

"They do. The relationship Benjamin and Isaiah shared was unique. They did not let their religious differences interfere with the love they had for one another." Malachi saw the startled looks and quickly shook his head. "They were brothers." He set his eyes back on the road and continued driving on in silence.

Scott returned his gaze to the book in his lap and started reading where he'd left off.

Testament of Solomon<br>
Book of Tobit<br>
Haggadic Legend

The Asmodeus in TESTAMENT and the Asmodeus in TOBIT seem to be the same as the "Ashmedai" of rabbinical literature. The Haggadah relates that Solomon did not know how to shape the blocks of marble without using an iron tool (Ex 20:25,26). His wise men urged him to obtain the "Shamir" (a worm that could cleave rocks). But not even the demons knew where the Shamir could be found. However, they reasoned that Ashmedai (Asmodeus), King of the Demons, knew of the place. So they (the demons) told Solomon of the mountain where Ashmedai dwelt and the manner of life he conducted there...

Scott skimmed down past the plot to capture the demon, scanning the text until his eyes were captivated by some severe underlining.

Solomon sends <u>BENAIAH ben Jehoiadah</u> to capture Ashmedai (Asmodeus). He gives Benaiah a <u>chain with a ring on it</u> (some translations say it was engraved with the Tetragrammaton). Then Benaiah pours wine into the demon's water well and makes him drunk. Once he has fallen into a deep sleep, Benaiah throws the chain around his neck and says, "The Name of thy Lord is upon thee."*

   -Connection of Solomon with magical ring is first documented by Josephus, who also describes him as a magician (Ant. 8.2.5).

Scott had no idea what all this meant, except that it sounded similar to what was in the *Testament*. "Do you know about this Benaiah guy Solomon gave a ring to?" he asked Malachi.

It seemed Benjamin's death was beginning to weigh on Malachi, and it was through a softer, more sullen voice that he answered. "Nothing more than what *Tobit* says of him."

"The priest underlined it..."

"Keep reading, Mr. Scott." He sighed and leaned to his left, putting his weight against the door.

"You okay?" Scott asked.

"Fine."

Scott went back to reading.

> Solomon tells the demon that he only wants the worm, and Ashmedai (Asmodeus) reveals its location. However, he remains with Solomon until the Temple is completed. Solomon then says to Ashmedai that he does not understand the greatness of demons if their king can be bound by a mere mortal. Ashmedai responds to this by suggesting that Solomon remove the <u>chain and lend him the magic ring</u>. Then would he reveal to Solomon his greatness. Solomon agrees to this, and the demon stands with one wing touching heaven and the other reaching earth before he snatches up Solomon (who had parted with his <u>protective ring</u>) and flings him 400 parasangs away from Jerusalem. From that point on, Ashmedai poses as Solomon in his stead.
>
> After wandering for a long time, Solomon eventually returns to reclaim the throne, telling his story to the people. At first, they think him mad. And then they begin to consider the strange behavior the king had recently exhibited, for his marital affairs were no longer being kept in accordance with Jewish law, and not even Benaiah was permitted in his presence anymore. <u>Solomon is then provided with another ring</u> and when he appears before Ashmedai with it, the imposter takes flight.

Then there were written some words that Scott couldn't decipher, and his head seemed to throb even more. He flipped through the rest of the book just to see how much further he had to read. It looked like there were only four or five pages left, so he took a deep breath and pressed on.

> Midrash Tehillim 78:351—353; Midrash Al-Yithallel (Sefer ah-Likkutim I, 20–22, ed. Gruenhut); Midrash Sir HaShirim

29a–30a; B.Berakhot 6a; Zohar III, 309a; Emek ha-Melekh,
12. Adolf Jellinek's Beth ha-Midrasch. Maasebuch.

He figured they were references to what followed—more Jewish folklore.

> Ashmedai throws <u>Solomon's ring</u> into the sea in hopes that no one finds it and discovers his true identity. Meanwhile, Solomon finds himself in a field, his appearance that of a merchant. He wanders the countryside as a beggar and cries out declarations that he was once the king of Israel. People think he is crazy, children throw stones at him. For three years, Solomon wanders foreign lands until he comes to Ammon and is hired as a cook. There he falls in love with the King's daughter, and the King expels them both into the wilderness, not wishing to see their forbidden love or their deaths. They come to the seashore and buy a fish, and when they cut it open, <u>Solomon's ring is found in it</u>. He puts it on and his rags are instantly turned to velvet. So he goes back to Jerusalem and shows the king's ministers <u>the ring</u>. Then he confronts the demon posing as him, and the demon flees back to his mountain. Solomon then marries the king of Ammon's daughter, and she gives birth to Rehoboam.
> -Other legends tell of the Sanhedrin giving Solomon <u>another</u> ring once they believed it was not Solomon sitting on the throne.

There was a loose piece of paper resting between the last two pages, just as there had been loose pieces in the *Testament*. And, like the ones in the other book, they seemed to be filled with random notes. References to Josephus, something about Mormonism, the Talmud, Kabbalah, five-pointed stars... There was a picture of a bright star floating in a triangle surrounded by more roses. The words "Blazing Star" were written across what looked to be a sketch of the American flag. The phrase "as above, so below" was written across a pool of water with the number 007 hovering beside it. There was a statue called *Destiny* sitting over a line that was labeled "Pennsylvania Avenue—the hypotenuse of the Federal Triangle." Six stars were arched over the statue's head. And then there was the crucifix, standing in front of the double-headed phoenix again...

Scott closed the book and took another look at the passing scenery. They were getting into the mountains now. He closed his eyes and tried to forget about the books in his lap, the ring, the Resistance sitting in the back seat, and the Mossad driving their stolen car.

Ten minutes later, after his brain subconsciously worked through the bizarre text, most of which meant absolutely nothing to him, his eyes snapped open.

According to the priest's books, there were *two* rings.

# 30.

*"A really efficient totalitarian state would be one in which the all-powerful executive of political bosses and their army of managers control a population of slaves who do not have to be coerced, because they lover their servitude. To make them love it is the task assigned, in present-day totalitarianism states, to ministries of propaganda, newspaper editors and schoolteachers."*

—Aldous Huxley, 1946

**M**alachi turned the Mustang onto a dirt road and, after two hundred yards, pulled up alongside an old farmhouse on their right.

"This it?" Scott asked.

"Yes," Malachi answered.

The BMW they were following didn't stop with them. Instead, it continued on past the house and disappeared down the road behind a wake of dust.

Mayhew sat up. "Where are they going?"

"To the rendezvous point." He looked over at Scott. "I am sorry about your friend, that we could not do more to help her."

"Me too."

Malachi pulled a phone out of his pocket and handed it to him. "You can use this to reach us. Just hold down the number one key. Use it once and then get rid of it."

Scott held it in his palm for a second. Would accepting it mean accepting their mission as his own? Reluctantly, he slipped it into his pocket. "What do we tell this guy?"

"Tell him that Benjamin sent you and show him the priest's books. He will believe you."

"And what exactly is it that we're supposed to learn from him?"

"That is up to him, I guess."

"Right," he mumbled. He pushed open the door.

"Hold on a second," Mayhew suddenly protested. "Where are *you* going?" he asked Malachi.

Malachi turned and looked at him. "Secret."

For a moment, Mayhew seemed to hesitate. Like he didn't want to leave the car. He looked up at Scott, then back at Malachi. Finally, he threw open the door and got out.

Scott bent over and stuck his head back into the car, through the open passenger window. "Thank you."

Malachi smiled. "I will see you soon." He put the car in drive and pulled back onto the dirt road. The Mustang raced after the BMW, leaving Scott and Mayhew standing there in the middle of nowhere.

"You trust them with the ring?" asked Mayhew.

"It's not mine to trust them with." And he started walking up the path toward the house.

Clouds were rolling in from the north. It was cold, and it felt like it might snow. Scott crossed his arms across his chest and tried not to think about why the Mossad would want him to have the phone. Why they would have a vested interest in him at all. None of it made any sense, but playing this game was the only thing that had been keeping him alive. So he'd continue to play it for now, even though he still didn't know his role or any of the rules.

The house was two stories tall. A portion of it was old stone, probably from the early nineteen hundreds. There was a newer addition to it that was covered in yellow siding. An old pickup truck poked through a tiny garage beside the house, but otherwise the surrounding property was bare. Scott could picture the empty fields being harvested fifty years ago, back when farming in the country still existed. He thought there were probably remnants of an old barn somewhere nearby, though he couldn't see it from the path. He stepped up the porch steps and approached the front door. Got a glimpse of his reflection in the glass window. His hair was matted with dry blood, and a plethora of cuts crisscrossed his forehead. Including the one from the sniper's bullet. His eye, from when he'd fallen headfirst onto the street last night, looked like a cheese grater had been used on him. His clothes were dirty and charred, and the army jacket he'd taken was now tattered in spots. He turned and looked at Mayhew. He didn't look much better. *Okay, Alice, let's see just how deep this rabbit hole goes, shall we?* He rapped his knuckles against the door.

After a few seconds passed, the door cracked open.

"Who is it?" a voice called from the other side.

Scott exchanged a quick glance with Mayhew before answering. "My name is Matthew Scott, and this is Titus Mayhew. We were sent here by Benjamin."

A pause. "Why?"

"To be honest, I'm not really sure."

Silence.

Scott tried explaining further. "We have something to show you, something we were told you would understand." He took the books from Mayhew.

"What?"

"Actually, they're books. Written by a priest." Trying not to move too suddenly, he slipped the books into the opening between the door and its frame.

The person inside snatched the books and shut the door.

Mayhew looked up into the sky. "Looks like snow."

Scott shoved his hands into his pockets. "Yeah."

The door swung open to reveal Mr. Smith come back from the dead. He was holding the books in his hands. "Are you armed?" he asked in a deep voice that was not Benjamin's.

Scott remembered that this was Benjamin's brother. But if not for the different voice, he could've passed as Mr. Smith for sure. The similarities were uncanny. "No."

The man nodded his approval and turned away from the door, looking through the books. "Come in and shut the door. They're calling for snow." And then he whispered under his breath, "Or *making* it."

They entered the house and closed the door behind them.

"Are you hungry?" the man asked, leading them into the kitchen. He set the books down on a hutch that stood beside the kitchen's entrance. "You look like you haven't eaten in quite a while. Or slept for that matter."

Scott noticed a slight limp in the man's step. "Your name is Isaiah?" he asked.

"Yeah. I'm Benjamin's older brother." He opened a cabinet and pulled out a box of crackers. "Here, you can snack on these for now. Until I know what all this is about." He set them down on a round table occupied by two lonely chairs. "Have a seat." He went to the refrigerator. "Something to drink?"

"Please, thank you." Scott looked around as he sat.

"Actually, would you mind if I used your bathroom?" Mayhew asked.

"Down the hall and to your right," Isaiah answered without taking his head out of the refrigerator.

Mayhew walked out of the room and left Scott with the crackers.

Isaiah brought over a pitcher of water from the fridge and some glasses over to the table. "Go on, help yourself," he said.

Scott obeyed, reaching for the crackers and pouring himself a glass of water. "So you're Jewish?" He gulped down the water.

Isaiah leaned against the kitchen sink. "Messianic Jew."

"Meaning that you believe Jesus Christ to be the prophesied Messiah?"

"That is correct."

"Don't have too many Jewish friends, do you?"

The man laughed. "Out here?"

"But Benjamin..." He stopped himself before he could use the past tense.

"He is Orthodox, though I believe the Lord is working on his heart." He was watching Scott intently, doing a little profiling of his own. "How is my brother?"

Scott stopped chewing and avoided Isaiah's eyes.

Which was all Isaiah needed to add things up. He sighed deeply, and his eyes filled with bitter tears. "How did he die?"

The man was strong emotionally. He was battling the feelings while quickly assembling a dam to keep out the tsunami of terrible comprehension he knew was on its way. The dam seemed to be constructed of cold and calculating analytical processes. But Scott knew it wasn't enough. Never was. It might buy him some time, but it would crumble soon enough.

"He was shot by an imposter."

Isaiah closed his eyes, and a tear rolled down his cheek. Then he looked up to the ceiling, took a couple of deep breaths while rubbing his swollen eyes, and whispered, "Forgive me."

"I'm sorry you had to find out this way," Scott said.

"I never suspected that old age would be the means of his departure." He leaned forward and off the sink. "But I can't do anything for him now, can I? So we should find out why he sent you here." He pulled a pair of reading glasses from the chest pocket of his flannel shirt. Then he walked over to the doorway and picked up the two books. Sitting down in the empty chair across from Scott, he wiped his eyes and slid the glasses up over his nose. "This came from a priest, you said?" He opened the first page.

"Yes."

"Ah. The *Testament of Solomon.* Father Baer."

"You knew him?" Scott asked, surprised.

A modest smile. "Yeah. I knew him. But since you have his books, and my brother sent you here with them, I'm guessing he's dead as well."

Scott nodded.

Isaiah flipped through the pages.

"How did you know him?" Scott asked.

Peeking over the top of his lenses, he answered, "A while back, before things really started changing, he was working with my brother and some others on a secret project. These are some of his notes."

"What kind of project?"

"A sort of treasure hunt. But the world being what it is now, they decided that discovering this 'treasure' would lead to certain ramifications they wanted no part in. So they decided not to pursue it after all, to let God deal with it in His own way, in His own time."

"Are you saying these books are part of some old quest to *find* something?"

"In a way, yes. Though the most important one is missing."

"What do you mean?"

Isaiah looked up at him. "He had at least three books that I know of. You only have two."

"Could the priest have lost one?"

Isaiah smiled. "You didn't know him, did you? No, that would be impossible."

Scott thought back to the warden's house and wondered if David could have taken it. "What was in the other book?"

Isaiah held up a finger. "Hold on. Let me look at this for a minute." He was going through the text, paying careful attention to the drawings while simultaneously trying to hold closed the floodgates of sorrow.

Mayhew walked back into the room, and with both chairs occupied, just leaned against the doorframe.

After a few minutes, Isaiah closed the book and opened the other one. "It's been a long time since I've heard any of this," he said. "This riddle they worked on." He looked up and stared out the kitchen window for a few seconds. "I can't imagine what would make them pick it up again."

"Why is that?" asked Mayhew.

Isaiah shifted his red eyes to him. "Because they'd chosen to abandon their work on it, to never touch it again."

"Why?"

"They didn't know what would happen if the world was awakened to its existence, what the consequences would be."

"You're talking about the ring of Solomon?" Mayhew asked.

"And what it unlocks."

Scott pointed at the books. "And these books give clues as to what that is?"

"Not really. These were the first books he kept, when their investigation was still in its early stages. These are just records of literature referring to the ring, their efforts at trying to establish a historical basis for its actuality on the physical plane."

"I was told that there was perhaps a truth behind the legend," Scott said.

Isaiah shrugged. "Maybe. I don't know. I don't know how anyone *would* know unless it was actually found."

Scott squinted. *"Found?"*

"The ring."

Scott stared at him. "They *did* find it."

Surprise animated Isaiah's face. "What?"

"You didn't know?" Mayhew came off the door and stepped closer to the table.

"When did this happen?"

"A couple of weeks ago," Mayhew answered. "They found it somewhere in the Middle East. We're not sure where."

"And my brother and Father Baer?"

"They had it in their hands," Scott said.

Isaiah pushed himself off the table and leaned heavily against the chair, his hands grasping the table's edge. He looked stunned. "I don't believe it," he whispered. Then he looked up at Mayhew, then over to Scott. "Tell me what happened."

Scott said, "A woman named Melissa Strauss brought the ring into the country."

"Melissa Strauss… I saw her on the news."

"Yeah, well, she was no terrorist. She sent the ring to a friend of mine, and NAU Intelligence tracked it to his house. I intervened, which is how I ended up here."

Isaiah looked at Mayhew. "And you?"

"I'm a member of the Resistance. We were positioned in Adirondack Park, in a captured gulag. Mossad agents showed up with the priest."

Isaiah studied him. He didn't seem to care one way or the other whether or not Mayhew was in the Resistance. "How'd you meet my brother?"

Scott related the rest of the story to him.

Isaiah took his glasses off and massaged the bridge of his nose. "Where's the ring now?"

"It just drove off down the street," Mayhew said with a hint of frustration in his voice.

Scott clarified. "Benjamin's men have it. They said they were taking it to their boss. Whoever that is."

Isaiah pushed the chair back, stood up, and walked over to the kitchen sink. Staring out the window again, he asked, "You have no idea what is happening, do you?"

Their silence affirmed his suspicion.

Snow began to fall.

"Do you know what the Copper Scroll is?" Isaiah asked, tracking the flakes with his eyes as they drifted past the window.

"No," Scott said.

But apparently Mayhew didn't share the same ignorance. "Spring of 1952, found in 3Q near Qumran. Took them four years to figure out how to open it because of how brittle the oxidization had made the copper. It's supposed to be some kind of treasure map indicating where the priests hid the Temple treasures before the Romans came."

Isaiah sighed, but it wasn't a sigh of relief. Instead, it sounded as if a huge burden suddenly landed square on his shoulders. "Let's go for a walk," he said.

# 31.

*"Truth is so obscure in these times and falsehood so established, that unless we love the truth, we cannot know it."*

—Blaise Pascal

The wind began blowing the snow across the open field as Isaiah led them across it. His hands were in his pockets, and his mind seemed elsewhere. No doubt wrestling with the news of his brother's death.

Scott watched his own breath crystallize in front of his face as he pulled the jacket a little tighter. The field was quickly turning white, and the trees that were scattered around its edges were creaking as they swayed. Other than a few houses way off on the horizon, the area was void of any human activity. He hoped it would stay that way. He turned toward Mayhew, who had gotten a warmer jacket from Isaiah, and asked, "What's this Copper Scroll you were talking about?" He didn't want to interrupt Isaiah's current thoughts with unnecessary questions.

Mayhew answered him, his words forming clouds of their own. "The Dead Sea Scrolls were found in 1947," he began. "Then over the next few years, they discovered more than eight hundred scrolls and more than a hundred thousand fragments."

"Of what?"

"Old Testament manuscripts, partial manuscripts, commentaries…" A large snowflake landed on his nose. "But in 1952 they found a scroll that was different from all the others."

"One made of copper."

"Yeah. It took them four years just to come up with a plan on how to open it without destroying it."

"What'd they do?"

"They cut it into strips. Though they lost some of the text when they did it."

Scott watched a fox run across the field and into a wooded area two hundred yards ahead. "Did they decipher any of it?"

"Yeah. I think it consisted of a version of ancient Hebrew that was different from the other Dead Sea Scrolls and some Greek cryptograms."

Scott watched the snow dance across the field, twirling in little tornados. "I don't know what that means."

"I think there were sixty-four lines, each one describing a treasure. They estimate the whole list to be around two hundred tons of treasure when all added up."

"An inventory? From where?"

"From the Temple in Jerusalem. Nebuchadnezzar carried it all off to Babylon, but Nehemiah and Ezra would eventually see that it was returned."

"The Temple had that much wealth?"

"In the book of Ezra, it says that Artaxerxes authorized a four-*ton* contribution to be given to the Temple's reconstruction efforts. And when Herod expanded the Second Temple, the wealth only increased. Even Jesus made reference to the Temple's gold."

Scott frowned. "That's what it is? A treasure map to the Temple's lost wealth?" He wondered if that could be what everyone was after, mere *gold*. It was a timeless tale, but somehow Scott didn't think the world's elite would be all that concerned with wealth. Not when they controlled global economies, owned the world bank, and ran it all through a digital currency of their own making.

"That's the general belief, but as far as I know, most of the locations listed only bear evidence of earlier excavations."

"So what would this Copper Scroll have to do with the ring?"

"No idea."

At that point, Isaiah suddenly turned and said, "He doesn't know, because he completely misses the essential mystery of the scroll." He slowed down and waited for them to catch up. "A common belief regarding the scroll is that the priests of the day, believing Ezekiel's prophecy of Gog and Magog to be upon them, didn't just hide the Temple's treasures but also anything that would be essential to maintain the practice of their religion. Those who take this view date the scroll at AD 68, two years before the Romans burned Jerusalem to the ground. There are others, however, who believe the scroll was made much, much earlier. Before the *Babylonians*, not the Romans, destroyed the city." He held out his hand and caught a couple of flakes on his palm. Seemed to study them.

"Either way," he continued, "the Copper Scroll is, as Mayhew suggested, an inventory of the Temple's hidden treasures and religious instruments. The sixty-fourth line in the scroll mentions another scroll. Some believe it is the key to unlocking the secrets within the Copper Scroll itself." He turned and looked at Mayhew. "*That* is the mystery."

Scott asked, "Another scroll?"

"Some think it might just be a copy of the same scroll..." He fell silent for a moment, contemplating. "In the book of Jeremiah, God promised that the Temple treasures would be restored after the captivity in Babylon. A common theory is that that promise is also applicable to *our* time, that the treasures will be found in the not too distant future and will provide the final incentive needed to construct a new Jewish Temple." He cupped his hands together and blew warm air into them. "The Temple Scroll, found at Qumran in 1956, describes a Jewish Temple that hasn't yet been built. It also mentions ritual cleanliness, the sacrifices and offerings according to the festivals, and statues of the king and his army. Along with the preserved instructions in the Temple Scroll, the Copper Scroll may provide what's needed to reestablish Judaism's sacrificial system and to erect its next, or final, Temple."

"Your brother took issue with that," Scott stated softly.

Isaiah managed a small smile. "He knew that any temple requiring UN sanction could never be the one that Ezekiel prophesied about, the true and final Temple that the Jewish people have been waiting for. As a Messianic Jew, I tend to agree with him."

"Why is that?" Scott asked.

Isaiah set his eyes on the distant woods. "I don't know what I believe when it comes to end-of-days theology. But if I were to take the premillennial view"—he waved his hand as if to indicate that he was perfectly aware the word meant nothing to Scott—"then I would believe that the prophet Daniel, aware that the Babylonian captivity was about to come to an end and inquiring about Israel's future, was given by God not just an immediate revelation, but a vision of Israel's entire future. If so, then the last part of that vision pertains to the last chapter of Israel's history. A specific period of seven years that the prophets call 'the Time of Jacob's Trouble.'"

Scott looked at Mayhew and wondered if he knew what this guy was talking about. He seemed to be tracking okay, which only made Scott more frustrated.

Isaiah continued. "Jesus Himself said that the second half of those seven years would be 'a time of such great tribulation such as the world has never seen.' And then would come the Antichrist, 666, and all the stuff in Revelation they used to make movies about."

"Stuff Christians have been arguing about for over a thousand years," Mayhew said.

But Scott recalled something that he'd heard Edward or Jack once say. "Isn't this Antichrist supposed to make some kind of deal with Israel that he ends up breaking?"

Isaiah nodded. "It's what Daniel called 'the Abomination of Desolation.' Jesus told his disciples that when they saw that take place, the people in Judea were to flee into the wilderness in hopes of escaping the coming tribulation."

"Some people believe that was already fulfilled," Mayhew interrupted again.

"True. From Daniel's perspective, it would seem that the abomination that makes desolate could have been fulfilled by Antiochus Epiphanes when he captured Jerusalem and sacrificed a pig on the altar of incense in 168 BC. And a lot of ancient Jews believed it at the time. However, the lynchpin of Daniel's prophecy was the decree to rebuild Jerusalem in 444 BC, which would make the events of 168 too soon to be the prophecy's fulfillment."

Scott was about to ask why, but again Isaiah waved him off. "More important than that, at least for someone like me, is that, as I already said, Jesus referred to Daniel's prophecy as something still yet to come." He walked shoulder to shoulder between the two of them as if playing the role of teacher or scribe. "At least not its *whole* fulfillment."

"But—" Mayhew started to say.

"Yes, I know," Isaiah said, cutting him off. "AD 70 is a different story."

"AD 70?" Scott asked. He recalled hearing Benjamin mention the same date.

"The date that the Romans destroyed the Temple." Isaiah looked over at Scott. "Those days, much like the days of the Holocaust, were a tribulation, no doubt. Many scholars today believe that Daniel's prophecy was fulfilled then. And maybe they're right. I don't know. Or maybe neither position is wrong. Or at least not totally correct."

"Meaning a dual fulfillment?" Mayhew asked.

"Maybe. I'm not a scholar. All I know is that it is prophesied that Jesus Christ will return and build that final Millennial Temple that Ezekiel spoke of, and that all of Israel will then be saved and worship their Messiah."

"According to a dispensational premillennial view," Mayhew stated. "But then you have to account for Pierre Poiret."

Isaiah looked at him, his eyes squinting ever so slightly, almost suspicious. "You know your history," he said. "John Darby is most often credited with dispensationalism, but you're right. It can be traced back to Pierre Poiret."

"Who was a French mystic and student of Antoinette Bourignon. Wrote her biography."

Isaiah turned to Scott, attempting to keep him in the conversation. "She was charged with sorcery." Then he looked back to Mayhew. "I don't know. Maybe there is no physical Millennial Temple that the Messiah will build. Maybe Jesus Himself will be the Temple. All I know is that a lot of the things the premillennial crowd has been warning about seems to be unfolding. Which tends to make me think they could be right about the rest of it too."

"Or," Mayhew said, "maybe that's a self-fulfilling prophecy. Maybe Poiret's connection to the occult is what influenced his hermeneutic, the occult dream having always been a one-world utopian society."

Again Isaiah fixed him with a curious look.

Scott shook his head. "I'm sorry. Maybe you're using too many Bible words, but I'm not getting it. What does all this have to do with the ring?"

"You asked if the Antichrist breaks a deal he made with Israel."

Scott nodded.

"The deal is a seven-year covenant. According to the Scriptures, he stands in the Temple and breaks that covenant at its midpoint, which is when the Jewish people realize they have been deceived by a false Messiah, and they begin running for their lives." He started leading them back toward the house. "So according to this particular end-times view, there *will* be a Temple in Jerusalem during the last seven years, built by the Antichrist, with animal sacrifices taking place. But, again, this Temple cannot be the one the true Messiah builds, but will be the one He *destroys* upon His return. That's why my brother is"—he choked on the word and corrected himself—"*was* opposed to its being built."

"And why are you opposed to it being built?" Mayhew asked.

"My Christian theology of grace, the finished work of Christ on the cross, and the writings of Paul make it impossible for me to recognize a rejuvenated system of Judaism as something that can possibly bring honor to God. As Jesus said, 'If you reject me, you reject the Father.' A new Temple with a reinstated sacrificial system meant to atone for sin already paid for would be a rejection of Christ's work."

Scott slowed to a stop, trying to connect the dots. "So you're saying that Daniel's prophecy includes a Jewish Temple being built in Jerusalem. Put in place by the Antichrist, who I'm assuming you believe to be the coming leader of the New World Order."

"Exactly."

He started walking again. "Okay, so how does the ring and this Copper Scroll play into all that?"

"As your friend Titus said, the Copper Scroll contains sixty-four distinct sections. And each one begins with the description of a hiding place and ends with a description of what can be found in that hiding place. Most of the treasure is described as silver, gold, or some other precious material. Except for the last one. In that case, the treasure described seems to be of some other nature while also including what many believe to be the key needed to decipher the scroll. I can't remember exactly what the sixty-fourth section says, but I know that Father Baer had it written down in one of his books."

Mayhew hadn't been in the room when Isaiah mentioned the priest having additional books, so Scott was looking for some kind of reaction from him. But the reference must've passed over his head, because he didn't even bat an eye.

"The list seems to be written in some kind of code, but in order to decipher it, one needs the key. And the key was hidden along with the copy of the scroll in the last described hiding place. There are also mysterious Greek letters in the margin of the first columns. No one knows what they are, but it's believed that they can be explained with the key."

Scott's brow furrowed, and he slowed down. "You said *was* hidden."

"That's because it *was* hidden. A long time ago."

"Did they find it?"

Isaiah began walking faster. "It's possible that the treasures listed are comprised of sacred objects reserved for the priesthood. In the text describing the last treasure, there are seven letters followed by a gap that was caused by deterioration on the far edge of the scroll. There's a lot of speculation around those seven letters, whether they're two words or one. Father Baer, through his studies, came to believe that it was one word, a Greek loanword meaning 'the first sheet of a papyrus roll.' The Copper Scroll's first sheet was blank, but Father Baer believed that the description at the end of the scroll referred back to the 'first sheet' of the corresponding duplicate, since the duplicate is associated with the interpretive key and is part of the last treasure. In other words, Father Baer came to the conclusion that what was omitted at the beginning of the Copper Scroll was, in fact, included in its duplicate. He believed the duplicate scroll would also have a blank spot that could only be filled in by the Copper Scroll."

"So only a person with both scrolls would be able to find the treasures," Mayhew said.

"Yes. My brother believed that the last treasure would comprise a duplicate scroll, a key that could explain or decipher it, and that together they would lead to the items dedicated to the priesthood."

Scott's head was beginning to throb again, and he wanted to get back inside the warm home. Maybe curl up under a blanket and sleep until all this end-of-days prophecy stuff worked itself out. "So to summarize for the idiot in the group, the Copper Scroll would play an important role in getting the Temple rebuilt."

"If it reveals the location of the hidden instruments dedicated to the priesthood, then yes."

Isaiah led them onto a concrete path and took it to the back door of his house. As he opened it, he said, "I said *was* hidden because the secret societies found the duplicate scroll a long time ago."

Scott stopped. "What?"

"And what about the key?" Mayhew asked.

"Only a ring." And then Isaiah walked into the house.

"How do you know that?" Mayhew asked, going in after him.

"Because one of the Templars who found it said so in his journal. Father Baer read the Knight's account with his own eyes."

"Where?" asked Scott.

"The Vatican. Where else?"

# 32.

*"Shall we expect some transatlantic military giant to step over the ocean and crush us at a blow? Never! All the enemies of Europe, Asia and Africa combined, with all the treasures of earth (our own excepted) in their military chest; with a Bonaparte for a commander, could not by force, take a drink from the Ohio, or make a track on the Blue Ridge, in a trial of a thousand years...If destruction be our lot, we must ourselves be its author and finisher. As a nation of freemen, we must live through all time, or die by suicide."*

— Abraham Lincoln

Isaiah hung his jacket over a kitchen chair. "Have a seat. I'll make you some lunch."

Scott and Mayhew didn't object, and they pulled off their own jackets before sitting down at the table while Isaiah opened the fridge.

"Grilled cheese okay?"

"Yes," they both answered in unison.

Then Scott leaned back and folded his arms. "So the ring is the key the Copper Scroll mentions?"

"Appear so," Isaiah answered.

Mayhew frowned. "I don't understand. You said the secret societies found it a long time ago. But this ring was just found."

"The ring that my brother and Father Baer were searching for wasn't the one the Templars found."

Mayhew thought about it. "So the Templar Knights found the duplicate scroll and the ring beneath the Temple Mount?"

Isaiah nodded, though Scott found it odd that Mayhew didn't have a reaction to finding out there was a second ring in play.

"And the secret orders have been passing them down through the centuries, unable to use them without the Copper Scroll...which was discovered in 1952. But now they do have all three things."

Scott tapped the table. "Yet they're still trying to get this other ring."

Isaiah flipped the sandwiches in the pan. "I'm assuming the explanation was in one of Father Baer's books. As for myself, I don't know. Benjamin called me once, excited that they'd found another piece of the puzzle. Said he wanted to stop by and show me, but then all of a sudden they decided to drop it. I never found out what it was they'd discovered."

"They weren't just after the Temple's treasures listed in the scroll," Scott realized. "They were specifically after the sixty-fourth line. Why?"

"Whatever it is," Isaiah answered, "it would undoubtedly provide justification for building the next Temple in Jerusalem. And so they decided that whatever it was, it should be left in the hands of God. That actually finding it would only lead to the very thing they opposed. If the Temple was going to be built, they didn't want it on their hands. If a Judas had to betray Jesus, they didn't want it to be them."

Scott took a deep breath, suddenly unable to grasp how he'd gotten here. Just a few days ago everything was normal. And now, just because he happened to catch the tail end of a news report, here he was. Stuck neck deep in some kind of international treasure hunt that would somehow decide who ruled the world. "Do you have any idea what it could be?"

But it was Mayhew who answered in a whisper, his lips barely parting. "The Ark of the Covenant."

Isaiah flipped the grilled cheese again. "Yes."

****

After having not eaten anything in over twenty-four hours, Scott let the melted cheese and buttered bread take his mind off the four puzzle pieces that were somehow supposed to fit together to reveal the hiding place of the lost Ark of the Covenant.

The sandwich tasted so good that it somehow triggered a memory of his wife. Which made him think of Cindy. And then the enjoyment of it was gone, and he finished the rest of it in two bites.

Though Mr. Smith—*Benjamin*—hadn't mentioned the Ark, Scott was now able to return to their conversation and fill in the blanks accordingly. It was the Ark that everyone was after. Not to create an invincible army like the Nazis had wanted in that old *Raiders of the Lost Ark* movie, but as an incentive to rebuild the Temple and to rebuild it on the finder's own terms. "Can the Temple be built without the Ark?" Scott asked, breaking the silence that had come over the room.

Isaiah, sitting in a folding chair taken from a closet in another room, swallowed a bite of his own sandwich. "The last Temple was without it, so I suppose so. Something extraordinary needs to push the world into allowing it though."

"Benjamin told me that if it is found, it'll propel the Jews into a war with the Muslims and that they'll destroy Mecca and reclaim the Temple Mount by force."

"I know. It grieves me as both a Jew and a Christian. It's exactly what the globalists want, a war between Jews and Muslims. Albert Pike, the head of Scottish Rite Freemasonry, wrote about a final war which he thought would be necessary to usher in the New World Order. He said that igniting a crisis between Islam and Judaism would create a conflict between two superpowers, and that the Order would rise in its aftermath. They're using Zionism and radical Islam as a means to destroy both religions." He got up from the table.

"Fulfilling H. G. Wells's vision put forth in *The Shape of Things to Come*?" Mayhew wondered aloud.

"Ah." Isaiah smiled. "The 1933 story that describes a future world government that persecutes and destroys Christianity and all other religions. Something that's presented as a good and necessary act." He took a drink of water. "That's their ultimate agenda, an anti-religious world order, though in reality it'll be very religious. The Theosophical Society of which most of these people are members is a spiritual and religious society that is waiting for their *Masonic* Christ, or their so-called 'perfected man.' What some might call the Antichrist." He paused. "Coffee?"

"That would be wonderful," replied Mayhew.

Scott gathered the dishes and took them to the sink as Isaiah went about making a pot of coffee. As he rinsed the plates, Scott asked Isaiah what his story was. How he ended up here.

"My father and mother came over from Israel just two years after they married. Benjamin and I were both born here. By the time I was five years old, my mother was desperate to see the family she'd left behind in Israel. There was no way my parents could afford for all of us to go, so they decided my mother would go with Benjamin, who was only one at the time. A few days after she arrived, my mother was killed by a suicide bomber while out shopping with my aunt. Benjamin was left to be raised by my mother's family in Israel. It wasn't until after college that I saw him again. He'd come back over to the States, working for the Mossad. At that point, I was into the whole Kabbalah thing, and we found that his Orthodoxy and my mystic training didn't get along very well. But we were blood, and that ended up being enough to ensure our friendship. A few years later I became a Messianic Jew." He smiled. "Benjamin couldn't understand that one. At first he wouldn't speak to me, but love covers a multitude of sins, and he got over it." He poured water into the machine. "Not that we didn't try converting each other every chance we got."

Scott dried the plates with a towel as the machine began to percolate. Isaiah turned and leaned against the counter, facing them.

"He'd give me reports on the happenings in Israel, the clashing ideologies of the religious and the secular. His heart had always been for the Jewish people to return to God, and by then it had become my heart as well, though obviously in a very different way. So we shared our love for the Land and for her people. Only he saw a need for them to return to the Law, and I saw only a need for them to acknowledge the Messiah who had already fulfilled the Law. His orthodoxy insisted that the Messiah would come and set everything in order in His time, seeing any human interference as sin. He was strongly against the Temple Movement." He smiled again and then switched gears a little. "It was always a dream of his to find the Ark. And then one day he met Father Baer in Jerusalem. Despite their obvious theological differences, their mutual obsession with finding the Ark overlooked anything else they might disagree on. But"—he pushed himself away from the counter—"like I said, they had an insider's perspective into what was happening in both the Vatican and in Israel, and they saw what was coming. They knew they weren't the only ones looking for the Ark, that there were other forces after it. And, after much soul-searching, they determined that they wouldn't aid them in the search, that the Ark should remain hidden until the Messiah came back and settled everything on His own terms and in His own time."

He pulled at an itch on his earlobe. "Why they decided to get involved again after all this time… I can only imagine they caught wind of the second ring having been discovered and wanted to prevent it from falling into the Illuminati's hands."

"The Illuminati?" Skepticism accented Mayhew's voice and his face.

But Isaiah didn't elaborate. He just poured three cups of coffee and walked into the living room.

The room contained a bookshelf and a few tables that served as platforms for lamps. Some pictures hung on the wall beside a window, and three armchairs were positioned in the corners.

Mayhew watched the snow fall past the window as he sat. "What made you decide to move out here in the middle of nowhere?"

"You mean instead of joining your Resistance?"

"Yeah."

"The church was given a different mission, Mr. Mayhew."

"Sounds like a cop-out."

Isaiah's eyes twinkled at that, and the lines around his eyes tightened. "Nowhere are Christ's followers instructed or encouraged to kill so that their way of life may be preserved or even bettered." H shook his head. "The faith has become imperialized again, and the church can't even find her way through all its doublespeak. Love your enemies: kill terrorists. Turn the other cheek: defend your way of life. The shroud of Turin a nation's flag. The church was played by the Establishment. Enough patriotism sprinkled onto pulpit and pew to make people like you"—he stared unwavering into Mayhew's eyes—"pick up a gun and join in whatever war was being waged against the Gospel of Democracy." He waved his hand as if to dismiss what he just said. "I'm sorry. You didn't come here to be lectured on Patriotic Christianity and its share of responsibility in all this."

"Don't you worry out here all alone?" Scott asked.

Isaiah smiled. "You mean, if they come for me? My time on this planet and the means to its end was determined before I even took my first breath on it. No one can change that."

Mayhew folded his arms across his chest. "You say that now. What about when they're pushing you into an oven?"

Isaiah took a sip of coffee. "Let me tell you a little story." He looked at Scott as he began. "Assyria was the first to put their reason for attacking other nations into writing. They said they did it because the gods told them to. They were perhaps the most vile and wicked army of all time. Anyone who refused to declare their allegiance to them was flayed alive, crucified, or impaled, their skin actually used as wallpaper. King Ashurnasirpal actually bragged about his atrocities, what he did to men, women, and children. Their people were so cruel that nations would simply surrender to them. It was the Assyrian army that the three hundred Persians fought. It was also Assyria that God sent the prophet Jonah to. No wonder Jonah didn't want to go. Not only did he risk having his flesh wallpapering the king's chambers, but he didn't want them to repent of their wicked ways and come into God's good graces.

He wanted God to judge them. So he tried running away, but he ultimately found himself telling the Assyrians that they needed to repent. And they didn't skin him alive or impale him. Instead, they did repent. Eventually, they fell back into their wicked ways and were about to destroy Israel when an angel of the Lord showed up and killed all one hundred and eighty-five thousand Assyrian soldiers. Soon after that, Assyria disappeared beneath the sand. God took care of them, and Israel didn't have to lift a finger."

He took another sip. "My point is two-fold. First, how can the church know to whom God wishes to extend His grace." He looked at Mayhew. "Actually, we do know, don't we? He wishes to extend His grace to everyone. And the church is supposed to be the vehicle through which He makes it known. The church is supposed to *be* Him. And in that way, we are all Jonahs, aren't we? Running from our calling. Secondly, God protected Jonah through his task and then miraculously defended Israel. So again, I'm not afraid of any man or what he can do to this mortal coil"—he patted his chest with an open palm—"so I don't particularly concern myself with your Revolution."

"So you just let the world burn around you while you sing hallelujah?"

"On the contrary. I believe the church is very much concerned with life because God is concerned with life. But that's not what I'm talking about and you know it."

Scott lifted the mug to his lips and hoped the hot liquid would dispel the fatigue fogging his brain. He didn't know which end of this dialogue was up. Could hardly think straight. But he could sense a silent debate raging between these two, an argument being communicated through sideways glances and theological innuendo.

"You two are free to stay here as long as you want," Isaiah said, apparently picking up on Scott's mental exhaustion.

"Thank you," Mayhew replied, finally setting aside their differences.

But Scott found his hand subconsciously feeling for the phone in his pocket, and again he wondered what Isaiah could possibly tell him that would make him want to use it. Or perhaps this was just Benjamin's way of informing his brother of what was happening, a message sent from someone he would be more likely to trust. He sipped more coffee and gazed out the window. "You sound like Jack. The guy Melissa Strauss sent the ring to."

"Jack Cairns?"

"Yeah, you heard of him?"

"I have two of his books."

"Small world."

"Indeed it is." He took a sip of his own coffee. "It's two o'clock. If you want, you can shower and get some sleep. I have two extra bedrooms. One of them has a sofa bed, the other a single."

It sounded like one of the best things Scott had ever heard in his life.

"Don't mind if I do," Mayhew said. He stood up, and Isaiah signaled to where the bathroom and bedrooms were.

"There are towels and washcloths under the sink. There's a washer and dryer in the closet up there too if you want to wash your clothes."

"Thank you again, Isaiah." And then Mayhew walked out of the room and disappeared up the stairs.

"The rings, do you know what they are? I mean, how they could work as a key?" Scott asked. He hoped Isaiah wasn't getting tired of answering his questions. He had a few more.

"I have no idea. And I don't know if my brother knew either. If they did, I imagine it would be in Father Baer's other books."

"Do you think that the book of Tobit and the *Testament of Solomon* could be accurate in their supernatural description of the ring?"

"You mean, do I think they actually controlled demons? I doubt it. I don't think demons really built the Temple. Could there be some kind of mysterious power exhibited by the rings? I don't know. You've seen one of them, I haven't."

Scott thought about it, remembered how it had so transfixed him. "The centerpiece seems to be some kind of polished lens.

A clear gem that's open underneath. The band looked like gold."

"I don't know."

Scott tried another question. "When I first met Father Baer, he said something about Roswell."

"Roswell…" The word seemed to stick on his tongue for a moment. He was thinking. "Are you sure?"

"Yeah. He asked me about July 1947."

He took another sip, mulling it over. "Interesting."

"You know what he meant? What he was talking about?"

"No, not really. But there has been talk within some eschatological circles of some kind of coming UFO deception."

Scott frowned. "For what purpose?"

"Something to do with establishing a single world religion. The New Agers have been teaching for a long time that one day our 'space brothers' will show up and save us, reveal our individual godhood and the such. Panspermia, life originating from another planet, our ET ancestors holding the keys to the universe. Some prophecy buffs even believed that the Antichrist would be perceived as an alien."

"An alien?"

"I'm not saying they're right, but they've been expecting that some kind of ufology will be part of the deception. What that has to do with the rings, I have no idea. Again, I imagine it would be in his other books."

But Father Baer hadn't said anything about any other books, and again he wondered if maybe David could have taken them. He remembered the loose piece of twine in the bag that had presumably held *all* the books together… But if David took them, why would he leave any of the others behind? Because the priest would've noticed if the bag was empty? "What about the drawings in the two books we do have?"

"Now you're peeling the lid off a whole other can of worms. The triangles, the pentagrams, the rose and cross, the double-headed phoenix…the occult agenda."

"You talking Illuminati stuff?"

He stifled a yawn. "The Apostle Paul called Satan's plan to usher in a world leader 'the mystery of iniquity' in Second

Thessalonians chapter two. He said its operation was underway even in his own day—two thousand years ago. That was a long time for Satan to be conspiring on the world stage to ready the nations for his Antichrist." He lifted his frame out of the chair and stretched. "Here," he said, walking over to a bookshelf. "I have a little book of my own on that agenda. Keep in mind, however, that I penned it well before the Transition and the formation of the NAU." As he pulled a composition book out from between two large titles, he continued to say, "Many people don't realize this, but the America for which the Resistance is fighting was far from being founded as a Christian nation. Here." He handed the book to Scott. "The triangle and the pentalpha Father Baer drew are products of Pythagoras. The pagan trinity found in the forty-seventh proposition of Euclid. Hermeticism." He waved the book. "It's all in here. Enough of it, anyway."

Scott took it from his hands, unsure if he could handle yet another layer of this multidimensional puzzle. "Father Baer called something out to me before he died, but I couldn't hear it all. Sounded like he said 'rose.'"

"Mmm… Rosicrucianism. A secret society said to be the forerunner of modern Freemasonry. They like to trace their origins back to the mysteries of ancient Egypt. It was the first of the secret societies to establish itself in the New World, in Ephrata, Pennsylvania. Francis Bacon was even the chief of the Order." He stared at the book in his hand. "Remember the image of the double-headed phoenix standing behind Christ on the cross, the Latin phrase taken from Psalms 17:8? It's a Rosicrucian piece of artwork that's in the Library of Congress." He looked up from the book. "Do you know what the symbol of the cross represents?"

*Death. Torture.* "Christianity?" he asked instead.

"And the rose?"

"Secrecy."

Isaiah nodded. "Representing the mystery religions. The rose and the cross are the joining of the two."

"The occult and Christianity?"

"Because Rosicrucianism bordered on being witchcraft, it had to find a way to stay hidden from the church. It did this by adopting Christian rhetoric, making themselves appear as servants of God. Professing Christ in the open, they swam in the occult at night. Perhaps that's how someone like Charles Thompson, a person closely related to Peter Miller and a well-known Rosicrucian and *leader* of the Ephrata community, could translate both the Old and New Testament while at the same time approve the all-seeing eye of Horus floating in the detached capstone of the Great Pyramid on the US Seal. Even helped Franklin translate the Declaration of Independence into a number of European languages." Another sip of steaming coffee. "This is why many of the Founders, known Freemasons, could pass as Christians. It's how America could be considered a so-called Christian nation while its capital is a monument to pagan ideology and humanistic philosophy. If you want to understand what is happening now, you have to understand the past and all the things that led us here."

"And what led you here? To this stuff?" Edward had never mentioned anything about this.

"My interest in Kabbalah, which is the Jewish adaptation of the occult, opened my eyes to certain things. But when my son was born, somehow I knew that I should protect him from the esoteric things I had dabbled in. So I began to process what I learned from a different angle. When Benjamin told me that the Star of David was the star of Rephan referenced in the book of Amos—"

But Scott cut him off. "You had a son?"

"I had a family. A wonderful wife and two little boys." He stared down into the mug. "They were all killed in a car accident. Other driver was texting, wasn't watching the road."

Scott didn't know what to say.

"I imagine I'll be seeing them soon." It was a statement that he seemed to find comfort in.

After a few quiet moments, once they could hear Mayhew turning on the water above them, Scott asked his final question. "What exactly is the Ark of the Covenant?"

Isaiah smiled through wonderful memories, and the pain they provoked, before turning back to the bookshelf. He pulled out a large book and handed it to him. "Look it up."

It was a Bible encyclopedia.

"Go on," he instructed, "get washed up and get some rest. We'll talk later." But before he left the room, he met Scott's eyes. "I think God has a special plan for you in all this, Mr. Scott."

"That's what your brother said."

"My brother was a smart man."

Scott stood and nodded. "Thank you." He reached out his hand, the two books cradled in the other.

Isaiah shook his hand. "You're welcome. I hope you figure out what Benjamin wanted you to see here."

"I'm beginning to think that this was more about you and him than me."

Isaiah's lips spread in a warm but sad smile as his eyes seemed to acknowledge the fact that his brother had just said goodbye to him through the words of a stranger. "Remember," he said, "Satan doesn't deceive by revealing himself as the Devil, he deceives by masquerading as an angel of light, as a servant of God. His real work is never done out in the open but under the cover of some grand illusion. Many have fallen victim to his deceptions while believing it was actually the voice of God they were obeying."

"I'll keep that in mind."

They shook hands again, and then left the room through different avenues. As Scott climbed the stairs, he could hear Isaiah begin to cry.

"Your turn," Mayhew said as he walked past him, his hair still wet. His shirt was only buttoned halfway, and Scott could see that a tattoo covered his chest. It was a cross.

"Thanks." The image brought back pieces of Isaiah's words, all of which followed him into the shower.

# 33.



*"We are dominated by a relatively small number of persons... It is they who pull the wires which control the public mind and who harness social forces and contrive new ways to bind and guide the world."*

—Edward Bernays

Scott opened his eyes to a blinding light. Immediately, he sat up, ready to fight whoever was standing there beneath the bare bulb hanging from the ceiling. But it wasn't a bare bulb that was blinding him, and he wasn't in a concrete room in Iran.

Once his mind caught up to his current circumstances, he turned away from the lamp on the nightstand and looked to the window. It was dark out. He'd slept longer than he'd intended. He sat up in the bed and rubbed his eyes. Then he reached for the two books that Isaiah had given him.

He opened the first one to a random page and began skimming the text.

Francis Bacon.

He flipped to another page.

Rosicrucians.

He yawned and kept turning pages.

Stonehenge. The 77th Meridian. New Atlantis. Charles L'Enfant. William Morgan. The Hell-Fire Club. Aleister Crowley. Francis Dashwood. Manly P. Hall. The Pythagorean Theory. John Dee. Knights of the Helmet. Shakespeare. Apollo and Athena. Columbus. Knights of Christ. Rosslyn Chapel. Baal. Osiris. Skull and Bones. House Resolution 33. The New Deal. The Hermetic axiom. The Federal Triangle. Destiny.

It nearly sent him back to sleep with a new headache, so he decided that book would have to wait until morning and a couple of cups of coffee. He replaced it with the encyclopedia, and turned to the As. He found what he was looking for after "Arkite" and before "Arm" and "Armageddon."

Ark of the Covenant, Ark of the Testimony.

He started reading.

> The Ark of the Covenant was constructed while the Hebrews were wandering in the desert and was used until the destruction of the First Temple. It was perhaps the most important symbol within the Jewish faith and was the only physical manifestation of God's presence on earth.

> According to Exodus 25:10–22 and Deuteronomy 10:2–5, God instructed Moses to make the Ark out of acacia wood. After constructing it in accordance with God's precise directions, he was to overlay it with pure gold inside and out. Rings of gold were to be put at the corners where staves covered with gold could be inserted for carrying the Ark. The kapporet, an atonement cover, was to be made of gold and was to have two gold cherubim flanking the mercy seat, the mercy seat to be sprinkled with the blood of a sacrificial bull once a year on Yom Kippur.

> *And thou shalt put the mercy seat above upon the ark; and in the ark thou shalt put the testimony that I shall give thee. And there I will meet with thee, and I will commune with thee from above the mercy seat, from between the two cherubims which are upon the ark of the testimony, of all things which I will give thee in commandment unto the children of Israel (Ex. 25:21,22).*

> *And the LORD said unto Moses, Speak unto Aaron thy brother, that he come not at all times into the holy place within the veil before the mercy seat, which is upon the ark; that he die not: for I will appear in the cloud upon the mercy seat (Lev. 16:2).*

Scott skimmed over the dimensions of the Ark, their meaning, if there was one, lost on him.

He came to another section.

> The Ark of the Covenant was used to carry the tablets containing the Ten Commandments after they were revealed to Moses on Mount Sinai. The Ark of the Covenant disappeared after the Babylonians destroyed Jerusalem in 597 BC. Until that time, it was kept within the Holy of Holies, the most sacred area of the Temple, accessible only to the High Priest on Yom Kippur.
>
> The Ark is described as being very powerful. It went before the Israelites in the wilderness journeys to "find them a place of rest (Ex. 40:20)." It was instrumental in the crossing of the Jordan (Josh. 3) and in the capture of Jericho (4:7-11). Joshua prayed before the Ark after the defeat at Ai (Josh. 7:6) and after the victory at Mount Ebal (Josh. 8:33). Eli's wicked sons took the Ark into battle against the Philistines, and it was captured. At which time "the glory departed from Israel (1 Sam 4:3–22)." The Philistines eventually gave the Ark back after a plague came upon them.
>
> The whereabouts of the Ark are not mentioned again after the Temple's destruction. Many historians believe that it was probably destroyed, but some traditions report that it was removed or hidden before the Babylonians invaded. One account credits the Jews for this possibility, while another credits the Ethiopian Emperor Menelik I—the alleged son of King Solomon and the Queen of Sheba.
>
> The book of Hebrews (9:4) says that the Ark contained a gold jar of manna, Aaron's budded staff, and the stone tablets of the covenant.
>
> The fate of the Ark of the Covenant will likely remain a mystery for the foreseeable future.

When Scott turned to the next page, he found two loose pieces of paper folded in half and tucked between the pages.

He unfolded them and saw that someone's small handwriting covered both sides of them.

*During King Solomon's reign, and just several years after the Ark was placed within the newly built Temple, the Queen of Sheba came to visit him. Ethiopian history declares that the Queen married King Solomon and that together they had a son. The Ethiopian Royal Chronicles recorded their son as actually being Prince Menelik I of Ethiopia. While living in Jerusalem and being educated by the priests of the Temple, Menelik is believed to have become a strong believer in the God of Israel. In 1935,* **National Geographic** *interviewed priests from different parts of Ethiopia, and all of them had only one story to tell: that the Queen of Sheba had a son with King Solomon (Menelik I) who was educated by Solomon until he was nineteen. Their story goes on to say that the boy later returned to Ethiopia with a large group of Jews and with the true Ark of the Covenant. Many of these people believe that the Ark is now in some church along the northern boundary of present-day Ethiopia, near Aduwa or Aksum. The* **Encyclopedia Britannica** *also tried to confirm this tradition…*

*Menelik I was the founder of the longest-lived monarchy in history, and former emperor Haile Selassie actually claimed direct descent from the line of Solomon. In 1974, the emperor was imprisoned during a Communist Coup and died a year later under mysterious circumstances while in jail. Some of his family, however, managed to escape. One of his family members, living in Toronto, was said to have confirmed that the Church of Zion of Mary, in Aksum, was reported to be the storehouse of the Ark of the Covenant. Glory of the Kings, the official Ethiopian national epic, tells a story of how the Ark was transported out of Jerusalem. Along with this story were a couple of Ethiopian murals depicting Prince Menelik I taking the Ark to Ethiopia for safekeeping. According to the story, Solomon, after the Queen of Sheba had died and Menelik I was preparing to leave for his own kingship in Ethiopia, made a replica of the Ark to send with him, knowing that his son's long journey would prevent him from ever worshiping in Jerusalem again. But Menelik had been greatly concerned with Israel's state of affairs, with his father's idolatry and his allowance of pagan idols to be placed within the Temple. So after Solomon gave a banquet for his son and the priests were all drunk, Menelik and his loyal followers switched the replica ark with the real one, taking it all the way to Ethiopia with them. A group of priests, with representatives from each of the tribes of Israel, went with him, taking the Ark for safekeeping until Israel turned from her idol worship and came back to worshipping the one true and living God. However, Israel never wholly returned to worshipping God, and so the Ark has never been returned.*

*The descendants of Menelik I and his followers from the various tribes of Israel called themselves Beta-Israel — today called Falasha Jews. Other theories, however, take the Ark even beyond Ethiopia. In 1935, a Jewish magazine stated that the Ark of the Covenant had been removed from Ethiopia and taken to the mountain strongholds of Abyssinia for safekeeping due to the impending Italian invasion. There was also a 1981 report by the* Toronto Star *that told of a 1936 attempt to get the Ark insured against war damage...*

Scott folded the first paper and stared at the wall. He was surprised to discover that he'd apparently gotten over being confused by all this nonsense, it having apparently become his new normal. He didn't bother wasting time on wondering how he'd ended up here either. He was past those questions too.

He looked down to the second page, on which a portion of Matthew chapter six had been written out by the same hand.

*Take no thought for your life, what ye shall eat, or what ye shall drink; nor yet for your body, what ye shall put on. Is not the life more than meat, and the body than raiment? Behold the fowls of the air: for they sow not, neither do they reap, nor gather into barns; yet your heavenly Father feedeth them. Are ye not much better than they? Which of you by taking thought can add one cubit unto his stature? And why take ye thought for raiment? Consider the lilies of the field, how they grow; they toil not, neither do they spin: And yet I say unto you, That even Solomon in all his glory was not arrayed like one of these. Wherefore, if God so clothe the grass of the field, which today is, and tomorrow is cast into the oven, shall he not much more clothe you, O ye of little faith? Therefore take no thought, saying, What shall we eat? or, What shall we drink? or, Wherewithal shall we be clothed? (For after all these things do the Gentiles seek:) for your heavenly Father knoweth that ye have need of all these things. But seek ye first the kingdom of God, and his righteousness; and all these things shall be added unto you. Take therefore no thought for the morrow: for the morrow shall take thought for the things of itself. Sufficient unto the day is the evil thereof.*

He closed the encyclopedia on the loose pages and set it back on the nightstand. Then he turned over onto his back and stared up at the ceiling, Jesus' words picking at his brain, bringing up his past.

A picture hanging on the wall caught his eye. It was a picture of Jerusalem with a verse written across it.

*I will rejoice over Jerusalem and take delight in my people. The sound of weeping and of crying will be heard in it no more. Isaiah 66:19.*

Scott wondered if that verse would ever be realized.

****

This time when Scott opened his eyes, there were men standing around his bed. He tried blinking them away, but the men in ski masks and carrying automatic weapons stayed right where they were.

An unmasked face came into the frame, peering down at him. "Hello, Joshua."

Scott shook his head. "Think you got the wrong house, mister." The last time someone addressed him by his real name, things hadn't turned out so great. And Cindy had wound up dead because of it.

One of the masked men reached down and grabbed him, dragging him out of the bed and dropping him onto the floor.

Scott sat up and looked around at all the guns aimed at his head.

"Don't do anything stupid," the unmasked guy said. "I know you were CIA, but they're Delta."

"What do you want?" Scott asked as more plastic wire ties were zipped onto his already wounded wrists.

"Stand up."

He thought about making a grab for one of their guns, but the guy across the room was aiming an M26 Modular Accessory Shotgun System at his face. An M4 with a shotgun mounted to the handguard. No way he was dodging all that.

He struggled to his feet. "I'd salute too, but you tied my hands behind my back."

The man ignored the comment. "We have a job for you."

Now Scott wasn't so sure he was awake.

"You're going to get the ring back from your Mossad friends and give it to us."

"I am?"

He nodded patiently. "Yes, you are."

"I don't know where they went."

The guy walked over to the bed and pulled the tiny phone that Malachi had given him out from beneath the pillow. "But you know how to get in touch with them."

Scott had no idea how he could've known about the phone.

"We're willing to erase you from our records, to forget you ever existed. We'll even set you up in Canada with a new life.

That's where you wanted to go, right? All you have to do is get us the ring."

"I have a better idea," he answered. "Why don't you just go to hell instead?"

"You'd rather die than help us, is that it?"

He feigned thinking about it. "That's about the sum of it, yeah."

"Even if we were to use a rusty saw blade?"

Scott blinked and hoped the guy couldn't see the hairs that just stood up on his arms and neck.

"Here." The guy held a manila folder out to him.

"Cute."

Now it was the guy having fun. "Sorry." He opened up the file and spilled its contents onto the bed so that Scott could see them.

Someone's personal file.

He almost shrugged, lost as to what it was supposed to mean to him. And then his heart froze in his chest, and he couldn't breathe. His muscles bulged, the plastic reopening the cuts in his wrists, veins surfacing in his neck.

There was a picture with the printout.

Jennifer May Cavanaugh.

His wife.

In an attempt to keep her safe, he'd gotten rid of all the pictures he had of her. And so this was the first time in over ten years (other than the picture hanging before his mind's eye), that he'd seen her face. Naturally, she looked older than he remembered, but she seemed to have aged well. She was beautiful.

Lifting his eyes from the only person he'd ever really cared about, or who had ever cared about him, he stared at the man, daring him to even utter her name.

"I guess you recognize her," he said. He crossed his arms.

Scott didn't respond.

"She's in a camp. Picked up yesterday after martial law was declared in her city. That would be Buffalo, New York. I'm guessing not far from where you were hiding. She moved in with her sister when you never came home. She thinks you're dead."

Still Scott said nothing.

"Don't worry, we took the liberty of informing her of your well-being. Though, I think she may have gotten the wrong impression. About why you left her, I mean." He sat on the edge of the bed. "She's a very attractive woman. I'm sure she'll have no trouble making all kinds of new friends at her new home."

Scott re-evaluated the situation and realized that they actually did need him to help get them the ring. Which meant that the guy with the shotgun wasn't really a threat after all.

The man continued, "Have your friends come pick you up. Then all you have to do is grab the ring when you get a chance. Your wife will be let go, and you can spend the rest of your lives together out in a log cabin somewhere."

It would be tempting if it were true.

"What do you say?" he asked.

And before he could stop himself, Scott lifted his leg and planted his foot right in the guy's chest. The guy, CIA or NAU Intelligence no doubt, flew backward and tumbled off the other side of the bed.

Scott's face was suddenly pressed into the floor.

Rubbing his chest and wincing from a cracked rib, the guy walked over to Scott and kicked him in the face, which only made him wince more.

Scott felt blood rush out of his nose.

"Your friends told you to toss the phone once you contacted them," the man said. "Don't. Keep it and call us when you have the ring. You have three days. By then your wife will be of no value to us." He turned toward the door. "If you waste that time trying to look for her, I'll see that whatever you do find will be in really small pieces." He left the room, and the soldiers followed him out.

Scott got to his feet and ran after them, reaching the stairs just as the last of the soldiers was walking out the front door. It slammed shut, and the house was plunged into silence.

"Isaiah!" Scott called out, running down the stairs with his hands still bound behind his back. "Mayhew!"

No answers.

He went into the kitchen and retrieved a knife from a drawer by the sink. After cutting the bands, he ran throughout the house, calling out for Isaiah and Mayhew.

He found Isaiah still in his bed. His throat had been cut, and there was blood all over the sheets. Arterial spray had even reached the wall beside the bed.

Scott left the room in search of Mayhew, sure he'd find him in the same condition.

But there was no sign of him anywhere.

He didn't understand. How had they found him? How did they know about the Mossad and the phone they'd given him? How did they know about his wife?

Then it clicked. He knew exactly how. He just couldn't believe it.

He went back upstairs and pulled on the rest of his clothes. He grabbed Isaiah's book and went to get the priest's books too, but those were gone.

He got the phone and activated the preset number with a trembling hand.

# IV.

# ORDER OF SECRETS

*"And he causeth all, both small and great, rich and poor, free and bond, to receive a mark in their right hand, or in their foreheads: and that no man might buy or sell, save he that had the mark, or the name of the beast, or the number of his name."*

– Revelation 13:16–17

The ocean looked like an infinite sheet of glass that reflected the brilliance of the hanging moon as the three ships gracefully cut a pioneer's path through its silver waves. They were being propelled by a steady wind that filled their white sails—sails splashed with the Red Cross of the Knights of Christ—while an esoteric knowledge of the Earth's great circles, of the lines of power, acted as their secret guide through the night.

The three ships that were sailing had been acquired in Palos de la Frontera, two of which came through an order issued by the Royal Council. The command ship was named *la Callega*. At least until the captain renamed it after a monastery in Huevla— the monastery where he'd met Father Juan Perez de Marchena, the humanist astrologer and cosmographer. The ship was a three-masted square-rigger that carried about forty men, and though Juan de la Cosa was the owner and master of the ship, he was not her captain.

The second ship in size was a three-masted square-rigged caravel carrying twenty-six men, Martin Alonso Pinzon her captain. A four-masted caravel carrying twenty-three men and around sixty tons of cargo was the third and smallest and was captained by Vincente Yanez Pinzon.

The captain of the first ship sat hunched over one of his logbooks. He had two, in fact. One book that recorded the truth and the other his clever tales of deceit. It was important that his men not know how far they had actually traveled. With no real place to sleep or any proper food, things were beginning to grow tense. They had already asked him to turn back more than once, so to prevent a mutiny, he had begun a false account of their journey, letting them think they were better off than they might actually be.

It was the eleventh day of October now. They had left from Palos on August the third, and the only course he'd given his men was that of a westward heading. They eventually reached the Canary Islands and had to remain there for several weeks due to unfavorable winds. They finally left on September sixth after the ships had been repaired.

He looked back through his log to the ninth.

> *Sunday, 9 September. Sailed this day nineteen leagues, and determined to count less than the true number, that the crew might not be dismayed if the voyage should prove long.*

They had sailed sixty leagues on the tenth, but he told the crew it had only been forty-eight. If they discovered his lies, they would surely throw him overboard. He glanced at the previous day's account.

> *Wednesday, 10 October... Here the men lost all patience and complained of the length of the voyage...*

Thankfully, he was able to convince them to continue on for three more days. Rubbing his weary eyes, he prayed again for land, swearing that it had to be close. He shut the true logbook, which he intended to give to the King and Queen, and hid it carefully in the desk, leaving the false one out on top for all to see.

He pulled a key from his pocket and unlocked another drawer. From this one, he retrieved a cluster of old maps and charts. He spread them out across the top of the desk, staring at them beneath the candlelight.

The maps and charts had come from his father-in-law, Bartolomeu Perestrello, the first governor of Madeira and, more importantly, the Grand Master of the Order of Christ—an offshoot of the Templar Knights. The captain had collected them and other writings as part of an inheritance when his father-in-law died. Having been passed down through the Order for centuries, the maps were believed to contain directions leading to a secret land, a land ripe for molding. For putting to practice an ancient philosophy.

He returned the secret maps to their drawer and stretched. It was almost ten o'clock, and he would return to the deck. Though he wasn't looking forward to the plethora of unpleasant looks that would be made at his back.

As he returned to the cool night air, he approached Pedro Gutierrez, making small talk with him while gazing out over the rolling sea. His thoughts were not on the conversation however, but rather how much time he had left before the dark void around him would prove to be his fate.

And then they saw it, both of them.

A light.

"Did you see that?" asked the captain.

"Yes, I did," Pedro answered, peering intently into the night.

But it was gone. They looked for it a while longer but saw no other sign of it.

"Strange, was it not?" The captain sighed and was about to turn when suddenly it appeared again. "There!" He pointed.

"I see it!" yelled Pedro.

The strange glimmering light was some distance away, shooting up and down in quick streaking motions.

Excited by the bizarre phenomenon, they found Rodrigo Sanchez of Segovia and begged him to look, but by that time it had vanished again. Disappointed, the captain walked back to the deck and stared once more toward the spot the mysterious light had shown itself.

He saw it again.

Like the light of a candle moving up and down through the sky.

By now others were beginning to see it too. It was appearing and disappearing out over the ocean, far in the distance. Or perhaps over their destination.

The captain instructed a strict watch be kept upon the forecastle, everyone to be looking for any sign of land.

Turning to the waters behind them, he could make out the two other ships following in their wake. He smiled. Then he retreated to his quarters and hurried to his logbook. He had something fascinating to write about on this eleventh day of October, 1492.

After fumbling about trying to retrieve the genuine logbook from its secret compartment, Christopher Columbus finally had it open on top of the fraudulent copy. Finding the correct spot, he began to record history.

While he wrote, the *Nina*, *Pinta*, and the *Santa Maria* crept closer and closer to a land that would indeed be considered new to the world. However, it would not be the first time that the white flag bearing a red cross had made the journey across the Atlantic.

And despite the evidence of prior visits to the New World (dating all the way back to the time before Christ), and though the Vikings had been there five hundred years before, and of course completely disregarding the natives who were already living there, history would record Christopher Columbus as being the one who *discovered* America. A statue of him would stand in Washington, DC, with an inscription declaring that his "faith and courage gave to mankind a New World."

# 34.



The man had gotten off a plane and into an unmarked black sedan. It was midnight, and he was tired from the long flight. Still, as they drove through the countryside of southern France, he found that he couldn't sleep. He was too scared to sleep. The collection of medals pinned to his chest beneath the sweatshirt did nothing to alleviate his concern. He was dreading this meeting. Last time it had been in New York. He supposed he was glad it wasn't in Dubai or Babylon. Though the next time he had to meet with these people (if there was a next time), he was sure it would be in Babylon. In the renovated UN headquarters.

Anger began to edge the fear. He hated these men. Hated that he was enslaved to them. It was his own fault, of course. He had agreed to their terms a long time ago. Back before he knew what he now knew.

A proud neoconservative, he had openly dedicated his career to helping America become the empire he believed she should be. To his way of thinking, it was her only chance at survival. The republic had stalled at the crossroads and had faced one of two options. Empire or self-destruction. So he had justified the wars, the globetrotting, the coups, and the omniscient military presence as being necessary for her very survival. A different America, he reasoned, was better than no America at all. A ratified Constitution was better than none. And New York as the world capital was better than the absence of New York.

But he knew now that he had been wrong. That he had been used. At first, the people he was on his way to meet had seemed supportive of such an agenda. Which was why he'd agreed to help them. It wasn't until a few years ago that he had learned their true intentions. Their entire scheme.

He shuddered as he thought of them, the tug-of-war game between fear and anger going back and forth. Andrew Jackson and Abraham Lincoln had warned of them. The rulers of the world. The elite. Yet they weren't presidents, prime ministers, kings or queens. They didn't head the CIA, NSA, Mossad, Opus Dei, or even the NAU or UN. They had no traceable ties to the CFR, the old Trilateral Commission, the Club of Rome or any of the old hats the conspiracy theorists had been calling out for a century. No, these men killed presidents and kings.

They were the ones who controlled the planet. The ones who owned the whole world. And they stemmed all the way back to the first international bankers—the Templar Knights. They controlled the money, the markets, and thus the media, the government, and even what most people thought.

These were the people he was going to see. The wizard behind the curtain. The faceless puppeteers. And they scared him to death. Especially now. Now that he knew what they were going to ask of him. Not that he had a choice. If he were to refuse, there would be no return flight home.

He watched as the headlights swept up and onto a path that led to a huge iron gate.

His heart began to beat faster. At first he had seen America's dominance as a promise of permanence. But now he knew that America, like him, had just been used. Used by these men to set the stage for *their* permanence. Used like a rag to wipe away any who stood in their way. And though it was democracy that had been promised, it was something else entirely different.

The Middle East, Russia, China, Venezuela, and all the nations that had stood in the way of their so-call utopia. He had believed they were enemies of democracy, of America. That they stood in the way of his empire. But it was really the elite they had positioned themselves against. And so the moneymen employed the use of America to remove the obstacles, and when they were done, they washed their hands of her, flushing her down the toilet like so much refuse.

No America. No empire. Just the NAU taking over a country teetering on the brink of total collapse.

The headlights illuminated the bars on the gate as it slowly swung open. He could see the huge mansion at the top of the hill. The lights were on. They were waiting for him.

How could he have been so blind? But he knew how. Back when everyone had compared America to Rome right before Rome fell, he had disagreed. Instead, he argued that America was in the exact position Rome had been in before the *Republic* fell, *before* it became an empire. And that was why he did what he did. The ends justify the means and all that.

But now they were going to ask him to do something in which there would be no end to justify. It would just be the end.

And how could he object?

It was now survival of the fittest, and that meant picking a side. He didn't like it. Hated it even. But the choice was obvious.

The car pulled up to the front of the mansion and stopped. Someone opened the back door, and he stepped out, the hood up over his head and concealing his face. Once he was inside, he removed the hood and looked around.

They were all there, waiting for him. Staring at him.

****

Two hours later, he was in the car and headed back to the airport, the meeting playing over and over in his head. He knew he had sold his soul to the Devil tonight, but at least his family would be safe from what was to come.

They had promised him that, at least.

What was to come was a nightmare. A billion more people about to die. Maybe more. Probably more. They said it was part of the overall plan. That NASA and the Pope were waiting. They didn't tell him what they were waiting for, and he didn't ask. They told him he was the most qualified to do what needed to be done, that his service had pleased them in the past.

He looked out the window. He couldn't see anything, but that didn't matter. His mind had no trouble filling the empty space with visions of dead and dying people piling up all along the sides of the road, their flesh rotting away.

He closed his eyes. It didn't help.

Though he'd heard rumors of plans to reduce world population down to five hundred million, he never imagined they would actually attempt to achieve it. Sure, reduce population through sterilization, promoting homosexuality, abortion, or whatever would prevent new births. He was fine with all that. But this?

He began to tremble. Then he wept, hating what he had to do.

Hating that he was too weak to say no.

# 35.



*"The greatest triumphs of propaganda have been accomplished, not by doing something, but by refraining from doing. Great is truth, but still greater, from a practical point of view, is silence about truth."*
— Aldous Huxley, 1946

Malachi had told Scott that a chopper would come by to pick him up in about three hours. In the meantime, Scott had gone outside to bury Isaiah.

The blisters on his hands from the shovel's wooden handle were begging him to slow down, but he couldn't. And even though it was snowing, he was stripped down to his waist and dripping with sweat. So much death.

Tears dripped off his chin as he moved loose earth over Isaiah's body. It seemed as if every person he'd met over the last couple of days had ended up here. The priest. David. Cindy. Benjamin. Isaiah. And of course it had all started with Edward and the three dogs. Would his own wife be next?

He covered Isaiah's face with dirt.

****

He stood beneath a stream of hot water while a torrent of emotion paralyzed him against the shower stall.

Finally, once he could move again, he let out a

shout and threw a punch at the tiled wall, shattering one of the squares. He turned the water off and went to get dressed.

He borrowed a hooded sweatshirt from Isaiah's bedroom closet and then sat down in the very chair Isaiah had been sitting in just a handful of hours ago and talking about Rosicrucianism. He faced the window and watched the snow cover the fresh mound of dirt that was now sitting in the yard. It rested beneath the shadow of a makeshift cross he constructed from the shovel he'd broken in half once he was finished with it.

Sitting there, his mind drifted away from all of the recent global developments (the nuclear bomb in Texas, the President and Prime Minister assassinated) and even the aforementioned list of dead associates. Everything paled in comparison to the person who had just been thrust back into his life.

Jennifer.

She was alive, thank God, but she was a POW in a war she had nothing to do with. She needed him. And *this* was his chance for redemption—not for all the destroyed lives billed to his account, but maybe, at least, for his marriage.

Maybe.

But who was he kidding? The idea of some happy reunion was just a tease. There was no way they would let them live once they had the ring. And they'd kill her if they didn't get it. Or worse. If killing himself would remove her from the equation, then he'd go do it right now. But if she was already in a camp, they wouldn't go through the trouble of releasing her just because he was dead. The guy was right, she was beautiful, and there was no doubt as to how she would be treated in such a place.

He looked at the photograph the guy had left on the bed, and it was like he was seeing her for the first time. The reality of her had diminished over the years, and the pictures he'd stored in his memory had begun to fade. But here she was. She was real. *They* were real. Or had been. He ran his fingers over her face, remembering the feel of her skin, her touch. But even if some miracle did put them back together, would she forgive him? Did she even remember *them*?

He heard the sound of rotors in the distance and stood. Wiped his eyes. As the chopper grew close, the pictures on the walls began to rattle. He put the picture of Jennifer in his pocket and grabbed his jacket off the back of another chair. Then he grabbed Isaiah's book and went out the front door, reverently closing it behind him.

The helicopter was an old UH-60 Black Hawk with a red cross inside a white box painted on its door, indicating its designated use for medical and evacuation missions. It circled the house once before setting down in the field and turning the grass beneath it green once more. Scott climbed inside and found three men waiting for him. Then the earth fell away, and Isaiah's house and fresh grave was fading into the distance.

"Where's your friend?" the man next to him shouted over the chopper.

Scott shook his head.

One of the two pilots turned and looked back. When the agent beside Scott gave the signal to proceed, the pilot gave a thumbs-up and then set the Black Hawk on a new heading.

Scott could tell they were heading northeast, and though the ceiling for the Black Hawk was 19,000 feet, they remained steadily at one hundred. He closed his eyes as the white mountains transitioned into soggy countryside. "How far we going?" he asked.

The man beside him leaned closer.

"How far?" Scott repeated.

"About two hundred miles," he shouted back.

Scott did the math in his head. One hundred and seventy-three miles per hour was 2.9 miles per minute, which would make the ride around an hour and ten minutes long. Heading northeast would take them somewhere in Pennsylvania, maybe near Lake Erie.

The guy leaned over again and more or less confirmed his guesswork. "McKean, Pennsylvania," he said.

It was a few counties away from Erie.

"What's there?" Scott asked.

"You'll see!"

*Great.* These guys excelled at not answering questions. He closed his eyes and let himself drift away to the *whoop-whoop-whoop* of the rotors spinning above his head.

Before he even got a chance to realize he'd fallen asleep, a nudge against his shoulder startled him awake. The Israeli guy was still sitting beside him and was pointing to something on the ground. Scott leaned over and peered down into the wilderness below.

"Over there!" the guy yelled, still pointing. The other two men were focused on the same spot.

The helicopter rose another hundred feet, and then he saw it too—train tracks stretching across the forest floor and leading to a huge compound.

"Here!"

There was a tap on his shoulder again, and he turned to see the guy next to him offering a pair of binoculars. He took them and brought them to his face, quickly focusing on the sight below before it was gone.

Razor wire.

He moved the binoculars to the left and saw boxcars lined up alongside a looming gate. People were being prodded off them like cattle. There was only one historical memory that such a scene provoked, and chills raced up his spine. He looked closer and could see NAU troops forming the people into separate lines before moving them through the gates. A few bodies lay sprawled on the ground by the last box car, and he saw four more get tossed out of it. A military truck pulled up, and soldiers were jumping out and loading the bodies into the bed. He spotted a Buffalo Bills jacket on one of the bodies.

*Buffalo.* Where his wife had been living with her sister.

As they flew out of range, he saw that the separate lines were being determined by gender. And before the wilderness swallowed the camp whole, he saw men and women fighting to stay together as soldiers tried pulling them apart.

He closed his eyes. Could this be the camp his wife was at? He fought the urge to make them go back. To use the M240H machine gun on the guards. To let him run through the camp and look for her.

He wondered if the camp was the result of some Readiness Exercise 1984 thing (REX 84 for short). The program disclosed during the now ancient Iran-Contra hearings of 1987 that oversaw more than eight hundred camps with railroad access built across the US for citizens deemed national security threats. "What do you know about that place?" he yelled. The first thing that went through his mind was all the talk of microwave termination facilities and gassing/crematory facilities he'd heard whispered about over the years. "Do you know what it's for?"

The agent shook his head.

Scott looked back down, but the only thing to see now was the multi-colored inferno that was the fall season in Pennsylvania.

*Microwave termination…*

Then they were descending.

The pilots set the Black Hawk down in a clearing and killed the engine.

Scott hopped out with the other guy and stretched, his body sore from being beat up and digging. He took in the surrounding woods. Saw a handful of men emerge from the forest, carrying a camouflage tarp. They ran over and began pulling it overtop the Black Hawk.

"It is a half-mile walk from here," one of the Israelis said to him as he headed for the woods.

Scott followed after him.

Fifteen minutes later, they were walking down the main street of what looked like an old summer camp, cabins sprinkled randomly throughout the nearby woods. There was one building bigger than the rest, and Scott figured it must be the mess hall or the town hall or maybe both. It had a porch and an old church or town bell fixed above the door. People were walking around and staring at him with curiosity. Two boys stood throwing a baseball back and forth while some girls jumped rope and other kids played a version of freeze tag. A few adults who had been sitting and watching the kids were now studying the procession of armed men making their way through the quaint town.

They turned off the dirt road (Main Street, Scott guessed), and took a path through the grass that led to a large olive-green hospital tent. As they approached, Malachi came out of it, his hand extended toward Scott.

"So Isaiah told you what you needed to hear?" he asked.

"Where else was I gonna go?" Scott shook his hand. "What is this place?"

"Come in," he said.

Scott went in with him while the others dispersed, going their own separate ways. He joined Malachi at a table that was cluttered with equipment. He looked around. Sleeping bags were scattered across the floor, weapons stacked atop more tables. He figured the place was home to about fifteen of Isaiah's Mossad agents.

"It's a Christian commune," Isaiah explained.

Scott leaned back in the chair. "I have a hard time believing you were invited here."

"Our presence makes them nervous, but their hospitality has been without fault. They just ask that we leave as soon as we can."

"What are they doing? Hiding?"

"They have been here for years. They foresaw the coming persecution and decided they would rather forsake society than watch their children fall victim to it. They call it Bethany. There are Christian communities like this all over the country. So far most have fared okay."

"So far. Except that you're endangering them by being here."

"Though they take the role of pacifists, they are sympathetic toward our mission. Many of the Christian communes believe that we are in the Great Tribulation that Jesus spoke of in Matthew twenty-four. They have fled into the wilderness to wait it out as they believe He instructed."

Scott rubbed his head. He didn't care about any of that prophecy stuff anymore. He just wanted to find his wife. "The ring is here?"

"Yes. We have it and will take it to a safe place. But there is one thing we must do first."

"That's why we're here?"

He nodded. "Did you see the camp?"

"I saw it."

"There is an important man there we need to extract."

"Who?" Scott asked.

"A scientist in the employ of NASA."

"NASA?"

"He knows what they have in store for the ring, their whole agenda."

"Who cares? You have it. Just bury it. No one will ever find it out here. Story over."

"No." He held up a finger. "I cannot do that. Some day it may be needed by the Messiah to gather the hidden instruments and the Ark itself. Our mission must now be that of guardian. And so we cannot destroy it or lose it, and understanding what their plan is for it will help us to better know how to keep it from them."

This was the first time Scott was hearing anything about the ring being needed by the Messiah to fulfill the prophetic writings of the Bible. He wondered if Malachi was operating according to Benjamin's convictions, or if he had an agenda all his own. He didn't care. "You know the guy's probably chipped. They'll know where you take him."

"We need only half an hour with him."

Scott paused, keeping his shaking hands hidden beneath the table. "You want my help in extracting this guy?"

"You would be an invaluable asset to us."

"Then I want your help in return." He reached inside his pocket and slid the picture of his wife across the table, hoping he was doing the right thing.

# 36.



*"Today, America would be outraged if UN troops entered Los Angeles to restore order. Tomorrow they will be grateful! This is especially true if they were told that there was an outside threat from beyond, whether real or promulgated, that threatened our very existence. It is then that all the peoples of the world will plead to deliver them from this evil. The one thing that every man fears is the unknown. When presented with this scenario, individual rights will be willingly relinquished for the guarantee of their wellbeing granted to them by the World Government."*

—Henry Kissinger

With nothing to do at the moment, Scott decided to take a tour through the community. The two boys he'd seen throwing a baseball earlier were still going at it, and as he walked by, an errant throw rolled across the grass and came to a stop against his foot. He bent over and picked it up. Tossed it back to them.

"Thanks, mister!" they shouted.

"No problem." *Kids,* he thought, and wondered what life would have been like if he and Jennifer had had one or two of them. Considering the way things had ended up, it was probably best that they hadn't.

He continued to walk, exchanging courtesy nods with others as he passed them, until he spotted a flat rock resting in the midst of a green patch of grass that looked rather inviting to his sore back and legs. He made his way over to it and sat down, leaning against the rock while watching the activities around him. From what he could tell, it seemed like the people here had settled down into a nice and simple off-grid way of life. How long it would stay that way once Malachi's men raided the prison camp was another matter. A day? A week? The whole area would be analyzed by satellites, drones, and MAVs while recon teams searched for signs of "terrorists" living outside the System. Everyone here would end up in a camp. Or dead.

The camp.

But he didn't want to dwell on Malachi's promise to look into Jennifer's whereabouts. Didn't want to get his hopes up. Yet, he needed to decide what to do about the phone still in his pocket. The one Malachi had told him to get rid of.

"Hello," a voice sounded out from behind him.

Scott turned and looked up at a man standing over him. Dark clouds haloed around his head. He wore jeans and an oversized sweater. His hair was short, and he had a black beard. "Hi," Scott said. He didn't get up.

The man reached down to shake his hand. "I'm Dan Ralston."

Scott took his hand and shook it. "Matthew Scott."

Dan Ralston stood back and smiled. "I hope you don't mind me saying so, but I think God gave me a message for you."

Scott raised his eyebrows. "God gave you a message for me?"

His smile faltered a bit. "I think so."

"Any reason God can't tell me himself?"

He squatted down in front of him. "What would be the fun in that?"

Scott blinked.

"It's a verse," Ralston continued. "Actually seven verses. Do you mind?"

"What the hell."

"It's from Psalm thirty-seven. 'Wait on the Lord, and keep His way, and He shall exalt you to inherit the land; when the wicked are cut off, you shall see it. I have seen the wicked in great power, and spreading himself like a native green tree. Yet he passed away, and behold, he was no more; indeed I sought him, but he could not be found. Mark the blameless man, and observe the upright; for the future of that man is peace. But the transgressors shall be destroyed together; the future of the wicked shall be cut off. But the salvation of the righteous is from the Lord; He is their strength in the time of trouble. And the Lord shall help them and deliver them; He shall deliver them from the wicked, and save them, because they trust in Him.'" He studied Scott, searching for a reaction.

Not knowing what else to say, Scott mumbled his thanks.

"Does it mean something to you?" Ralston asked.

"That the wicked have it coming to them? Yeah, that'd be nice. Haven't quite seen it go down that way though."

"Which side of the fence would you fall on, do you suppose?"

Scott stared at him.

"I'm sorry. It's none of my business, is it?" His bright blue eyes flashed warmth as he stood. "I hope you figure it out. The verse, I mean. It was nice to meet you." He waved and walked away.

*Well, that was weird as* — but he stopped, the words circling back around and coming at him again. *I have seen the wicked in great power, and spreading himself like a native green tree. Yet he passed away, and behold, he was no more; indeed I sought him, but he could not be found.* It wasn't hard to apply the words to the world rulers, the ones running the show and orchestrating all this madness. *But the transgressors shall be destroyed together; the future of the wicked shall be cut off.*

Together.

Ralston's question about which side of the fence he would fall on gave him pause. For his sins, there was no doubt that he would be counted among the very people he hated, who ruined his life. Who made him do what he did. And wouldn't that be ironic.

But now wasn't the time to start thinking about repentance and forgiveness and second chances and spiritual awakenings. Not with what lay ahead of him. With what he had to do. He'd already felt the vulnerability of such a heightened conscience when he began shooting at soldiers' legs instead of their heads back in the woods of Vermont, and he couldn't have that interfering with the people who would need killing if he was going to get his wife back.

He took Isaiah's book out of his coat pocket and decided he'd try it again now that he was actually awake. He opened it to the first page and saw, written in big bold letters, a title.

*LUCIFER'S GLOBAL COMMUNITY*

Scott sighed. More New World Order stuff. He started to read.

> There has been a dream among men throughout history—a perfect society through which all people will finally be satisfied.
>
> Utopia.
>
> Within the following pages, we will look at how this dream has been unfolding throughout history and how, recently, it has become something more than a dream but a probability. For the sake of time and practicality, we will not start so far back as the Tower of Babel or even the Garden of Eden, but only mention such ancient examples as it complements more recent history.
>
> So let us go back about 2,500 years and start with Plato and his work *Critias*. For it was within that work that he wrote of such a utopia.
>
> He called it Atlantis.

*Roswell and now Atlantis?* This was beginning to sound like one of those old sci-fi reruns he used to watch as a kid. He skimmed through Isaiah's account of Plato's Atlantis, trying to get right to his point rather than wade through the theories that supported it.

> ...For centuries, esoterics have claimed that Plato's Atlantis once existed as a great empire that covered the entire world. And some even believe that the ancient wisdom of Atlantis has been preserved within the secret

orders, destined to one day be reborn. And while it is true that secret societies have been working for over 3,000 years to create a background for which an enlightened world democracy would be necessary, Plato is perhaps the most popular person to have first expressed a philosophical basis for it.

Let us fast-forward nearly a thousand years and look at Francis Bacon, the leader of England's secret societies during the seventeenth century and chief of the Rosicrucian Order. The author of *New Atlantis*, he described within that work a nation that was marked by its scientific advances. Though what is most interesting about his vision of this *New Atlantis* is that he referred to himself as the "Herald of the New Age" and has been credited as America's true founder—even a 1910 Newfoundland stamp reads "Lord Bacon: The Guiding Spirit in Colonization Scheme."

History has told us of those coming to the new world for supposed religious freedom, but it has done quite well in hiding yet another group of people who came with an agenda all their own. People sent by Francis Bacon to establish his vision of a philosophic world empire.

At least, Scott thought, Isaiah had intended his research to be either a series of articles or a book, which made it easier to read than Father Baer scribbling thoughts around partial passages of mysterious texts.

Scott skimmed further, his eyes picking up on paragraphs concerning something that Isaiah called "ley lines." He said it was believed the five Revolutionary War cities had been built in perfect alignment across the eastern seaboard (Boston, New York, Philadelphia, Washington, and Baltimore), that the ancient alignment of cities and other important sites had often been associated with a series of "great circles" that encompassed the Earth ("ley lines" or "lines of power")—the equator and the meridians of longitude the most famous of these lines. Apparently, it's believed by some that the ancient builders were aware of these lines and used them deliberately, that they were even perceived to be portals through which spirits could travel between the different sites.

He turned the page.

Something about the 77th meridian, or "God's longitude." About Washington, DC, being built on it. That Sir Walter Raleigh, a member of Bacon's secret society, actually established the colony of Roanoke while searching for it. That his true mission had been to establish the New World's philosophic capital. Meridian Hill in Washington, DC, still marks "God's longitude."

Scott rubbed his eyes.

Bacon was the grandfather of the English enlightenment, the father of modern science. He coined the phrase "knowledge is power", believing that mankind possessed the ability to transform into the highest enlightened state— godhood even. He was so influential in his time that Thomas Jefferson considered him to be one of the three most important people in history (along with John Locke and Isaac Newton). He is considered by some to have been the grandmaster of enlightened Freemasonry, having laid out the ambitions of all secret societies—the establishment of a new Atlantis.

But how did he expect to accomplish this? We will come to that. But first I would like to consider the fact that Bacon is often cited as having been a follower of Christ. But which Christ? The Jesus Christ as revealed in the Holy Writ, or as He is revered in Freemasonry and the mystery religions—of which the Order is simply a fountainhead? For the ancient mystery religions recognized a Christ figure in their divine trinity too—within the 47th proposition of Euclid (the Pythagorean theorem). The right triangle, Masonic philosophers insist, is the symbolic representation of this ancient trinity, the perpendicular being the masculine father, the base being the feminine divine mother, and the hypotenuse their offspring, the divine child (or Masonic Christ). But this "divine child" offers salvation through knowledge and science rather than the atoning work of Christ on the cross and His resurrection from the dead. In fact, Bacon's interpretation and use of the Bible was more in line with the mystical philosophies of Kabbalah, aiming to achieve a godlike status through an enlightened state (thus Hitler's obsession with the occult as he tried to create a perfect race of humans through which to rule a new utopia).

But we will revisit the right triangle and its true meaning within the mystery religions later...

Scott found that he was actually being drawn in to this bizarre world of esoteric mystery, secret societies, and ancient conspiracy, and he wondered if the Rosicrucian Order could still be at work, as Isaiah had suggested.

Reading on, he read about a Dr. John Dee—Bacon's mentor and personal astrologer and spy for Queen Elizabeth. A mathematician, mystic, and Rosicrucian who was deeply invested in esoteric study and frequently tapped into the spirit world in order to communicate with angelic beings, he coined the phrase "Britannia" and was credited with laying the philosophical foundation for Britain's empire. He trained the first great navigators and made maps charting northeast and west passages. He is said to have been the inspiration behind Shakespeare's Prospero in *The Tempest*; along with Doctor Faustus, Gandalf, and even James Bond (he would sign his communiqués to Elizabeth "007," making him the true spy "On Her Majesty's Secret Service," and why the priest had scribbled the numbers in his journal). He apparently passed on all of his esoteric knowledge to Bacon.

> ...John Dee believed that the New World was the lost civilization of Atlantis, and when Elizabeth took the throne, his dream of colonizing America as the new Atlantis had suddenly fallen within reach. But then the church excommunicated Elizabeth, and Lee and Bacon would form a Rosicrucian intelligence network to protect her from spies and assassins over the following years...

He read that Bacon had been working on a book he called *New Atlantis: Land of the Rosicrucians* when he died. And Father Baer's last word ricocheted through the corridors of his mind.

*Rose...*

But had the priest been referring to something backward, indicating the history of this grand conspiracy and wanting him to appreciate the scope and magnitude of what it was he had become part of? Or had he been pointing at the Order for the things now unfolding? Was it possible that what he was trying to tell him was that the Rosicrucians were also after the ring?

Scott skipped past the explanation behind the rose and cross symbology since Isaiah had already explained it to him. A cold breeze blew across the grass and ruffled his hair. He looked up and watched the people for a few minutes, then dropped his eyes back into the depths of a hidden history.

> …So how did Bacon hope to spread his philosophy of a New Age and manifest it on the physical plane? There were two major ingredients that helped set the stage for his New Atlantis. One of those ways was a worldwide revolution against established monarchies. The other was the development of a universal language. Bacon realized that in order to unite mankind through the spread of information, the confusion caused at Babel would have to be reversed. So to accomplish this impossible task, he created a literary society called the Knights of the Helmet, which was responsible for the explosion of literature during the Elizabethan era as well as translating the works of Plato and other ancient wisdom texts into English. It is said that up to 2,000 works passed through Bacon's hands on their way to the public. Though his true purpose in promoting such literacy was to prepare the people of the Old World for the colonization of the New.
>
> The Knights of the Helmet society was named after the Greek goddess Pallas Athena, who wears a helmet that signifies secrecy or invisibility (for no one can see her when she is wearing it). Interestingly enough, Bacon's spirit encounter was supposedly with Athena, whereby she told him that the Divine Majesty delights to hide his work according to the innocent play of children and that he should "follow the example of the most High God, putting away popular applause, and, after the manner of Solomon the King, compose a history of the times and fold it into enigmatical writings and cunning mixtures of the theatre."

Scott read of Bacon's "enlightened" entertainment and more of his intention to educate the English people in preparation for world democracy.

> With no concern for the praises of man, many believe that Bacon and his literary society wrote under the guise of another.
>
> William Shakespeare.
>
> Now if you are not familiar with this old debate, it may sound strange and farfetched to you. However, in 1909, Mark Twain wrote an entire book making just this claim. And isn't it interesting that Shakespeare is synonymous with Apollo and Athena? Both meaning "shakers of the spear" and representing the light of knowledge being shaken at the dragon of ignorance? For Apollo and Athena are considered to be the great shake-spears.
>
> Also of interest is that an anagram of William Shakespeare could be "here I was, like a Psalm" from Psalm 46. And in the King James Bible (1611), the 46th word from the beginning of the 46th Psalm is "shake" while the 46th word from the end of the 46th Psalm is "spear." 46 was also his age when the KJV Bible was printed, as well as the sum of 23 and 23—the days of both his birth and death.

Though he was interested in the famous Baconian/Shake-spear debate, he understood Isaiah's point and just skimmed all the other facts that seemed to make laughable the idea that an actor like William Shakespeare could be responsible for developing more than twenty thousand words in the English language, or somehow know quite intimately and in great detail the inner workings of the court.

> ...Manly P. Hall (Masonic philosopher) wrote in his book *Secret Teachings of All Ages*, that "Sir Francis Bacon, the Rosicrucian initiate, wrote into the Shakespeare plays the secret teachings of the fraternity of the Rose and Cross and the true rituals of the Freemasonic order. The Bacon-Shakespeare controversy...involved the most profound aspects of science, religion, and ethics: he who solves this

mystery may yet find therein the key to the supposedly lost wisdom of antiquity."

Perhaps here is a good example of the Rosicrucian method, for Shakespeare clearly attempts to represent Christianity through over 1,200 biblical references, yet his Christian themes are interwoven with the occult wisdom of the mystery religions. And of course, we can easily see just how effective his work (commissioned by Pallas Athena) was, for "Shake-spear" has long been a mandatory requirement within the American education system.

He skipped to a section that touched on the religious aspects of this utopian dream.

…Within the scheme to unite mankind, we can see a clear trend toward universalism being the preferred religion of the one-world crowd. And perhaps there is no clearer picture of this than Rosslyn Chapel in Scotland.

The Knights Templar, while stationed in the Middle East, began mixing their Catholic beliefs with those of Islam, Judaism, and the Hashishim. In so doing, they adopted the teachings of the esoteric religions as their own. Later, while being hunted by the Catholic Church, they found refuge within the Masonic Lodge, and though Freemasonry existed before that, the Templars are credited with the development of its modern philosophy. It is Rosslyn Chapel that clearly connects Freemasonry to the Templar Knights, and Christianity to the ancient pagan religions (Constantine's total merging of the two notwithstanding).

The Chapel was built by William St. Clair in the fifteenth century. Within it, one can find 110 sculptures of the ancient fertility god sprinkled throughout the many crosses and roses with no clear indication of what is supposed to be worshiped. There is also evidence in the artwork that suggests an influence from the New World— and that from before Columbus! The chapel was finished in 1492, yet there is Indian corn found carved around the windows, corn indigenous only to North America and not grown in Europe. There are also cactus plants carved along the chapel's arches and a type of clover leaf that botanists insist could only have been found in America. So just how far did the Templar Knights escape the Catholic Church?

Columbus's father-in-law was the grand master of the order of the Knights of Christ, an offshoot of the Knights Templar, and many insist that Columbus had been given secret charts and diaries that he used to reach the New World...

Scott looked up from the composition book and thought back to everything he'd been taught about his former country's founding, about the fight for religious freedom. Suddenly, the idea that Jesus would lead His followers onto a battlefield to fight for a person's right to worship any god or demon they wanted seemed utterly preposterous from a Judeo-Christian perspective. As did the battle cry of the Revolution, "We have no king but King Jesus." Yet it had been a common Christian belief. Patriotic Christianity, Jack Cairns had called it. Deception. Scott didn't know much about the Christian faith, but he did know there seemed to be a stark contrast between the Jesus of the New Testament and the Jesus people wrapped up with a flag. Jack was always quoting Jesus as saying, "If my kingdom were of this world, then would my servants fight."

He looked up at the sky and took note of the darkening clouds.

...The secret societies would convert the Old World through the example of the New. And though most "Americans" did not fight the Revolutionary War intending to promote a global revolution, it is indisputable that the secret societies played an important role in America's independence. And the American revolution would be the first of many.

The American Revolution was the first move on a worldwide chessboard, and Benjamin Franklin was perhaps one of the game's key players. An active member of Freemasonry and other secret societies both in England and France (including the Hell-Fire Club), Franklin—

A raindrop landed on Scott's head and exploded his concentration. He watched as men and women began running back and forth, trying to retrieve clothes that were drying on clotheslines. Soon they would be running for another reason.

He flipped the collar of his jacket up and returned to the text about Franklin and his involvement in this Hell-Fire Club, which apparently had been forced underground after accusations of Satanism emerged. Their motto had been, "Do what thou wilt shall be the whole of the law." Isaiah went on to say that it was the very philosophy that Aleister Crowley (the famous British occultist, Freemason, and Rosicrucian) had adopted a century later, earning him some of the credit for sparking the Cultural Revolution of the 1960s.

> ...What was Franklin's involvement with these people? Sir Francis Dashwood was the club's founder, a member of British Parliament and a close friend and advisor to King George III (much of the club is said to have been comprised of English nobility). Franklin reportedly visited with Dashwood in 1758 to discuss the future of the American colonies, which made some believe that the Hell-Fire Club was just a cover for British intelligence and that Franklin was actually a British spy known as #72 or "Moses." Though I believe it is more plausible that he was working alongside the Hell-Fire Club to ensure the society's esoteric goals.
>
> British intelligence referred to Franklin as "Moses" because he was seen by them as leading the colonists away from King George like Moses had led the Israelites out of Egyptian captivity (and Franklin's original design for America's seal was that of Moses standing on the shoreline as the waters were collapsing onto Pharaoh's army, the inscription reading, "Rebellion to Tyrants is Obedience to God"). So it would seem that British intelligence was actually working with the secret orders in undermining King George, attempting a world democracy through an American revolution that favored Bacon's vision of a new World Order. And haven't we seen that more recently? America being used as the spearhead of democracy throughout the world? But we shall come to that...

As the American ambassador to France, Franklin's ideas played a large role in leading to the French Revolution. And since Franklin managed to get the King of France to fund America's revolution, it is ironic that its success later inspired the very revolution in France that overthrew the King!

The raindrops were falling more regularly now, and Scott had to quickly skim through the rest of the book.

...Thomas Paine, a friend of Franklin and a Mason, wrote *Common Sense* and helped inspire the American Revolution... Voltaire was a Mason, and his writings helped lead to the French Revolution...

...This "virtuous" revolution was, however, something new. For no one had ever thought it right and proper to rebel against kings who had supposedly been appointed by God...

...Manly P. Hall stated that the secret societies helped establish the country for a peculiar purpose known only to the initiated...

...During the American Revolution, there existed a secret order in Germany that many believe was responsible for most of the wars and conspiracies that would take place over the next few hundred years. General William Huntington Russell created the order as a means to reconcile the esoteric orders with the mainstream European movements, since he believed that Rosicrucianism and Freemasonry had started to drift away from their roots. He brought his order to North America, and we know it now as Skull and Bones...

...Intended to change the organized system of religion and government, the revolutionary ideology of the eighteenth and nineteenth centuries was not just shaped by the rationalism of the French Enlightenment but also by German occultism...

Scott forced himself to slow down when he saw stuff about Pythagoras again, how he was driven from Greece to southern Italy and had purportedly established a religious-philosophical brotherhood that was intended to transform society. Isaiah then revealed the relation between Pythagoras and the French Revolution by pointing out that Pythagorean symbols dominated the revolution, that Adam Weishaupt (the leading revolutionary/Bavarian lawmaker who founded the Illuminati) wrote a blueprint for politicized Illuminism during the first years of the revolution that he called *Pythagoras*. And though the Illuminati was disbanded by the Bavarian government in 1786, their doctrines had managed to make it all the way to America, for in a response letter written by George Washington to Rev. G. W. Snyder (who sent Washington a copy of Robison's *Proofs of a Conspiracy against All the Religions and Governments of Europe*), Washington admitted that he was in fact persuaded of the Illuminati's active presence within America. He also associated the Illuminati with Jacobinism, the radical group that was responsible for starting the French Revolution.

> ...But, in point of fact, the Illuminati was the power behind the Jacobins! The Bavarian Illuminati put a "fire in the minds of men," compelling them to join in the global revolution that would change the world!
>
> Perhaps the presence of the Jacobean hat (the Phrygian cap, dating back to ancient Rome and said to have been worn by slaves who had obtained their freedom) found on the seal of the US Army, several figures of liberty in the Capitol Building, and all over the Library of Congress reveals the overall role America was to play in the Utopia scheme...
>
> ...The caps are depicted as being worn by the Magi as they followed the star to Bethlehem (Freemasonry teaches that the star was Sirius and that the Magi were followers of Zoroaster). The hat is also associated with Ganymede, the mythical figure carried away by Zeus and made cup-bearer to the gods, Zeus giving him a place within the heavens, where he becomes the constellation Aquarius. And though it will be of greater importance and textual relevance later on, we must note that throughout the twentieth century, esoteric teachers had been declaring that mankind was in the process of entering this New Age, or the Age of Aquarius. And does this "liberty hat," used by the

Illuminati-backed Jacobeans, and inserted by Freemasons into America's artwork, spell out a connection between these different things, linking the discovery of a Christ to the birth of the new age? If so, who do the secret orders say this Christ is? For the answer to that question is the crux of the whole matter. Otherwise, we would be tempted to support such global efforts at a one-world democracy. Why wouldn't we? It seems that the utopian dream would be the natural goal for the future of humanity. Unless, of course, the symbol for such a new order happens to be a swastika...

Benjamin's words came scrolling back through Scott's mind. *How could one know all that the Devil has been up to for the last six thousand years, and that within every society of which he has been working to prepare the way?* Lucifer presents himself as an angel of light, he had said, many people believing they are obeying the voice of God when in fact it's Lucifer's agenda that they're working for.

*Deception.*

Then the heavens opened, and the rain started coming down in sheets. Scott closed the book even as part of him wanted to reject it all as sheer nonsense. But the day in which he lived made such an easy dismissal nearly impossible. Either all this stuff had been orchestrated as Isaiah said, or everything all these people had been talking about (whether as prophecy-believing Christians, those fighting the NWO, the global elite who included such things in their memoirs, or the Freemasons boasting of such a future) had just happened to come true as a matter of coincidence, no power behind the scenes working to bring it about at all.

Whatever the case may be, at least he now understood what Isaiah had been trying to tell him about the Rosicrucians. And what Father Baer had meant to warn him about.

The rose and the cross.

The deception lurking within the shadows of a patriotic religion. Lucifer's working throughout the centuries to bring about a platform on which his New Order could arise, the promise of liberty his *modus operandi.*

Scott tucked the book into his jacket and ran down the main street and back to the tent.

Thunder shook the forest.

As he walked past Mossad agents planning their attack on the prison camp, he again felt the form of the phone through his jeans.

"Hey."

Scott looked up and saw Malachi coming into the tent.

"It's confirmed," Malachi said.

Scott blinked, everything he'd just read disappearing like a shadow struck by light. "What's confirmed?" His heart began to race.

"She's there. Your wife, Jennifer May Cavanaugh. She's in the prison."

"The same one?"

Malachi nodded.

If there were warning bells, Scott didn't hear them. He *needed* it to be true. "So you'll help me?" he asked.

"If you help us."

"When?"

"Tonight."

# 37.

*"It was not my intention to doubt that the doctrines of the Illuminati and the principals of Jacobinism had not spread to the U.S.... On the contrary, no one is more truly satisfied of this fact than I am."*

— George Washington

All fifteen of them had been on foot and well into the five-mile journey to the prison camp when the rain turned to sleet. Then the sun dipped beneath the earth, and big flakes of snow began to flutter through the black hours of night. They were all in black and equipped with silenced weapons and grenades, their night-vision gear transforming the darkness into green day. The op was simple: neutralize the prison's guards, infiltrate the structure, and find the scientist. And somewhere along the way they would find Scott's wife. Once they had her secure, they would fade back into the night.

Or something like that.

But as Scott followed the men in front of him, his conscience began to stir. What would happen to the prisoners they would be leaving behind? And what about the commune? It was sure to be targeted as a result of their raid on the camp. Malachi might be okay with "the end justifies the means" mantra or maybe the one about the greater good, but neither could erase the simple fact that actual innocent people were going to be slaughtered as a result of what they were doing.

He adjusted the silenced submachine gun that was slung over his shoulder.

Malachi's men had given him a black jacket, pants, boots, flight gloves, and a ski mask. They'd also given him the submachine gun, a silenced pistol, three grenades, a combat shotgun, and two knives. Mags for the submachine gun were tucked into sleeves across his chest, and shotgun shells and mags for the pistol filled the ammo belt hanging low around his waist. A knife was positioned at the base of his spine, another strapped to his ankle.

By the time they reached the camp, it was around 3 a.m. They were positioned at the edge of the woods, the fenced enclosure a hundred yards ahead of them. Snow was falling harder and now covered the mountains in white sheets.

The open space between the woods and the fence was overseen by two guard towers standing in the corners of the camp. The cloud cover would help to prevent moonlight from reflecting off the snow, while the snowfall would hide their approach and cover their tracks. Not that the guards in the towers would even be looking in their direction. They were mostly there to monitor the happenings within the camp, not to protect it from unknown enemies outside.

As his heart raced, Scott tried to recall his bird's-eye view of the camp from earlier that day. He knew the train tracks ran east to west and passed the prison's entrance, and that the large loading platform stretched along most of the front fence. Three large antechambers were constructed on top of the platform and led to fenced-off areas within the camp, separating the men, women, and children. He shuddered as he thought of Jennifer stepping off a train and onto the platform, being separated and herded toward one of the three tunnels like an animal, standing in a line with women who were screaming for their husbands and children.

Malachi gave a signal, and they readied their weapons. Then they were moving out.

They took off in a straight line, moving as a single shadow across the white ground. The guards positioned in the towers were put down with silenced rounds before the Mossad team even reached the fence, which wasn't electrified and was easy enough to cut through with a pair of bolt cutters.

Once through the fence, two of the men immediately broke off toward the guard towers just cleared. They hurried alongside the fence, running in opposite directions until they reached the towers. Then they climbed up and replaced the guards they'd shot, taking up an overwatch position from which to direct the rest of the team. They aimed their rifles across the camp, to the other guard towers standing across from them in the other two corners, and shot those soldiers too.

Scott and the other dozen operatives crouched low by the hole in the fence, waiting for the all clear from Overwatch.

*"Two targets, northwest corner."* The whispered voice crackled over the radio from one tower to the other.

*"Affirmative. One southwest, another walking your way."*

*"Got him."*

Scott saw a muzzle flash up in the northeast tower. Then another. Two seconds later, and after a shot from the other tower, a third and final flash blinked through the quiet night.

*"All clear."*

*"All clear."*

Scott followed the men in front of him to the southern corner of a large warehouse. From there they could see the front of the camp, the train tracks on the outside of the fence and the loading platform that stretched out past the three antechambers to meet them. There were signs on the fence designating specified zones, but whether they were for new arrivals or those moving on, Scott couldn't tell.

They broke into three more groups. One group heading for the other two towers, another to search for the scientist, and the third group to find the computers. Scott was on the team designated to find the computers—where he hoped to find a record of the interns.

Scott had the submachine gun tight against his shoulder, sweeping it back and forth as they moved. Malachi was in front of him, two others behind. They were heading north toward the back of the camp, making their way between the warehouse on their right and a few other buildings to their left, one of which was two stories high, its windows boarded up with plywood.

The ground they were covering was void of any other footprints, which Scott found to be strange. Only four guards in the towers, a handful of waltzing soldiers, no electric current running through the fence, no lights, no LZ for a helicopter, no wind markers, no dogs…

When they came into view of the north side of the compound, they saw a row of trailers lined up against the back fence. There was a light on in one of them. Malachi ran up the wooden steps that led to the trailer's door and put his back up against the wall beside it.

Scott went to the opposite side of the door, where he could try the handle. It was unlocked. He pushed the door open a centimeter, just far enough so the latch was free from the frame. A line of light filled the crack. He flicked the night vision off.

He raised a finger. Two. Three.

He kicked the door open and spun back out of the doorway as Malachi entered with the other two agents on his heels, their weapons coughing as they went.

By the time Scott got in the trailer, there was an NAU officer lying on the floor beside a desk with blood pooling around his head, and one of Malachi's men was already working a multi-touch table, everyone else gathered around him. Scott looked around. The room contained filing cabinets and a bookshelf in addition to the table. He went back to the door and stared out across the grounds, thinking. He remembered that the agent in the helicopter had said there was an underground facility beneath the camp.

"I'm in," declared the agent working the touchtable.

Scott turned toward him and held his breath.

"Melissa Strauss," Malachi whispered, pointing at the image before them.

Scott took a step toward them. "What did you say?" He walked over to the desk and looked at the image himself. "What's going on?" There was a layer of ice in the question.

Malachi lifted his eyes to Scott's. "She was the one who brought the ring into the country. She was part of the research team preparing a diagnostic report for the NAU."

"I know who she is."

"She could know how it works."

*Because if the Messiah needed it for some reason, he wouldn't be able to figure it out on his own once he got here, would he?* "Where is she?"

The guy at the desk answered, "General population. The ground floor of the two-story building."

Scott pointed back to the monitor. "And what about my wife?"

His fingers danced over the glass surface, each letter he pressed lighting up in response. He shook his head. "She's not listed here."

"What?"

"We may be too late," Malachi whispered.

*No.* Turning, Scott hit the button on his goggles, activating the night vision, and ran out of the cabin. He sprinted toward the two-story building, passing one of the Mossad teams that seemed to already have the NASA scientist in custody.

Reaching the doors, aware that Malachi and the others were following behind, he pushed them open and stepped into a world of cruelty.

Bunk beds lined both sides of the walls, and he paused only long enough to glimpse the green faces occupying the beds. His heart pounded in his chest as he frantically moved from one bed to the next. "Jennifer!"

The prisoners began to wake up.

"Jennifer!" he yelled, growing more desperate the closer he got to the end of the room. But only the nutrition-deprived faces of women he didn't recognize stared back at him, their eyes glowing in the night vision as if they were ghosts about to exact their revenge on him for the part he'd played in making all this possible. Ignoring the haunted stares, he burst through another door and found himself in another section of the building. More bunk beds. More sleeping women. "Jennifer!"

"Over here!" someone called out in the darkness. "I'm Jennifer!"

He raced to the voice, to the godforsaken bed it was coming from.

But it wasn't her.

He swore, leaving the woman groping in the darkness for a hope that would never be. He kept calling out.

Then he saw Melissa Strauss.

She was just getting up to her elbows, trying to make sense of what was happening. He ran right past her. But a second later, he could hear Malachi and the two other agents wrestling her from the bed, taking her out into the snow. He didn't care. He continued searching beds, beds that were running out. *No.* This couldn't be happening. She had to be here. He needed her to be here. "Jennifer!" he screamed again.

The next door he went through took him back outside. *No!* He turned back and went for the stairs to the upper floor, took them three at a time.

The male population.

He felt dizzy, his world spinning. He leaned against the wall for support before making his way back down the stairs. "Jennifer!" He stumbled outside just as Malachi and nine others ran past him. The scientist was with them, helping Melissa along. Feeling for the picture in his pocket, he ran after them.

He caught up to them at a toolshed. Except, upon entering, he saw that there were no tools of any kind. Instead, the Mossad agents were all standing around the scientist as he worked a series of buttons on a concealed keypad fixed to the wall. Then the floor suddenly retreated, and a descending staircase appeared at his feet. Without pause, the scientist began leading them down into what Scott assumed to be the underground facility. But why? They already had everything they'd come for. Except his wife, of course.

There was a large steel door at the bottom of the stairs, which required the use of the scientist's ID card to bypass. The door opened, and they descended another short flight of stairs before coming to another, even larger door. This one required the scientist's eyeball, voice, name, access code, and fingerprint.

The large vault-like door swung outward with a beep only to reveal yet another stairwell. Three flights descended into the earth, cinderblock walls surrounding them, emergency lights flickering above.

Scott pulled the night vision from his head and stole a glance at Melissa under the artificial light. She looked terrified, a far cry from how she looked on her NAU identification photo that the news had posted when labeling her a terrorist. Big black circles surrounded her eyes, and her skin was pulled tight against her cheekbones and neck. She looked like a prisoner in a concentration camp. Her hand was pressed firmly against her stomach.

After coming to another door, the scientist turned and whispered to Malachi, "There's a guard on the other side of this door. I'll swipe my card, and the door will release. I'll go in and walk past him, get him to turn his back to the door. Then you can do whatever it is you do."

It was pretty clear to Scott that the real reason they were here was not for the scientist, but for something else. That Malachi hadn't trusted him with that information suddenly had him on edge. And he didn't like the fact that he was the only one without a radio.

He observed the scientist, saw that he was old, the hair he had left whiter than the falling snow. His shoulders were hunched forward from what could have been a life spent leaning over a computer or microscope, but Scott could tell from his eyes that it was actually from the burden of shame that he carried.

"There's a long corridor stretching north and south, connecting the laboratory with offices, barracks, and quarters. The whole sublevel is networked into the surface, most buildings having a way up and down." The scientist swallowed. "At the end of this hall, there's another door. Behind that door is a long corridor, and there's usually one or two guards patrolling it. We're going south, or left. I don't advise going right. Fifty sleeping soldiers are that way." He took another breath and continued, "There's another door in the corridor, and then the one that leads into the lab. You'll be going in at six o'clock, west. A guard will be on the other side of the door, positioned at the top of the stairs. To the right, or five o'clock, is another door and staircase with a guard. Directly beneath you will be a long conference table. There are usually two scientists working through the night and two patrolling guards. Once you get what you need, there's an elevator on the east wall. It's a freight elevator they use to transport the subjects, and it's connected to the warehouse. You may have to make two trips."

"What about the biohazard protocols?" Malachi asked. "Are you sure we are able to gain access to these levels?"

"Given the nature of the work conducted here and the complete lack of government oversight, such regulations are irrelevant. Oh, and you should know that every soldier has the ability to sound an alarm." Then he dipped his head and swiped the card. The door released, and he walked through it.

Malachi peered through the crack left open in the door, and once he could tell the guard was walking away from them, he quietly pushed the door open and shot him in the back of the head. He collapsed on the floor beside the scientist.

The agents retrieved the body, dragging it out of the corridor and into the stairwell.

The scientist looked unmoved by the violence, his eyes sad and tired. He was desensitized to death, which was a realization that only compounded the guilt sitting on his shoulders. Whatever it was he'd been doing here, Scott knew it couldn't have been anything good.

When they caught up with the scientist, he was already at the end of the hall and swiping his card, pressing his thumb onto a shiny surface while orally dictating a code.

The door rose into the ceiling like a blast door, and the scientist ducked under it. He was standing at the top of a T. He looked to his left and right. Waved a hello to the right. "I'm sorry," he called out to whoever was there, "but I think something might be wrong with the door down here." He pointed behind him, to the other end of the corridor and the entrance to the lab.

A few seconds later, a guard walked straight by the open corridor that Scott and the Israeli team were standing on either side of, crouching in the corners where the walls met beside the open door.

Again Malachi stepped into the adjoining corridor and shot his target in the back of the head. And again his men dragged the body back into the stairwell.

They continued on to the lab.

But before reaching the door, Scott grabbed the scientist by the arm and asked through his mask, "What is this place?"

The scientist looked confused, by both the question and the American accent asking it. "It's a research facility."

"Sponsored by who?"

"It's not officially sponsored by anyone."

"Unofficially?"

"The men who comprise our world government, of course."

"The NAU?"

"Such people as these are above territorial designations and their governing philosophies."

"Who's running it, then?"

"A secret faction of the new CDC oversees it."

"And what's going to happen to the prisoners?" Scott asked.

The scientist looked away. "They're all implanted with microchips. They can't cross the electromagnetic perimeter that surrounds the camp."

That would explain the lack of security, Scott thought. "What about her?" he asked, looking over to Melissa.

"Hers has been removed."

"When?"

But Malachi interrupted. "Let's go."

The scientist went to work opening the door while Malachi checked in with the four agents manning the guard towers.

"*All clear*," came the response.

Scott could feel everyone around him growing more tense, the pressure in the room increasing as they prepared to enter this secret laboratory.

The door slid open to reveal an even brighter length of corridor, and their black uniforms presented a stunning contrast as they moved through it.

"Remember, there's a guard on the other side of the next door, another guarding the door on the right, and one standing down on the floor against the left wall. There are two patrolling guards and at least two scientists working. You need to take them all at once, or they'll trigger the alarm." The scientist raised his card to the mechanism beside the final door.

"Wait," said Malachi.

He paused, his hand elevated over the swiping mechanism.

"How long will we have once the alarm sounds?"

"Five minutes."

"And the alarm, how far does it sound?"

"Like I said, this is a black site, and whoever the new president is, I guarantee you that he doesn't know about this place. It would light up a few switchboards across the country, but any outside response would take at least a day."

"Okay," Malachi said.

The Mossad agents gripped their weapons tight, ready for a swift surgical strike.

"What're we doing here?" Scott quickly whispered in Malachi's ear.

Malachi brushed him off.

They went through the door and piled onto the metal staircase that overlooked the enormous room, shooting immediately. The guard who was standing right beside the door went backward over the railing. A soldier standing by the elevator sprayed blood up the wall behind him while the third guard atop another metal staircase took bullets in the shoulder, chest, head, and stomach before he could even raise his rifle. The two scientists at the long conference table were thrown backward away from their work, landing on their backs and shooting blood across the floor from pulsating neck wounds. One of the patrolling guards did have enough time to raise her weapon, but she got no further than that. A line of holes punched through the dividing wall she was standing behind, tracing upward and eventually into her head.

"Where is the other guard?" Malachi asked over his shoulder, his weapon still aimed intently beneath him.

"No trace of him," another responded.

Malachi immediately began descending the metal stairs, sweeping the sights of the suppressed M4 back and forth throughout the room.

The entire assault took less than two seconds, and when Scott stepped out onto the staircase, all he saw was red splashed across the glowing white floor and walls. He took in the room, its magnitude overwhelming. It reminded him of some old science fiction movie, something from *Star Trek* maybe. The floor was forty feet below him, and the room was the size of an aircraft hangar. It was divided into three sections by two standing walls, but the walls were meant only to separate, not conceal. The front of the room, a large open space stretching from the elevator doors on the left to the other staircase on the right, faced no obstructions. Anyone sitting at the work table would be able to see into any of the three sections. And what they would see, what Scott was seeing now, was science's version of hell for any unfortunate soul who managed to find themselves here.

Rows of beds, lined up in a twelve-by-twelve grid, filled the center section alone. There were people strapped to them, low blinding lights lighting them up for display.

They were naked, and wires snaked in and out of them before running along the floor and connecting to the dividing walls.

Scott's throat tightened at the sight of the digital charts shining from the multi-touch computer walls while continuous three-dimensional readouts fluctuated stats on huge plastic display screens. Images of the brain, DNA strands, a model of the human genome, and other chemical properties that Scott couldn't decipher, all seemed interfaced with the biology of those asleep in the beds. But then his eyes drifted right, and he noticed other subjects submerged in tanks full of fluid. Hoses were coming and going from the glass-like coffins. "What is this?" he whispered. He was standing alone with the scientist and Melissa at the top of the steps while Malachi and his team were busy at the computers.

"Transhumanism," the scientist replied. "Our brave new world."

Scott ran down the stairs, thinking only of Jennifer. He ran down the rows of naked and sedated prisoners, his heart beating with a sense of dread so powerful it was almost paralyzing. He forced his panic-filled eyes on one unfamiliar face after another, but the more he saw, the sicker he felt. Men and women, both old and young, all stared blankly into the light shining above them.

*Transhumanism.*

All these people, and who knew how many more over the years, lay here sacrificed on the altar of man's ego. The thought of Jennifer put through such terror was too much for his rational mind to process, and as he neared the final bed, he was no longer sure if he wanted to find her here or not. He didn't know if what had been done to these people was reversible.

The last pale face he came to was not Jennifer's. It belonged to a younger woman, though just as beautiful, her nude body strapped to this horrible gurney so far beneath the earth's surface and robbed of every ounce of dignity she'd ever had. Brought down by her captives to the basest level of life — that of lab rat. An experiment. Her hopes and dreams, her *humanity*, crucified by an insane world.

Despair and hope collided into him from opposite sides, for though this wasn't his wife, it could be someone else's. Someone's daughter, sister, friend. He tore the ski mask off his face and stormed past the agents, approaching the scientist again. The old man was standing at the foot of the steps and staring out over his past work as Melissa sat down on the floor and began rocking back and forth. "What the hell is this?" Scott yelled, pointing behind him.

The scientist sighed and set his weary eyes on Scott. "An experiment."

"For what?"

"I told you. Transhumanism. Each subject has been chosen according to their unique genetic makeup."

"And how did you get that?"

He blinked. "The cataloging of every newborn's DNA has been going on for a very long time."

"For this?"

He shrugged. "If not the intent, this was always its natural destination." He paused. "The post-humanist agenda. Eugenics. The advancement of the species... It was decided a long time ago that biological evolution was too slow for the human species, that we could no longer sit back and wait for it. So this"—he waved his hand—"is our attempt at speeding up evolution, at achieving our godhood."

"At the expense of innocent blood?"

"Of course. Do you think people would actually *donate* themselves to such a cause? Many of the medical 'blessings' we enjoy today came as the result of experimentation on unsuspecting peoples...or populations. My god, the Nazis could probably take the credit for most of what we thank God for today. And people don't cry about it as long as they're the ones benefitting from it."

*Eugenics.* Biotechnology.

Scott turned and looked back over all the comatose people, hating how their bodies had become fodder for these sick vampires. "Is this why you're here?" he asked Malachi as he walked by. "You could have told me."

"No." He looked over to the scientist. "Let him tell you."

Shame loosened the scientist's lips farther than the question demanded, his soul venting. "Everyone always argued whether the world would turn in favor of Huxley's vision or Orwell's. No one seemed to notice that we were combining them, that biotechnology had opened the door to their marriage. Cloning and genetic engineering were just the beginning, bioethics no longer part of the debate. After all, *progress* couldn't be hampered by some archaic notion of morality. Not when utilitarianism was the governing religion—the greatest good for the greatest numbers, eliminate useless eaters burdening society...

"T. H. Huxley's eugenics influenced so much, attempting to reduce the population of inferior classes. Gene patenting, genetic discrimination, germline intervention… We may not have created the dust that formed life, but we manipulated the process so that we could get the desired results, creating man in *our* own image. Cybernetics, joining man and machine…" He was beginning to descend into an incoherent ramble. "The Tuskegee Experiment, third-world depopulation procedures, sterilization of races, Hitler's Final Solution…" Then he looked up into Scott's face, and there were tears in his eyes. "You have no idea the magnitude of this dream."

Scott didn't need persuasion. "What is this?"

"A virus. They're going to blame Russia for a biological attack in order to justify a nuclear response. An antidote has been prepared for those who willingly submit to chip implantation, relocation, or whatever else they're told to do in order to ensure true *World* citizenship."

"These people were test subjects for that?"

He nodded. "Originally for the vaccine. Now for genetic classification. We've unlocked the human genome. We can now target the genes incompatible with where it is the world is heading."

"Genetic discrimination on a global scale."

"Eventually. Used to determine everyone's role in society, even their right to live within it."

"This *biological* attack, when is it supposed to happen?"

"Within the year, at least."

Scott thought of the Georgia Guidestones that Edward used to talk about, their advice not to let the population exceed five hundred million and calling for an age of reason that resembled the Earth Charter and Thomas Paine's little book of the same name. It sounded like they were now actually going through with it. Two objectives accomplished through one false-flag attack.

A loud blasting siren suddenly exploded throughout the lab, and they all turned to see the last guard standing in front of a closing door above the other staircase. They swung their weapons up and sent off a barrage of bullets that tore through the soldier before he could fire his weapon, but he'd already triggered the alarm.

Malachi began shouting over the siren. "We almost there?"

"Ninety percent," the man at the computer shouted.

He turned to the scientist. "Get that elevator down here."

The old man ran to the keypad on the east wall, almost slipping in the blood that covered the floor.

Scott and the other agents took up strategic positions throughout the room, waiting for soldiers to come running through the doors, while Malachi raced up the stairs and began leading Melissa back down to the elevator.

"Ninety-five!" yelled the agent.

"How is the elevator coming?" Malachi shouted to the scientist.

"It's on its way."

The door above Scott opened, and when a soldier came through, Scott shot him three times. The soldier dropped to the metal grated platform, his body wedged in the doorway and keeping the door from closing.

"Okay, I have it!" the guy at the computer yelled, waving a disk.

The elevator opened.

"Get in the elevator!" Malachi ordered.

The agents began backing out of their positions, guns still trained on the exits while jumping aboard the elevator that was already occupied with Malachi, Melissa, and the agent with the disk.

But there was no room for Scott or the scientist.

"We'll send it back down," Malachi said as the doors closed.

"You gotta be kidding me," Scott mumbled, but the sirens drowned out his voice.

Then the door atop the other staircase opened, and two more guards came in. Scott swung the submachine gun up and shot them both before they could spot them. The next person to walk through the door must have thought it was a false alarm, because they didn't even have their gun in their hands. Scott squeezed off a burst that ripped through his chest and sent him bouncing down the stairs after the other two.

"What's going to happen to all these people?" Scott yelled over to the scientist.

"They will never recover."

"How could you do this?"

A tear rolled down his cheek. "I didn't realize that I was."

And Scott could certainly sympathize with that. He went to the scientist and pulled out the picture of his wife. Held it up to his face. "Jennifer Cavanaugh. Have you seen her here?"

He rubbed his eyes and squinted through his tears. He shook his head. "I never knew any of their names."

"You knew Melissa Strauss!"

"Only because of the instructions I received."

"From who?"

"In my attempt to purify what is left of my soul, I contacted the Resistance and told them of this place."

"The Resistance told you about her?"

"I was informed that the Mossad was interested in her, that they were corroborating with the Resistance in a mutual effort to obtain any knowledge that she might have."

"Knowledge of what?"

"They didn't tell me, but I assumed it had something to do with NASA's plan to orchestrate some kind of god hoax."

"You're a *NASA* scientist?"

"I worked *with* NASA, as we all did. But I am not employed by them."

Scott shook his head. He wanted to know more, but there wasn't time. He'd have plenty of questions for Malachi later on though, that was for sure. "How do we shut down the security net so the prisoners above can escape?"

"You have to disable its power source at the other end of the corridor by the barracks. But—"

And then both doors at the top of the staircases banged open, and guards started firing down at them.

Scott pushed the scientist into the first section of subjects and slammed him up against the dividing wall so that he was out of sight. Then he leaned around the corner and returned fire.

The elevator opened.

Scott shouted to the scientist, "Go! I'll cover you!" He stepped out from behind the wall and ran for the north staircase, shooting at the other stairs as he went.

The scientist was able to scramble into the elevator, but bullets were tearing up the ground at Scott's feet and preventing him from joining him. And then he heard the very distinct sound of a heavy metallic object bouncing across the floor. He turned just in time to see the grenade skip into the elevator, slipping past the door just before it finished closing.

The explosion tore the door in two, half of it jettisoning across the room in red rain while the other half crumpled outward like tinfoil.

Without hesitating, Scott pulled the pin from one of his own grenades and tossed it onto the platform above him. It landed on the body that was still wedged in the doorway and rolled into the corridor behind it.

The explosion rocked the staircase, and cries of pain echoed from the hall down into the lab. Scott ran back to the elevator, his ears ringing, and concentrated fire on the door atop the other staircase, keeping the soldiers from coming through.

The elevator was destroyed, and there was so much blood that it was dripping from the ceiling. What was left of the scientist was strewn all over the floor and hanging from the handrails. The guy had gotten off easy. Dead before he even had a chance to realize it. But now Scott was going to have to escape by going back the way they'd come in. Which meant he'd need the scientist's key cards.

He stepped into the elevator and looked around, ignoring the blood dripping down on him and wondering where the guy's hips might've ended up. He poked his boot at a pile of guts and found what he was looking for underneath it. A pocket. And miraculously, the key cards were inside it, still intact. He slipped them out of the slimy fabric and put them into his pocket. He ran back to the north stairs, careful not to slip in the blood, and fired until the submachine gun clicked empty. Throwing it aside, he grabbed an M4 from one of the dead guards and took the steps three at a time. When he got to the platform, he fired the gun at a soldier who was just coming through the door, the sound of the blasts rebounding off the walls. He swung into the corridor. It was clear.

He left the lab and headed toward the very place the scientist had warned them not to go. Toward the barracks.

But he didn't get far before he was at the huge steel door. It was closed, and though he had the scientist's cards, he didn't have his thumb, voice, or eyeball. None of that existed anymore.

He could hear the footsteps of more troops descending the west stairs, reaching the laboratory floor, and running over to the stairs that would lead them up to him. He ran back to the door to the lab, the dead body still wedged in it despite the explosion, and tossed another grenade down the steps. When it exploded, the force of the blast lifted three of the soldiers up into the air and tossed them off the stairs.

Scott ducked low and fired around the door, punching holes through two more guards on the stairs across from him. Then he looked at the staircase he'd tossed the grenade down and saw that its metal framework was leaning away from the wall, twisted and bent from the blast. They wouldn't be able to come up that way anymore, so his back side was safe. He turned away from the lab and began jogging back to the huge steel door at the top of the T, trying to think of a way to get past it.

But it began opening even before he got back to it.

He ran as fast as he could, up on the balls of his feet, and threw himself forward through the air. He landed on his stomach and slid across the polished floor, passing beneath the rising door and maneuvering onto his side and bringing the M4 around. The soldiers standing there waiting for the door to open looked down at the black shape streaking past them, but it was too late. Rotating onto his back, Scott fired at the back of their legs, and they dropped to the floor. When Scott sat up, they were right there in front of him, and he finished them off with headshots. Getting back to his feet, he ran down the corridor and passed straight by the door leading back up to the camp.

The next door he came to opened with the key card, and he found himself in a maze of tunnels. He decided on the most direct route and headed straight down the hall. Individual rooms that he figured to be living quarters began passing him on both sides.

The card worked for the next door too, and he entered a dark room. But the lights were motion sensitive, and they blinked on as he stepped forward. Computer stations were everywhere, digital charts and maps, desks, file cabinets… It was a big operation for not having any official funding.

He walked cautiously through the room, realizing that most of the soldiers must have gone topside to try to head off Malachi's escape. That was fine with him. He needed all the time he could get to find the controls to the perimeter fence and figure out how to shut it down.

"I don't think you're supposed to be in here," a voice rang out from behind him.

Scott froze. Then turned.

And came face-to-face with Titus Mayhew. Only now the Christian was aiming a pistol at his chest.

# 38.



*"...Some even believe we are part of a secret cabal working against the best interests of the United States, characterizing my family and me as internationalists and of conspiring with others around the world to build a more integrated global political and economic structure — one world, if you will. If that is the charge, I stand guilty, and I am proud of it."*

— David Rockefeller, *Memoirs*

The smile on Mayhew's face confirmed what Scott suspected had happened to him back at Isaiah's house. But even still, seeing him here, in *this* place, right now, Scott could barely believe it.

Mayhew took a step forward. "So how'd they get you to come along? Wait. Don't tell me. They told you your wife was here."

Scott fixed him with an icy gaze. "You took the priest's other books, didn't you?"

"Guilty." He patted his coat pocket with his free hand. "Had them the whole time. Guess Father Baer never got to tell you how many there were or what was in them." He shrugged. "It was fun listening to you try to make sense of it all, though. I left the two most obscure and pointless books behind. The ones without any real answers. At the time, though, I didn't know I was leaving them for you. Didn't know he was going to trust you with them. How could I?"

Here it was on full display. The rose and the cross, Rosicrucianism hiding behind the veil of Christianity. That *was* what Father Baer had tried to tell him, why he had said not to trust anyone. *Satan doesn't deceive by revealing himself as the Devil, he deceives by masquerading as an angel, as a servant of God.* Scott began tracing the M4's trigger with his index finger as it hung at his side. "So you're one of these Rosicrucians, then?"

"Are you surprised?"

More things began dropping into place. "That's why you made a fuss about Malachi driving off with the ring."

"A curveball I wasn't expecting."

"But you had the ring when we were in—" He stopped. "You called the cops on me at the restaurant." He thought spilling the coffee was what had gotten the cop's attention.

He pulled out a cell phone and waved it in his free hand. "I was almost 'Scott' free." He smiled.

"Cindy?"

"She was slowing you down."

"What do you mean?"

"You started looking after her, too. Which split your attention in half."

"You were using me?"

"Absolutely. You think I would've made it this far without you acting as my personal bodyguard? Only cost me a ride, a room, and some sob story about wanting to get back to fighting the New World Order."

"So you didn't pray with Cindy."

"No. I picked up a piece of twisted metal and plunged it into her back while she was lying unconscious in the road."

Scott took a deep breath, the hand holding the M4 beginning to tremble as guilt and shame tag-teamed his conscience and slammed it into a wall of blame. "I'm going to kill you."

Mayhew shook his head and took another step forward, waving the pistol. "This is a classic .50-caliber Mark XIX Desert Eagle. You think you can get past it? No, you're not going to kill me, Matthew. Or whatever your name is." He squinted. "I'm guessing you read Isaiah's book?"

"Some of it."

He raised the Desert Eagle higher, aiming it at Scott's head. "Did you at least skip to the end? To see how it all ties together?"

Now Scott was the one squinting.

"Oh," Mayhew said, waving the pistol, "I read it while you were sleeping. I was going to take it, but I had to leave you some kind of clue as to what was going on. This wouldn't be any fun at all if you didn't know the stakes, if you died completely clueless as to how you'd been used."

Scott wanted to shoot him then and there, but he knew that he had to hear him out. Egomaniacs like this derived pleasure from their work only when their work could be recognized. If not able to reveal their evil genius, then they'd get little satisfaction out of being an evil genius. He needed to spill it all, to let him know exactly how he'd been used and how it was all going to end. Needed to see the hopelessness in his eyes before he killed him. They were all the same. Which was why so many of them had spelled it out in letters and memoirs over the centuries. They just couldn't help it. They laughed amongst themselves, gloating about the power they had, finding it even more amusing that they could publish it all right out in the open and that the dumb sheep they ruled over would still manage to talk themselves out of believing it.

"The secret symbols all over our former nation's capital, the esoteric agenda spelled out in stone, Sirius portrayed by the five-pointed pentalpha, the Blazing Star the light shining behind the capstone on the dollar bill..." He paused, waiting to see if any of that would provoke a response from him.

Scott shook his head, hoping that it would keep him talking.

Mayhew dropped his shoulders. "Really? None of that?" He sighed. "Well, go ahead and drop your gun."

Scott dropped the rifle, and it bounced at his feet. But unfortunately, it didn't go off and hit Mayhew in the mouth.

"Manly P. Hall? Masonry's greatest philosopher?"

"I remember his name, you insane piece of —"

Mayhew raised the pistol and fired it at the ceiling, the explosion banging throughout the offices, the muzzle flash blinding even in the artificial light. The empty casing rattled on the floor. "No, Matthew," he said, wagging the gun back and forth like it was an extension of his finger. "You don't get to call me names." He pointed to his left. "Go sit."

Scott walked over and sat at a computer console. He knew the magazine in the Desert Eagle held seven rounds, and the more Mayhew fired the monster, the more fatigued his arm would become. He hoped he would keep up the act.

"Put your hands on your knees where I can see them," Mayhew ordered.

Scott obeyed.

"Hall founded the Philosophical Research Society in California. It was his attempt at bringing back the Alexandrian Library, though his research was mostly dedicated to discovering what America's true purpose was. *Is*."

"Really?" Scott turned his head and spit on the floor.

"He was convinced that America had a secret destiny dating all the way back to the ancient world. FDR believed America had a date with destiny too. A Russian mystic and Rosicrucian named Nicholas Roerich… You heard of him? Nominated for the Nobel Peace Prize three times, member of the theosophical society? No? Anyway, he was the spiritual mentor of Henry Wallace, FDR's vice president, and it was his influence that convinced FDR to put the reverse of the seal on the back of the dollar bill with the words 'New Order of the Ages.' How about that? You think maybe FDR thought his New Deal was the beginning of the New Order?"

"Is this going somewhere, because I have to pee."

"World democracy, my friend, is the main reason for all the wars throughout the last century. A fair world in which a world court sows forth justice, a world police keeping the peace, and no one in need of anything. For three thousand years, our secret societies have been working to bring this about."

"I'm not your friend. And you just said 'no one' in need."

"That's right."

"Don't you mean those who are left?"

Mayhew smiled. "The scientist explained it to you?"

"Transhumanism? Playing God? Your little virus to cull the population?"

"Not playing God, Matthew. *Becoming* God."

"Oh."

"You remember the part in Genesis where Lucifer tells Eve that if she eats of the tree of the knowledge of good and evil, her eyes will be opened, and she'll be like God?"

"Sure."

"Well, that's exactly what happened, and mankind has been writing about that illumination ever since. The Greeks, Persians, Babylonians…you see it all throughout history, even today. Especially today."

"You're talking about the new age stuff everyone's been peddling?"

"Everything God wanted to keep for Himself." He looked in the general direction of the lab. "But the philosophers understood that a perfect society could only come about through perfected men. *That* is what we're doing here."

"Oh. You're Nazis. Why didn't you just say so?"

"We're on the verge of accomplishing something Hitler barely even scratched the surface of."

"You're gonna burn in hell with him just the same."

"You don't believe in hell, remember?"

"You're quickly changing my mind."

Mayhew smiled again. "The way the rose infected the cross… I don't know that even the great architects of that plan could have foreseen how effective it would be. And just printing 'In God We Trust' on the currency was enough to convince most people that the country was founded on Christian principles, the founding fathers on par with the apostles. We convinced them that the nation was first theirs, entrusted to them by God, so we were able to manufacture this whole patriotic version of American Christianity that was so easy to use for our purposes. To get God's people more concerned about politics than heaven, to have them endorse wars in God's name, to promote democracy throughout the world." He laughed. "In God's name, and with a rose in their chest pocket, they paved the way for their biggest enemy."

Scott knew all this from Jack. It was what his book had been about. The church turned first into an institution and then into a political tool. Though it was nothing new. From Constantine to the Reformation to Manifest Destiny to a hundred years of war. The church had always found itself being manipulated by some political agenda.

Mayhew waved the gun again. "I can tell you're getting bored, so I won't mention the number thirteen and its relevance in numerology, why it was all over the dollar bill—"

Scott laughed.

"I'm sorry, are you the one trained in the esoteric arts, the mystery religions and their ancient practices? No. So then you wouldn't understand that these things were all crafted into plain sight where their meaning would be clear and obvious to the initiated. You think it's a coincidence that Washington was constructed by Freemasons and that the imagery for this whole ancient plan is spelled out in its architecture? You do know that Congress passed HR 33 to honor Freemasonry's role in establishing the country, right? So don't laugh at things you know nothing about."

"I have an idea," Scott stated dryly. "Why don't you let me finish reading the book myself so that you can shut the hell up?"

Mayhew stared at him for a long moment, and when he spoke again, his voice was as level as a frozen pond. "The scientist didn't recognize your wife, did he?"

Scott didn't answer.

"Maybe that's because, like I said, Malachi and his Mossad friends lied to you. What was it they said they were after? The scientist? Information about the biological agent?" He shook his head. "They don't care about any of that. They only care about the ring. They came here for Melissa Strauss."

Scott had figured as much.

"And for information about the planned deception. The role the Ark of the Covenant is going to play in it."

"Can you please just shoot me?"

"I heard you talking about Roswell with Isaiah."

"The priest mentioned it."

"He would. New Mexico, 1947, first week of July." He began pacing, his gun arm now bent at the elbow, getting tired. "A local rancher discovers a huge amount of unusual debris while checking on his sheep after a night of thunderstorms. Some of the debris appears to have strange physical properties, so he goes to get the sheriff. The sheriff contacts Roswell Army Air Field, and they investigate. But the military shows up and seals off the area, closing it for days while retrieving the wreckage. Whatever's found is first taken to Roswell Army Air Field, but is then loaded onto B-29s and C-54s and flown to what was then Wright Field." He raised his eyebrows. "July 8th, 1947, the commander of the 509th Bomb Group, the only atomic bomb group in the world at the time and one of the most elite units in the world, issues an official press release stating that they've recovered the wreckage of a crashed disk. The statement makes headlines in over thirty US magazines that afternoon. But within hours, a second press release is issued from the commander of the Eighth Air Force at Fort Worth Army Air Field in Texas. Four hundred miles away. Evidently, the 509 at Roswell mistook the wreckage of a weather balloon and its radar reflector for a crashed disk.

"The incompetent commander who couldn't tell the difference between a weather balloon and a flying saucer? Well, he'd later become a four-star general and vice chief of staff of the US Air Force. But other witnesses, such as two brigadier generals, testified that the commander's first report was correct." He licked his lips, not used to talking this much. "Investigators got copies of the 1947 Roswell Army Air Field yearbook, and they tracked down witnesses. The intelligence officer of the 509 was the first to testify. He was one of the first two military officers to the actual site, and he said that what they found wasn't of this earth. And then he went on to prepare the report on the Soviets' first nuclear detonation for Truman. Before he died, the chief of staff at Eighth in Fort Worth testified that he'd received the call from Andrews Army Air Field in DC, commanding a cover-up." He waved the gun in circular motions again. "The testimonies go on and on."

"So what?"

"So what if this information, and tons more like it from all over the world, was suddenly admitted?"

"I thought they already admitted UFOs exist."

He smiled. "They admitted enough to get the public thinking about it, but I'm talking about something on a whole other scale."

"We're being invaded?"

"No, we're being *summoned*."

"Summoned?"

"What do you think the masses would do if NASA suddenly proclaimed they found an extraterrestrial substance with all of earth's religious texts engraved on it? And what if that material was the same material Solomon's rings were constructed of? Or the Ark of the Covenant itself, for that matter? Do you think that people might begin to think of God a little differently? The Jews using an alien instrument as a radio through which to talk to their creator?"

"You're crazy."

"It's practically New Age doctrine, Matthew. Has been for a very long time."

"For what purpose?"

"One world religion, humanism, the occult dream."

"You think the Jews and the Muslims are going to go along with that?"

"Seems to me that the ones who won't are busy killing each other. Though, according to Isaiah's version of the Bible, the Jews are going to fall in line with the whole program anyway, making a covenant with the Antichrist."

Scott clenched his teeth. He couldn't take much more of this. The Desert Eagle weighed four and a half pounds, and its sights were beginning to dip lower and lower in Mayhew's hand. "What's the point of all of it?" He needed to keep him talking just a little longer.

Mayhew blinked, confused. "The point? The point is power, control. That's *always* the point. We will evolve and be gods of this world."

"Ruling over who?"

"Everyone else. All the good little world patriots who will proudly submit to microchip implantation."

"So you can have complete control over everyone."

His lips spread away from his teeth. "Matthew, we have to differentiate between terrorists and innocent civilians, eliminate fraud, get rid of germ-ridden cash."

The huge pistol dropped another inch.

"What does that have to do with this alien crap?"

"World democracy can't become a reality with our present concept of God, of religion. It's too divisive."

Scott laughed again. "Says the atheist who is planning to murder half the population."

But Mayhew ignored him. "Some of the most atrocious things in history have been orchestrated by religion."

"Religion *used* by people like you."

"Faith is a powerful thing and very useful when controlled. But it has no place in the coming empire. Our space brothers will come to save us, to illuminate our way of thinking, to reveal the true concept of the divine. They will have the answers man has been searching for. Answers we will want to hear. How we are all of the same spirit, part of Gaia."

"Is this before or after you kill everyone? Forget it, I don't even care. Did you kill Isaiah?"

"I slit his throat. What does that have to do with anything?"

Scott was counting on the heftiness of the Eagle to give him a fighting chance. Because of its size, weight, report, and blinding muzzle flash, the Desert Eagle was relatively clumsy for these types of situations and the reason it had become a relic among pistols. The Mark XIX that Mayhew was wielding had a ten-inch barrel opposed to the six that other models had. If he fired it with his fatigued hand, the report would jack the barrel of the gun almost straight up into the air, pulling his whole arm up with it. He would then have to bring it all the way back down before getting off another shot. Scott just needed the first one to miss.

"How do I turn off the fence?" Scott asked, wondering just how far Mayhew was willing to take his little tell-all.

"You think you're going to get a chance to turn off the fence? Matthew, Matthew…you're not getting out of that chair. You're never going to see another face again. Never going to breathe fresh air or see the sky. I'm going to blow your head apart right where you sit."

He shrugged. "Just supposing."

Mayhew sidestepped over to a console and brushed his fingers over the touchpad. "There. It's off."

Scott just stared at him.

"Not that it matters, because I already knew the scientist was planning his little act of penitence. Why didn't I stop him? It brought the ring back. And yes, I know all about the little Christian commune. Don't worry, every last one of the bores will be dead by tomorrow night. So even if the prisoners here got away somehow, they'd just be hunted down and shot."

"You don't think they'll get information from Melissa Strauss?"

"Do you know what they did to her? Before they threw her off a bridge?" He drew a finger across his stomach. "She's a vegetable. Besides, they'll all be dead soon, and I'll have the ring."

"The ring that leads to the location of the Ark?" Scott was ready now. He just needed Mayhew to move the pistol to his left hand. That was when he'd make his move. The psychopath had been talking for nearly ten minutes. It had to be coming. No way he'd shoot him now with his right hand. He'd transfer it to his left and give his right a rest before transferring it back and then shooting him.

"It's the last piece of the Jewish puzzle."

"Everyone's always taking from the Jews."

He shrugged. "I didn't judge them."

This was it, he could feel it.

"You know, years ago we actually lost track of the other ring. What a mess that was. But you don't even know about the other ring, do you? What it is?" Mayhew brought his left hand toward his right.

Scott tensed, only needing to confirm that he was in fact transferring it and not just getting a firmer grip with an added hand.

The gun rotated sideways, the barrel shifting up to the left ever so slightly. But ever so slightly spread out over distance could prove to be the difference between life and death. Granted, there was only thirty feet separating them, but it was his only chance.

The weight of the Eagle was now mostly resting against his left hand, his finger off the trigger and out of the trigger guard, his right hand releasing the gun.

*Now!*

Scott pulled the silenced pistol out of the holster strapped to his thigh even as he moved forward up and off the chair. He threw himself sideways, diving for the cover of a desk.

Mayhew quickly fired the Desert Eagle, but he hadn't had the time to aim. That and he'd used his left hand. Still, the bullet passed just inches from Scott's head, tearing half the table apart.

But now Scott had the advantage. He crawled across the floor between rows of desks, heading for the far right wall. Once there, he sat with his back against it.

A whistle echoed through the room. "That was fast."

Scott aimed the pistol at the farthest light and squeezed off a round. The bulb shattered. He did it three more times, creating more shadows in the room.

"I know what you're up to," Mayhew said. "Don't think I didn't see that night vision hanging around your neck."

Crawling across the floor, Scott made his way along the wall and toward Mayhew's last position. Then he stopped and listened.

The console next to him exploded, shooting a debris trail across the floor away from him, which told him that Mayhew was coming up behind him. He spun around and fired off a few shots just as Mayhew peeked out from behind a row of desks. More touchscreens shattered, and Mayhew ducked back out of sight. But not before Scott saw that he had an M4 in his hands.

Scott dove into a tuck and roll as Mayhew fired a burst from the M4 that cut into the wall above his head and shattered the closest desk, filling the air with loose papers. Back to his feet, Scott replaced the pistol's empty mag and fired again in Mayhew's direction, shell casings bouncing off the floor at his feet.

Mayhew returned fire, and the muzzle flashes from the M4 were like a strobe light in the darkness. Scott ducked back down. And then silence.

Scott looked up over the shattered desks but saw no sign of him. Then he walked in a low crouch down the aisle where their confrontation had begun. Still no sign of him. The sound of sizzling and popping electronics accompanied the glass crunching under his feet. He swept his aim from right to left.

And then he sensed something behind him. Whether a shadow or movement in his periphery, he didn't know. But he broke out into a full sprint just as Mayhew's M4 erupted, and everything around him exploded.

Diving onto his stomach, he slid across the floor. Reached out and grabbed a desk leg, swinging himself around behind it. The shooting stopped, and the sound of the empty M4 clattering against the floor echoed in the sudden silence.

Scott hopped to his feet and emptied the rest of his magazine in the direction he'd heard the gun drop. He ducked back low to reload, then ran across the aisle, back to the right side of the room and toward the wall. Swinging around the corner, he found only the M4 lying in a puddle of casings.

A door banged shut somewhere in front of him.

He followed the sound to the door, saw that it swung on hinges and didn't require a key card. He turned the handle and pulled the door open as he dropped to a knee and raised the pistol.

No sign of Mayhew. Just an empty corridor.

He stepped into the artificial light and removed his night vision. He followed the hall to another adjacent wing that was also empty. He stood there at the top of another T, not sure which way to go, when the report of Mayhew's Desert Eagle suddenly sounded from the left. Scott took off in that direction and came to one of Malachi's men lying facedown on the floor, blood flowing from his body. Scott stepped over him and continued on.

There was a gradual incline to the corridor now. Drops of blood dotted the floor, stretching all the way to the end of the passageway. Malachi's guy must've managed to get a silenced round off before Mayhew shot him. Hopefully that would slow him down.

Another door, and Scott swiped the keycard. Immediately he saw Mayhew thirty yards ahead of him, limping, dragging his left leg, going for a huge white door that sat above a small set of metal stairs. Above the door, in big red letters, was the word EXIT.

Scott raised his pistol and lined the back of Mayhew's head up in his sights just as Mayhew turned and fired the Mossad agent's silenced submachine gun at him. Scott threw himself to the side of the corridor, squeezing off a few rounds as he did so, and Mayhew fell with a moan. The submachine gun skidded across the floor away from him.

Scott stood, his chest heaving, the veins in the side of his neck bulging against his skin. "Well, Titus, doesn't look like you'll be around to see your New World Order after all." His words echoed through the corridor. He took his time reaching him, walking slow. Now it was his turn to savor the victory. "I'll be sure to send you a postcard though. Let you know how it's all playing out without you. Except that I hear there's only outer darkness where you're going, so you probably won't be able to read it." He stood over him.

Mayhew tried to raise the Eagle.

Scott shot him in the arm.

Mayhew started to scream and curse, fuming like a man possessed, kicking against the angels of death as they began to drag him toward the heat. And then he stopped and smiled.

"Something funny?" asked Scott.

He nodded. "It is." He laughed. "It really is."

Scott kicked the Eagle aside. He reached down and grabbed Mayhew's collar with one hand. Lifted him to his feet and shoved him up against the wall.

Mayhew licked his lips. "Remember how I sort of insinuated that your wife isn't here?"

Scott stopped breathing.

"Actually, she *was* here."

Scott shifted his hand from Mayhew's collar to his throat. Began to squeeze. "You're a liar."

"Sticks and stones," he whispered through his constricted larynx.

"Where is she, then?" His whole body was convulsing with rage now, and he had to keep from snapping his neck. The muscles in his forearms were stretching the black fabric of his shirt.

Mayhew raised a finger and tapped it against Scott's hand.

Scott loosened his grip, and Mayhew gasped for air.

"I said…she *was* here. Once we're done with the subjects — people who died in the nuclear attack, of course — we have to remove any trace of them."

Scott started shaking.

"You didn't see the incinerator?"

Scott didn't know what happened next, only that Mayhew was suddenly beneath him and his face had somehow turned into bloody pulp. He brought his hands up to his face and saw that they were covered in blood.

And then a severe stinging sensation in his right arm.

Everything stopped. Sound itself vanishing. Slightly aware of someone to his right, he tried turning his head in that direction but it seemed to be taking forever. Finally, an NAU soldier pointing a rifle at him came into view. But then just as quickly, the soldier was on his back, blood spurting from his body. More time dragged on, and he was looking back down at Mayhew. Only he wasn't there anymore.

A loud blast from somewhere far away. Something slamming into his back, and the floor was slowly coming up to meet his face. He tried to put his arms out, to brace himself, but he couldn't move them. It seemed like he might lie down gently. Then his face hit the floor, and everything went black.

He opened his eyes a second later (though it could have been a hours for all he knew) and realized right away what had happened. The news of Jennifer had sent him into a frenzy, and he'd thrown Mayhew to the floor and proceeded to beat his face in. Which was when the NAU soldier came around the corner and shot him in the arm. The impact had spun his upper body while he fired off a shot or two of his own.

But the force that had knocked him down…

He rolled onto his side and saw Mayhew standing over him, the Desert Eagle back in his hand, its barrel smoking.

"Didn't know you'd take the news so bad," he said, blood oozing from his mouth.

Scott's mind whirled through the chaos. Jennifer was dead. Nothing mattered anymore.

"Guess I'll be the one sending you the postcard after all." He spit blood across the floor, and a tooth went bouncing through it. He laughed.

But then Scott realized that something did matter. There was a phone call he had to make. He arched his back and reached his hand behind him like he was in pain from the gunshot. But it was the shotgun on his back that had taken the brunt of the blast. He put his hand at the base of his spine and slipped the knife from its sheath.

Mayhew crouched beside him and glared at him through bloodshot eyes. He raised the Eagle and pressed it against Scott's head.

Seeing stars, Scott could only pray that Mayhew needed to get in another blow before shooting him. That he'd want to inflict more pain before ending all of it.

And that was exactly what happened.

Not content to transport him from one place to another with a single bullet, he changed his grip on the pistol so that he was holding it like a hammer. He raised it, intending to beat Scott's skull in with the butt of it. He swung it down hard and fast.

But not fast enough.

Scott raised his arm and blocked the blow while pulling his other hand out from behind his back and lashing out with the knife. It flashed under the lights like a streaking missile before plunging into Mayhew's flesh.

Mayhew screamed and backed up, dropping the pistol and grasping his arm.

Scott leaned forward and swiped the blade across the front of his shins.

Mayhew fell over.

Scott struggled back to his feet. He took the bent shotgun off his back and tossed it away.

Mayhew was sitting on the ground and pushing himself backward toward the exit. The knife had cut through his pants and all the way to the bone.

Scott bent over, picked up the Desert Eagle, and fired its last round into Mayhew's knee, shattering his kneecap like glass.

Mayhew screamed at the top of his lungs, and Scott threw the empty gun at his face. Mayhew clutched his nose, more blood oozing between his fingers. He rolled onto his side and yelled in agony.

"You know what I'm gonna do for you?" Scott asked. "I'm gonna let you sit here and think about your life. Or maybe you can try calling your space brothers for help. Or, hell, maybe you'll find a way to achieve godhood in the next twenty minutes and you can give yourself eternal life."

Mayhew tried to move but couldn't. "Please…"

Scott paused. "Please? *Please?*" He began to tremble. "Is that what my wife said before you stuck her in a microwave?" Then he lunged down at him, the knife flashing back and forth, blood spraying all over the corridor walls. Mayhew screamed, held up his hands. Scott just cut through them.

When he was finally done, exhausted and shaking, craze still in his eyes, Scott wiped the blood splatter from his face. Somehow he'd managed to miss cutting through any major arteries, but no amount of plastic surgery would ever fix Mayhew's face. He'd never walk on his own two legs again, and he might be a little slower in the head, but he might still live. If he got some serious medical attention fast. But that wasn't Scott's problem. He bent over to take the books from Mayhew's jacket when he noticed something through Mayhew's torn shirt. He grabbed the shirt and ripped it in half, down to Mayhew's stomach. The tattoo he'd gotten a glimpse of at Isaiah's was indeed a cross. But not only a cross. There was a rose wrapping around its base and a double-headed phoenix standing behind it. Scott stared at the Rosicrucian symbol for a second before grabbing the books. There were two of them. "Thanks," he mumbled. He turned and headed for the exit.

"See you in hell, Matthew," Mayhew called out.

"You'd better hope not," he said. He climbed the stairs and used the key card on the door. It opened, and the cold night stood before him. Mayhew's voice echoed after him.

"Your wife died squealing like a pig! She screamed like a little—"

Scott popped the pin, and the sound of it stopped Mayhew in mid-sentence. He tossed the grenade over his shoulder and stepped into the open air.

Mayhew looked around, trying to get a glimpse of the thing bouncing down the corridor toward him. He craned his neck and saw the grenade roll to a stop just five feet from his head. It sat there, staring at him. But he couldn't reach it. Could only watch it and wait. Wait for hell to come get him.

Scott collapsed into the snow, barely acknowledging the dead NAU soldiers who were sprawled out around him. Malachi's men must have mowed them down as they exited the facility.

He heard the grenade go off and turned. He stared at the door that had closed just seconds before, and then vomited.

*Jennifer…*

He rolled onto his back and lay there, motionless, staring up into the darkness as snowflakes melted on his face.

But the stillness was interrupted by a sudden burst of static that came from somewhere beside him.

*"Fifteen minutes."*

It was illusive, like a dream. He couldn't pinpoint what it meant or where it was coming from. It sounded like it had come right out of the snow.

*"Fourteen minutes."*

And then he understood.

He stumbled back to his feet and pulled the night vision back over his eyes. Saw one of Malachi's men lying amongst the soldiers. The voice had come through the radio still strapped to his chest. Scott took it and started to run. He fell, got back up, and fell again. But he kept going. He had to get to the building they'd found Melissa in. To all those people.

*"Twelve minutes."*

Scott stumbled through the snow and to the building. He threw the door open and fell inside. "Get up!" he yelled, getting back to his feet. "Come on, wake up!" He made his way through the room, urging the women to get out of their beds. "Get out of here!" But they just sat there and stared into the darkness.

"Come on! Get out of here!" He climbed the steps to the second story and tried stirring the men who were being housed there, but they just stared at him with the same dumbfounded expressions. "Get out of here!"

"Who are you?" someone asked.

"Just get out of here! Run! I'm rescuing you!"

"Rescuing?" the voice came back. There was no comprehension in it.

*"Ten minutes."*

Scott looked up and down the rows of beds, the room beginning to spin around him. No one was moving. *They're sedated*, he realized. He swore and made his way back downstairs.

*"Nine minutes."*

There was no more time. He looked through the night vision at all the innocent women, took in all their confused faces. Thought of Jennifer. But there was nothing he could do. "Get out of here!" he yelled again. "Or I'll shoot you!" He pulled the pistol out, removed the silencer, and shot a round into the ceiling. But instead of creating a panic, the noise had the opposite effect, and they all just recoiled into the corners of their beds.

"Please," Scott begged. Tears filled his eyes. He couldn't save them.

*"Six minutes."*

"I'm so sorry," he whispered through quivering lips. He turned back into the snow. And as he began making his way back to the fence, he spotted a little boy standing in front of another building. Behind him, in the windows of the building, were a dozen more little faces. Children who had been living normal lives just a few days ago. All of them about to die. Maybe it was a mercy.

Scott knew he'd never make it to the kid in time, but he waved for him to run toward him.

But the boy shook his head and instead turned and ran toward the other building, where he thought maybe his parents were.

Scott wiped his eyes and turned away.

He went through the hole in the fence and continued toward the woods, completely unaware of his bleeding arm and his bruised back, his body as numb as his mind, the look in the children's eyes hypnotizing him.

A deafening roar filled the night, and the forest ahead of him lit up like midday as the ground shook beneath his feet. The underground facility exploded, tearing open the earth above it and turning the whole camp into a crater. But he didn't turn to see it.

As he walked from tree to tree, leaning on them for support, he took out his phone and brought up the number the intelligence guy had programmed into it. He hit CALL, and a voice answered.

"I have the ring," Scott said. "Now where do I meet you?"

# 39.



He had no idea how many hours it had taken him to traverse the five miles back to the commune, only that dawn was now breaking over the horizon. He'd moved one foot in front of the other over and over again while his mind wandered light-years away from northwest Pennsylvania. Instead, it had been called away to an invisible court held in the metaphysical. He remembered Edward telling him about God's instruction to Israel through the prophet Isaiah to "Come, let us reason together." Only he found that the courtroom was empty, God wasn't there, and that there was no *reason* at all. And so all his accusations against God he just flung into a silent emptiness where they would go forever unanswered. And Scott hated Him for it.

He walked out of the woods and saw the commune sitting just a hundred yards away. The morning breeze sent wisps of swirling snow across the ground at his feet, and he watched it dance in the golden glow of a new day. And before he knew it, he was staggering down the commune's main street. It was empty, everything still and silent. He headed to Malachi's tent.

He saw that there were lights on inside it, and silhouettes were walking back and forth across the tent walls. He could hear whispers drifting along the freezing air. He climbed the steps and stood there for a moment, allowing his eyes to adjust. Some men were asleep on cots while others were having their injuries looked after. He found Malachi sitting on a table with his back toward him.

Scott told his legs to start moving again, and they reluctantly obeyed, even as the ground seemed to rock unevenly beneath them. He reached out and grabbed Malachi's right shoulder. Malachi turned his head, and Scott sent him crashing to the floor with a right hook to the face. Scott swayed as fireworks popped in his head, his right shoulder an erupting volcano spewing pain up and down his arm. His vision faded, and he pitched forward onto the table, rolled off, and landed on the floor.

"Are you awake?" Scott heard someone say.

He blinked, recognizing Malachi's voice, and tried to find him.

"You will be sore for a while," Malachi said, "but you will be okay. You should take it easy until you regain your strength."

Scott saw that he was standing over him, his head blocking the sun. The side of his face was bruised. Good.

"I am sorry that I lied to you, but we needed you with us," he continued.

Scott sat up, and it felt like his back had been wound as tight as a piano wire. Or struck with a sledgehammer. He tested his arm and found that it worked okay. Saw that he was in a sleeping bag near the edge of the tent. "Why?"

"Because we know what happened to Isaiah. And since you survived, we presumed they offered you a deal. When you mentioned your wife, I knew that was probably the leverage they were using. I needed to keep my eye on you."

Scott closed his eyes and looked down, stretching the muscles in his neck and back. "They know about this place. They know you're here with the ring." And then he whispered, "All these people are going to die today." Then he fixed eyes of fire on him. "You killed all those people…"

"The prisoners? Some might consider what happened to them an act of mercy. Besides, would you rather the transhumanist agenda continue?"

Scott didn't know what to say to that, and Malachi began walking away.

"Whatever they offered you, you would be a fool to trust them. Even if you could get the ring away from us."

"I was a fool to trust *you*," Scott shot back.

"Yet you are still alive."

He got to his feet and needed to lean against one of the tent poles for support as his vision went dark and the room seemed to spin. Once it passed, he stood straight and noticed there was nothing beneath his jacket but gauze and tape, which explained why he was so cold. He pulled the jacket closed, flipped up the collar, and left the tent. He could smell breakfast being made, and once again the smell of bacon brought Jennifer back to him. She turned from the stove and smiled. Brushed a strand of hair behind her ear.

"Hi."

The voice shattered the memory, and he turned to see someone holding out a plate of eggs.

"Hungry?" Dan Ralston asked.

He nodded and accepted the plate. "Thanks."

"Here, you can sit down over here." Ralston started walking toward a table that was set up outside one of the smaller cabins.

Scott sat and started eating. "You're the leader here?"

Ralston shrugged. "More or less."

"You don't seem the type."

"What do you mean?" Ralston asked.

"A cult leader."

He laughed. "You think we're some kind of doomsday cult?"

"You do adhere to the New World Order conspiracy theory, don't you? Where were you on the first of January 2000?"

Ralston smiled, amused. "The FBI's *Project Megiddo*..." Scratching an itch over his eye, he said, "I'm pretty sure the cat's out of the bag by now, their 'strategic assessment' having been a little off the mark."

The project had stamped anyone who believed in the second coming of Christ and His millennial Kingdom, the Antichrist and the New World Order as potentially dangerous conspiracy theorists.

"You sure you're not one of those neo-Nazi groups, then?"

Again Ralston laughed. "Look around; you won't find a single weapon."

"Well, that's just stupid," he said through a mouthful of egg. He was about to say something else when a shadow fell across the table, and a small *thud* sounded between them.

Malachi was standing over them. "I think these belong to you," he said, pointing to the books he just dropped on the table. And then he walked away.

With a casual glance, Scott recognized the two books he'd taken from Mayhew along with Isaiah's notebook. He continued eating, not really caring about anything other than eggs at the moment.

But Ralston was curious. "Diaries?" he asked.

Scott shook his head, no. He motioned toward them with his fork, indicating that Ralston was free to have a look. Which he did. As Scott finished his breakfast, Ralston flipped through the pages to one of Father Baer's books. One that Scott hadn't seen yet.

"Are you serious?" Ralston asked once Scott finished clearing his plate.

"What?"

He pointed to the open book in front of him. "Is this for real?"

"Who knows."

Ralston flipped through a few more pages. "This is incredible."

"What is?" Though he didn't care.

"The Ark of the Covenant."

"What about it?"

But Ralston didn't seem to hear him, just kept turning pages. "I've heard of this before. Where did this come from?"

"A Catholic priest."

"Interesting." Then he spun the book around so that Scott could see it. "Look at this."

Scott forced his eyes to the pages and saw what looked like a two-dimensional diagram of some kind of underground contraption.

"This is supposed to be beneath the Temple," Ralston said. "*Jachin* and *Boaz*." He tapped the drawing, indicating what looked to be two pillars rising from the ground. Then he moved his finger to the left a little and said, "The Holy Place." And finally he touched what looked like a small room all the way to the left of the page, to some kind of protrusion on the floor. "The Holy of Holies."

"Solomon's Temple?"

He nodded. "*Jachin* and *Boaz* are the two pillars in front of the Temple."

"What's all this other stuff?" Scott was now pointing his own finger at the strange subterranean mechanism scribbled inside what he assumed to be a long cave beneath the Temple.

"Some sort of reverse lever system that was operated by sand hydraulics." He was smiling.

"For what purpose?" He faintly recalled all that stuff about demons building the Temple, but also knew offhand that Freemasonry took credit for building it too.

"Okay, look here. See this?" Down under the diagram was a list of Bible references. "First Kings 7:16." He pulled a small Bible out from inside his coat pocket and flipped it open. "Listen. 'And he made two chapiters of molten brass, to set upon the tops of the pillars: the height of the one chapiter was five cubits, and the height of the other chapiter was five cubits: and nets of checker work, and wreaths of chain work, for the chapiters which were upon the top of the pillars; seven for the one chapiter, and seven for the other chapiter...'"

"Hold on," Scott interrupted. "How long is this gonna take?"

"Okay, just note that when the pillars were built, they had five-cubit capitals of brass on top of them."

Scott's face was blank.

Ralston continued anyway. "Well, according to Second Kings 25:17"—he pointed to another reference on the page—"when Nebuchadnezzar came to Jerusalem some five hundred years later, the height of the capitals was recorded as only being *three* cubits."

"So the Bible's wrong. I already knew that."

"Jeremiah records that the Babylonians tore the pillars down and carried the brass back to Babylon. And the brass capitals they brought back were measured at *five* cubits."

Scott dropped his bored gaze back down to the diagram of the lever system and re-evaluated the two pillars. There were rods extending down from their bottoms and connecting to the short side of the lever.

Ralston said, "The Ark was kept here, in the Holy of Holies."

The lever stretched from beneath the pillars all the way to underneath the area Ralston just indicated, under the Holy of Holies. There was some type of protruding base that the lever rested on, closer to the pillars, giving it the appearance of an off-centered seesaw. Only connected to the right end there were rods or poles going up into the pillars, and on the left was some kind of underground compartment or elevator.

"Second Maccabees says that Jeremiah and the priests were warned in a dream how to hide the Ark from the invading Babylonians, and the theory is that a secret escape passage was built beneath the Temple, leading out beyond the walls of the city. That's what this is." There were steps leading away from the underground box below the Holy of Holies. "There were supposedly four keystones within the Holy of Holies that the priests of Levi would stand on to unlock the elevator."

"Elevator?" Scott raised his eyebrows in mock amusement.

"Yeah, basically. The lever system supposedly worked like this: while the priests unlocked the 'elevator' in the Holy of Holies, someone else would smash the base of the pillars. They were filled with sand, and as the sand leaked out, the capitals would sink down, the long rods connected to them engaging the lever. So, the rods would force that side of the lever down while the elevator atop the opposite end of the see-saw would rise out of the ground and into the Holy of Holies. A built-in sand damper system would allow the lever to operate slowly. The Ark of the Covenant would then be moved into the elevator, and the second sand damper would allow its descent back down into the subterranean cave, granting access to the secret tunnels below the Temple that led out of the city."

Scott yawned.

"That's why there's no record of the instruments from the Holy of Holies being carried off to Babylon. They weren't there when they arrived. They'd already been hidden. That's why the capitals were recorded as being two cubits short, but then full size again once the hollow pillars were broken apart. The French explored some of these tunnels in the 1800s. They found a half-carved cherubim that's now in the British Royal Museum. Second Maccabees states that a priest began carving directions to the Ark and that Jeremiah rebuked him, saying that the Ark must remain hidden in the secret place until the Lord brings it forth in the last days when His glory will be seen above the mercy seat as it was in the days of Moses and Solomon."

"I read that Solomon's son switched the Ark with a fake and carried it off to Ethiopia."

Ralston nodded. "That's another theory. The language in the text seems to give it some credence too. I'm just telling you what *this* is." He flipped the page, bringing to light something about a secret pact Solomon made with Hiram, the king who helped in the construction of the Temple.

Scott wondered what part the rings played in the whole Ark scheme, wondered about the Temple Scroll, the Copper Scroll, and all the other pieces needed to unlock the Ark from the mysteries of time. Then he thought about the things Mayhew had said about NASA introducing the Ark as something alien.

"Didn't expect to come across this today," Ralston said. He closed the book and stood, taking the plate from Scott. "I'll be right back. You stay here." He came back with a set of folded clothes in his arms. "I think these should fit you."

Scott was taken aback by the kind gesture and looked around. "Don't you need them?"

He shrugged. "Not as much as you do. Please take them. I'm cold just looking at you."

"I can't do that," Scott said, feeling guilty about what he knew was going to happen to these people.

"Come on, we insist. Besides, it's what the Bible commands. 'He doth loveth the stranger, in giving him food and raiment.' You can change at my place."

"Okay," he answered. He stood and followed him to his little abode and went in to change as fast as possible. Jeans, comfortable pair of socks, a white T-shirt, and another hooded sweatshirt. "Thank you very much," he said to Ralston, stepping back outside.

"You don't have to thank me. Treasures in heaven, my friend."

"Is that all you people think about? Going to heaven?"

"Considering what's become of this world, can you blame us?"

"You don't think your obsession with heavenly matters is what helped cause this mess?"

Ralston smiled, started walking. "On the contrary, actually." And then he asked, "Have you ever read the Bible?"

"Parts."

"Here." Ralston offered him his. "Take this."

Scott hesitated.

"Take it."

But Scott only leaned in and asked, "Is there a verse in there that explains why it pleased God to kill my wife?"

Ralston's whole demeanor instantly deflated. "I'm sorry."

"Yeah, me too." And then he grabbed the books Ralston had been holding for him and turned back toward the tent, leaving Ralston standing there with just the Bible in his hands.

When he reached the tent, Malachi was waiting for him with a cup of coffee. Scott took it.

"It was a necessary evil," Malachi began explaining. "We had to destroy their progress, their work."

"And of course you couldn't have just let them go," Scott answered back as he savored the hot liquid running down his throat.

"Go where? They would have died in the woods. And destroying that place may have saved millions of others from a similar fate."

Scott shook his head. "You don't care about their work. You just care about the ring. For all I know, you blew the place to cover your tracks so they don't know you have Melissa Strauss in your possession."

Malachi sighed, defeated.

"And what about these people? You just gonna hop on your chopper when the army shows up?"

"Not everything can work out the way we wish it could. Unfortunately that means the safety of a few will be compromised for the safety of many."

"Are you quoting *them*? Because I'm pretty sure that's exactly what the scientist said they were doing."

But Malachi didn't answer him.

"Where are my sneakers?"

Malachi pointed.

"Thanks." Then Scott brushed past him and went to put them on. He tilted the coffee back and drained it all at once, setting the cup down on a table as he passed it. He had some walking to do, and he preferred sneakers over boots to do it in.

As he sat and put the sneakers on, he noticed a table laid out with guns. He tied the laces and stood. Walked to the table and snatched a pistol from it. He felt the cold steel against his skin as he tucked it into the back of his pants. He picked up a shotgun, a few magazines, a pocketful of shells, and then he was on his way.

He needed to find the train tracks and follow them west to a bridge. He had almost a full day to get there.

A day he was sure would be his last.

# 40.

*"The real truth of the matter is, as you and I know, that a financial element in the larger centers has owned the Government ever since the days of Andrew Jackson."*
<br>— Franklin D. Roosevelt

He had the hood pulled up over his head in an attempt to shield himself from the biting wind, his hands thrust deep into his pockets. He was miserable, and he felt like the Reaper must be playing a drum solo in his body, amping things up for the grand finale. Stomping on the bass pedal, the beater swinging up and smashing into his back with every step he took. The little flame flickering in his shoulder the hi-hats rhythmically clanging shut. The machine-gun speed of the snare and toms pushing him ever closer to the edge of sanity and into Mr. Grim's boney embrace.

*I'm losing it,* he thought. He looked up at the dark clouds. They were threatening another unhappy night. He returned his gaze to a spot up ahead where the ground began to slip down out of sight. The sound of a nearby stream trickling over rocks drifted to him, and the soothing noise had him closing his eyes. He stared at the picture of Jennifer. Cindy was there too, but she'd faded into the background of another room. He tried to reach out and touch his wife, but as soon as his fingers were about to make contact, the picture disappeared. Replacing it was a video of her being thrown into an incinerator. Her face staring out of a glass window, her fists pounding against the steel door. And then flames.

He took the actual picture of her out of his pocket and stared at it while he walked. But after only a few steps into it, he lost sight of her behind a veil of tears.

When he'd called the intelligence operative on the phone, he said he wouldn't have the ring on his person but that he would have it hidden somewhere nearby. Hopefully that meant he wouldn't be shot as soon as he walked into their crosshairs. All he needed was to stay alive long enough to do what he needed to do. He didn't care about anything else. He blinked, and the new, older Jennifer appeared again. As he stared at the picture, he rehearsed what it was he would do.

He found himself at the top of a sloping hill and slipped the picture back into his pocket. Grabbing onto saplings that were shooting up through the hillside around him, he worked his way down to the stream. Once he was beside it, he began to follow it south. And as he walked, he let his mind out of the cage, free to roam and wander wherever the wind blew it.

He realized that he wasn't so much mourning the life that he had with Jennifer as much as the hope of what it could have been. In truth, their marriage hadn't been easy, not with his line of work interfering with every aspect of it. She'd deserved much more than the secrets and lies that were his wedding present to her. But it was the unfulfilled promises and all they'd envisioned their future to be—the sons and daughters they would have, and just growing old together—that Scott found hurt the most.

He walked on and found that he didn't want to let his mind roam free after all. So he began reeling it back in, choosing instead to think about why Malachi would have lied to him about wanting the ring. He knew that he wanted it to find the Ark, that he wasn't planning on hiding it until the Messiah showed up and asked for Melissa Strauss's explanation on how to use it.

He looked up to the sky and figured it was around one in the afternoon. His breath was no longer appearing in front of him, and the snow was beginning to melt from the branches above. Then he spotted a set of train tracks in the distance. He sighed.

It was time for a rest.

He sat against a large evergreen, and his body thanked him for the break. The ground around the trunk was dry, the thick pine needles above having acted as an umbrella during the snowstorm and keeping the area from accumulating more than a mere dusting. He put his legs out in front of him and felt the pleasant stretch in his hamstrings as his muscles began to relax. He massaged his quads, hoping he wouldn't start to cramp when it was time to start moving again. His back still felt like an elephant had tried to play chiropractor on it, but it was starting to loosen up. He leaned his head back against the tree and closed his eyes.

But there she was. Only it wasn't the picture he'd been staring at for the last ten years, but the new picture. The one in his pocket. The one that came to life and began banging against the window of a sealed vault. He opened his eyes. Figured he wouldn't ever sleep again. Not until he was dead.

So he pulled the last of the priest's books from his jacket and moved off the tree, relieving the pressure on his bruised back. Turning onto his side, he leaned his head against his hand, which was bent at the elbow and resting on the ground. He'd use his injured arm for the light task of turning the pages.

When he opened the book, he recognized the handwriting right away. It was of a more formal construction than the sketches and random notes though, like it had been a letter to someone else rather than just musings meant for himself. And, in fact, after reading the opening, he knew that was exactly what it was.

> My dearest friend,
> I believe that I have uncovered a puzzle, though a puzzle neither of us suspected even existed at the start of our proud adventure to locate the most sacred object the earth has ever known. All that we have seen and everything that we have done and all that we have worked for over the years has now led me to yet another discovery. It is a discovery of great importance and one that all of our endeavors must be checked against. It is the past,

my friend. The hidden things, covered by time and secrecy. I long to see you again, to show you what it is that I have found within the ancient records, in the records of the Holy See. I feel as though I have only just begun to understand something that someone like myself could ever hope to grasp. I need your help, your knowledge of things Jewish. But I have probably said too much and will await your reply before mentioning anything more. And though I cannot say why, I must ask you, for both our sakes, to cease immediately from any further mention of our discoveries concerning the resting place of the aforementioned. Trust me, Benjamin. May God bless thee and keep thee.

Recalling what Isaiah had told him of Benjamin and Father Baer's passion, Scott knew that the priest was referring to the lost Ark. Reading on, however, it appeared that the letter gave way to a private journal. Perhaps intended for Benjamin in the event that Father Baer never got the reunion he was seeking.

It is my sincere belief (and that through much research conducted by both my colleague and I) that the Temple of Solomon was built with a secret chamber below the Holy of Holies itself. A chamber through which the Ark of the Covenant and the other priestly artifacts could be taken away and hidden in the event of an enemy invasion. I believe, because of our studies, that this chamber led to an underground passageway that perhaps stretched beyond even the city walls. It is here, within these secret tunnels, that I believe the Ark may still rest.

Scott flipped open the other book, the one Ralston had fussed over, and paid closer attention to the sketches drawn of the Temple and what supposedly rested beneath it—to the reverse lever system that provided access to a secret chamber. He flipped through more pages and realized that the book was mostly concerned with the Temple—sketches of caves and secret rooms, Bible verses, and quotes from Josephus and Maccabees. He went back to the other book.

The legend of Solomon's ring (though it shows up everywhere from the apocrypha to witchcraft and the occult), I believe to be based on a truth. While no one is quite sure what that truth might be, it is clear that, based on the writings in the book of Tobit and the *Testament of Solomon*, it has something to do with the Temple. Various works together actually make a case for two separate rings. They are presented within those texts as being a sort of spiritual tool. And though I do not believe they were used to make demons build the Temple, I do believe that they were used for something else.

I have come across (or have been divinely directed to) an obscure and mysterious document, a scroll that I cannot substantiate as being authentic or fake. No one seems to know anything about its origin or when it even arrived within the archives. This scroll speaks of two rings made from the lights and perfection stones contained within the breastplate of Aaron. The Urim and Thummim.

The scroll goes on to describe how the two rings were fashioned so as to function together as a physical key, one that could unlock the secret chamber housing the Ark of the Covenant. Being that the high priest alone would be in possession of the Urim and Thummim, the only one worthy to enter the Ark's presence, and the only one able to determine the time in which it should be restored, the scroll insinuates that this secret was made known only to the high priest.

Scott vaguely remembered reading about the Urim and Thummim, something about Mormonism and Joseph Smith out in the woods with an angel and special glasses. He wished he had Isaiah's Bible encyclopedia with him now.

Ethiopian history tells that Solomon had a son with Queen Sheba—Menelik I. Raised by the priests to fear the God of Abraham, Menelik feared the ensuing consequences of his father's gradual slip into idolatry. Foreseeing the possibility of judgment upon Israel for Solomon's blasphemy, he created a counterfeit, replica Ark. And then he switched it with the real one, not able to bear seeing its desecration. He then, at the age of nineteen, carried the Ark to Ethiopia, the land of which he was prince, where he intended to keep it for safekeeping until Israel repented and turned back to her God.

Another version states, however, that Solomon himself made a replica Ark to accompany his son on the long journey to Ethiopia and that Menelik, fearing the fate of the real Ark, subsequently switched the one his father had made with the authentic one, carrying it out of Jerusalem and to Ethiopia, where it still rests. If this is so, then the reports of people actually seeing the Ark below the Temple would either have to be false or they would have had to have seen the replica ark. If so, then perhaps that would explain why they lived to tell about it. And maybe Second Chronicles 35:3 could also be explained this way, the reason why the mentioned ark could be handled so easily (as opposed to when Uzzah was struck dead for reaching out and touching it, and when the men of Bethshemeth looked inside it and over fifty thousand people died as a result, and when it circled the walls of Jericho and dried up the Jordan).

However, my research has led me to some ancient texts that suggest an alternative to even the Ethiopian account. Texts that give some credence to <u>both</u> historical views—that of the Ark being carried away <u>and</u> that of it being hidden below the Temple. Whether or not the records can be trusted is known only by God. I know only what they say, and they say that Benaiah, the captain of Solomon's army, assisted Menelik in escorting the Ark to Ethiopia. Only he could not bear to actually take the Ark from Jerusalem. So, unbeknownst to Menelik and all those traveling with them, he did <u>not</u> switch the Ark. Instead, they transported the <u>replica</u> to Ethiopia—this being something that only Benaiah knew about at the time. Conceivably, his purpose was to create an air of mystery around the fate of the Ark that would keep Israel's enemies guessing as to its true location, while the Ark itself never became lost at all.

But could this actually be true? Did Benaiah deceive Menelik and, in so doing, thousands of people throughout the ages? I cannot know for sure, but it is worth noting that I have been able to find other documented sources connecting Benaiah to the mysterious fate of the Ark of the Covenant (though admittedly this is somewhat confusing since some scholars insist upon four different Benaiahs all living within the same timeframe).

Regardless of my own opinions and the subjectivity of the records I have found, I am fully convinced that years and years later, just before Israel was invaded by Babylon, the prophet Jeremiah hid the Ark and the Temple treasures around the city. And though I believe he hid the Ark in a secret chamber (along with the other holy instruments) beneath the Temple, I cannot be sure as to whether or not they remain there still. Many seem to think that Second Maccabees actually suggests Jeremiah hid the Ark in a cave on Mount Nebo, but from my own studies I believe that view ignores an in-depth analysis into that passage. Some believe that Jeremiah had Haggai and Zachariah construct a pair of unique scrolls that together would reveal his true hiding places. And though I have not found any evidence to support this, the scrolls undoubtedly do exist and have indeed been found (Copper Scroll). It is also clear that whoever designed them did so in such a way that they were both needed to interpret the other. For this reason, they were hidden separately. Perhaps Jeremiah's thinking was that only the high priest would know where both scrolls were hidden, trusting him to determine when the treasures should be revealed. But if the Ark was sealed under the Temple, is it possible that the record contained in Maccabees (as concerning Jeremiah's hiding of the Ark) was nothing more than another preventative, a false lead held out to those not of Levitical standing who might try to locate the Ark before the appointed time?

Haggadic legend tells that Solomon sent Benaiah to go after Ashmedai (or Asmodeus, king of demons) with a chain holding a ring. Supposedly the Tetragrammaton was engraved onto the ring and enslaved Ashmedai once it was thrown around his neck. Benaiah then took him back to Solomon, where Solomon had him build the Temple. In addition to this legend, I have found scattered pieces that, once put together, may suggest Benaiah did indeed have one of these rings on his person while escorting the replica ark to Ethiopia with Menelik. If that be the case, then this ring, one of the two fashioned by Solomon needed to unlock the Ark itself, would have been lost along with Benaiah, sharing the same mysterious fate. Or, was the fate of the ring actually known by the priesthood and passed down to Jeremiah's day?

Eventually, Israel was taken into captivity, and the Ark was never seen again. The most important Jewish relic, mentioned about 194 times between the books of Exodus and Second Chronicles, suddenly dropped off the pages of history with no explanation at all, leaving us with only fractured legends and obscure documents to wonder over. The next Temple that was built (Zerubbabel/Herod) was without the presence of the Ark, so the Ark was obviously taken somewhere. It was not recorded as being taken by the Babylonians, and one would certainly think it would have been had they found it. But history says they found brass, not gold. Herod's Temple was destroyed by the Romans in AD 70 when they burned it and later pulled every brick apart to get the melted gold that settled between the cracks. History makes no mention of the Ark being found by them either.

Many years later, Constantine became emperor of the Holy Roman Empire and declared Christianity to be the state religion, thus granting the church with unprecedented powers. Christians at this time believed that the nation of Israel had been replaced by the church, and so the church took an extreme interest in the Holy Land, a land they now viewed as theirs—the Kingdom of God. Then war broke out with the Muslims, and the Crusades were underway. The Muslims were able to take control of Jerusalem, and they built a mosque over the holy site. But then the Crusaders beat them out of Jerusalem and built a church overlooking the Temple Mount.

When the Crusade ended, the soldiers returned to England to spend their booty, leaving behind many bitter Muslims who would attack pilgrims journeying to the Holy Land. A handful of knights then appeared on the scene, presenting themselves to King Baldwin of Jerusalem and offering to protect the pilgrims. Impressed by their piousness, Baldwin housed them over the very site on which Solomon's Temple once stood. I believe, as many have suggested over the years, that it was here that the knights were able to go about their true mission, perhaps one drawn up by the Pope himself—the search for the lost Temple treasures (the same ones that Jeremiah hid around the city) and particularly the Ark of the Covenant.

For seven years they excavated the site, somehow managing to accumulate a surge of wealth that made them one of the most powerful societies of their day. While some of their fortune could be explained by generous contributions, tax exemptions, and land donations, the fact that no one knows just exactly what they were doing for seven years and how they so suddenly became one of the most powerful forces in the world seems to lend some level of credibility to the claims of discovery. But just what exactly did they discover?

I have uncovered, within the Vatican's secret archives, a document that makes mention of the diary kept by one of the original Knights Templar—Gondamer. While it tells of their search for Temple treasure, it is silent as to whether they found any. However, it does mention two peculiar discoveries: a scroll made of copper (that seemed to them to be an inventory of hidden treasure) and a mysterious ring. The writing gives the impression that Gondamer was weary of the ring, that it troubled him for some reason (though there was nothing more specific as to why that would be so). Perhaps there was an element of truth to the apocryphal accounts of the supernatural properties of the ring. Though Tobit was never considered an integral part of the Tanakh, Hebrew fragments of it were discovered in Cave IV in Qumran in 1955, and it is considered part of the Catholic and Orthodox biblical canon (Council of Carthage and Council of Trent).

Scott flipped the page, his mind suddenly and mysteriously captivated by what he was reading. He couldn't believe that Mayhew had had this on him the entire time they were together. All the guessing as to why the ring was so important had been right next to him for two whole days. He wondered if he would have done anything differently had he known this from the start, if *this* was what he'd opened up in the restaurant instead of all that other stuff about demons building the Temple. He silently cursed Mayhew before going on to read what Father Baer had intended for him to have read from the start.

It is not far-fetched to assume that the scroll they found led them to chambers full of hidden treasure. That would account for their sudden great wealth and power. Also in Gondamer's account, he mentioned another scroll that they found, one speaking of the ring's purpose. Though that scroll is most likely gone or still being kept with the scroll of copper they found, I believe it explained exactly how the rings worked. They never found the other ring or the other scroll of copper, so they were never able to properly interpret the scroll of copper they did find, leaving them clueless as to where the secret resting place of the Ark was and the means by which to unlock it. I believe that they spent the remaining time there searching for the other ring and the other scroll, and that this is the true reason the Crusades continued after the Muslims retook Jerusalem.

There is not much known about the Urim and Thummim, as they are never specifically described. Exodus 28:30 and Numbers 8:8 suggest that they were stones placed in the breastplate of the high priest, something that he wore when entering into the presence of God to determine His will. Some believe that they were used as lots to be cast, the result being God's answer to a particular question or matter. And yet another theory is that they served as a symbol of the high priest's authority in seeking God's will, which was revealed through an inner illumination of sorts. The words in Hebrew mean "lights" and "perfections."

Some scholars believe that "Urim" is derived from the Hebrew term "Arrim," which means "curses," and that Urim and Thummim mean "cursed or faultless" within the context of someone accused. It appears in the Vulgate as "revelation and truth." The Septuagint version of First Samuel 14:41 states that the Urim would indicate Saul and Jonathan while the Thummim would indicate the people (see account). Some even believe that they could have been tablets of wood or bone. Most Talmudic rabbis (and Josephus) believed that "Urim" meant "lights" and thus argued that the Urim and Thummim involved questions being answered by great rays of light shining out of certain jewels within the breastplate. They believed that each jewel represented different letters and that sequences of light would spell out an answer. It is interesting that Joseph Smith claimed an angel named Moroni appeared to him and provided him with a pair of stones bound together by silver bows that functioned as a set of spectacles, for he later claimed that these stones were the Urim and Thummim and that they helped him interpret the Golden Plates into the Book of Mormon.

Whatever they were and however they functioned, the scroll I found claims that they were fashioned into the two rings. It is possible, according to some writings, that one appeared as a black stone while the other was white. Gondamer's diary hinted at the ring they found being of a dark color, set in bronze with Hebrew script engraved around the band. He also claimed that Hugues de Payens put the ring on. Given his troubled feelings about the ring and the Templars' sudden involvement with the occult, perhaps there <u>was</u> a curse ascribed to those who had no business handling the priestly objects (as was the case with the Ark). The breastplate the Urim and Thummim were inserted into was commonly referred to as the breastplate of judgment, and assuming that the ring was passed down through the secret societies of which the Templars were the founding fathers, perhaps the ring provided a stronghold for Satanic influence. But I am only speculating at this point. I do find it interesting, however, that Solomon claimed (at the end of the *Testament*) that his experience with the occult and the mystery religions of his pagan wives had made him the sport of demons. Perhaps this ring somehow turned the Templars and their successors into the sport of demons as well.

Scott thought about the ring he'd once held in his hand. A clear gem, transparent, like a lens. Could it be meant for the passage of light, and if so, how could it possibly be used as a key? *Could I have held in my hands the Urim or Thummim?* He tried to remember all the things Isaiah had said about the rings, about the Copper Scroll and its duplicate. The last line, the key needed to interpret it…

The Copper Scroll was found in 1952, and then the world went on a treasure hunt. But they never found the second scroll. My suspicion is that it never left the possession of the Templars. I know that many of them escaped the King of France before the 13th of October and that they made their way to Scotland with some eighteen ships (unless they sank during the journey). I know that Rosslyn Chapel connects the Templars to both Freemasonry and the New World. So it is not outside the realm of possibility that the ring and the scroll went with them. If so, after 1952, three of the four elements needed to locate and unlock the Ark of the Covenant would have been accounted for. The only one remaining would be the other ring. But which one? Lights or perfection, cursed or faultless, revelation or truth? And where could that other ring be? Where could Benaiah have taken it? Could it still be connected to the chain, wrapped around a skeleton somewhere in the desert, buried beneath thousands of years of sand? Or was Benaiah somehow able to pass it down through the priesthood?

Though the document I found tells of a scroll the Templars found, explaining how the rings function together as a key, I have found nothing of the sort and thus have no idea how the rings could possibly work as such.

That was how the section ended, indicating to Scott that whatever had turned them away from pursuing the Ark had taken place between the priest's letter to Benjamin and this entry. Turning the page, he found another unsent letter.

A squirrel skittered down a nearby tree, paused, and stared at him. He stared back, reminded of how much Jennifer hated the bushy-tailed rodents. One had gotten into her hair when she was a child, and she had resented them ever since. He smiled at the critter, and it continued on its way. He set his eyes back into the book before they could fill with more tears.

Benjamin, I must write you now to tell of a sudden conviction, one that has shaken the very ground I walk on. It appears as though your Protestant brother may be right, leaving you and I standing on opposite sides of the truth. I have stumbled across something big, whispers echoing down the halls of the Vatican. Maybe you have heard similar things from within the Knesset.

The Holy See is awake and searching for the very thing that has occupied our own interest over the last few years. Surely your people look for it in Israel as well, but what I have heard, the rumors I have caught wind of, suggests a more sinister reason for locating the holy instrument than anything I could have ever imagined. I know that the Vatican is spotted with sinful men and thus sinful action, but I have always held fast to my faith in the Holy Father. No longer. I wish I could speak to Isaiah now, for his thoughts on this matter would fall on open ears.

All that I will say for now is that the beliefs the Reformers held concerning Mystery Babylon, the woman on the Beast, the revived Roman Empire, and even the Pope, are not looking so ridiculous from my current position. The Vatican has an agenda, an agenda that I cannot take part in. It pertains to our archeological pursuits, of resurrecting the presence of God on earth. I always believed that such a discovery could only be good, to prove to the nations that God does indeed exist. No longer would atheism have a shred of validity while being blinded by the light of the shekinah. But it seems as though I was wrong, that I underestimated Lucifer's cunning ways.

As you know, many have assumed that the treasures listed in the Copper Scroll were from the Second Temple, that the Essenes hid the Temple treasure just before the destruction in AD 70. But you and I both know that the things listed in the scroll are objects from the First Commonwealth, not the second! As you pointed out earlier, the authors used Mishnaic/Aramaic spellings and a style of letters other than archaic Hebrew, pointing to an alphabet and writing style a couple of centuries earlier than what is commonly believed. In addition, Josephus recorded the treasures as still present within the Temple when the Romans took it.

But, Benjamin, if the Copper Scroll is indeed an inventory of the treasures from the First Temple and was written under the supervision of Jeremiah, then I must ask myself, why did they not recover the treasure for the Second Temple? If we are right about Haggai and Zachariah being involved in the process, why then would they have kept the instruments secret, being that both of them witnessed the destruction of the First Temple and the rebuilding of the second? The only answer that I can find being of any satisfaction is that they both wrote about the <u>Messianic</u> Temple being the ultimate glory and <u>not</u> the Second. Perhaps they knew the fate of the Second Temple before it was even completed. And that line of thought takes me to Second Maccabees...

"It was also in the writing that the prophet, in obedience to a revelation, gave orders that the Tent and the Ark should accompany him, and that he went away to the mountain where Moses went up and beheld God's inheritance. And Jeremiah came and found a cave-dwelling, and he took the Tent and the Ark and the Incense Altar into it, and he blocked up the entrance. And some of those who followed him came up to mark the road, but they could not find it. When Jeremiah found out about this, he reprimanded them and said, 'The place shall be unknown until God re-gathers the congregation of His people together and shows His mercy. Then God will show where they are, and the Glory of God will be revealed as it was revealed in the days of Moses.'"

If that account is true, then Jeremiah never intended for anyone to find the Ark. And if so, then maybe what your brother believes about the Third Temple is correct, that it will not contain the Ark and will fall short of bringing to fruition the Messianic era. Perhaps we should give another look at the that particular view of eschatology, of the Tribulation and the Temple built by the Antichrist. I am wary to write that for so many reasons, but my worldview is crumbling with every new step I take.

There is an agenda to find the Ark, and those behind it are not interested in God's glory. I do not know that I want to help them find it, not if Jeremiah locked it in a chamber for which he did not have the key. If he did that, then he must have fully expected the Messiah to come and reestablish the Ark's presence along with the rest of the nation. As long as the second ring is lost, the secret societies that wish to gain access to the Ark and use it for their own purposes can do no such thing. Perhaps the two Copper Scrolls have led them to the location, that together they reveal the sixty-fourth treasure to be the Ark, telling even where it rests. But without that ring, I believe they will stand just outside its location for as long as it takes their mortal bodies to turn to dust. In some unknown way, it is hidden from mankind, and only Solomon's rings can unlock its secret location.

That must have been what Father Baer finally realized, that the Ark was never intended to be found once it was hidden. Benjamin said that his brand of orthodoxy believed the Messiah would be the one to sort everything out and that any efforts by man to do so were nothing short of sin. He said religious Zionism and the Temple Movement were attempting to create an atmosphere in which the next Temple would *have* to be built, but a Temple that would fall far short of being the Messianic Temple that Ezekiel described.

Father Baer and Benjamin must have realized that a third Temple would somehow function as a major piece in an established New Order of the Ages and thus wanted no part in it. But then the second ring was found, and all the pieces were suddenly out on the table. That drove them back into action, not to find the Ark, but to keep it from being found, from being used as a tool to jump-start the building of the next Temple and the rise of the Antichrist—the establishment of the New World Order. He remembered Benjamin saying that if the Antichrist's Temple had to be built, he hoped it would be built without Jewish hands having to kill Muslims. Of course he didn't go so far as Isaiah in suggesting that accepting the Antichrist's Temple was a sign of accepting the Antichrist himself, but was there a difference? Though Father Baer hadn't mentioned the agenda to eliminate the Muslims, to destroy Mecca and the Dome of the Rock, it had been of major concern to Benjamin.

And then Scott remembered what Benjamin had said about Israel having to be purified before the Messiah could come. And that purification, if he'd interpreted it correctly, was the Great Tribulation itself.

He closed the book, finally beginning to understand the predicament he was in, why the ring was so important. The world had just been waiting for it to show up. And then it had…right in his lap.

He stared into the woods as the branches above him swayed to the soft beat of a cool breeze. He figured it all came down to what Melissa Strauss knew about the ring—why the government wanted her dead, and why the Mossad needed her alive. But he wouldn't be around to see how it played out. And that was just fine with him.

# 41.

*"What is the purpose for which Masonry exists? Its ultimate purpose is the perfection of humanity. Mankind itself is still in a period of youth. We are only now beginning to acquire a consciousness of the social aim of civilization, which is man's perfection."*

— Albert Pike

It was Jennifer. She was standing beside him and looking into his eyes with hopeful passion. Her lips were moving, but he couldn't hear her voice, though he didn't need to. He knew what she was saying.

"I forgive you."

His heart dropped into an abyss, and tears welled up in his eyes. He grabbed her hand and pulled her into him, enveloping her in his arms. His face was buried in her hair, and the familiar smell of it broke down the dam that had for so long suppressed the memories of this love. They kissed, her lips against his striking a symphony of words that no language could contain.

He opened his eyes with a smile on his face before realizing it was only a dream. His personal storm had shifted to the perfect position where it could better beat him down, his heart a lightning rod erected in the midst of it.

He hadn't even known that he was falling asleep, and now it looked like the sun was getting ready to set. The air was colder too. He brought his hand to his face and felt a teardrop on his cheek. He cursed the dream. Or reality for interrupting it. He dropped his head back to the earth and took a deep breath, pulled the hood down over his eyes. He wanted to scream, to shout, to let loose the rage, the hurt. But what good would it do?

He worked his way to his knees and finally back to his feet. Stumbled to the train tracks. They stretched out before him and disappeared around the trees some two hundred yards away. He began walking, the dream hovering over him like a ghost, haunting every step. He wondered how sleep had managed to get around the picture of Jennifer. Or the children's faces.

He stared down at the wooden slats, watching them pass beneath his feet one at a time, and didn't even notice that it had gotten dark.

He slowed, suddenly conscious of how cold his feet were in the sneakers. The way the stone was crunching under his feet. It seemed loud out here in the middle of nowhere. He stepped up onto the frozen rail and looked ahead. All he could see was a dark void mocking him with its blank expression. The stars were blotted out with clouds, so the tracks were now his only reference point, his only map.

A voice seemed to come out of the void. "Do you think she wouldn't have forgiven you?" it asked. "Is that why you went and hid from her, because you'd rather her think you were dead than find out what you did? You couldn't bear the thought of her knowing, could you? You thought she'd leave you, that she would think you were a monster."

*That's not why.*

"You hate what you look like through her eyes. Through anyone's eyes. That's why you hid. You hate yourself. Your selfishness, your inability to face the consequences. You left her defenseless. A widow with no one to protect her from the soldiers. From the tests."

*Stop.*

"Don't you see? Your inability to deal with your guilt has only made things worse for everyone."

*And how am I supposed to get rid of my guilt?*

"You can't, obviously."

*So then what the hell is the point?*

"The point is that you need help. You need to escape the burden you're carrying."

*It's a little late for that, isn't it?*

"It's never too late."

*Will it bring her back to life? Will it bring all those people back?*

"No."

*Then why should I care? Let me pay for what I've done.*

"You think this is adequate payment?"

*It's all I have.*

"That's pathetic. Community service would reap better results. You think that hating yourself means anything to anyone? You think Jennifer is happy being dead now that you hate yourself? What do you want, people to feel sorry for you?"

*No. I want to stop the pain.*

"Is that why you wish the rusty saw had taken your head? You think that would've been retribution enough? Well, you're wrong. And unless you get that burden taken care of, this is just the beginning of your pain."

*What about Cindy?*

"What about her?"

*What of her pain?*

"I can't say. I wasn't there when she died."

*Is it possible?*

"What?"

*That she found freedom?*

"In death?"

*Before death.*

"Anything is possible."

*I hope she didn't die the way that Mayhew said she did.*

"It's not your problem."

*The hell it isn't. I'm the one who got her killed.*

"You're not accountable for her soul. Only your own."

*That's convenient.*

"It's true. Think about all the things you heard Jack talk about."

*I don't want to.*

"Why not?"

*I don't know. Leave me alone.*

"Fine."

He wrestled with himself like that for another hour before sensing a change in his surroundings. The air around him was hollow, empty, the wind now coming up from beneath him. Things sounded different too, a broader emptiness echoing through the black, the faint sound of trickling water accenting the freezing wind. He no longer had the sense of forest trees peering down at him. He was in the open. On the bridge.

Feeling his way off the tracks, he made his way to a stone wall and sat down against it.

And waited for the dawn of his last day.

****

When the darkness finally gave way to daybreak, Scott wasn't surprised to find that his last day was a cloudy one. It seemed fitting that this unintelligible drug-crazed dream that no actual sense could be wrung from would end under dark and bitter skies. Oh well, not everyone got to live the good life, he supposed.

He struggled to his feet and looked around. Despite being masked by heavy clouds, the dawn offered enough of a glow for him to make out his surroundings. The bridge he'd spent the night on stretched over a gorge that rested maybe two hundred feet below, a trickling stream snaking steadily through its center. The bridge itself was a hundred yards long with short stone walls on either side. He figured there had to be a nearby road that provided access to the tracks. Either that or they were coming to meet him in a helicopter. He looked up into the clouds and waved to the NAU satellites he was sure had his heat signature—if not a live ultra-definition close-up of him (through clouds and all)—on some large screen in a room full of shady men.

He turned toward a distant noise and quickly rechecked the two weapons he had, wishing he'd taken the time to grab a grenade or two. That's okay, he told himself. Only need to get one of them. He walked away from the wall and stepped onto the tracks as the sound of an engine grew nearer. He made sure he was standing in the middle of the bridge, over the lowest point of the valley and the spot he'd be aiming for in just a few moments.

He could see fog floating through the air now. It was riding along the current below, the temperature warming. It wafted up over the bridge and crossed over it like a veil separating the two sides. He could make out the bare trees on the other side of the bridge, their needled fingers poking through the mist. They seemed to be waving goodbye. *Yeah, goodnight, trees. Goodnight, sky. Goodnight, water and birds and air…it's time for me to die.* He didn't know where that had come from, the singsong rhyme stolen from the children's book his mother used to read him.

His mother.

His father.

His childhood…

The memories had broken out of a crypt long lost and forgotten. But why now? Why just moments from taking his last breath? It was almost too much, the sudden emotion of it all. Life. All the things that comprised it. The things that tethered him to it. Love, beauty, hope… Even if those things had taken off on him a long time ago, he still had the taste of them.

Jennifer.

And suddenly he was scared. Scared of losing what he hadn't even realized he'd had all this time. Connection with the past, of those he cared about. The feelings and memories, the record engraved into his mind of their having been. Would it all disappear when he joined them in oblivion? Did they only exist as long as someone was left behind to remember them? His hands trembled. Suddenly the air seemed precious. The sound of the water below a symphony of grace. Life. Existence. It was beautiful. Even in the midst of the hell they'd managed to make it, there was still the scent of wonder above all the corpses.

The sound of tires bouncing over the tracks came overtop the water, and with it came all that stood in contrast to what he'd just felt. Here came the black hole that consumed everything that was good in this world, a parasite feasting on innocence. He hoped the intelligence operative he'd spoken to over the phone was with them so that he could look him in the eye when he blew his head apart with the shotgun. The man who had fueled his hopes and dreams with a lie, who had used his precious wife to get to him just as he feared they always would.

Headlights came bouncing through the trees, cutting into the fog, and then swung around and settled before him, shining in his face. He shielded his eyes with his hand and thought he could make out more than one vehicle.

Whatever kind of vehicle it was, it didn't come out onto the bridge. Scott lowered himself down, not wanting them to shoot out his knees. He'd need them to make it over the side of the bridge. Taking the shotgun off his shoulder, he laid it down next to him. He heard doors open and watched as silhouettes stepped in front of the headlights.

"Hello again, Joshua."

The voice matched the one he'd heard over the phone and the face he'd seen at Isaiah's. *Good.*

"Do you have the ring?" His voice echoed through the canyon below.

"I can't see you," Scott yelled back.

The headlights flicked off.

"Do you have the ring?" he asked again.

Scott closed one eye, attempting to adjust to the darkness as quickly as possible. He was seeing spots from the headlights. "Do you have my wife?" He was going to have to get closer if either of the guns were going to be effective.

"Of course."

"Show her to me!"

The guy made another gesture, and two huge men in black suits opened the back door of the car and pulled someone out into the morning mist. There was a bag over their face.

"Now, again, do you have the ring?"

Scott noticed some other guys in camouflage standing behind what he could now see was another vehicle. He looked back to the person wearing the bag. Could definitely tell by their figure that it was a woman. Probably an agent with a knife up her sleeve or a small pistol at her back, or maybe it was just some girl they picked up off the street on their way here. "I told you I wouldn't have it on me. How stupid do you think I am?"

"Where is it, then?"

Scott grinned. "You have some woman with a bag over her face standing fifty yards away from me, and you think I'm gonna tell you?"

"How do I know you even have it?" he asked.

"Can you take the chance?"

"Can you?" he shouted back.

"I have nothing to lose."

"You have your wife to lose, Joshua."

"Well, you're going to have to prove that to me. Send her out here."

The guy stood there for a moment, thinking about it. And then he nodded, saying something to one of the suits. The huge guy pushed the girl in the back and started walking her toward him.

*This is as good as it's going to get*, Scott thought. He'd shoot the huge guy in the head, grab the girl and use her as a shield. Though the guy would make for a better shield, he probably weighed two hundred and fifty pounds. The girl was more like one-twenty. He could move with her.

He waited until the man and the woman were positioned between him and all the guns on the other side of the bridge before standing. They stopped ten yards away. "Come closer," Scott ordered. His whole body was tense. He didn't notice the pain in his back anymore, his arm silent too. He was shaking with anticipation, with adrenaline and anger. Maybe even with fear. *This is it.* They stepped closer, within five yards. *I'm living out my last seconds.* Three. *What if Jack and Edward and Isaiah are right about what comes next?* Ten feet. *What if—*

Five feet.

They were standing right in front of him, and his heart was pounding in his chest. So ironic how life was surging through him in the face of death. So alive one instant, so dead the next. At least he wouldn't have to watch himself rot away like he'd watched others in his life rot. He hated that process. Still, even a quick death was still so…final.

It was too late now though. There was no way out of this. And he wanted to kill this guy more than he wanted to live, so he'd wait until the guy pulled the bag off the girl's face. Wait until it was in his hands. While he was distracted.

He was a huge specimen of a man, bigger than he was. But bullets generally didn't discriminate. Not at this range anyway. The man had a .45 SIG P220 hanging loosely at his side. He wouldn't be able to draw it in time.

"Take it off," Scott told the guy.

He reached up and pulled the bag off the woman's head.

And Scott's whole world imploded.

It *was* Jennifer.

# 42.

*"This regionalization is in keeping with the Tri-Lateral Plan which calls for a gradual convergence of East and West, ultimately leading toward the goal of one world government. National sovereignty is no longer a viable concept."*

—Zbigniew Brzezinski

For five seconds, time ceased to unwind. Or had at least slowed down long enough to incorporate hours' worth of thought and emotion. The first second was just pure shock accompanied by a mental debate as to whether or not she could even be real, the next second pronouncing a verdict on the reality of her presence, while the third opened the floodgates of relief, wonder, elation, and even excitement. There she stood, and even with half her face obscured by a blindfold, she was beautiful, even more beautiful than he remembered. The fourth second brought the realization that Mayhew had lied to him, that for his own sadistic pleasure, even in death, he wanted to inflict as much pain as possible. And second number five told him just how much everything about this moment had changed, things suddenly much, much more complex. He would not be using her as a shield in order to make his way over the side of the bridge after all. Life, all of a sudden, was worth living again. Love and purpose had re-tethered him to this earth. He needed to get them out of there alive. Without the ring. And fast.

Impossible.

*No.* He refused to accept death now.

Halfway through the next second, Jennifer spoke, her hesitant voice full of uncertainty. "Josh?" A tear slipped from beneath the blindfold and rolled down her cheek. "Is that you?" Two more tears.

He stepped toward her and pulled the blindfold off. Watched her green eyes adjust to the closeness of his face. He could see thousands of questions and feelings running through them as her bottom lip began to quiver under the weight of so much doubt. He wrapped his arms around her as tears streamed down his own face. He could feel her sobbing, squeezing him. He closed his eyes, and everything around them disappeared.

Until he forced himself back into the present, knowing that he had precious little time to figure this out if their reunion was to extend beyond the next few seconds.

He looked down at her as she lifted her head off his chest. "Did they hurt you?" he asked.

She shook her head, no.

The large guy in the suit carrying the SIG stepped back a few paces.

The guy in charge, the one Scott wasn't as eager to kill now, yelled to him, "There, you have your wife, just as I promised. Now where's the ring?"

Even as the intelligence man's lips formed the words, Scott's eyes dropped down in search of answers to another question that he'd been harboring for years. And relief flooded his chest when he saw that the rings he'd given Jennifer so long ago were still there right where he'd left them, nestled together right below her knuckle, fourth finger in on her left hand. His heart leapt, and another tear slipped.

"Joshua," the guy called again, "the ring!"

He looked up to him through the spreading fog. "How do I know you won't grab us once I tell you?"

"If I wanted to, I'd have already grabbed you, started cutting her up right in front of you until you told me everything I wanted to know." He paused. "If I wanted to."

It was a very good point. He never thought the conversation would get this far, never thought out an actual location to give them. Wherever he supposedly put it would have to be somewhere behind him, since it was possible that they had been tracking his route via the cell phone. But that was the very direction he'd have to flee in too. "You understand my hesitation to trust you," he said.

"All I want is the ring."

"Why?"

"Because I was told to get it."

"Do you know what it is?"

"I'm beginning to think you're stalling, Josh. And why would you be doing that?"

"Give us a head start."

After a glance at his watch, thrusting his hands in his pockets and looking back and forth impatiently, he nodded. "Fine. You've got half an hour."

Scott took a couple of steps backward, pulling Jennifer along with him. "I'll tell you from the other side of the bridge." Then he turned with her and covered the fifty yards to the west end, leaving the shotgun lying on the tracks. When they reached the other side, he turned back, his mind racing.

"Well?" called the man, his voice echoing back and forth through the gorge.

"Follow the tracks for a mile or so west. You'll see a marker. Go north. You can't miss it." His sentence rebounded overtop of itself and continued on down the canyon.

"A little vague."

"You can't miss it."

"Okay, Joshua. But I want you to know that if it's not there…well, let's just say we've taken precautions. You won't get far. And when we catch you, we'll probably be pretty pissed at having been lied to."

He looked down to Jennifer.

"I think they put something in me," she whispered.

Scott nudged her west and away from the bridge. "Go."

"Oh, and Joshua," the voice boomed after them, "does Jennifer know about Los Angeles? Maybe you can tell her about it on your way."

He pushed her along. "Keep going. Don't look back." They began jogging over the tracks.

"Does she know how many lives you took that day?"

The question went back and forth across the ravine, rebounding off its sides and repeating itself over and over again, a knife thrusting into his stomach with each echo. His dark secret laid bare to the wilderness of Northwestern Pennsylvania.

And to his wife.

But all he could do to escape the rebounding accusation was to move faster.

"What kind of shape are you in?" Scott asked.

She looked over at him. "What do you mean?"

"How long do you think you can run?"

"As long as you need me to."

"Two miles?"

"I'd run a thousand for you," she replied.

He smiled and had to resist the urge to sweep her up into his arms and kiss her. "We need to move fast. As fast as we can."

"What's going on?"

"There's no time to explain. But when they find out I don't have what they want, they're gonna come after us, so we need to get as far away from here as possible."

After seven minutes, they stopped to catch their breath. Scott needed to think of something that would buy them a little more time. Even if the guy kept his word and didn't come after them for another twenty-three minutes, it'd only take them two or three minutes to reach their location in their vehicles. That was four minutes lost, meaning they really only had a twenty-six-minute head start.

Jennifer dropped her head down between her legs, trying to fill her lungs with the air they were screaming for. The cold air burned going in.

"I need to make a marker," Scott mumbled. He started walking off the tracks, toward the woods.

"Wait," she gasped. She stopped him by grabbing his arm, spun him so that he was facing her, and then threw her arms around his neck. She pressed her lips onto his, kissing him with a passion no words could describe, ten years' worth of feeling and emotion in their embrace. They held on to each other so tight, fearing that if they were to let go, they might lose each other forever. Again.

A million things were sprinting through Scott's head, questions he wanted to ask her, things he wanted to say, but the clock wasn't going to wait for them. Pulling away, he dragged her back toward the woods. "Come on!"

"Josh."

He turned to look at her, and the sight of her, the way she was standing there staring at him… She looked like an angel, the wind carrying her strawberry blond hair across her face and over one eye. He could have exploded right there, the emotion he felt surging within almost too much to bear, his very existence no match for the love swelling in his heart. "What?"

"I love you."

More water filled his eyes. He couldn't believe it. After all this time… "I love you."

"I never stopped."

"Me neither."

She stepped off the tracks after him.

"We need to make a marker," he said.

So they made a small pile of rocks and stuck a long tree branch into the middle of it so that it stood in the air like a flagpole.

Another two minutes had passed.

"It needs something more obvious," Scott said.

"You can use my jacket," Jennifer offered.

He shook his head. "No, I supposedly did this last night." He quickly unzipped his own jacket, pulled the hooded sweatshirt up over his head, and then took off the white T-shirt. The cold blasted his bare skin and spread goose bumps over his flesh. He noticed Jennifer staring at him. He smiled. "What're you looking at?" He tied the shirt around the top of the branch, making a white flag out of it.

She blushed. "My long-lost husband."

*God, please get us out of this.* He walked over and picked her up, kissing her. She wrapped her legs around his waist and kissed him back hard. Tears fell between their lips. With all the willpower he had, he set her back down. "Come on," he said. He grabbed his sweatshirt and jacket and put them back on as he led her up into the woods and away from the tracks.

"Where are we going?" she asked, panting.

"To see some people about whatever they put in you."

"What about the ring they want?"

"Hopefully they waste a lot of time searching the area around the flag before they decide to come make me show them where it is." He helped her up a steep slope. He wanted to reach the commune before the Mossad abandoned it to the coming soldiers. He was hoping Malachi's men could take out whatever it was they'd put in Jennifer.

But only minutes later, Jennifer was already growing tired, running out of energy. Her steps were slowing, her breathing more strained.

"Come on, Jen. You can do it," Scott urged.

It was growing lighter, though the clouds still hadn't broken. They navigated through the trees, fully aware that their time together was already running out.

"How much farther?" Jennifer asked.

"I don't know. A few more miles maybe."

"I won't make it." She tripped and fell.

Scott went back, helped her to her feet.

"I can't breathe," she said.

"Come on, we have to make it." How could they be reunited after ten years just to be torn apart within an hour? He wrapped his arm around her waist and helped her along. He refused to accept it.

Tears welled in her eyes, and she started to cry. "I'm going to lose you again."

He shook his head. "No you're not. I'm not going anywhere. You hear me?"

"But I can't make it."

She was right. By now the intelligence guy would already be on the tracks, looking for their marker, and soon they'd be right behind them, tracking whatever was in her. Scott didn't know how many of them there were, but he was pretty sure the guys he'd seen in camouflage were NAU Special Forces. He wouldn't stand a chance against them, not with one pistol. He pulled the phone out of his pocket and tried dialing the number Malachi had given him.

Disconnected from network.

He swore and threw the phone against a tree.

They pressed on, slower, and now Scott knew it would take a miracle for them to get out of this alive. He figured they had about an hour before everything came to an end in a shower of blood and bullets. He offered a silent prayer, not caring if it made sense or if he even knew to whom he was praying. He held the gun in one hand and Jennifer's hand in the other.

Ten minutes later, the clouds let loose a freezing rain over them. Within seconds, Jennifer's hair was soaking wet and matted to her face. She was shivering, arms folded, teeth chattering.

"Here," he said, and took off his jacket, putting it over hers.

"Thanks."

He pulled his hood up. "You don't know what's going on, do you?"

"They said they found you, told me to go with them. Next thing I know, they're injecting me with something. I'm put into a car, blindfolded and brought here. To you." She paused. "That's what I know."

The rain erased any snow that still remained from the day before, and once again the forest floor was covered with leaves. The rain echoed off them, and he had to speak up so that she could hear him over the sound of it. "There's more you need to know. Something I have to tell you."

"About what he said? About Los Angeles?"

He clenched his jaw. He'd spent the last ten years trying to avoid this very moment, and now here it was. Only he didn't know how to do it. How to look her in the eyes and say it.

She touched his face with a trembling hand. "I know."

"What do you mean?" She couldn't possibly *know*. She must be thinking of something else. Something not as forgivable.

"I mean I know. I know that it was a false-flag operation." She ran her hand through the side of his hair, over his ear. "I know about the drills, about what you used to do. I know what you *did*."

He looked down. She couldn't know, or she wouldn't be here looking at him like this. "I don't know what you think you know, but—"

Raising her voice over the falling rain, she cut him off. "After you disappeared, I got a visit from the CIA. They told me they had reason to believe you were still alive. They wanted to know if you'd contacted me. The agent told me about what happened in Iran. He told me they set you up, tried to get rid of you. Because of what you knew."

His mind churned. The Agency had admitted they'd set him up? No, it had to have been a trick to get her to talk. "And did he tell you what I knew?"

"Pieces of it. But that's all I needed. I went online and started investigating everything I could. Found that there was this whole movement dedicated to exposing the government's involvement in the attack and trying to reveal the role of terrorism within the globalist plot to usher in a New World Order."

Scott knew of those groups. They'd been around forever. He knew their theories were sometimes close to the mark—once you got past the line of straw men the government propped up to discredit their messages. "What did he say?"

"He said the government was lying about what really happened. He said somehow you were involved. He claimed to be your friend, said he wanted to help you."

"Yeah, right," he muttered.

"I know all about what happened. Well, as much as anyone can, I guess. I know you were involved."

Water was dripping down her face, but he could tell she was trying not to cry.

"I don't care," she said.

He stared at her.

"I forgive you. I don't care."

Her gaze was piercing, and he couldn't stand it. More tears began to swell in his own eyes.

"I know you're torn apart by what they made you do. I know that's why you disappeared."

"So many people," he whispered. "Thousands in LA. Millions more in—"

She grabbed his sweatshirt. "Let me help you bear the burden of it."

He couldn't hold it back any longer, and the dam that had been holding back all the guilt cracked and then finally crumbled. He buried his face in her chest and sobbed.

She wrapped her arms around him and cried with him. "I forgive you," she kept saying.

He collapsed to his knees, pulling her down with him. And there, in the mud, beneath curtains of freezing rain and with soldiers hunting them down, they held on to each other again.

"I'm sorry I left you. It was the only way I knew how to protect you," he stuttered. He was running his hands over her face, brushing the hair out of her eyes.

"I know," she said, still crying. "I thought you were dead, but then they came, and I…"

"They told me you'd been killed in a camp. Incinerated. I wasn't there to protect you…"

"I'm here. I'm fine." She slipped her hand into the hood and gripped the back of his neck. "Where were you? Where have you been?"

"Vermont."

She laughed and choked on her tears and the falling rain. "So close…all this time. I missed you so much."

He kissed her, and she kissed him back, their hands moving up and down each other's bodies with a frenzied passion. Bodies that were once so familiar now ten years older. They groped and squeezed and petted and clawed as if it was the only way they could convince themselves it was all real. That they were together.

Forgetting about what they were running from and where they were going, they rolled atop the matted leaves until Scott came up on top of her. He traced her face with his hand.

"I'm sorry I wasn't the husband you deserved," he whispered.

She leaned up and kissed him. "I didn't appreciate how hard you tried until you were gone. Every day I wished that I could go back and do it differently. To be there for you."

"No. You were right. I should've quit when I had the chance. I didn't know —"

"Shhh." She put a finger over his lips. "God's given us a second chance." And then she grabbed the back of his head and pulled his face back down to hers.

He was lost in a dream, lost in over a decade of futile hopes he never thought could be realized. Only now they had been. And it changed everything. Changed him. He could feel it already. He didn't know what it meant or where it would lead, but he could tell that the conflict he'd been feeling over the last few days was somehow coming to a head.

Lost in each other's arms, they were not aware of the cold, the rain, the mud…

Or the men closing in on them.

# 43.

*"The very word 'secrecy' is repugnant in a free and open society; and we are as a people inherently and historically opposed to secret societies, to secret oaths and to secret proceedings."*

—John F. Kennedy

He spotted them from the corner of his eye. Soldiers sneaking in on them from out of the woods and rain. His first instinct was to reach for his gun, but he thought better of it. Instead, he rolled off Jennifer and slowly raised his hands into the air. It was the only thing he could think to do that might buy them some more time. And it was all about time now, every second suddenly important. Precious. Forcing a gunfight would only get both of them killed right here and now. And if they tried running for it, they'd just be shot in the back. But he knew these guys wouldn't kill them if they didn't have to. They still needed to know where the ring was.

Jennifer looked up, trying to see why her husband's hands were no longer on her, and she saw them too.

They came closer, materializing out of the rain like apparitions. Scott blinked.

He recognized them.

They were Mossad.

Scott lowered his hands, but before he could say anything, one of the agents put a finger to his lips, instructing Scott to be quiet.

Scott bent over and pressed his lips against Jennifer's ear. "Stay still." He pulled out the pistol.

"*Psst.*"

Scott looked behind him and saw another of Malachi's men slithering through the undergrowth beside them.

"There are three left," he whispered. "We lost them a hundred meters northeast." Then he disappeared back into the woods.

Scott lay down beside Jennifer. "Lay on your stomach," he whispered.

She was confused, her eyes darting back and forth and full of worry, but she obeyed.

Scott climbed on top of her, shielding her. He held the pistol out in front of him and aimed into the woods.

Two minutes later, one of the NAU Special Forces soldiers came walking out of the rain and stood right in front of them. He couldn't see them though, not with the rain splashing mud all over them and blending them into their surroundings. Although if he stood there long enough... Scott held his breath and made sure Jennifer's wasn't drifting up into the air in frozen signal clouds.

Both he and Jennifer watched as the soldier moved his weapon back and forth, searching. Scott prepared to shoot, and he could feel Jennifer's shivering body tense up beneath him as she braced for the coming shot. He hoped she wouldn't have to see it, see what he had grown so callous to over the years.

But she did.

The soldier's eyes fell on them, and the rifle in his hands began swinging in their direction.

Scott squeezed the trigger three times.

The 9mm bullets struck the soldier in the shoulder and side, twisting him to the ground as the assault rifle in his hand erupted in a reactionary burst that splashed mud and splintered wood.

More gunshots suddenly exploded from out of the forest, and the soldier, still struggling to maintain his balance, disappeared beneath a hanging red mist.

Then the whole area blew up in an exchange of firepower.

Jennifer squirmed under her husband, trying to cover her ears against the sound of SAWs working through belts of ammo and grenades from grenade launchers shaking the ground. But after a few minutes, the battle began to drift away from them, the gunshots heading southeast.

"Come on," he said to Jennifer, getting to his knees and pulling her up. She was covered in mud and freezing. "Stay with me. We can do this." He led her west as thunder drowned out the battle behind them.

They walked, hand in hand, for what seemed like an hour before Scott came to an abrupt halt. "Hold on." Jennifer's teeth were chattering so hard, he was sure it could be heard over the rain.

She looked around. "What?"

"Shhh." He peered through the rain as he raised the pistol and began circling around her. He could sense them closing in.

But again, it was one of Malachi's men who came bursting through the undergrowth.

Scott relaxed and let the pistol drop to his side as two more agents appeared, one holding his shoulder and the other limping. Scott tucked the 9mm into the back of his pants. "Thank you," he stated. Whatever their intentions, they had saved their lives.

The uninjured Israeli, the one who had whispered in his ear back there in the mud, acknowledged the thanks with a simple nod before looking over to Jennifer. "Are you alright?"

Jennifer nodded her head, though her face was as pale as a ghost's.

"Malachi sent us to keep an eye on you, to make sure you did not get yourself killed," the agent said to Scott.

Scott didn't believe that.

"What did you tell them?" the agent asked.

"I told them I buried it out in the woods, but they would've followed us back to the commune. They put a microchip or something in her."

"We can take care of that when we get back."

"You think we could do it here?"

"If you are worried about the commune being discovered, I am afraid there is nothing that can be done about that now."

Scott thought of Ralston, of the children throwing the baseball. "They'll be slaughtered," he said.

"Malachi explained their situation to them. He encouraged them to leave in advance."

"To go where?"

"There is another community in New York, about a hundred miles northeast."

"And how are they supposed to get there?"

But he just said, "Come," and the three of them turned and began heading back through the woods, leaving Scott and Jennifer to fall in line.

Scott grabbed Jennifer's hand and led her after them. "How are they supposed to get there?" he asked again.

It wasn't fair. But was it his problem? A few hours ago, the answer would have been absurdly obvious to him. But now, after looking into Jennifer's eyes…

Somehow, he needed to find a way to help them too.

****

Scott led his wife into the commune and toward the tent serving as the Mossad command post. He helped her up the steps and out of the rain.

"You survived."

Scott spun to see Malachi walking toward them. There was a small smile on his face.

"Yeah." He didn't return the expression. "Thanks for the backup."

"What are friends for?" He turned his attention to Jennifer. "I hear you have a little problem."

She instinctively grabbed the back of her neck.

"I think it's a microchip," Scott said. "A transmitter."

"We will get it right out." He motioned for some of his men to come over. "Lie down on your stomach, please," he told Jennifer.

She gave Scott a nervous glance as she took his jacket off and handed it back to him. Then she took hers off too.

"It'll be okay," Scott said.

She lay down on the table, her body shaking from a bitter chill that seemed to be in her very bones.

Scott watched as they extracted the tiny chip from beneath the skin on her neck, and he knew that he needed to get her someplace warm fast. If she got sick, with her body already exhausted and vulnerable, there would be no hospital available to her.

One of Malachi's men bandaged her neck while another dropped the chip onto the ground and crushed it with his heel.

Malachi looked at his watch, then at Scott. "We cannot all fit on the Black Hawk, so we will make two trips. You and your wife will make the second. In the meantime, you might as well get a fire going."

A female agent handed Jennifer a blanket, and Scott nodded his thanks to her as Jennifer wrapped herself in it.

"I'll be right back, okay?" he said to her. Even if it wasn't, she was too weak to protest. He kissed her on the forehead, put his jacket on, and went after Malachi. He grabbed his elbow when he caught up to him.

Malachi turned. "What is it?"

"Did you talk to Melissa?"

"Yes."

"And?"

"And she told us everything that she could."

Scott leaned closer. "And what was that?"

"You suddenly care?"

"Maybe. What did she say?"

"She told us what she learned from studying the ring. Did you read all of the books?"

"Yeah."

"So you know about the rings, about the Copper Scrolls, and what many have theorized they point to."

A burst of wind blew through the opening in the tent and made him cross his arms over his chest. He hadn't gotten any drier or warmer since when they were out there in the mud, and he hoped he wouldn't get pneumonia either. He nodded, understanding now that Malachi had lied to him in the car on the way to Isaiah's. He obviously *had* read the books, or at least knew what was in them.

Malachi continued. "Father Baer's writings tell of a scroll the Templars found, one that explained how the rings worked. That scroll, as far as I know, has never been found. Maybe it was handed down through the generations of secret societies along with the other ring, but I doubt it. If they still have the instructions, then why would they need to study it so extensively? I think they only had bits and pieces of the whole to work with. When they finally had both rings in their possession, they still did not know what to do with them."

Scott pondered this, wondering if it was possible. *Of course it's possible.* But was it likely? Why would NASA be studying it? If they simply hoped to unlock its secrets, why not use gemologists or archeologists? Why NASA? He figured it was more plausible that NASA's interest in it had more to do with that whole extraterrestrial god hoax Mayhew had blabbed on about.

Malachi pulled the ring out of his pocket and held it up so that Scott could see it. "This ring, along with the other one, functions as a key that unlocks the secret chamber the Ark now rests in. But, even more importantly, it leads to the *location* of that chamber. We do not believe that gaining access to the chamber will be very difficult. We expect opening it with the rings to be somewhat self-explanatory. The problem has always been finding it."

Scott stole a glance at Jennifer and the agents around her packing up to leave.

"Melissa confirmed that the gem is actually a sort of lens, an instrument maybe used for viewing coded texts. The top is polished, but the underside is refracted."

"You're saying it's like a decoder ring?"

"Maybe the first." He turned back toward the tent. "The Urim and Thummim stones were somehow used to interpret the will of God. This ring that Solomon built out of the Urim seems to also function as some kind of an interpretation device, as well as being a key. Perhaps light would shine through the lens and illuminate a word or letter, or maybe the refracted lens would unscramble a text. Who knows? But we do believe that this ring is the key that the Copper Scroll speaks of."

"The key that was supposed to be with the duplicate copy."

"Yes."

"Except that the duplicate copy was found by the Templars along with the other ring."

He shrugged. "Maybe the key that the 1953 scroll speaks of is the key to the Ark, and the key that was supposed to be with it was the one that was supposed to interpret them both. I guess no one can really know until they try reading it through the lens of the Urim. In any case, all four objects are needed, and until recently, only one was missing."

"That would explain the strange letters throughout the scroll, if they actually appeared as something else through Solomon's ring."

He nodded. "The scrolls were fashioned in such a way that only the ring could decode them."

"That would mean that Benaiah was somehow able to get the ring back into the possession of the priesthood."

"In order for the rings to be compatible with the scrolls, yes, Jeremiah had to have had access to both of them."

"What about the other ring?"

"Melissa said that her team was given the description of another material, a dark geological object. She was told to find similarities between the two. It would stand to reason that this was a description of the other ring, crafted out of the Thummim stone. They wanted her to figure out how the two could function together as a single unit without exposing her to the ring itself."

*Or that's what they told her while NASA constructed their hoax around both objects,* he thought.

"What did she say about the other one?"

"She said that the material they described, the data they sent her, was unlike anything she had ever seen before."

"What do you mean?"

"Nothing. She just said she did not understand what it was they gave her and why they assumed the two substances had any relation to each other."

"That's it? Nothing else?"

"Nothing."

"What do you think?" Scott asked.

"I think that Father Baer might have been right about it being some kind of judgment on those unworthy of its use. I think it has supernatural ramifications. Perhaps more so than this one."

"That's it? That's all she had?"

"More or less."

*No, they would have already known that.* They didn't need Melissa or NASA to find that out. This knowledge, if it were true, had been passed down to them from the Templars. They wanted the diagnostics of the rings to better work them into their planned deceptions. "What are you gonna do?"

"I am going to take this to my boss."

"Why not just get rid of it?"

"Because that is not what I was told to do."

"But that's what Benjamin was planning on doing, wasn't it?"

He stopped. "The intention is the same. The ring will not be attained by those who want to use it for evil."

"Benjamin thought that *any* use of it would be evil."

"I assure you, the Temple will not be built through the use of this ring."

"Then why not make sure of it?"

But instead of answering, he just smiled and clapped him on his good arm. "Take care, Joshua. We will send the Black Hawk back to get you. It will take you to New York."

Scott knew he was lying about the ring, that he was hoping the Ark might restore Israel as God's center of the world, that with its power they might cast off the globalist yoke, the very thing Benjamin had been trying to prevent. "Are you leaving now?"

"In ten minutes."

Scott reached out his hand. "Thanks again."

Malachi shook it before stepping out of the tent and into the rain, toward the helicopter.

Scott let his gaze drift over the commune and didn't see any sign that preparations were being made to leave. He looked back to his wife, then to Malachi. Scott found himself in the center of a triangle, three different points all shouting for his help. He swore under his breath and ran after Malachi. "Wait!"

Malachi stopped.

His feet sloshing through the mud, Scott tried to slow down when he reached Malachi, but his foot slipped, and he went barreling into him, almost knocking him down.

"Sorry," Scott said.

Malachi fixed him with an irritated stare.

"I slipped," Scott said.

"I have a flight to catch, Matthew, Joshua, whatever your name is. What do you want?"

"What about Melissa?"

"She is sleeping. Ralston said they would care for her."

"You're just leaving her?" Scott asked in mock disbelief.

"She is in no condition to travel. I am surprised she is even still alive after what they did to her."

"After all she went through, you're just gonna leave her out at the curb with the trash? The only reason you have the ring is because she risked her life to steal it."

"As you said, *she* risked her life. Nobody forced her to."

Scott turned away from him. Was anything fair in this life? "Whatever, Malachi." He started walking away from him. "Take care of yourself."

Malachi shouted back to him, "Be ready and stay with my men. The helicopter will be back in a few hours. Do not miss it." And he turned and trotted off into the woods, toward the hidden chopper.

Scott returned to Jennifer's side. Her lips were a shade of purple, and her face hadn't regained any color.

"Aren't you cold?" she managed to ask through rattling teeth.

"I'm fine." His sweatshirt had managed to open a little beneath the jacket, and he zipped it tight. "I'm gonna start a fire, okay?"

She didn't say anything but was able to work her lips into a thin smile.

"Hang in there." He kissed her frozen lips and had to fight the urge to linger. He left the tent and saw three remaining Mossad agents still packing up some items as the Black Hawk rose above the trees and then swung away. He stood there and watched it disappear into the rolling sea of dark clouds.

"You're back."

Scott was surprised to find himself smile a little at the sound of Ralston's voice.

"Yeah, I'm back."

"And you brought a woman with you."

This time he couldn't suppress the smile, and it spread over his whole face. "My wife."

Ralston's eyes lit up, and his smile was just about as big. "Back from the dead…"

He nodded. "Back from the dead."

"She looks cold," he stated. "Come on, Mr. Scott. Let us help you."

He didn't protest this time. "I'd appreciate it."

"Go get your wife and bring her over to my home."

As he began walking away, Scott called out to him, "Hey, Dan? Sorry about before."

"No need for an apology. I can be a little forward sometimes. I'm just glad you're still alive."

By the time Scott had Jennifer to Ralston's door, Ralston had a fire going, and his place was nice and cozy. In another room, Scott helped Jennifer out of her wet clothes. She looked slightly embarrassed though, like this wasn't how she wanted him to see her their first time back together—half naked, soaking wet, shivering, and purple. So he just wrapped the blanket around her and held her for another minute, praying they could escape the coming soldiers. "Go sit out by the fire," he whispered. "I'll be right there."

Once she left the room, he took the books from his jacket and checked to see if they had been ruined by the rain. He was surprised to find them still in decent shape. Some of the edges were wet, and the ink on one of the first pages had started to bleed a little, but that seemed to be the extent of it. He picked up Jennifer's jacket and checked the pockets to see how wet they were. There were two outside pockets on both sides and then one large zipper pocket inside at the left breast. He stuck his hand in it. It was dry. The jacket was heavy, water and wind resistant, and 100% polyester on the outside. The pocket was big enough, so he slid the books inside it.

Then he took the ring out of his pocket.

The one he'd picked out of Malachi's pocket when he pretended to lose his footing and fall into him.

He looked at it for a second, pondering just how Malachi had planned to use it without having access to the other ring and scroll. Or maybe he *did* have access to them. Maybe Malachi had been working with the secret societies. But that didn't make sense. Then again, who knew how many different groups wanted it and for how many different purposes? Father Baer had told him not to trust anyone for a reason. Or maybe Malachi hoped that the "lights" ring and the 1953 Copper Scroll together would be enough to reveal the Ark's location.

It didn't matter now. He dropped it in the pocket along with the books and zipped it. Then he walked out of the room and joined Jennifer and David.

****

Jennifer was curled up in a fetal position with her head resting in Scott's lap. She'd fallen asleep after drinking a cup of hot tea, and now Scott was moving his fingers through her hair while he talked with Ralston.

"You know what's going to happen when they come, right?" Scott asked him. Their eyes were locked on the fire, its sporadic dancing hypnotizing.

"Whatever God wants to happen."

"You're not gonna do anything?"

"Like what? We have nowhere to go, and we have nothing to fight with even if we wanted to."

"You'd stand a better chance if you made a run for it."

Ralston smiled. "No, it'd be better to face our fate together than to all die alone." He poked a stick into the flames. "When they came for Jesus, to crucify Him, Peter fought to protect Him. He took out his sword and cut off one of the guard's ears. Jesus told him to put away his sword, that all who take the sword shall perish by the sword. He said, 'Don't you think that I can pray to my father, and he can give me more than twelve legions of angels?' And then when He was talking to Pilate, He told him, 'My kingdom is not of this world. If it were, my servants would fight to prevent my arrest by the Jews. But now my kingdom is from another place.'"

"His kingdom being heaven?"

"I think His kingdom is wherever His authority is being manifested."

Scott frowned, not understanding his meaning.

Daniel chuckled. "The church, and I don't mean this political institutional thing you're probably picturing in your head—steeples, pews, pulpits, offering plates, and flags—but the *ekklesia*, the living organism that is Christ's body on this earth."

Scott scratched his head. "Sounds a little existential. You're saying the church is Christ's body?"

"That's what the Bible says. Each of His followers are members of His body, and when we gather together, we literally *assemble* into a physical manifestation of His presence on this earth. Each one of us has a spiritual gift and a piece of God. When we get together, we share those gifts with each other. And with Christ as the head, He directs the rest of His body however He sees fit. As long as we are submissive to His headship, that is."

"Well, that's the thing, isn't it?" Scott said.

Daniel looked sad at that. "Unfortunately, the church of Laodicea seems to be the church's legacy as a whole throughout most of the centuries. Since Constantine imperialized the faith and opened the door to an untold number of pagan practices and customs that to this day are still held with greater reverence in the church than Christ Himself. Even the Reformation was political at heart, and because western Christianity saw its roots in the Reformation rather than in the book of Acts, we, for the most part, never got back to what first-century Christianity was." He sat back. "I'm sorry. I don't mean to bore you with a bunch of church history and ecclesiology." He laughed. "I don't even remember what your question was."

"I was trying to figure out why you won't run."

"Or fight." He nodded. "I remember. The Gospel of the Kingdom. We're not afraid of death, Matthew. The Apostle Paul said that to be absent from the body is to be present with the Lord. We all believe that. Besides, how can we fight the very ones we're supposed to love? How are we to be Christ's body to the world around us while fighting for our own freedoms? Jesus laid down His rights, His life, *for* His enemies. And He's called us to do the same."

"But the church will die out..."

"The religious will fight their wars just as they always have in the name of God or whatever else they want to slap His name on, but the true church always thrives in persecution." He scratched his jaw. "When Communism came to Russia, it came to a dead religion propped up by tradition and ceremony. Priests and cathedrals. When the government closed down the church buildings, so-called Christianity died overnight. But when Communism came to China, where the people were coming together and functioning as Christ's body, the true church went underground, and Christianity there exploded." He poked around in the fire some more. "The question had always been what would happen in America. Would we be Russia, or would we be China?"

"And which were you?"

He sighed. "I'm afraid we were more Russian than Chinese."

Scott tried to grapple with such a bizarre worldview, and wondered why he hadn't heard more of it from Edward. He looked down at Jennifer's sleeping face, at the shadows shifting back and forth across it.

Ralston continued to talk. The fire had him in a near trancelike state. "Jesus was in Israel while it was under Roman occupation, most of the Jewish people awaiting a Messiah who was going to come and cast off that yoke. And it was within that sociopolitical and religious context that Jesus laid down the example His followers were to emulate. No talk of revolution or war, patriotism, or anything like that at all. He even declared that a certain centurion had more faith than what He had found in all the rest of Israel. He cried out for God to forgive those who had crucified him. So, no, Matthew, I can't take up arms against those coming to harm us. Not if I'm claiming to be living by His Spirit."

"Do you think this is the end times? That the Antichrist is coming and all that?"

"I'm not sure I have an opinion on that."

That caught Scott by surprise. "What do you mean?"

He shrugged. "I admit that it seems the world has certainly been trending that way for a long time. Things the prophecy buffs have been talking about since the 1980s. A One World Order, a cashless society, the Temple being rebuilt..."

"But?"

"But things have been going very badly for so many people in so many parts of the world for so long, that I think it's presumptuous and maybe even arrogant for Americans to think that God's tolerance threshold is solely based on what happens in this country. It's insulting to the people who have been starving for centuries in Africa, or who have been executed for following Christ in China. The Black Death. The holocaust. Slavery. Genocide. To say that God didn't care about any of that, that the line He will not allow to be crossed is another Democrat in the White House, is—forgive my language—asinine."

"So..."

"So maybe this isn't the end of the church, but the beginning of a new revolution of the church. Maybe the old systems, all the strongholds left in place from Constantine that have had us majoring in minors and missing the point, needed to be destroyed. And out of the ashes, we can assemble as His body once more. Not getting caught up in nationalism or globalism or any of the other things that distracted us from being what God called us to be—a colony of heaven on earth. Maybe, Matthew, this is just the beginning and not the end at all." He smiled.

Scott looked back into the flames, thinking. "I saw what they were doing to the prisoners in the facility…"

"The people who are coming for us need to see His love just as badly as anyone else. How else will God's Kingdom spread if we don't present His love to wicked men? That was the other major failure of the church. We shut ourselves off from the outside world. Declared them enemies and washed our hands of *them*. Yet Jesus himself ate and drank with sinners and prostitutes and tax collectors." He laughed. "The only people He ever lost His patience with were the religious leaders who were misrepresenting Him."

"So you'll be missionaries to prison guards? You're crazy."

"There have been many prison guards throughout history who have fallen in love with God through such witnesses. Who knows? Maybe like Shadrach, Meshach, and Abednego, God will deliver us. In the meantime, if He wants us to be Jonah to those caught up in this evil system, then we cannot refuse."

"Jonah did."

"And look where that got him."

"You understand that I can't sit back and do nothing. Let them just walk in here and carry you and your children away."

"I appreciate your concern, but you need to look after your own wife. And to be honest, I'm not so sure that either one of you is ready for death quite yet."

His gaze fell back to Jennifer, his finger tracing her cheekbone. "I have to make amends, to give back some of what I've taken."

"Wrong. You can't *earn* redemption. And even if you could, do you know the price? Is it the same for everyone? How will you know when you've finally satisfied God's hatred of sin? You can't. That's what the Gospel of the Kingdom is all about.

God's eternal purpose has always been to have a family that He can share His life and love with. To have many sons and daughters. And those sons and daughters were to live by His own empowering by eating of the Tree of Life that had been transplanted in the Garden. But man ate of the other tree instead, and rather than relying on God's life, they relied on their own understanding to determine right from wrong, making and legislating rules and codes and religion. But the Tree of Life is now Jesus, and all those that partake of Him have new life. *His* life. And He is reversing Eden's curse and making all things new. And now we live in this divine parenthesis where we are governed by His life and present in His Kingdom, yet not completely. You trying to earn your redemption is you partaking of the wrong tree. The only thing that can help you, that can bring you into the beating heart of God, is eating from the Tree of Life — who is Christ."

Scott rubbed his eyes. "Wow."

Ralston laughed. "And I just gave you a year's worth of Bible in about ten minutes." Then he grew quiet. "All this talk about the Ark of the Covenant..."

"Yeah?"

"Jesus said that the Scriptures spoke of Him, meaning the Old Testament." He looked into Scott's eyes. "Jesus is everywhere in the Hebrew Bible. Everything is a type or shadow of Him. Like the Passover lamb. Everything. Including the Ark."

"How so?"

"The Ark housed the Ten Commandments, right?"

"Okay."

"What are the Ten Commandments? They are the expression of an invisible God. They give us an idea of what He is like. He is jealous. He is holy. He is righteous. He is love. The Commandments, the manifestation of God, were put into the Ark. As Scripture says of Christ, the fullness of God dwelt within Him. Paul said that Christ was the image of the invisible God. And the Ark expresses the two natures of Christ. It was made of wood and overlaid with gold. Wood being a representation of human nature, while gold represents the divine. He is the God-man, with God Himself dwelling within Him. He is also the Mercy seat." He poked at the fire. "I could go on and on about the feast days, the Land of Canaan, the manna, the tabernacle, and even the Urim and Thummim itself, but you get my point. It's all about Jesus, and that's all it's ever been about. All this stuff about the Antichrist and the false prophet and the mark of the beast... If that's all people come away with after reading the Revelation of Jesus Christ, then they miss the point of the letter."

Scott's brow turned into a series of Vs. "So if the Ark was a picture of Christ, then why when He comes back would He need rings and scrolls to find it again? Why would He even need it since He Himself is the actual thing?"

Ralston smiled. "You're quick."

"So this whole game played out across the centuries to find the Ark—"

"Might turn out to be pretty silly." But then he shrugged again. "Or maybe not."

Scott thought his mind might explode. He'd never heard this stuff before, and he could tell Ralston had only scratched the surface of something that would redefine his entire perspective of religion. But there was still the matter at hand. "I can't leave you here. I won't."

But before Daniel could respond again, there was banging on the door. As he went to answer it, Scott woke Jennifer.

"Take your clothes and get dressed," he told her.

Getting up, she noticed the concern in his eyes and quickly reached out of the blanket for her damp clothes. Then she retreated into the other room.

Ralston opened the door, and the three Mossad agents were standing there in the rain.

It hadn't been three hours yet.

"Is Cavanaugh in there with you?" one of them asked.

Ralston looked confused. "Who?"

Scott walked past him, placing a hand on his shoulder. "I'll be right back," he said. He shut the door behind him and stepped back into the rain. "What is it?" he asked them. "I'm getting wet."

They had their weapons with them. "Malachi called us."

*Uh-oh.*

# 44.

*"Doublethink means the power of holding two contradictory beliefs in one's mind simultaneously, and accepting both of them."*

—George Orwell

They took a step closer, and the agent on Scott's far right moved a hand toward his holstered weapon. Scott quickly tried going over his list of options, but it was all blank. He didn't see how this could end well for anyone. Of course, he could just *give* them the ring.

They took another step closer, and he held his breath. The one in the middle was the biggest, so he'd have to hit him first. Then the one on his right since—

A distinct sound cut through the rain and reverberated over the treetops—the *whoop-whoop-whoop* of rotors beating the air.

The three Israelis turned and looked back over their shoulders, toward the incoming helicopter, and Scott could tell by their reaction that something was wrong. This wasn't the Mossad returning for them.

Scott bolted back to Ralston's place and burst through the doors. "They're coming!"

Ralston jumped to his feet and ran to the door.

Scott turned back to the agents, but they were already gone, abandoning their orders to secure the ring in favor of dealing with the more immediate and potent threat.

The choppers were dotted along the gray horizon now.

Scott grabbed Jennifer's hand and pulled her past Ralston. He led her out into the rain and back toward the tent.

"What's happening?" she yelled, trying to keep up with him.

"I have to get you out of here!"

"What?" The implication wasn't over her head, and she began to pull against him.

"There's no time for this," he said. But then the helicopters began drifting east. They were heading to the facility. He relaxed a little. "It's okay," he said. But it wasn't. They would be here soon.

When they got to the tent, they found that it was completely empty, the area surrounding it eerily still. Branches swayed slowly in the wind as rain smacked against the tent's sides.

Something felt wrong.

An enormous explosion rocked the forest, fire shooting up above the tree line and into the sky.

Scott pushed Jennifer down below an empty table, whipping out his pistol.

Another explosion. This one a hundred yards south of the first. Scott realized that Malachi must've set up a defensive perimeter around the commune.

And then a third explosion, and this time some of the Christians came out into the rain to see what was happening. The lingering smoke hugging the treetops had them congregating in close, curious circles.

And then a nearer, fourth explosion went off behind them, and a wave of uneasiness ripped through the crowd.

Still kneeling beside Jennifer in the tent, Scott was waiting for some kind of clue as to whether or not the forces surrounding them had all been eliminated by what he knew to be claymore mines, or if soldiers were still coming.

Machine-gun fire ricocheted through the trees southeast of his position, answering his question. He looked at Jennifer and saw that her lips were forming a series of inaudible prayers.

"They are coming from the east and from the north," a voice called out to him.

He looked up and saw the three Israelis sprinting past the tent. One of them continued straight into the commune while the two others broke off to the right and headed east.

Seconds later, more gunfire erupted, and now the crowds of people were scrambling to get back indoors, babies crying as mothers tried to hush them, frightened children pulled along by more frightened adults.

Scott could tell from the shooting that a good number of troops had survived the claymores. The Israeli agents were far outnumbered. He didn't know what to do. The Mossad needed his help, the community needed his help, and Jennifer needed his help.

"Listen." He took her face in his hands and watched tears appear in her eyes, the sudden reality of their situation striking home. "I want you to run south. And just keep running."

She shook her head, and the tears fell. "I can't."

"You can!"

"I can't!"

"Jen, please. I need to help them now. I'll catch up with you."

Her tears turned to sobs, and she threw herself around his neck. "I won't leave you," she cried.

His eyes began to tear up too. There was no doubting that this was it for them, their final moment together. He supposed he was glad for it, that he hadn't put a bullet in his head so long ago. It had been worth the wait, even if the reunion was short-lived. He supposed if he was going to die anyway, he was grateful he got to see her again, to know she forgave him and still loved him. He kissed her, knowing it was their last kiss.

Their last kiss…

"Go," he whispered.

"But I don't want to live without you," she said.

"I'll catch up, I promise."

Then came another sound, suddenly rising over the symphony of death.

A helicopter.

It was coming in from the south.

The Black Hawk.

*Oh God, please.* Scott grabbed her shoulders. "Forget that. See that helicopter?" He pointed.

It was hard to see through the clouds, but she nodded.

"It's gonna land nearby. Make sure you get on it, okay? That's Malachi's men coming back for us. You get on that helicopter and keep your head down. Nothing else matters."

"What about you?"

"Someone needs to cover your escape." He smiled. "Would you at least let me do that? For all the grief I've put you through over the years?"

"I've already forgiven you."

He pulled her close, put his lips against her cheek. "Get on the helicopter, Jen. I'll find you." Then he helped her out from under the table.

"Josh," she started.

Hearing her say his real name superimposed years of old memories on top of the recent ones, and the image it created was confusing. "Yeah?"

Her lip began to quiver, tears and rainwater still dripping down her face. "In case I never see you again…"

"You will! *Go!*"

The helicopter was getting closer, but so was the gunfire.

The two Mossad agents appeared, backpedaling out of the woods, SAWs firing relentlessly from their shoulders. Then, turning toward the tent, they called out, "It's touching down in the clearing! We are going now!"

Scott led Jennifer down after them. "Take her with you!" he shouted at their backs.

They turned and stopped, their weapons falling to their sides as they motioned urgently for them to catch up. "Where is the ring?" one of them yelled.

"I don't have it!" Not waiting for a response or an argument, he said, "Take her with you, and I'll cover you!" He threw down the pistol and held out his hands to receive the huge SAW from one of the Israelis. When he had it in his hands, they all sprinted for the clearing. The Black Hawk was almost over them now.

When Scott turned to cover their backs, he saw the third Mossad agent running after them with a few camouflaged soldiers chasing him. Scott moved to his left in order to clear the Israeli from his line of fire and pulled the M249's trigger. The machine gun rocked back and forth in his arms as empty shells sizzled in the rain. The soldiers were thrown backward, shredded by the barrage of 5.56mm rounds, but Scott could see more of them through the surrounding trees. He sprayed some cover fire at them, finding out that the ammunition was mixed with tracers. He used the TOT (tracer on target) to home in on the them, keeping them pinned behind the trees. "Go! Go! Go!" Scott screamed at the Mossad agent. The Israeli ran past him and continued toward the descending Black Hawk.

Scott stole a glance at the helicopter as it touched down seventy yards behind him, and watched as the Israeli agents had to physically drag and pull Jennifer up into it. His heart broke in two at the sight. But at least it wasn't an incinerator she was being forced into.

Fire was now being directed at him from the woods, so he had to move. As he ran for cover, he tried not to think of his screaming wife while the Black Hawk rose into the sky and banked away.

****

Jennifer screamed as one of the Israelis struggled to hold her head down, bullets clinking around the inside of the helicopter from small-arms fire below. With her head in her lap, she watched the form of her husband become smaller and smaller as he ran toward the landing zone, firing aimlessly over his shoulder in an attempt to keep the soldiers' attention on him and off the escaping chopper. She saw the whole commune and the NAU troops, how they were circling around Josh's position like wolves surrounding their prey.

Then the helicopter banked again, and she lost sight of him. Struggling against the agent, she turned her head and looked out the other door and saw a tinier version of her husband exchanging fire with some troops who were positioned in the trees. She reached out her hand as if she could snatch him out of harm's way. "Josh!" she yelled, fighting against the agent's grasp, though whether it was to get a better view or to join her husband in death, she wasn't sure. Only that her helpless anguish seemed too much to bear. *"Josh!"* she screamed hysterically, and another agent had to help hold her down. She saw Josh fall to the ground, and then the whole world seemed to fall away, and he was gone.

****

Scott was struck in the shoulder and side, and he went down hard. As he rolled onto his back, he got one last glimpse of the Black Hawk as it disappeared over the horizon, his wife, the books, and the ring of Solomon along with it. He clenched his teeth and tried to move, but he knew the soldiers were already closing in.

He reached out and grabbed the SAW, pulled it back to his side. He tilted the barrel up and was able to squeeze the trigger just as two soldiers burst through the woods on top of him. Their feet flew out from beneath them, and they landed, unmoving, ten feet away.

He dropped his head back to the ground and stared up through the raindrops splashing against his face. He looked into the clouds and wondered what, if anything, was beyond them. Was it too late, or was Ralston right about only needing to believe? Could it be that simple? Even with the blood of so many on his hands?

Someone else came pounding out of the woods, and he tried to raise the machine gun again, but he had no strength left in that arm. The recoil from the last burst had torn too much muscle. He closed his eyes, thought of offering up a prayer, but didn't even know what to say. How to do it.

"Hey."

It came carried on a whisper, and when he moved his head to locate its source, he saw Ralston coming over to him. "What're you doing here?"

Ralston kneeled beside him, taking in his wounds. "I wanted you to have something. Thought maybe you'd take it this time." He held up the same Bible he'd tried to give him before.

Scott shook his head. "Your family needs you. Get out of here."

"I will, but first I had to make sure you got this." He examined the entry wounds.

"What're you doing?"

"I used to be a medic."

"What?"

"Army."

He would have been shocked had he not been so preoccupied with the pain. "So am I gonna make it, doc?"

"If we can stop the bleeding." He reached out his hand. "Come on, I'll help you."

"Help me what?"

"We have to get you back."

Struggling to his feet, Scott noticed the sudden absence of soldiers. "Where'd they go?"

"They headed back to the commune."

Ralston led Scott into one of the houses that bordered the woods, even while the soldiers were at the other end and rounding everyone up. He stripped Scott of his jacket and sweatshirt and immediately went to work removing the bullets. "The one in your side went straight through," he said. "The one in your shoulder's going to take some digging. This might hurt."

"You don't have to do this."

"Yeah, I do."

"They need you out there."

"You need me in here."

Scott stared at him. "But why?"

"Because I'll be with them forever..."

He gripped the sides of the table he was on, grinding his teeth and trying not to pass out from the pain of having Ralston's fingers moving around inside his arm.

When he was done, Ralston said, "I could be fancy and try burning the wound shut like they used to do in the movies, but

I don't think it's necessary. What do you—" And he jabbed a needle through his skin.

Scott curled his toes, and his eyes rolled up into his head as he groaned.

"Sorry," Ralston apologized.

Ten seconds later, the hole in his shoulder had a single piece of fishing line holding it together. Thirty seconds after that, he had a clean rag taped over it.

"Hopefully this doesn't get infected before you can get some real care. But at least you won't bleed to death."

Scott sat up and gingerly touched his side. It was a good tape job.

And then came shouting from just outside. A soldier was asking if anyone was in the small home.

"You should hide here," Ralston said as he wiped his hands on his pants.

"Where are you going?"

"Like you said, I need to be with them." He handed the Bible to him and then gave him a quick hug. "Make sure my sacrifice isn't in vain." He patted him on the back. "It was a pleasure meeting you, Matthew Scott."

"It's Joshua, actually," he replied.

Ralston only smiled, turned, and walked toward the door. He whistled an old hymn as he went.

But instead of hiding, Scott went after him. He reached him just as the door swung open to reveal a line of soldiers standing in the pouring rain. Most of the commune was rounded up with them, being held at gunpoint. Ralston's effort to save his life seemed pointless now.

"Friends!" Ralston shouted, getting the soldiers' attention.

"Come out of there!" one of them yelled.

Ralston raised his hands in surrender but didn't make any effort to comply. "My friends, we are nothing to you, so why have you come here to torment us?"

"Get out here!" the soldier screamed again.

"No, you come in here. Come in out of the rain, and let us serve you. Are you hungry? Thirsty?"

Scott didn't know what Ralston was doing, but the soldiers were clearly growing anxious as a result of it.

Ralston looked over his brothers and sisters in the faith, meeting each one of their tear-filled eyes with an expression of encouragement and understanding. "I love you all," he said.

"Ralston, they're gonna shoot you," Scott whispered from behind him.

But he ignored him. "'Behold, I stand at the door and knock. If any man hears my voice and opens the door, I will come in to him and sup with him, and he with me.' My dear soldiers, Jesus loves you—"

Guns went off, and the stunned community watched as Ralston and Scott fell backward in seeming slow motion.

The smoke from the soldiers' guns lingered in the deafening silence that followed until a song broke out among the crowd. At first it was just a line mumbled in a woman's trembling voice, but then another voice joined it. And another. Until they were all singing a song about "that glorious day." The song echoed in the rain and drifted up to heaven, escorting their brother home. Then the soldiers started shouting orders, telling them to be quiet.

Scott began moving beneath Ralston's weight, trying to get out from under him.

"Stay still," Ralston whispered. He said it strictly, with no give in his tone. And then he added, "Take from the Tree of Life, Matthew. Search…for the true Ark of…the testimony."

So Scott stayed still, feeling blood flow down his neck and beneath his shirt. He lay there listening to the people singing and the soldiers trying to shut them up. But eventually, the song grew distant as they were marched off to waiting vehicles.

Silence. Nothing but the sound of the rain. It seemed as if time stopped, and it wasn't until he could hear the faint sounds of wildlife returning to the forest around them that Scott finally moved.

"I think it's okay now, Dan," Scott said.

No response.

"Dan?"

Again, nothing.

He maneuvered out from beneath him and saw that his eyes were closed. He pressed two fingers against his neck. No pulse. Then he saw Ralston's chest and stomach and looked down at his own, amazed to find that none of the rounds had made it through to him. At that range, with those weapons, he should've been full of holes too. But the blood he'd felt flowing over him had not been his own. It had all been Ralston's.

He shuffled backward until he came up against a wall. Then he slid down to the floor and sat staring at Ralston's bloody body.

He sat there for an hour before finally reaching for the Bible that lay sprawled open on the floor beside him. There was a bookmark in it, a verse in red print underlined. It read, *And fear not them which kill the body, but are not able to kill the soul…*

And right there, sitting in an empty commune in the middle of nowhere and sitting next to a dead man he'd met just the day before, his entire life changed in an instant.

# V.

# NO MORE SECRETS

*Why do the heathen rage, and the people imagine a vain thing? The kings of the earth set themselves, and the rulers take counsel together, against the Lord, and against his anointed... He that sitteth in the heavens shall laugh: the Lord shall have them in derision. Then shall He speak unto them in His wrath, and vex them in His sore displeasure.*
—Psalm 2:1–2, 4–5

The sun shone through the green-needled canopy in rays of misty light, melting snow wherever it touched. The mountains surrounding the area were silent and still, as they had been for a very long time.

Jennifer folded her arms across her chest, trying to retreat further into the warmth of the bearskin coat. A few of her neighbors exited the longhouse beside her, and they waved as they set out for their morning fishing trip. She smiled and turned around. Lifting the flap to the wigwam, she ducked back inside.

She had come to love this new way of life. It was so different than anything her westernized worldview could have prepared her for, but it felt like home almost immediately. The natives had accepted her as one of their own right away, so her education into the ways of a simpler life had begun almost the moment they'd crossed paths. There was definitely a learning curve, but her new family was patient and kind, and she soon caught on. Maybe it was the community life here that she so loved, so connected with. Unlike her upbringing in the West where individualism and independence reigned and everyone had been separated by fences, political parties, denominations, and even sports teams. But here… They lived in a shared-life community where everyone seemed to function as a whole, and the love they had for each other defined their existence. It was completely unlike anything she'd ever experienced before, something she didn't even know she had been missing.

She only hoped that it would last. So far, the little corner of the Canadian wilderness had yet to be touched by the NAU or any other element of the emerging New World Order. Sometimes she even forgot about the horrors that were taking place in the world just beyond the mountains. About the esoteric conspiracy she'd read about in the books Joshua had put in her jacket pocket.

She approached a figure that was sitting on the floor beside a small fire, the smoke it expelled drifting up through the hole in the ceiling of their simple abode. She placed her hands on his shoulders and asked, "How is he?"

Joshua Cavanaugh turned his attention from the newborn baby cradled in his arms and looked up to his wife. "Sleeping."

She sat down beside him and rested her head against his shoulder, and together they watched their son sleep.

They'd been here for almost a year, living amongst the indigenous peoples in relative peace and quiet. No one had come looking for them yet, and they could only pray they never would.

Leaving the empty commune behind, Joshua had made his way back to the house in Vermont, intent on getting the duffel bag of cash and false identities he'd left in the park. Because his house was associated with a false identity, he didn't think anyone would be able to trace it back to him. But when he entered his home, he found that there were people there waiting for him. People with guns.

The Mossad.

And they had Jennifer with them.

Apparently, at some point while he was sleeping in the commune, Malachi had injected a transponder beneath his skin. So the Israeli agent knew he'd survived the assault on the commune and was able to track his movement east through the mountains and back to Vermont. So they'd settled in and waited for him to complete his journey home (it being too dangerous to try to pick him up). Of course, it wasn't just a neighborly act of kindness through which Malachi was seeking to rejoin husband and wife. He wanted the ring back, and as far as he knew, Joshua still had it. He'd planned on making an exchange, the ring for Jennifer. But Joshua didn't have the ring, which was evident after a thorough strip search.

Because Jennifer had read the books Joshua had hidden in her jacket, she had come to understand that the ring was best left undiscovered, and so kept her possession of it a secret. Malachi and his men were forced to leave Vermont empty-handed. As for him and Jennifer, they'd finally made good on his escape plan to Canada.

Joshua handed baby Daniel to her and reached beside him for Ralston's Bible, turning to the book of Jeremiah.

With the holy book opened on his lap, he took the ring from his pocket.

Jennifer stared at her husband, amazed at how much he'd changed over the past year. The things Ralston had shared with him seemed to have finally set him free. She leaned in close, always fascinated by what was about to happen.

Turning the ring over in his hand, Joshua's mind turned with it, wondering again about the deception the secret societies had planned for it. Did they have a plan B? Would NASA still come up with an extraterrestrial hoax via some other means? Or maybe, as Daniel suggested, this was just another blip down history's long highway. He didn't really care. He knew where it ended even if he wasn't sure how it would get there.

The things that Ralston had said to him had so changed him that he couldn't help but talk about it. First to Jennifer and then—as he used his talent for picking up languages and began learning their words—with their new family too. He had no western agenda, no imperial goal, just a Tree that he wanted to tell people about. And so far, the things that Ralston had said about the members of the body assembling together to construct the whole, each one exercising gifts to edify the other (things he'd read in the New Testament since), seemed to be taking place rather organically. It wasn't anything like he'd perceived "church" or religion to be, and as he read through the book of Acts and the rest of the New Testament, he couldn't help but wonder if Ralston was right about the old things needing to be destroyed so that the original intent could be reestablished.

Placing the ring on the open page of Jeremiah's text, light from the fire shone through the ring's lens and fell onto the English words. The words, however, suddenly appeared raised, hovering over the page like some kind of three-dimensional hologram. Only the words floating through the air weren't the words of the prophet, at least not as they appeared on the page in English, but were actually rearrangements of the letters the inspired prophet had used.

"What does it say this time?" Jennifer asked, trying to make sense of the shining display.

That the ring worked to rearrange an English translation of Jeremiah's work seemed impossible. But there it was. A single sentence hovering in midair, words chosen from the page and miraculously assembled into a single sentence. "It says, 'I am with you always, even to the end of the age.'"

She smiled and squeezed their child tighter as Joshua kissed her on the forehead.

SELECTED BIBLIOGRAPHY

This list was originally comprised in 2011 upon completion of the novel's first edition. In checking the links prior to this new edition, I discovered that most of the links are no longer available. I have therefore removed all internet links, though I have kept the sources.

Bacon, Francis. "New Atlantis." <u>Great Books of the Western World #30 Francis Bacon.</u> Ed. Robert Hutchins Maynard. Chicago: William Benton, 1952. 198-214.

"Copper Scroll." <u>Wikipedia.</u>

*Eerdmans Handbook to the Bible.* Oxford: Lion Publishing, 1983.

<u>The Great Secret of Solomon's Temple and the Hiding of the Ark of the Covenant.</u> Dir. Michael Rood. A Rood Awakening, 2000.

Hall, Manly P. *America's Assignment with Destiny.* New York: Penguin Group, 1999.

Hall, Manly P. *The Secret Destiny of America.* New York: Penguin Group, 2008.

Hall, Manly P. *The Secret Teachings of All Ages.* New York: Penguin Group, 2007.

Hieronimus, Robert. *Founding Fathers, Secret Societies: Freemasons, Illuminati, Rosicrucians, and the Decoding of the Great Seal.* Rochester: Destiny Books, 2006.

Jeffrey, Grant R. *Armageddon: Appointment With Destiny.* New York: Bantam Books, 1988.

Jones, Vendyl. "The Copper Scroll." <u>Vendyl Jones Research Institutes.</u>

Kah, Garry H. *En Route to Global Occupation: A High Ranking Government Liaison Exposes the Secret Agenda for World Unification.* Lafayette: Huntington House Publishers, 1991.

"Larry McDonald on the New World Order." <u>Crossfire.</u> 1983.

"Lou Dobbs-North American Union." <u>Lou Dobbs Tonight.</u> 21 June 2006.

Lundberg, Marilyn J. "Copper Scroll." <u>West Semitic Research Project.</u>

"Masonic Rosicruciansim." MasonicDictionary.com

Mitchell, Chris. "The Mystery of the Copper Scroll." Christian World News. 19 Oct. 2008.

Mock, Robert. "The Hebrew Account of Hiding the Ark, the Sanctuary and the Treasures of Solomon's Temple." BibleSearchers.com. Nov. 2002.

*New International Bible Dictionary*. Gen. Ed. Merrill C. Tenney. Grand Rapids: Zondervan Publishing House, 1987.

North American Union. Council on Foreign Relations.

The Northwoods Documents.

*Old Testament Pseudepigrapha: Vol. 1*. Ed. James H. Charlesworth. New York: Doubleday, 1983

Ovason, David. *Secret Architecture of Our Nation's Capitol: The Masons and the Building of Washington D.C.* New York: HarperCollins, 2000.

Paul, Ron. "A North American United Nations?" Texas Straight Talk. 28 Aug. 2006.

Peterson, Joseph H. "The Testament of Solomon, translated by F.C. Conybeare." Twilit Grotto—Esoteric Archives. 1997.

Price, Randall. *The Coming Last Days Temple*. Eugene: Harvest House Publishers, 1999.

"Rebuilding America's Defenses." Project For New American Century.

Resources for the Study and Praxis of Rosicruciansim. The Hermetic Fellowship Website.

Robison, John. *Proofs of a Conspiracy Against All the Religions and Governments of Europe, Carried on in the Secret Meetings of Freemasons, Illuminati and Reading Societies* (1st ed. 1798). FQ Publishing, 2007.

Roper, David H. "King Solomon's Ring." PBC Library.

The Rosicrucian Academy.

Schrigner, Linda S., and et al. "Bacon's 'Secret Society'- The Ephrata Connection." 5 May 2002.

Secret Faith of the Founding Fathers. Dir. Christian J. Pinto. Adullam Films, 2010.

Secret Mysteries of America's Beginnings: The New Atlantis — Volume 1. Dir. Christian J. Pinto. Antiquities Research, 2006.

Secret Mysteries of America's Beginnings Volume 2: Riddles in Stone: The Secret Architecture of Washington D.C. Dir. Christian J. Pinto. Antiquities Research, 2007.

Stryz, Jan. "The Alchemy of the Voice at Ephrata Cloister."

Wigston, W. F. *Bacon, Shakespeare, and the Rosicrucians*. Whitefish: Kessinger Publishing Company, 1993.

Wolters, Al. "The Last Treasure of the Copper Scroll." Journal of Biblical Literature. 107.3 (1988): 419-429.

*The Works of Josephus*. Trans. William Whiston. Peabody: Hendrickson Publishers Inc., 1987.

World Transhumanist Association.

The Story of Solomon's rings
continues in the prequel spin-off
*The Judgment Key.*
Available now!

# ABOUT THE AUTHOR

Shawn Hopkins lives in Pennsylvania with his wife and children. He holds degrees in theology and biblical studies. He is an avid football fan, enjoys the weight room, and loves reading. He is busy working on the next novel.

If you enjoyed the story, he would really appreciate if you would take a minute to leave a review.

Visit his site shawnhopkins.com to get on the mailing list and grab a free book!

www.ingramcontent.com/pod-product-compliance
Lightning Source LLC
Chambersburg PA
CBHW030814110726
47900CB00006B/1623